WILEY BROOKS

The Next Best Thing

I hope you find this to be a fast & fun read.

Wiley

First published by Wiley Brooks 2019

Copyright © 2019 by Wiley Brooks

Library of Congress Control Number: 2019907191

Cover design and map illustration by Maria Stoian

First edition

ISBN: 978-1-733177-10-8

This book was professionally typeset on Reedsy.
Find out more at reedsy.com

Contents

Dedication

To my sweet wife, **Marianne Bichsel**. You've always believed in and encouraged me. Every day that passes I'm thankful that you agreed to marry me those many years ago.

To my dear friend, **Monty Dennison**. This book had languished for 32 years until one Tuesday last August when, after a very dry Bombay Gin martini and a glass of red wine, you said to me "Just write the damn book." So I did.

Map of Malaysia

MAP OF MALAYSIA

Prologue

Some things never leave you. I lost my daughter thirty-two years ago. You know that cliché about time healing wounds. Don't believe it. If time had healing power, three decades should be more than enough. But I long for my sweet baby girl every day. Every day, there is a moment when my heart cracks. I can feel it. Physically. It's like something gives way in my chest.

Anything can trigger it. Yesterday there was this little girl – I'd say she was three, maybe four – literally ran right into me on the sidewalk outside the Winn-Dixie. She was wearing a bright yellow dress and laughing up a storm. Then she looked up at me with her beautiful blue eyes with that half-guilty, half-frightened look that only a child can give. I gave her a big smile; her expression changed back into glee once again. She turned, darted off as her mother came running down the sidewalk, bags in both arms, yelling for her to stop that instant. As the little girl scurried away, my smile melted from my face. Those blue eyes could have been Amanda's. The terrible emptiness gripped me yet again.

It's awful to lose a child. It doesn't matter if she is two or twenty-two. I suspect that almost all dads have a clear picture in their minds of their kid's future. From the time Amanda was a baby, I could see her in cap and gown, or walking down the aisle, me at her side. In my mind, Amanda was going to take over the business I had founded. I pictured her sitting behind my desk looking every bit the successful woman that I knew she would become. And, of course, I saw her as a mother. She'd be a great one. I think all fathers have these visions

1

of their children. Amanda, though, was my only child, so maybe mine were more vivid.

I'm getting old. I was forty-eight when Amanda died. Last week I turned eighty, but I stopped celebrating my birthday thirty-two years ago. On my birthday this year, I ran into my friend, Amal, at the gym. Amal is about twenty years younger than me and one of the most outgoing fellows I know. He retired a year ago and started showing up to work out at about the same time as me every day. We became gym pals. Well, last week when I told Amal that it was my birthday, he insisted on taking me to lunch.

—————

"My friend, eighty years is a long life," Amal said to me as we waited for our food. "A chance for many blessings. Tell me, what are you most grateful for?"

Amal and I were not deep friends. I had never told him about Amanda or much of anything that was truly personal. "That's easy," I said. "Amanda." He looked puzzled at the name he had not heard before. "Was that your wife?" he asked.

I'm sure he didn't expect to spend the next four hours hearing about my sweet girl, all the things we did together, her years away at college and finally her post-college adventure. "You know, Amal, I wasn't thrilled that she was going to travel the world – by herself, no less! But the world was a far safer place back in the Eighties. Or so I thought. And Amanda was a smart kid. Lots of common sense. She'd be fine. I was wrong."

And with that, I told Amal about Amanda's murder. Savage. Brutal. I told him how it gutted me and emptied my soul.

"I couldn't imagine how I could go on, yet here I am thirty-two years later. Nothing had meaning then. You know the stages of grief? I moved to the anger stage quickly. I wanted to find the sonofabitch who did it and kill him. I hatched a plan and hired a guy to find him."

"Did you?" Amal asked. "Find him, I mean."

"Oh yeah," I answered.

2

"And what did you do?"

I stared at Amal. His question hung in the air. What happened that hot afternoon on a jungle trail in Southeast Asia had stayed there. Only three other people knew the story. I've since shared it with no one. But as I sat there with this casual friend sipping on a Diet Coke and waiting for my burger to arrive, I knew the time had come. I told Amal the whole story.

He wept.

So did I.

Day 1

Amanda boarded the bus this morning in Melaka. Truth is, she was glad to be moving on. Visiting Melaka was like visiting Oakland before its renaissance. Best, perhaps, to not linger. Melaka's "charms" were pointed out in her travel guide and the yellow book had rarely misled her. And make no mistake; there was history here. And maybe, someday, Malaysia would get it together enough to do it justice. After all, Melaka had once been the center of an empire. One would never guess it now.

Once a busy port on the Strait of Malacca, Melaka was showing its age. Tired, rundown and dirty. It was hard to escape the stench of raw sewage that flowed into the river that meandered through town.

During the Vietnam War, ports throughout Southeast Asia bustled with business. It was in a prime and safe location. Near Singapore, Melaka held a strategic location on the Strait that hugs the west coast of Malaysia all the way to Thailand. But when the war ended, things slowed. Fewer and fewer ships called on Melaka. The city looked weary. As did its people.

Amanda was traveling alone. Her dad had worried about that before she left Tampa. But the fact was that she was rarely actually alone. The road is sprinkled with travelers like her from all over the world.

Backpackers, it turns out, are a friendly bunch. They engage easily with each other, form bonds, share stories, sometimes more and then move on. The membership of their little bands ebb and flow, constantly changing. It had become the aspect of travel Amanda most enjoyed.

Bus routes crisscross Malaysia. While some backpackers stuck out

4

their thumb for rides, most relied on going from point A to point B by bus. Buses were cheap and fairly reliable. Some were even air-conditioned coaches with TVs showing movies. Others were less well appointed; basic school bus seating with windows that move up and down to allow in cooling air, at least when the bus was moving. That's the kind of bus Amanda found herself getting on for the upcoming four-and-a-half-hour ride.

When she boarded, a petite redhead with her hair tied back in a ponytail was already sitting midway back next to an open window. Amanda grabbed the seat directly across the aisle. The two young women smiled at each other.

"Tioman?" Suzanne asked as Amanda took her seat.

"Yep. I've really been looking forward to it, especially after this place." She used her head to indicate Melaka, the place they were leaving.

"I'm Amanda, by the way."

She reached out for a brief handshake.

"Suzanne. Just call me Suzy."

As the two young women chatted, a petite blonde girl took the seat one row up. Behind her was a slim guy who sat next to her. The only other passenger to board was another backpacker who offered a big smile and took the seat across the aisle from the young couple. Everyone else on the intercity bus was either Malay or Chinese Malay.

Suzy looked over to Amanda and raised her eyebrows and mouthed the word, "hunk." She was referring to the last backpacker to board the bus. Amanda smiled back.

Truth is she had seen him earlier at a restaurant in town and felt a twinge of excitement when he boarded her bus. He was a good-looking guy, though he ignored her at the restaurant.

The driver closed the door and the bus pulled away. The destination sign on the front said Mersing, which explained the backpacking travelers. Mersing is a small fishing port on the lower east coast of Malaysia and the jumping off point for Tioman Island.

"How long you been traveling?" Suzy asked.

"I left home about six months ago," Amanda said. "Started in India and worked my way east. I'm giving myself a year. At least that was the plan when I left home. Not so sure now. Might be longer."

"It will be," Suzy said. "When I left home, I told my folks six months. I couldn't imagine then that I'd want to be away more than that."

"How long ago did you leave?"

"Nine months now. And no plan to stop anytime soon. You meet all these people who have been on the road for way longer. I traveled with an Irish guy in Laos who had been traveling for four years. Blows my mind. Four fucking years. Can you believe it?" Amanda shook her head no.

"When I asked him about his plans," Suzy continued, "he would just say something like, 'Suze, you have to let go of your American fixation on 'building' a life. Life happens, babe. It's the journey. Just love the journey.'" She said it like a stoner with an Irish accent.

Amanda put her thumb and index finger together as if holding something, raised it to her lips and made a sucking sound.

"You got that right. Colin took getting high to a new level. I was with him for about a week. Had to leave."

"Four years. No way I could do that. My dad and I are too close. I miss him. We're all we have. My mom passed a few years ago and I don't have any brothers or sisters. He flew all the way from Tampa to meet me for my birthday in Bangkok. Hung out a few days then flew back."

"Ah, that's sweet. It's great you're so close to your dad. My folks are divorced. I'm pretty tight with my mom."

"Yeah. My dad's great. But he thinks I'm too trusting. 'Do you really know these people you're hanging out with?'" Amanda said, giving her dad's words a false parental tone.

"Of course, I don't tell him when I'm traveling with a guy. I'll say I'm with a group. He would freak out if he knew how much sex I'm having."

"I just don't go there with my parents," Suzy said. "They would have

6

a meltdown if they knew I was an equal opportunity fornicator."

"A what?" Amanda laughed.

"A woman of the world. Damn, girl, why would I want to screw an American? I have the rest of my life to do that!"

They laughed.

"How about you?"

"Well, I'm not as well traveled as you," Amanda said, putting air quotes around well traveled. "There was an Aussie I traveled with named Bryan. We were together for, like, three weeks."

Amanda paused. A devilish grin spread across her face. She lowered her voice slightly.

"What a lay!" They both did a soft giggle.

"Hey," Suzy said, "I'm thinking about writing an article about how people from different parts of the world say different things during sex. I think Playboy or Penthouse would buy it. You know they pay like a thousand dollars."

"Oh, they definitely would," Amanda said, "God, Bryan, you know, the Aussie, did this thing when he was getting close. He'd start softly repeating 'yeow, yeow, yeow.' The first time I wondered what in the hell that was about. It was actually distracting. But then, you know, it would happen and he'd shout, 'Whooaa.' The first time it was all I could to not laugh out loud."

They broke into giggles, much louder this time, drawing the attention of several passengers.

"You ever do it with a local?" Amanda asked.

"Once. In India. It was okay. He was good-looking enough. Nice body. Spoke English with a lilting English accent. I thought, why not? You?"

"No. At least not yet. Sounds like your guy had some sex appeal. I haven't found a local guy yet who gets my motor running. Know what I mean?"

Suzy nodded yes.

"I'm open to it, though," Amanda continued. "I think it would be part of the experience of traveling the world."

"Yeah. You could write a book, 'Screw the World' or, wait, 'Dicking Around.'" Both girls squealed.

Martin, in the seat in front of them, turned around with a big smile on his face. His girlfriend, though, was the first to talk. "I'd buy that book, sugar," she said in a thick unmistakably southern accent.

"Hi ladies. My name is Martin," the fellow said and it was obvious that he was from Germany. "I'm from Bonn. This is Crystal."

"Hi y'all," Crystal said. "From Little Rock."

One row up from Amanda, Joey was debating with when to join the conversation. Now was as good a time as any.

"Hey guys, I'm Joey," he said. "I grew up in a little town no one has ever heard of in North Carolina." He shook hands with everyone.

"You're an American?" Martin asked, the skepticism clear in his tone. "You look like you might be from here."

"Yeah, I have some Malay blood in me, but I'm all USA, the whole kit and caboodle." Then changing the topic, he quickly added, "Hey, everyone headed to Tioman? It's awesome."

Nods all around.

"You've been there?" Suzy asked.

"A few months ago," Joey answered. "I was there for five days. Would have stayed longer but I had to leave to meet someone."

"Is it as primitive as they say?" Suzy asked.

"I don't know if I'd call it primitive," Joey said. "Maybe pristine. Basic, for sure. There's not much development there. Just a little village. The jungle comes right up to the beach. All the places to stay line the beach at the edge of the jungle."

"Well, sweetie, that sounds danger-ass to me," Crystal drawled.

"What!" Suzy chortled.

"Yeah, dangerous to my ass."

"No, Crystal," Joey answered, interrupting the chuckles. "It's not dangerous at all. The only time I saw any jungle creatures was when a group of us took the trail over the mountain to the other side of the

8

island. We were walking down the other slope and facing us in the middle of the trail were two of the biggest monitor lizards I'd ever seen. I swear those guys were at least four feet long!"

"Christ!" Suzy said.

"It was okay," Joey said. "They didn't want to be around us either. They scurried off down the path away from us. Didn't see them again."

Joey said the best part of the jungle were the sounds. Birds, insects, monkeys. They all make their noises at the same time.

"It's really loud, but really beautiful, too," he said.

Joey told them that there are quite a few decent places to stay on Tioman. He stayed at a place called ABC Village. It was basically small A-frames with thatched roofs. Each hut had a wooden floor that raised it slightly off the ground to keep people inside and their stuff above the water when it's raining like crazy. A hut, he said, was only about two and a half dollars a night.

"The guy who runs it is a Malay named Baharom. Westerners throw in a T and call him Batharoom. He's good natured about it. Great guy. Most nights after dinner he plays guitar around a fire on the beach. It's really cool."

Amanda decided that she kind of liked this guy. He was good looking and had a nice quality to his voice.

"So, you're kind of a Malay and an American at the same time," she said. In her mind, she was wondering if he had been sitting just far enough away to not overhear her chat with Suzy earlier about screwing local guys. He hadn't said anything to hint that he had. And the bus was noisy, after all. Then again, Martin and Crystal had heard.

"You could say I'm the best of both worlds," he said with an infectious smile. She found herself smiling right back at him.

The five chatted a bit more, but eventually turned back in their seats. Martin plugged in his Walkman to listen to songs. Crystal stared out the window. Joey pulled out his yellow Lonely Planet guidebook.

Amanda and Suzy continued to chat, but at a level that those nearby wouldn't overhear.

The long drive to Mersing included a couple stops along the way. It was nearing evening by the time the travelers disembarked. All five headed toward the docks only to find out that the tide had crested a few hours before. All the boats for Tioman had left on the high tide. Next high tide would be at about eight the next morning.

The group headed back toward the center of town.

"Let's try this place," Martin said to Crystal, standing outside the Happy Song Hotel. "Lonely Planet says it's decent enough." Martin and Crystal went in. Amanda and Suzy followed. Joey said he was going to try another place he had read about and would catch them later.

Amanda's room was typical for a cheap Malaysian hotel. Nondescript, even starkly plain, but clean. It offered a full-sized mattress on a plywood base. The only light fixture was a fluorescent bulb hanging from the ceiling. It cast its harsh blueish light throughout the room. There was a small chest and a simple nightstand. While it was not much to look at, it was fine at just seven ringgits – less than three US dollars.

The room also boasted its own bathroom, which not all guest house rooms did. The hotel itself had two floors. The door to Amanda's room was midway down the hall on the second floor.

At the end of the hall was a back door that could serve as an emergency exit. Some of these low-cost places were firetraps, so she always thought through a get-out-fast plan. She tried the door to make sure it would open. It did.

She had just stepped from the shower when Suzy, whose room was a couple doors down, knocked and called in.

"Amanda. We're heading to the Portside Café. The manager recommended it. It's close. Want to come along?"

"Not ready yet," she answered back through the door. "I'll join you there."

A short time later, Amanda was out the door and on her way to the Portside Café. The others, even Joey, were there, drinking cold beers.

"Hey Amanda," Joey said as she walked through the door. "Over here."

She walked over and took the seat next to him. "How about a beer?"

"Why not?" she said. Joey signaled the bartender to bring her a beer. The beer came and she took a long draw on it.

"That hits the spot," she said, then turned to Joey. "So Joey, what's your story?"

"I didn't tell the whole truth and nothing but the truth on the bus. I was born here," he said. He took another pull on his beer, then continued.

"I never knew my dad. He was a British sailor. He was long-gone by the time my mom found out she was pregnant. It was just me and my mom."

"No other family around?"

"No. They shunned her. You know, the unwed mom thing."

"Sorry."

"My mom died when I was little."

"What? God. Joey, that's awful. I'm so sorry."

"Hey, the story gets better. Honest! An American couple adopted me and took me to Bentonville. That's in North Carolina. I grew up there. I have almost no memories of my life here before them. My dad was a preacher."

"Wait. You were raised in a small town in North Carolina but you have no southern accent. I've never met someone from North Carolina with no accent. How'd that happen?"

"It was my mom's doing. I already spoke a little English when they adopted me. Not much, mind you, but I picked it up quickly. Everyone in Malaysia learns English. Well, mom – that's my American mom - she said if I ever wanted to amount to anything, I had to talk like I was from someplace where they don't have an accent."

Joey explained how they would watch TV and his mom would have him try to repeat lines exactly like the speaker.

"We had a Betamax to record shows. We'd be watching and she'd stop the tape, back it up and have me speak the lines. We'd sometimes do it over and over. She really taught me how to listen to people. What

11

can I say? It worked. I can slip into a little North Carolina when I want to, though."

"Let's hear it."

"Y'all seed my new sheirt and paints?"

Amanda laughed.

"Yeah. There it is! Well, I'm from Tampa. But it's like Tampa isn't in the South anymore. My dad doesn't have an accent. He says he worked on getting rid of it. My mom didn't have one because she grew up in the Midwest before her family moved to Tampa."

Their conversation moved to college. He went to a small, unknown school called Barton. It wasn't too far from Bentonville. She was an English major at Brown.

"Brown? Wow," he said. "Ivy League girl. You must be, one, smart and, two, rich."

"Well, I was a pretty good student. And my dad does okay. He's a developer. Commercial office buildings."

"Brothers and sisters?"

"Nope. Only child."

"Me, too."

They spent the next hour with everyone getting to know one another better.

"I'm ready to head back," Suzy said. "We need to get up early in the morning. How about you guys?"

"Yep," Crystal said. "I'm plumb tuckered out. I need to lay my head on a pillow and visit Neverland."

"I'm not ready to turn in yet," Amanda said. "*L.A. Law* is on tonight. Maybe the bartender will put it on the TV."

The bartender, an Aussie no less, agreed to switch the TV to TV3, the new Malaysian station that carried English-language shows, mostly from the US.

Joey admitted he was an *L.A. Law* fan, as well. While waiting for the show to start, they discussed their favorite *L.A. Law* characters.

"I like Arnie," Joey said.

"He's a pig!"

"Yeah. That, too. Listen," Joey added, "since we're going to stick around to watch the show, we'll be late. I'll see that you get back to your hotel okay."

"Thank you," she said. "That's nice. It's not far, but a young woman on the street at night is probably not a great idea."

The others said their goodbyes and see-you-in-the-mornings, then headed out. Amanda and Joey chatted until the show came on the TV. She liked him. He was easy to talk to, funny, with a nice smile and was, she had to admit, not hard on the eyes. He was maybe an inch or two shy of six feet tall and looked fit. If his biceps were any hint, he even had some muscles.

Knowing his story, it was easy now to see that he was biracial. You could see the Brit in him. But she also understood why Martin thought Joey was a local. Martin probably had focused on Joey's complexion.

What you might see first if he were standing in a group of local men would be skin tone. Joey would fit right in with them. A Malaysian's skin tone is darker than Westerners but with a hint of yellow. The closest thing she could compare it to back home was people from Mexico and Latin America, except for the slight Asian hue.

The obvious comparisons to Malays pretty much ended there, though. Apart from the color, he had the face of a Brit. Joey's nose was narrower than the typical Malay nose and came to more of a downward point so that his nostrils were not so visible. Malays generally had high cheekbones on a squarish face. Joey's face was more of an oval. His head boasted sandy brown hair, several shades lighter than adorned the heads of the men from here. Even his light brown eyebrows set him apart from the locals. They were neither thick nor bushy.

It all came together quite well on him. Suzy was right, she thought to herself, he is a hunk. As he spoke, she found herself looking at his lips. He had nice lips. She had a brief thought that they were very kissable lips.

There was something else she liked about him. He made eye contact,

13

true lingering eye contact with his soft brown eyes. She felt it said something good about a man who is willing to maintain eye contact. The slight twinkle in his eyes made her feel immediately comfortable with him.

"Hey, you want to walk down to the docks to scope out the fishing boats?" he asked when *L.A. Law* ended. "One of them will be taking us to Tioman tomorrow."

"I don't know. You think it's safe to walk around there?"

"Amanda, this isn't a big bad city. They don't know how to spell c-r-i-m-e here. And I suspect I could handle anyone who even looks at us funny." He gave a grin and flexed a bicep.

"Yeah, like that would work against a knife," she said with a smile, then raised her eyebrows and added, "but I do have to say it looks good on you."

They walked to the docks. She was glad they did. A slight breeze wafted in off the water. It was a beautiful moon-lit night. Mersing is a quiet town and it felt as if they had the entire place to themselves. She hooked her arm into his as they walked along. At the end of a dock, Joey turned toward Amanda, gently touched under her chin and softly kissed her.

"That was nice," she told him.

"Yes, it was," he responded softly.

They meandered back toward the Happy Song.

"I'm another five minutes into town," he said when they got to her hotel.

"Listen, I'm not sleepy," Amanda said. "You want to come in for a bit?"

In her room, the only place to sit was on the bed. She rummaged through her backpack and found two candles. She placed one on the nightstand and the other on the chest. She lit them with a Bic lighter.

"I find rooms in places like this are always have those damn fluorescent lights. Way too bright. So I carry a couple candles with me." With that, she walked over, turned off the dangling light and the soft glow of the candles dimly lighted the small room. She sat on the bed next to him, leaned in and said, "I liked that kiss." She then kissed him again. And, of course, he kissed her back.

He laid her on the bed and nuzzled her neck. After a couple minutes, he moved his left hand under her Madonna Like a Virgin tee-shirt and caressed her breast. She liked it and kissed him a little more breathlessly. He sat up and pulled off his shirt. She took in his well-toned muscles. He helped her pull her shirt over her head, then unbuttoned her shorts and pulled them down and off.

She wasn't reluctant. She was doing this and she was liking it. He slid down and kissed her through her yellow dotted panties, then moved them aside and licked her. When he did, she made a soft purring sound and pressed herself against his lips.

"Take off your pants," she breathed. He did as he was told. He was clearly ready for her. She took him in one hand, stroking slowly. It felt solid. She kissed the side, then outlined the tip with her tongue. Joey was enjoying this.

Amanda looked up at him, scooted back across the bed and opened her arms. No words were needed. He climbed between her legs and entered her with a slow, smooth stroke. The tempo picked up. Then picked up again. Her purrs turned into more audible moans.

"Are you almost there?" he whispered in her ear.

"Oh God, yes," she whispered back.

He was good. She started taking short breaths. Amanda could feel it coming. She was so close. He changed his angle of penetration. She gasped, then shuddered. He slowed for a moment, then feeling his own orgasm nearing, he sped up again. With one hand, he moved her hips up so he could drive in deeper. Then, in a burst, he was done.

"My God," she said after they laid quietly for a moment. "Are all Malaysian men as good as you?"

"Only the ones raised in America," he said with a smile.

They lay together for a bit longer, then she said she needed to go to the bathroom.

She turned on the bathroom light and closed the door. She looked in the mirror. "That was intense," she said to herself. "I wonder if he'll be as good next time."

While she cleaned up, Joey was busy, as well. First, he moved his clothes out of the way to a corner of the room. From the left front pocket of his pants, he pulled a pearl-handled switch-blade knife. He opened the blade and watched a moment while the light from the candles flickered on it. He moved behind where the door would open and waited. He heard her turn off the water.

Amanda opened the door and stepped though.

"I was thinking…" was all she got out before he grabbed her from behind. His right hand covered her mouth. In one quick move, he wielded the knife, a beautiful pearl-handled stiletto with a five-inch blade, with his left hand and slashed deeply through and across the exposed front of her neck. It was over in an instant. He held her up for a moment, making sure she could utter no sounds, then let her droop, face up, across the bed. Her body twitched a bit and her blue eyes peered up at him in horror. She knew she was dying. He watched her as her life faded away. It didn't take long.

From the small day pack he carried, Joey pulled out his Walkman. He popped in his headphones and pressed play. The song he had queued had become part of his ritual. He, bopped his head to the beat and picked up part of the song, singing under his voice:

. . .*And another one gone, and another one gone*
Another one bites the dust
Hey, I'm gonna get you, too
Another one bites the dust

Keeping Queen's beat, he pranced around the small room as if he were Freddie Mercury himself. This had become his favorite part of the night. High on the adrenaline that always came with the squirts of blood, he danced over to the bed and used the sheet to wipe the blood from his knife. "I'm good at this," he thought. Then he got down to why he was there.

Her backpack contained a Nikon with a telephoto lens. That was a score. She also had a newer model Walkman – better than his. That Walkman could bring some bucks, but he just might keep it for his songs.

He also found her passport, ten like-new hundred-dollar bills in a money belt she usually wore under her shorts. The pouch also contained another fifteen-hundred dollars in traveler's checks and two credit cards. One was a gold Mastercard and the other an American Express. In the right front pocket of her shorts pocket was about hundred dollars' worth of Malaysian ringgits.

Finally, he removed the gold locket from around her dead neck. It was probably a gift from Daddy. He didn't know how much it was worth, but it had to have decent value. He was sure it was real gold. And he would bet that the diamond atop the heart was real and at least a carat. He took it to the sink and washed off all the blood and put it in his pack.

Joey washed his hands and splashed cold water on his face. He removed the condom he was wearing, flushed it, then washed his crotch. He returned to the bedroom and put on his clothes. He moved to the door and listened. No sounds. This, he knew, was the most dangerous part of his night. He had to get out without being seen. He cracked the door open, listened again, then peaked out. No one was in the hall. He slipped out, headed to the back door and left the Happy Song.

He moved swiftly through the night to a spot outside town where he had hidden his motorcycle two days before. He climbed on, kicked it to life and sped away.

Suzy knocked on Amanda's door the next morning. When there was no answer, she figured that Amanda had gone to Joey's place. They seemed to be getting it on last night. She, Martin and Crystal walked to the dock, suspecting that Amanda and Joey would be there. When they didn't show up, the backpackers shrugged and headed on to Tioman. "We'll probably see them tomorrow," Suzy said.

Joey rode all night. By noon the next day, he was home. Dead tired, he just wanted to collapse on his bed and sleep. But he knew that he couldn't do it just yet. He had to move the items.

Day 2

The shower and shave gave Joey a second wind. He made some toast and scrambled a couple eggs. He allowed himself one cup of coffee. Joey wanted just enough caffeine to keep him lucid through the next couple of hours.

His body still craved sleep. Understandable. He was now past twenty-four hours since he last closed his eyes and drifted off. It was okay. Part of the job. He'd have the rest of the day to crank up the AC, close both sets of curtains in his bedroom and crash. Time in his business was money. This was especially true for the traveler's checks.

Joey grabbed his day pack with Amanda's stuff, climbed on his Honda and headed into George Town. His destination was a nondescript tailor's shop in the old part of town. It was an easy twenty-minute ride.

Big Willie Chirathivat sat in the air-conditioned shop his family had run for three generations. The storefront was in a two-story building on a side street in George Town. The sign outside above the shop simply read TAILOR.

Willie had been called Big Willie since childhood. By ten, he was twice the size of his schoolmates. Now, thirty years later, Big Willie didn't know how much he weighed. Four hundred pounds? Maybe more. Remarkably, he seemed otherwise healthy.

His grandfather had moved his part of the family from Bangkok to Penang in 1932 as part of a plan to expand the Chirathivat crime network. The Chirathivat families were all tailors, so each set up a legitimate tailor shop in their new city. It would be a front for buying and selling stolen goods.

Big Willie was Joey's fence.

The Chirathivat family plan was simple enough. Move what you could locally, but make sure thieves knew that nothing was beyond the family's scope. Art masterpieces. Rare coins. Ancient artifacts. Jewels. The family could find buyers somewhere in the world for it all. Before the Japanese invaded in late 1941, the Penang branch of the family had already moved millions of dollars in art and artifacts up to Bangkok and on to buyers on four continents. The war changed all that, though.

Clearly, things didn't work out quite as the family had hoped back in Bangkok. While the Penang Chirathivats got through the war, it cost them dearly. Big Willie's only sibling, an only child at the time, was playing outside with friends a couple blocks away on December 8, 1941. That was the first day of Japanese bombing. Terrified, the young boy ran toward home as fast as he could.

He wasn't fast enough.

In the wrong place at the wrong time, the boy died instantly when the bomb exploded just feet from him. The family grieved. It was six years before they had another child, Willie. The Chirathivats survived the war by keeping their heads down. They fell back on their skills as tailors for the four long years of Japanese occupation.

Other branches of the Chirathivat family had established similar satellite shops in Kuala Lumpur, Singapore, as well as Chaing Mai in northern Thailand, the Laotian capital of Vientiane and Saigon. All suffered at the hands of the Japanese.

World War II threw a major wrench into the Chirathivat family plan to become the dominant crime family in Southeast Asia. Family leaders suffered and died at the hands of the Japanese. By the end of the war, the family's outposts, like its base in Bangkok, were shadows of what they were before the war. Family members still cooperated with each other, but the vision of the crime empire had faded.

The successes of the Communists in Vietnam, Cambodia and Laos eroded the family network even more. The Saigon branch thrived during the Vietnamese American war, but within a year of the fall of

Saigon several family members were dead, and others had fled back to Bangkok. It was a similar story in Phnom Penh.

Joey met Big Willie not long after he moved to Penang in 1981. By then, Joey had become a purse-snatcher. He was smart enough to know he was leaving money on the table with every purloined purse.

Here's what he would do. He'd target an older white woman and when he could see a clear getaway path, he'd grab the purse and run like hell. He always knew where he was running to: an out-of-sight place where he could take a moment, undisturbed, to dump the contents on the ground and quickly go through them. There was always cash and it went straight into his pockets. Then he'd look for anything that would be easy to pawn. Everything else he'd leave there on the ground then he'd slink away.

Every time he'd leave behind credit cards – all older white tourists carried credit cards – usually a book of traveler's checks and often a passport. Joey just knew those things just had to have some value to someone.

One day, the purse carried a small Leica camera. He took it to one of the handful of pawnbrokers he used. After telling Joey how much the camera was worth, the man eyed him closely.

"Look, kid," the shopkeeper said, "I have a pretty good idea how you got this camera and all the other stuff you've brought me in the past. I'm thinking there's more, right?"

Joey grew a little suspicious. His eyes darted around, but everything appeared as it had in the past.

Joey looked back at the man, who held his gaze, then pulled out a booklet of ten crisp American Express hundred-dollar traveler's checks. The man eyed Joey and the checks and chewed on his lower lip.

"I know someone," he finally said, "who might be able to help you. Tear out one of the checks. I'll show it to my friend and see what he says. Come back at eleven tomorrow morning."

Joey tore a check from the checkbook and gave it to the man. He returned the next day as instructed. The broker told him to go to a

21

nearby café for lunch at one o'clock. There would be a very big, well dressed Thai waiting for him.

"Everyone calls him Big Willie. You'll see why. Speak English when you see him."

Joey couldn't miss the well-dressed but obese Thai man sitting at a private table toward the back of the dining room. He walked to him.

"Big Willie?" he asked. The man nodded. "I'm Joey. I was told to meet you here." Big Willie pointed to the empty chair across the table from him. He signaled the waiter to serve them.

"Tell me about yourself, Joey."

So, Joey did.

He told Big Willie how he had arrived in George Town a few months before. He had been in KL briefly before, having moved there from Melaka. He then got into the more interesting part of his story.

"I was born in Melaka. My mother died when I was seven and I never knew my father. My mother said he was a British sailor."

"That explains your looks."

"Yeah, I don't look much like my mother. I suspect I have my father's eyes and nose."

"And hair," Big Willie added.

Joey nodded.

"So, tell me, Joey, what exactly do you do?"

A moment of truth, but Joey saw no reason to hold back.

"I grab purses from old white ladies."

Willie accepted that answer in a matter-of-fact way.

"I pocket the cash and pawn what I can."

"But you get things that you don't know what to do with."

"Yes. Like the traveler's checks. I always get credit cards, too. Sometimes a passport. I suspect the passport is worth something."

"Of course."

Joey immediately asked how much, but Willie shook his head. He focused on the beer the waiter had set before him. Neither uttered a word.

"How often do you steal a purse?" Big Willie broke the silence.

"Two, sometimes three times a month."

That was the right answer, as far as Big Willie was concerned. Most purse-snatchers get greedy and think they're never going to get caught. He had known young men who would go for purses every day. He would stop working with them because he knew it was just a matter of time before they were caught. When the police nab a young thief, they're going to drill him to learn who his fence is.

"Good answer. From now on, bring everything to me and I mean everything. And you have to follow my rules. OK?"

"What rules?"

"Well, rule number one is obvious, but it has to be number one. Don't get caught. If you get caught, you and I will never work together again. Have you ever been caught?"

Joey told him about getting caught in Melaka. It was a few months after Pastor Johnny had left. He said he could recall vividly being handcuffed and taken to the police station. It was an awful experience. He had grabbed food off a table – he was hungry, after all – and then had the rotten luck to turn and literally run into a police officer. He spent the night in jail but was released the next day.

The fat man gave a subtle nod of his head. He used a finger to trace a design in the lace around the flowers that sat on a centerpiece on the table.

"And what did you learn from that?" he asked.

"To always know how I'm going to get away."

Big Willie smiled a big toothy smile.

"That's right," he said.

"What about unexpected opportunities?" Big Willie asked. "Carpe diem, right? You see a little old lady walking alone with a big purse dangling from her arm. Almost too good to be true. What do you do?"

"If I see an old lady like that, I start looking around to see where I'd run and who might chase me. If it all looks good, then yeah, I'll grab it.

23

But if I see anything I don't like, I pass."

"Good. Good. Don't get greedy."

Joey frowned. He wasn't sure what Big Willie meant. Steal less? Big Willie saw that Joey was confused.

"Look, the more time you can put between grabs, the less likely you'll be caught. Do you know why?"

Joey peered at his curry, then looked back at Big Willie. "Less chance for people to remember what I look like."

"Excellent! You never want people to remember you. Never!" He paused and peered more closely at Joey's face. "That will be harder for you so it's even more important."

The waiter came and asked if they would like another beer. Big Willie's glass was empty, but Joey's was still almost full. The Thai simply pointed at his glass. The waiter left to get him another.

"Tell me, Joey. You speak English like an American. If I didn't know better, I might think you were an American. How did that happen?"

"After my mother died, I was taken in by an American pastor and his wife. They ran a mission school in Melaka. They had no children and treated me as a son."

"How very fortunate for you."

"Yes. My good fortune."

Joey explained that everything at home was in English. They watched a lot of American TV and movies on videotape. His American mom – what he called her – tutored him every day.

"She would play a movie on the Betamax," Joey said, "then pause the tape, back it up and replay a bit of the dialogue." He pantomimed pushing the buttons on the machine. "She'd then have me repeat it. My job was to speak exactly like the guy in the movie. Sometimes, we'd replay the piece eight, nine, even ten times. Mom said she was training my ear in order to train my voice. It sounds boring, but I loved it. I loved her."

"Are they still in Melaka?"

"No," Joey said, then explained that his mom went back to the States.

24

A month later, his dad packed up and left, too.

"He gave me some money and said he'd come back, but he didn't."

Big Willie's gaze drifted to an attractive Chinese woman who had just walked in. She was wearing a body-hugging red dress. She was well coiffed and carried herself with an air of confidence. She was hard to miss. Joey's back was to her.

"Always dress to blend in," Big Willie said, returning his eyes to Joey. He told the young man to never wear a shirt or hat that would be easy for others to describe with any detail.

"That hat you were wearing when you came in," he said to Joey as the waiter set his second beer before him.

"What about it?"

Willie paused to take a sip and savored it.

"That NY on the front," he said. "That's the kind of thing people remember."

Another point came to him. Mix up where you grab purses, the fat Thai continued.

"If you grab in front of Khoo Kongsi, don't go back there for at least a couple months," he said. "And never snatch near where you live or anywhere close to me.

"Listen to me, Joey. Never lead anyone to me. If you do, well, you'll never do it again."

Joey saw the deadly serious expression on Big Willie's face. He got the message. If Big Willie got arrested because Joey led the police to him, Big Willie would kill him. It was something he'd never had to think about before. But he understood it. If he was caught, he could never give up Big Willie. Besides, if he went to prison, he'd need Big Willie again when he got out.

"I understand," Joey said.

Big Willie paid for lunch, then told Joey to walk with him back to the shop. Joey needed to know where it was because that's where he would bring the things he stole.

"Bring me everything you get," Big Willie reiterated. "Well, you can just stick the cash in your pocket. But everything else. You might be surprised at what has value."

"Even the purse?"

"Yes. Obviously, you want to keep it out of sight. Some purses have hidden compartments. And some will be true designer bags. Those have value in and of themselves."

At the shop, Big Willie asked Joey for the rest of the traveler's checks. Joey handed them to him.

"And do you have this woman's passport?"

"I didn't keep it."

"Hmm. Too bad." He opened a file, withdrew a stack of twenty-dollar bills and counted out some for Joey. "If you had the passport, I could have given you twice as much for the checks and another three hundred dollars for the passport itself."

Joey's eyes widened. He had literally dumped and walked away from hundreds, perhaps thousands of dollars. Never again.

One day, Joey asked Big Willie how someone could travel with only two-hundred or three-hundred dollars on them.

"I know they use their credit cards and some of them have traveler's checks, but I bet when they left for their trip, they had a lot more than a few hundred dollars in cash."

"They wear money belts. It's where they keep most of their cash."

Joey had no idea what a money belt was, so Big Willie explained that it was a pouch that a tourist would wear under their clothing. Older tourists, Big Willie said, traveled with more cash than younger ones.

"Those old ladies you rob could easily have twenty hundred-dollar bills in a money belt," Big Willie said. "They only keep the cash in their purse that they think they might need that day."

He explained that many of the older folks go to a bank almost every day to convert dollars into ringgits.

Joey thought about all the old ladies he had robbed of their purses. How many, he wondered, were wearing a money belt with a couple thousand dollars in it. His mind went to work trying to figure out a way to get to all that cash.

————————

In the six years since that first meeting, Joey had seen Big Willie often. Big Willie became more than a mentor to him. Joey profited from the older man's advice. The average Malaysian was earning about a thousand dollars a year. Joey was pocketing three times as much. The two had grown much closer. Joey would show up with goods to fence and Big Willie would insist on taking him to a nice indoor restaurant. Joey found that if he went home and dressed in better clothes, Big Willie would take him to an even finer place. Joey even had what he thought of as his Big Willie dinner clothes.

At a quiet table over dinner one night about three years ago, Joey leaned in closer to Big Willie and said he had an idea for something bigger. Instead of snatching purses from old women, he would prey on young American women – girls really – traveling alone.

"It's all about getting to the money belt," he told Big Willie when he first laid out the plan.

To get to the money belt, he had to get them alone. To do that, he would need to win their trust or their lust. He suspected that playing to their lust was the easiest and fastest route.

"You've always said I could pass as an American," Joey said. "If I become just another American backpacker, but a charming one, I'll win them over."

Big Willie sat quietly, staring at the candle that flickered on the table between them. Finally, he looked back to Joey and said, "Yes. I believe you could."

Big Willie told him that he'd need a good backstory. It needed to be one he could deliver convincingly to each young woman he targeted.

"Keep your lies as close to the truth as you can," he said. "You'll be less likely to get tripped up."

Over the next hour, the two of them built Joey's new life story. It indeed stayed close to the truth with one huge difference. In the new version, the pastor and his wife adopted Joey and then took him back to live in North Carolina.

Joey's story began as it actually had. His mother was a Malaysian woman who met a British sailor who she knew only as Reggie. She was an attractive eighteen-year-old who worked at the port. One evening, the sailor was taking shore leave just as she was leaving work. He exuded charm and confidence. She was taken by him.

Reggie's ship was only in port for a few days. Reggie was long gone before his mother learned she was pregnant. It was tough being a single mother with a biracial son in a country where to be officially considered to be Malay you had to have a Muslim Malay father.

Even as a toddler it was obvious his father was not Malaysian. For some people, the first thing they noticed when they looked at the little boy was that while his skin tone matched theirs, little else about his appearance did. Eyes, nose, shape of his face, even his sandy brown hair clearly came from his daddy's genes. But his mother endured the ostracism and provided for him as best she could.

Then, when he was just seven years old, his mother was struck by a car while crossing a highway. She died at the scene. Everything about the story was true to this point.

Then the fiction took over. There was no one to take care of Yusof, his Malaysian name, so authorities placed him in an orphanage. They knew, of course, that no one would want him.

Luckily for Joey, the assistant director of the orphanage was a member of a nearby mission church run by an older childless couple. The gentleman brought young Yusof to church one Sunday and Helen Jackson, Pastor Johnny's wife, fell in love with him on the spot.

In the story that Joey would eventually repeat as if it were the gospel truth, the man from the orphanage was able to arrange for the pastor and his wife to adopt the boy by saying he wasn't actually a Malaysian Muslim, but the son of a Christian Englishman. That ruse might have worked in real life, but for Joey it never came to that.

The real story of Yusof's young life was that after his mother died, he lived on the streets. That's where Mrs. Helen found him one day.

He had survived as a seven-year-old thief and scavenger. He looked it. But Mrs. Helen saw a beautiful young boy, a gift from God. Pastor Johnny wasn't so sure, but he knew that when his Helen had her heart set on something that he'd best let it be. So, in real life, the pastor and his wife took young Yusof in and raised him like their own for the next ten years.

In Joey's new life story, the pastor and his wife's mission service ended the year after Joey joined them. When they had adopted him, they gave him an American name. Since Yusof is the Muslim version of Joseph, they renamed him Joseph Thomas Jackson, but simply called him Joey. He moved to North Carolina with them and they raised him as their only child. After high school, he attended Barton College, a small Christian college near them, and earned a degree in business administration.

It was a good story. Joey was able to make it sound real. Inspiring even.

Joey paid Big Willie to create a US passport and a North Carolina driver's license for him.

Joey's plan was to woo a young American woman traveling alone somewhere in Malaysia and get her to take him back to her hotel. Once in the room, he would gag her and tie her up, then rifle through her stuff. He was looking for her money belt and anything else of value.

Big Willie, though, saw a fatal flaw in the plan.

"You're not considering one of the key rules to not get caught, Joey. Blend in. You don't want anyone to be able to describe you. These girls are going to be able to tell the police exactly what you look like and even your American name. You have a very distinctive look, Joey. The police will come looking for you."

Joey nodded in agreement. "What can I do?"

"For starters, don't do anything in or around George Town. This is your safe place. Okay?"

"Okay."

"There are probably places these girls go to. That's where you should do it."

"Yeah. There are places. They go to a lot of beach areas. I see them all the time when I'm out at Batu Ferringhi."

"Too close."

"Yeah, I know."

"So, get to know the places they hang out, make a plan, go do it, then jump on your motorcycle and ride back here as fast as you can. Best case is that you're back here handing stuff to me before anyone ever finds the girl."

Big Willie thought some more then frowned.

"I don't know, Joey. That doesn't solve your biggest problem," he said. "The girls will be able to tell the cops a lot about you. It's only a matter of time before someone fits the pieces fit together. I don't like it."

The two men sat in thought. Then Big Willie spoke again.

"There is one way to keep them from telling anyone about you."

Silence separated the two men, a generation apart, mentor and student, but now more than that. They had become friends. Well, more than friends, really.

Big Willie was the last in the line of Chirathivats in Penang. He was alone and missed having family. As did Joey. The bond between the two had evolved. They might not have been family biologically, but they were becoming one emotionally.

Both knew that Joey faced the biggest decision of his life. Big Willie said the choice Joey would make would forever define him.

Does grabbing a purse from an old lady make him a violent person? The real question pushed its way forward in his mind.

Could he kill? That's what Big Willie was putting before him. Could he end the life of a young woman simply so he could do it again? And again?

When you make a living snatching purses from old ladies, you stop thinking of them as people. Often, the victim would not just be old, but elderly. Some even frail. They would usually fall to the pavement. Once, he yanked a purse so hard that he pulled the elderly woman into the street where she was struck by a taxi. He never knew what happened to her.

As he thought about that time, it dawned on him that he didn't really care what had happened to her. As he pondered it, he realized that she probably died. He let that sink in but felt nothing.

Nothing.

After some time, he looked Big Willie straight in the eyes. "I can do it," he said matter-of-factly.

The fat Thai simply nodded his head.

Two months later, Joey slit the throat of Annie Smith, a twenty-two-year-old graduate marine biology student at the Rosenthal School at the University of Miami. She was found in her room at a small hotel near the docks in Kuala Besut.

On her nightstand was a letter she had written to her parents dated the day before. In her last letter home, gathered up and shipped back to her grieving parents, Annie wrote that she was excited to share a boat the next day for the ninety-minute crossing to the Perhentian Islands. She told her parents that even before leaving Miami, Annie learned of Perhentian's stunningly clear waters, its fantastic coral reefs and its abundant marine life. One of her professors, who had been there himself, said it was one of the best undiscovered places to dive anywhere in the world.

But it wasn't to be. Like six young women after her, Annie would never make it to a special island. She would be charmed by a young American of partial Malaysian descent.

He would be a handsome young man whom a young woman would meet while sightseeing alone, or about to have dinner alone or doing something else alone. Always alone. A young man from North Carolina with a warm smile and beautifully expressive eyes would end up in her bed. He would make love to her and then she would die.

As he had meticulously planned, Joey would rummage through all her belongings. At the top of his list was always the money belt. Annie didn't disappoint him. She took it off as they were climbing into bed.

31

He watched her lay it on the nightstand.

He fought the urge to just kill her so he could see what treasure was hidden in the belt. But this would be her last night on earth. "I'm not an animal," he told himself. He wanted her to be enraptured right up until the end. He caressed her, treated her gently and then passionately. He waited for her to shake with pleasure before he cut her throat then watched her take her last breath.

He sat up and reached for the money belt. His heart raced. He realized that he was nervous. He needn't be. When he unzipped the money belt to look at what was inside, he found twelve-hundred dollars in cash, a passport, and three credit cards.

A new career was born.

That was two and a half years ago. On this day, Joey arrived at Big Willie's with everything of any value that he could find after blonde-haired, blue-eyed Amanda had bled out. He started the long motorcycle ride back from Mersing to Penang at about four in the morning. stopping only for food, gas and to relieve himself. He was exhausted with no sleep in more than a day. But Joey put the solitary ride to good use and added to it while taking a quick shower before going to Big Willie's. He developed a new plan for his life and was eager to get the fat Thai's take on it.

———————

The bells on the door jingled as Joey walked into the tailor shop. Big Willie emerged from the back room and broke into a big smile when he saw Joey. He wrapped his arms around him as if he were a son returning from overseas service.

They took care of business, then Joey said he had an idea that he wanted Big Willie to weigh in on.

"I'm not going to be able to do this forever," Joey said. "I'm good at it and the girls like me. But I'm not going to always have my looks. Look, my face is already starting to show its age."

"You're a good-looking young man and will be a for a while," Big Willie said. "And you are making what now, nearly six thousand or so dollars a year? You are living well, young man. Why mess with that? It works for you."

"Because it won't last," Joey responded. "Look at me. I'm looking older." He pointed to his eyes at lines Big Willie couldn't really see.

"You're nuts."

"No, I'm not. I need young girls to make it all work. I'm a little bit older than them now, so we're close. Five years from now, I won't look as good to them. I just won't. You know that."

Big Willie realized that Joey was dead serious. He looked at him closely, chewing on his lower lip.

"That may be true," Big Willie said finally, "but you have lived well off the young ladies. You might be hard-pressed to find something to match it."

"Maybe not."

"Why not just move up to older women?"

"First, there are fewer of them. Beyond that, though, older women are not as willing to take risks. I rely on the girls being willing to take me alone back to their rooms the night we meet. Some older women might do that, but not many. So, why not move on to something entirely different?"

Joey said his biggest asset wasn't how he looked, but how he acted.

"It doesn't hurt that they think I'm a good-looking guy. That gets me in the door. But it's my charm that makes them like me. It's what makes me safe enough to hang out with and take back to their room. There's no reason I should ever lose my charm. That's what I should be relying on. My charm."

Big Willie had never seen Joey in action but had knew from early on that Joey oozed with charm. He could see how it could be totally disarming.

Joey laid his idea out for Big Willie.

Between victims, Joey had traveled around the country. He did it for two main reasons. First, he knew it helped him with the break-the-ice conversations if he could talk about the places the young women were thinking about visiting. In the past two and a half years, he had been to all the popular islands, many of the beaches and even a few undiscovered gems.

The other reason he did it, though, was to scope good places to find, target, kill and rob a victim. That's why Amanda was murdered in Mersing and not on Tioman. Before her, he slit Sally Simpson's throat in Lumut, not on Pangkor. Even Annie, his first victim, was done in Kuala Besut, not on Perhentian Kecil where she was headed. All his victims fit this pattern. Each died not at their next destination, but where they needed to spend the night before getting there.

Amanda was a classic Joey victim. He didn't need to ask where she was going when he got on the bus in Melaka. Any backpacker getting on that bus was heading to Tioman Island. What he knew that she didn't, though, was that they'd arrive too late to ride the tide out of the harbor, so would need to stay one night in Mersing. He learned this the day before when he hid his motorcycle in the port town. While there, he checked the tides for the next few days. Once he knew the tides, it was easy to find a bus that would arrive after the last high tide of the day.

He then used his knowledge of Tioman itself to become a valued member of his new traveling band of backpackers, all of whom had just met that day on the bus. He regaled them with glimpses of what lie in store for them on the island. He talked about the cold water that cascaded from the waterfall near the top of the mountain in the center of the island. Hikers, he said, would strip naked and just let the water flow over them to cool off. It was so invigorating, he said. It felt wonderful. To those who heard his story, it felt exciting. They wanted to be there, stripping naked and feeling the water wash over them.

He might tell another story about the only bungalows and restaurant on Pulau Bumbon Besar that serves homemade fried chicken every Tuesday. After being on the road for months, a young woman's heart would skip a beat at the mere thought of fried chicken.

Backpackers stayed in what many referred to as bungalow villages.

They were small establishments that offered basic bungalow huts around a common, open-air restaurant overlooking a beach. They were just getting popular in Malaysia, but already were found widely on islands and beaches in Thailand.

He told Big Willie about a trip he had made to Koh Samui, a popular Thai island in the South China Sea. He explained that most were a collection of eight to ten bungalows built around a common restaurant, but sometimes more. There were even a couple bungalow villages with a larger hut that could sleep six to eight guests, like a hostel.

"These are happy places, Big Willie. Most of the guests are in their twenties. They like to party. The restaurant becomes the center of their world for the few days they are there. They eat all their meals there, then in the afternoon and at nighttime they sit at the tables playing games, talking about where they've been or plan to go, all the while drinking beer. Lots of beer. The restaurant is a gold mine."

"As I visited these places, Big Willie," Joey continued, "I realized that the difference between the ones that were hopping and the others boiled down to one thing. You know what it was?"

"Good food?"

"No. The popular places all had a guy that everyone loved running the place. And Big Willie, none was as charming as me!"

Big Willie frowned, clearly skeptical.

"What's the play here, Joey? I don't see the job."

"That's the beauty of it. There is no job. I want to build my own little bungalow village and run it till I die. It's totally legitimate. It's the best of everything. These places make good money. I'll be paid to be charming. I'll still get to screw beautiful young women. I just won't kill them. In fact, I'll want them to tell people about me and my place when they move on."

Joey was beaming. Big Willie wasn't.

"So," Big Willie said somewhat incredulously, "you want to buy a small hotel on a beach?"

"Not a hotel. And not buy."

35

"You want to steal one? I don't see how."

"I want to build," Joey said emphasizing the word build, "my own bungalow village and restaurant."

Big Willie whistled. "That'll take more money than you have."

"Yeah, but I have an idea how I can get the money. You're going to love it!"

He told Big Willie what he saw as the problem with young girls. You could take everything they travel with, but that was it. For the most part, his take would pay him usually about twenty-five-hundred dollars, sometimes more.

"That's a good payday for you, Joey," Big Willie said.

"No future in it," Joey quickly responded.

Big Willie tilted his head in thought, then slightly nodded that he didn't disagree.

"Older women have more money," Joey said. "I see them all the time at Batu Ferringhi. They stay in hotels, not bungalows or guest houses. They dress better. When they are in the cafes, you can tell they order whatever they want. They don't care about the price."

"But you will have the same problem with them you have with the young girls. They won't be traveling with a lot of cash. They're using credit cards, so they don't need so much cash. Sure, they'll have more than Amanda, but not enough to build your bungalow place."

"I know that. What they have, though, that the young girls don't is a lot more money back home in the bank. And if that older woman is traveling alone, I bet that she controls her bank account, not some guy."

"Wait a minute, Joey! You actually think you can get some woman you met last night to give you the keys to her bank account?"

"Yes! I'm sure of it! But no, not a one-night thing. It's a long play, Big Willie. It will take all my charms and a few weeks, maybe a month, but I can do it. I know I can."

"Hmmm. I don't know, Joey. You really think that some American woman is going to hand you – wait, how much do you think you need?"

"I can do the whole thing for fifty-thousand dollars."

"You're going to get a woman to give you, a stranger in a foreign country, fifty-thousand dollars?"

"She's not going to give it to me exactly. She's going to invest it in me."

"What?!!"

Joey explained that over the course of a few weeks, he would weave the two of them closer together. At some point, he said, the woman would want to know what he planned to do with his life.

"She'll bring it up. Not me. Here's the thing, I won't tell her that I'm going to build one bungalow village. I'll say I'm going to build a chain of them! Very American of me, don't you think?"

The Thai gave a look that said he still wasn't buying it.

"She'll get to know me as a guy with a business degree and a business plan. Build one location to establish the brand, then add more. If I choose my lady right, she'll like the idea. I'll have her wanting to invest. I'm sure I can do it."

"So, she invests," Big Willie said, adding emphasis to the word invests, "in your plan."

"Yes."

"And then what?"

"Same as the others."

"You kill her?"

"Yes. But I'll need to make it look like an accident. Too many people will know about me. I'll be distraught. Then, as soon as I can I'll disappear to become Yusof again."

Big Willie stroked his chin. He poured Joey and himself glasses of tea. There was a long silence.

"It could work," Big Willie finally said. "I bet, though, that you'll get tired of being a respectable businessman and get back to dabbling in ill-gotten gains," he added with a grin.

"I don't think so."

Joey told Big Willie that he wanted a better persona. Not a different one. One with a backstory that would build on the one he was already using. He needed to become the businessman he was going to pretend to be.

"I know Joey Jackson. We should keep him. I am Joey Jackson."

Big Willie thought for a bit.

"We need to make you look like a businessman," he told Joey. "You know what they say: Clothes make the man. You'll need new clothes, a completely new wardrobe. You've been dressing and acting like a backpacker. I'll give you a new look, top to bottom."

He thought some more.

"You think this woman will visit your apartment?"

"I don't know, probably. I'm thinking I'll find her at one of the hotels in Batu Ferringhi. I see no reason not to hunt where I live this time."

"Probably a benefit. You can take as long you need to find the right woman."

Joey became animated as he envisioned wooing a woman at the beach. He spoke about bringing her back to his apartment for a home-cooked meal and wow her with his kitchen skills.

Big Willie started to see where Joey was going with all this. His inner-tailor kicked in.

"You'll need nice things hanging in your closet and folded in your drawers," Big Willie said. "That's my department. A couple business suits, dress shirts, leather shoes, the works. Leave that stuff to me."

Again there was a silence as the two men thought through everything.

"If you were serious about this, you'd have a company set up," the fat Thai said. "A bank account, too. But not just any bank account. It'll look legit but once you have her money and are ready to stop being Joey Jackson, you can close it and not worry about it being traced back to you should anyone start to look. My family in Singapore can do all that. People hide millions of dollars in Singapore all the time, so fifty-thousand dollars will be easy for them."

Big Willie pulled a sheet of paper from his desk and a pencil. He made categories and put amounts next to them. He wrote a category called "pursuit," then looked at Joey.

"It's going to take some time – who knows how long – for you to find the right woman. You might find a good one right away, but probably not. You might have to – what? – date" – he said the word as if a question – "several to find the right one. You need to be able to pay for all of that. Dinners. Sightseeing. Taxis. Whatever."

Big Willie told Joey that the woman didn't need to think he was rich, but that he did have the resources to treat her well.

Joey agreed and they came up with a sum. Big Willie wrote it next to the word pursuit. When he totaled it all up, it came to ten-thousand dollars.

"You have to spend ten grand to get fifty. You sure you want to do this?"

"Yeah," Joey said, "It's fifty that will set me up for life. Here's a problem, though. I don't have that much. I have about seven-thousand dollars."

Silence again filled the space between them, then Big Willie spoke.

"Maybe you should do one more young lady. That would put you close enough. It could be your last. Well, next to last."

Joey left Big Willie thinking about finding one more girl to kill and rob. Of course, he would do it. He had a plan and Joey always stuck to his plan. The only question in his mind was where to do it.

He had held to Big Willie's rule to not work where you live. That's why he had never targeted anyone in Penang. But maybe, since this would be the last one, it would be okay to do it here. He knew exactly where to go in George Town. Besides, he hadn't lived in George Town itself in a while. As he rode his motorcycle back to his apartment in Batu Ferringhi, he decided that tomorrow he would go hunting.

Day 3

On any given day, there might be more backpackers in Penang than all the other islands combined. There are reasons why so many make it to the northwest corner of the country.

First, if you're coming south from Thailand, a direct train links Bangkok and Butterworth. Backpackers love reasonably priced yet comfortable trains. It's old world charm. Dining cars. Great views. Uniformed conductors. The constant yet soothing clankety-clank of the steel wheels on the tracks that soon fade into the background like a mom's heartbeat. It's no wonder that each arrival unloads scores of mostly twenty-something travelers. There are also trains arriving from Singapore and Kuala Lumpur.

Not far from the train station is the region's main bus terminal. It was always packed and reeking of diesel. Foreign nomads who have wound their way through and across peninsula Malaysia usually arrive by bus.

The airport south of George Town sits on the island itself. Some backpackers arrive by air. Not many, though, unless it is the first stop on their big adventure. Backpackers are frugal and while Asia offers some very low-fare airlines, nomad travel is not about speed.

Once on the road for a few weeks, everything slows down. The rhythm of daily life back home loses its pounding beat. The joy shifts to the journey. Seeing things anew. Being with them long enough to feel them seep into your being. That kind of thing simply doesn't happen at thirty-five-thousand feet.

Mary Higgins had arrived on a bus from Kuala Lumpur late in the morning. The guidebooks suggested little to see and do in Butterworth, but across the Penang Strait was George Town. It boasted a robust, fun-filled neighborhood that catered to young travelers. Mary shared a taxi across the newly opened Penang Bridge with George and Sam, short for Samantha. She had met the two Kiwis on the bus. They told the driver they were looking for an inexpensive hotel in the heart of George Town. He drove them to the Lum Fong.

The Lum Fong wasn't much to look at, but Mary had learned that the most important aspect of a travelers' hotel was whether it was clean, something not always apparent from the outside or even the lobby. The best advice Mary got before leaving Boston was from a friend who told her to always ask to see the room and to check out the bathroom. "Some are truly disgusting," he told her, "and you don't want to find that out after you've paid for the night and checked in."

Having been on her journey a few months, Mary had learned a few things about hotels herself. First, if you ask to see the room before registering, the hotel clerk will take you to the nicest room available. That can be a game changer for how well you sleep at night. Second, a place that kept the bathrooms clean tended to keep the entire place clean. As a result, not just the bathrooms smelled better, but so did the room itself and the hallways leading to it. And – this was a big one for Mary – you are less likely to come face-to-face with a rat or other vermin.

The older Chinese man at reception agreed to show her a room with a bath on the second floor, as she had requested. It was basic, but at ten feet or so by ten feet, it was bigger than some she had stayed in. She sat on the bed, a full-size mattress on a platform. It felt firm enough and the sheets on top, while showing age, had clearly been laundered. The test, though, would be the bathroom. While not up to Holiday Inn standards, it had a western toilet, a hand sink and a shower. Better, everything, if not shiny, was clean and there was a nearly full roll of toilet paper.

"I'll take it," she said. Mary threw her stuff on the bed and followed the clerk back down the stairs, filled out the registry, shared her passport for the old man to record, then paid the ten Malaysian ringgits – about four dollars – for the night.

The aroma of cooking wafted into the lobby from the hotel's main floor restaurant. It was tempting, but experience had taught her that the best meal to eat in the hotel was always breakfast, regardless of how good dinner might smell. Breakfast could provide reliable basics, like eggs over easy, local sausage and a side of toast. And hotel coffee was usually drinkable. In fact, she had developed quite a taste for Malaysian coffee with sweet condensed milk.

Lunch and dinner, though, were always best elsewhere. With that in mind, Mary headed back up to her room, took a shower, changed clothes then headed out to explore her little corner of George Town.

Mary strolled down noisy Leith Street, past shops, personal service vendors like tailors, hair salons and watch repair, as well as restaurants. She didn't know what she had in mind, but thought she'd know it when she saw or smelled it. At Chulia Street, she turned left. Chulia clearly was a magnet for travelers like herself. It was teeming with somewhat scruffy-looking, young tourists.

After a few blocks, she stopped outside a cute place called the Rama-Rama Restaurant. Everything was adorned with butterflies. Mary glanced at the menu, looked inside the open-air establishment, liked what she saw and walked in. A minute later, a young man also entered the Rama-Rama and took the table next to hers.

She couldn't help but notice him as soon as he sat at one of the few tables in the Rama-Rama. He was wearing a clean, white tee-shirt that was tight enough to show some muscles and a boyish face that made his age hard to predict. Mary tried not to be too obvious. Still, she lingered. She had a game she liked to play with herself whenever she met someone new. Where were they from? She was stumped.

"Would you bring me a Tiger beer, please?" he asked, then added a "Thank you" when the waiter nodded yes.

"You're an American?" Mary asked him, startling herself. She didn't mean to say it out loud.

"North Carolina. And you?"

"Boston."

Until he spoke, she would not have pegged him as being from the States, though she didn't have any other origin in mind. He just didn't look the part. Besides, you don't come across many Americans in Malaysia. Lots of Brits, French and Germans. A fair number of Swedes. The ever-obvious Aussies and the more gentle, quick to smile Kiwis. But Americans? Not so much. She forgave herself for not realizing right away he was from the US.

The fact was, though, that he didn't look like most Americans. He had a skin tone you didn't see in the States. It was, she thought, like the Malaysian men she had seen. But he didn't look Malaysian in any other way. His features were just too refined. Maybe British, she wondered?

They chatted for a bit before the waiter came back with his beer.

"Do you want one?" he asked her.

"I'm not a big beer-drinker, but, hey, it's been a long, hot day."

He asked the waiter to bring a Tiger for the lady, then looked back to her.

"May I join you? Maybe we could share a couple plates. I like to try as many dishes as I can."

"Sure. And sharing sounds great."

He moved to her table.

"I'm Joey," he said with a sweet smile.

"Mary," she answered, feeling good about how her first night in Penang was working out.

Together, they chose items from the menu, ordered, then focused on each other with the usual sharing of their trips. She described coming from Kuala Lumpur, after spending two weeks in Taman Negara, a jungle rain forest so thick and lush it would fit in right in the heart of Africa.

"I've been thinking of going to Taman Negara," he said, "but just the thought is intimidating. Good for you to do something so," he paused

43

to think of the word, then said, "extreme."

"Oh, you absolutely should go," she told him. "Yes, it's extreme, as you put it, but It's fucking spectacular. Did you know that it's the oldest rain forest in the world?" He looked skeptical. "Really," she continued, "I thought it would have been the Amazon, but it's not. I'd never even heard of Taman Negara before coming to Malaysia!"

"I guess the Amazon has a better publicity agent," Joey said with a chuckle. "What's so great about visiting a rain forest? I mean, I'm not sure I want to traipse around in constant rain and god-awful heat."

"I can understand that," Mary said. "It can be, like you put it, 'god-awful hot and humid.' But believe me, it's worth it. The jungle is so overwhelming. That place hasn't changed since before the Ice Age. Wrap your mind around that, Joey. Talk about going back in time."

She told him to forget about taking a bus or car somewhere. "There are no roads. None!" she continued. "The only way to get from Point A to Point B is on the river. Or hiking. But that's for crazy people."

She pointed out that even though she was in good shape, she was spent in about two hours on a trail. Too hot. Too humid. Too many bugs. "Did I mentioned the mosquitos?" she asked. "Too many bites."

"I hear it can be dangerous," Joey said. "Tigers and leopards and stuff."

"I never saw anything like that, but let me tell you, you can hear them!" Mary said with emphasis. "One night I was in a little hut and suddenly there was a loud roar. It sounded like it was right outside. Roared several times. Scared the shit out of me. Took me several hours to get back to sleep. The next day one of the guides told us that it was a tiger, but it really wasn't as close as it sounded. I didn't believe him. He told us the only thing we really needed to worry about biting us were the mosquitos and leeches."

Mary glanced over Joey's shoulder and saw Sam and George walk by.

"Sam!" she called out. The couple turned and seeing her, smiled and walked over.

"This is Joey," she said. "Joey, this is George and Sam. They're from

New Zealand. We met on the bus from KL. You guys want to join us?"

"We just ate and are checking out the area. Maybe next time," Sam said, then added, "Hey, George is going to a Bahasa language class in the morning. You want to hang out with me? Do a little non-guy sightseeing?"

"You bet! When do you want to go?"

"Why don't we meet for breakfast in the hotel restaurant at nine o'clock?"

They said their goodbyes and headed down the street.

"Hey, you want to do something fun?" Joey asked Mary.

"What did you have in mind?"

"Let's take the cable car to the top of Penang Hill," Joey said. "A guy at the hotel told me that if you are up there at sunset, it is incredible. You get the colors of the setting sun coming over your shoulder while watching the lights of the city come on."

"I read about it in my guidebook," Mary said. "Sounds great. Can we walk there?"

"No, but I'm sure we could take a taxi. Shouldn't take too long."

There wasn't much to see on the ride up, even at the stop midway to the top that seemed to be there mostly for local residents. But the view from the top of the hill was as promised. Spectacular.

He took her hand as they meandered along the lookouts, waiting for sunset. After twenty minutes or so, Mary linked her arm through his and they exchanged small smiles.

"It was great to meet you, Joey," she said. "Thank you for starting up a conversation back in the restaurant."

Sunset came, with its brilliant display of reds and oranges and yellows giving way to the bluish grey of the coming night. They turned back toward George Town to the east and watched as lights flickered on. Mary was taken by how colorful it was. And how silent. The viewpoints atop Penang Hill are nearly a half-mile above sea level, so the sounds of the city were lost well below them.

She leaned in and gave Joey a soft kiss. He smiled that beautiful smile of his, then kissed her back, gently, but, she felt, with a hint of promise.

They took the funicular back down to the bottom of the hill, then grabbed a taxi back to the city.

"Hey, you want to find a bar and get a drink?" he asked her.

"Sure," she said.

They took a taxi back into town and were cruising down a street when Mary shrieked to the driver to pull over.

"It's the Boston Pub," she said, turning to Joey with a huge smile across her face. "We got to go there. I can write home about it."

Several drinks later, he asked her where she was staying. She told him the Lum Fong Hotel. He feigned not being familiar with it. "Want to see my room? It's simple but clean." She was smiling, so he did, too. "I'd love to see your room, Miss Mary." They giggled.

They got to the hotel about one in the morning. Joey was prepared to turn his head away, but there was no one at reception. Her room was on the second floor, near the back of the hotel. She always asked for a room as far from the street as possible, she said, to avoid all the street noise and above the ground floor for safety. Joey noticed that it was also near the back stairs.

While no one saw them arrive, he was less sure that no one heard her moans during their making love. Women, he had found, were unpredictable about the sounds they made during sex. Some were quiet as a soft breeze. And then there were the Marys.

She wasn't a screamer – exactly – but she also didn't seem to care who heard her screwing some guy's brains out in the middle of the night. Maybe it was the alcohol. Since he never knew how noisy the girl would be, when it was time to fetch his rubber, he'd also squirrel away his knife. He hoped he wouldn't need to use it before they finished, but better to be prepared.

He entered Mary from behind and began to slowly and deeply take her. It was going to be her last time, so he wanted it to be good. And Mary was into it. Matching his rhythm by pushing herself back into him. That's when the moans started building. Please don't scream, he pleaded with her in his mind. Moans are okay. Screams bring attention and sometimes a knock on the door.

He picked up the pace, driving more deeply. When she came, she let out her loudest moan yet and at that precise moment, his knife sliced across the front of her neck. Her head was up, so the deep gash produced a gusher. She stiffened briefly, then collapsed unconscious as her blood soaked the sheets and into the mattress.

Joey rose, wiped his blade clean, went into the bathroom, took off his rubber and flushed it. He used her washcloth to clean her juices from himself. He walked back into her bedroom, fished what had been Amanda's Walkman from his daypack, pressed the play button. Again, he did his Freddie Mercury dance as he got down to the job of finding everything of value Mary had in the room. It was a good night. When satisfied that he had everything worth taking, he dressed.

Joey peeked into the empty hall, waited briefly listening for sounds. There were none, so he silently exited the back stairs.His motorcycle was in the parking spot that he had reserved for one Malaysian ringgit back near the Rama-Rama Restaurant. He rode back to his apartment in Batu Ferringhi and was asleep within twenty minutes of arriving home. He'd catch a few hours' sleep then would go to Big Willie's the next morning to cash out Mary's stuff.

Day 4

Blair Fitzgerald Fox, Fitz to his friends, was sitting at his desk in the Southeast Asia section of the State Department sipping his morning cup of coffee. His assistant, Jonathan, knocked on his door.

"Come in," Fitz said. Jonathan walked over and handed him an overnight fax from the embassy in Kuala Lumpur. A young woman's body had been found in a hotel in Mersing. The hotel clerk said the victim appeared to be the young woman who registered the night before, an American named Amanda Gayle Anderson.

"Shit," Fitz said. "Great way to start the day. I hate this part of the job. Look up her info and let's see who the next of kin is. We'll need to make the call today or tomorrow."

"Already did it," Jonathan said. "Her passport application listed a Robert Carson Anderson in Tampa. He's the father."

"So, let's do the usual. Run his name by the finance guys at both parties and check in with the White House to see if anyone knows him."

"What are the odds?" Jonathan asked.

"Between slim and none," Fitz said, "but it's the kind of thing you never want to have missed. Just make the calls."

Jonathan turned to leave, but at the door stopped, looked back at the deputy undersecretary for Southeast Asia. "You know, sir, if my memory serves, the same thing happened to another young girl in Malaysia about six months or so ago."

"Shit happens, Jonathan."

———————

The bell jingled as Joey walked into Big Willie's shop.

"That was quick," the fat Thai said as he looked up from a rack of suits. "What do you have for me?"

"It was a good day," Joey said. "I should have what I need. Maybe a little more."

Joey opened his bag. From it he pulled two books of American Express traveler's checks totaling eighteen-hundred dollars face value, Mary's passport, two credit cards, a gold bracelet and a Nikon SLR with a zoom lens.

"How much cash did you get?" Big Willie asked.

"Fourteen hundred dollars plus another hundred or so dollars in ringgits."

"Very good!"

Big Willie totaled up Joey's take on Mary's items and handed him the cash.

"Let's get started on Bungalow Paradise," Joey said.

"You've named it?"

"Yes. I named it."

"Hmmm. Why not Paradise Bungalows?"

"This is why I'm going to be so good at this, Big Willie. 'Paradise Bungalows' is just a place. 'Bungalow Paradise' is more than a place. It's a state of mind. A community of happy travelers that becomes a paradise."

"If you say so. . ." as he turned to pick up his tape measure. "Stand over here," Big Willie said. He motioned to a small platform in front of several mirrors and picked up his tape measure.

Joey stepped up and the Thai began taking measurements and writing them on a pad. He measured Joey head to toe.

"One street up is a shop called A. Chinn & Sons. He makes shoes. Tell him to bill me. That will keep him honest. Have him fit you with a pair of black wingtips. You might not wear them much, but when a woman sees them in your closet, she'll think more of you. Trust me on this. You should be able to try a couple pair on.

"You'll also need a pair of casual dress shoes," Big Willie continued. "Chinn will know what's best. And you'll want some sneakers. Maybe Nikes. Again, Chinn will know which brand will make the best statement."

"I have decent sneakers already," Joey said.

"This is a new you. I know more about this stuff than you. Just do as I say. Okay?"

Joey nodded yes.

Willie Chirathivat, the tailor, told Joey to come back late the next afternoon for a first fitting. He was going to make the young man two suits and a couple pairs of slacks, plus three or four dress shirts. He told Joey that in the meantime, he should go shopping for nice casual clothes.

"Buy underwear and dress socks," Big Willie said. "Keep them tasteful. You're a businessman now."

Joey asked the clothes he already had, adding that he had some things he liked.

"I'll tell you what, Joey," Big Willie said, "go home tonight and make two piles of clothes. In one pile put the stuff you really like and want to keep. In the other pile, put everything else. Then throw the second pile away. All of it. We're building a new you. We'll go through the first pile together."

As Joey was about to leave, Big Willie called after him. "You still live in the place I visited last year for dinner?"

"Same place."

"I remember it was a nice place, but I should visit it again. At some point, she'll want to see your place. We need to look at how it reflects on you the young businessman. Tomorrow evening won't work for me. How about the next day?"

"Sure. I'll make dinner."

"And tomorrow here for your fitting."

"Yes. I'll be back here around four o'clock tomorrow."

———————

"I heard back from the White House about Anderson," Jonathan said to Fitz in the older man's office later that day.

"They knew who he was?" Fitz asked, knowing that if Jonathan got an answer that quickly that there had to be a reason.

"Big time Reagan contributor," Jonathan said. "Big time. He gave $100,000 in the '80 campaign and $225,000 in '84."

Fitz whistled.

"He attended an inaugural ball for the first term. He was invited for the second one, too, but declined."

"Were they able to say anything else about him?"

"A little. The guys at the RNC had some background."

"Self-made," Jonathan continued. "He's a big-time commercial real estate developer. Very successful. He has projects in Tampa-St. Pete, as well as Miami, Fort Lauderdale and the Disney World area."

"Wife?"

"She died ten years ago. Cancer."

"War record?"

"I'm still waiting to hear back from DOD. One of the guys at 1600 said he thought he might have been a chopper pilot in Nam."

"What about other kids?"

"She was it."

Fitz grimaced.

"Thanks Jonathan. Someone will have to deliver this news in person. I need to tell the Secretary and see who he thinks should do it. I'm sure it will be me. God, tomorrow is going to suck. Why don't you call Mr. Anderson's office before it gets any later and see what his schedule looks like tomorrow. Tell his secretary that you don't have any details but that it is important. They'll want to know how long. Tell them it would be best if he could clear his schedule for the afternoon. They'll push back, but they'll do it."

"I'm on it. And if he's out of town, I'll find out where he is."

Fitz nodded his approval. He told Jonathan that he'd like to arrive in late morning, then return at the end of the day.

"Consider it done," Jonathan answered.

————————

Joey had never owned dress shoes, nor dress socks, for that matter. He walked out of A. Chinn & Son wearing his new Nikes with two pair of dress shoes in a bag. He felt good about himself. When he got home, he threw all his old clothes on the floor. "I have a lot of clothes," he said to himself, then started making the two piles. After about thirty minutes, he moved it all into one big pile and started carrying it out to the garbage. He saved just one pair of jeans, some shorts and five shirts, three of which were new tee-shirts, plus clean boxers to wear until he could buy the new ones.

Day 5

J onathan met Fitz at the Eastern Airlines gate at Washington National.

"I was able to get a fair amount of info for you. Some of it is hard to look it."

"Crime photos?"

"Yeah. He slashed her neck and I mean slashed. Her naked body was crumpled on the bed. Lots of blood. I can't imagine you would want to show it to Mr. Anderson. I included the photos because they were part of the police report that arrived in the pouch from KL. I knew you'd want to see them."

At thirty-five thousand feet, Fitz reviewed the full file. First, he read a summary Jonathan had prepared, then studied the supporting documents.

Bob Anderson was a war hero from his two tours in Vietnam in the sixties. He flew Hueys on medevacs. He was part of the famed 57th Medical Detachment. The Army promoted him to major shortly before the end of his second tour. That would have been '67. Not many of the pilots made it to major while still flying missions, Fitz thought. He figured Bob must have been fearless.

The file noted many commendations. Most notable was a Bronze Star with the V Device for valor in combat. A Purple Heart. Shot down three times.

Bob started his company developing office buildings in 1967, the same year he left the service. Amanda was just two at the time. She was probably the reason he became a civilian, Fitz concluded.

Bob's wife, Juliet, had died of ovarian cancer in her mid-thirties. Jonathan had noted that it was rare for a woman her age, but that it's more aggressive in younger women.

A copy of a business section profile of Bob from the Tampa Tribune was at the back of the file. It had been written two years ago. It told of his Vietnam years, but mostly focused on the office towers he had developed. His flying days didn't end in Vietnam. The story included a photo of him at the controls of his Bell helicopter, which he flew most days from his home north of Tampa to the helipad he made part of the design of the downtown skyscraper that housed his company's offices.

Bob told the reporter that he had always dreamed of being a helicopter pilot. Why copters? No logical reason beyond a child's fascination that he didn't outgrow. Toward the end of his senior year at the University of Florida, he met recruiters. The Army struck him as his best path to flying copters. He took a series of tests and did well enough that the Army flew him to Fort Bragg to do more tests and interviews. A few weeks later the Army called to offer him a commission in Army Airborne. The Army gave him a report date of September 1, which meant he'd have a few months after graduation.

He put it to good use. He and Juliet had been college sweethearts at Florida. They married shortly after earning their degrees. With the help of his parents, they found a nice home in the Temple Terrace suburb. The house was near King High School, where she would teach history. They just got settled in when he had to head out for training.

The world was a peaceful place when Bob signed on with the Army in 1961. John Kennedy was the new president and America was filled with hope and promise. Who could see just how awful the sixties would become? He had expected he'd be stationed in Germany. He told his college buddies while on leave back in Tampa that Germany had been good enough for Elvis and it would be good enough for him. He never made it to Germany.

President Kennedy quietly was increasing the number of US troops in Vietnam. Technically, they were "advisers." But their numbers were growing. Advising meant they were embedded with the South Vietnamese regulars who were taking the fight to the insurgent Viet Cong.

In the spring of 1963, the Army sent Bob to Vietnam. He was part of the first deployment to the war by the 57th Medical Detachment. By the end of the year, the number of US advisors had grown from a few hundred early in the Kennedy administration to sixteen thousand.

During that year-long tour, about eighty percent of the wounded soldiers he swooped in and took to hospitals were South Vietnamese soldiers. His copter was downed while landing in a firefight. Lieutenant Anderson suffered a flesh wound while defending the location until help arrived. His co-pilot, Sgt. Thomas Wilson, of Lancaster, PA, though, was shot jumping out of the copter. He died on the spot. He would lose other crew on future missions. Being on a medevac crew was among Vietnam's most dangerous assignments.

His tour ended after thirteen months, broken only for one R&R in Hawaii with his wife. Bob returned to the States and was posted to Fort Bragg, the big Army base in North Carolina where he had been flown when in college. Juliet joined him there and took a teaching job at Fayetteville High School.

Amanda was born in September of 1965. Juliet quit her job to be a fulltime mom. Then early the next year, Bob returned to Vietnam for another thirteen-month deployment. Juliet and Amanda moved back to Tampa to be near family. The following year, Juliet was able to resume teaching.

Between his two tours, Bob was promoted to captain. When he arrived in South Vietnam, he found it to be a much different war.

To begin with, American involvement in Vietnam had soared since his first tour. In 1963, American troops were primarily providing support for the South Vietnamese Army, which did most of the fighting. Four years later Americans were deep and broad in the war. It was largely President Johnson's doing. Johnson had become president when John Kennedy was assassinated in late '63.

In August 1964, though, just three months before America was to elect a president, the Johnson administration greatly exaggerated an incident to whip Congress into giving him broad powers. A US destroyer, the Maddox, was "attacked" by three small North Vietnamese torpedo boats in the Gulf of Tonkin in international waters off the North Vietnamese coast. While that incident, to some extent, actually happened, the Johnson administration made up a subsequent Tonkin attack a few days later.

Their propaganda campaign was so successful that the Gulf of Tonkin Resolution quickly passed Congress. There was little debate and virtually no opposition. In November, Johnson was reelected in a landslide against an arch-conservative Republican named Barry Goldwater.

The Gulf of Tonkin Resolution opened the floodgates for US troop involvement in Vietnam. In 1965, there was a nine-fold increase in the number of US troops on the ground there. By 1966, troop strength doubled again. One in every three troops on the ground was an American. US forces were everywhere.

The picture was starker if you looked at combat deaths. In all of 1963, just one-hundred-sixteen Americans died. In 1966, the war claimed six-thousand-one-hundred-forty-three American lives. Bob found that four out of five injured soldiers that he airlifted out of battles were Americans.

It was in 1966 that his actions earned him a Bronze Star with V device, the highest honor for a soldier short of a Medal of Honor. An Army unit set out to find and destroy tunnels used by the Viet Cong in a vast network in and around Cu Chi. VC in the area ambushed the unit. The soldiers were pinned down and taking heavy casualties.

Captain Anderson flew his Huey medevac into the firefight to ferry wounded soldiers to a hospital near Saigon, a short distance away. He made five trips to the besieged unit, taking heavy fire each time. On the fifth rescue mission, his copter was able to land, but was crippled by enemy artillery. It burst into flames.

There were three crew members onboard at the time. All three were injured in the hard landing and fire that erupted almost immediately. Captain Anderson carried each away from the chopper. He suffered a gunshot wound to his leg as he lifted the last man from the burning aircraft, but still managed to get him to safety. A month later, he was back in the pilot's seat rescuing more injured soldiers.

One hell of a war record, Fitz said to himself. The man's courage and sacrifice made him proud to be an American.

Fitz finally turned to the police report from Mersing. Apart from the grisly pictures, it shed little light. Amanda had checked in to the Happy Song Hotel in the late afternoon of the previous day. She was with another single girl and a couple. The two other women were from the States and the fellow from Germany.

The three others left the hotel early the next morning. They walked to the nearby docks to catch a fishing boat that would take them to Tioman Island. Amanda's body was found in her room later that day. The report noted that the three had not been interviewed since they had left Mersing before the body was found. They apparently were not seen as suspects by the short-handed Mersing police.

The report reconstructed the group's activities the evening they arrived in Mersing. The group of young travelers had dinner that evening in a restaurant near the Happy Song called the Portside Café. The bartender remembered the group and said that Amanda came in after the others.

After a couple hours, Amanda's other three friends left, but she stayed later with one of the men. The bartender said he first thought the fellow might be Malaysian but didn't totally look it. He added that the young man spoke, dressed and acted like an American. He put the man's age at mid- to late-twenties.

The bartender said Amanda asked him to tune into TV3, the new Malaysian network that aired current American TV shows in English. The two watched *L.A. Law* on the set above the bar, then left together shortly after the show ended. They were not kissing or holding hands or acting in any other way like a couple. The bartender said he had the impression that perhaps they had only recently met.

The report noted that police contacted other hotels in the area. None reported having a registered guest that night fitting the young man's description.

The murder itself appeared to have been swift. The single gash across her neck was deep and well placed, clearly meant to both silence and kill her. There were no other signs of injury or a struggle. The report noted that her vagina area had been cleaned. It speculated that perhaps she had cleaned herself in the bathroom after sex and that the killer took her as she stepped out of the bathroom.

Fitz closed his eyes and envisioned how he would tell Mr. Anderson about his daughter. There was no way to do it but to be direct.

———————

Joey showed up for his fitting with Big Willie at four o'clock. He walked in wearing a new pair of jeans with a brown leather belt and a nice Polo shirt. After the fitting, Big Willie handed Joey a large manila envelope.

"What's this?" Joey asked.

"A new US passport, driver's license and credit cards for Joseph Thomas Jackson of Bentonville, North Carolina," the big man said. "Check them out. Much higher quality than the passport you've been using. It also has immigration stamps to support your story. The passport shows you arrived in Kuala Lumpur six months ago. You've also been to Singapore twice for a few days each time and Thailand once, but you stayed a month there.

"Your story is that after you finished college, you took a job in Charlotte," Big Willie continued. "Your American dad died this past year – your mom had died a few years ago – and you felt it was time to revisit your roots and to explore Southeast Asia. About a month ago, you got the idea to build and run your own bungalow place."

He told Joey that the passport showed the two in-and-outs for Singapore. If asked, that when he went there to set up his company.

"Everyone knows that Singapore is a much safer, business-oriented place," Willie said.

As for the month in Thailand, it was pure pleasure.

"You're an American backpacker. Of course, you're going to spend time in Thailand. You need to think about where in Thailand you've been. Have you ever been to Thailand?"

Joey said he'd been a few times, His first trip was to Koh Samui. So many backpackers had been that he felt he needed to see what it was like. It was the same reason he went to Koh Phi-Phi.

"I took the train up to Bangkok last year. Hated it. Stayed for five days. Too big and too crowded. Sorry, I know your family is from there, but it wasn't for me."

Big Willie told Joey he'd need two or three days to finish his clothes, then said he was looking forward to a checking out Joey's apartment the next night.

"I've become quite the cook," Joey said.

"Just so you have cold beer," Big Willie answered.

———————

The view from the thirty-sixth floor of the Bayview Tower was stunning. Looking southwest across Old Tampa Bay, one could see MacDill Air Force Base at Tampa's far south end. Beyond the B-52s, the view continued all the way to the newly reopened Sunshine Skyway Bridge. The bridge, an engineering marvel, connects the southern tip of St. Petersburg with Bradenton. To the west of the bridge is the open water of the Gulf of Mexico.

From the high perch, Fitz could follow Bayshore Boulevard. The roadway lined the Old Tampa Bay heading south. Fitz was too young to have visited Havana before Castro took over. He imagined, though, that the Cuban capital might have a similar gently curving boulevard. The boulevard separated stately old Spanish-styled mansions from the water. Hundreds of palm trees that lined the drive lazily moved in the breeze.

"Mr. Fox," a thirty-something well-dressed and attractive woman said, approaching him. "Mr. Anderson will see you now."

Fitz took a deep breath and followed her back to Bob Anderson's office. It was understated, yet personal. One wall boasted photos of Bob with various political leaders. There were, of course, photos of Bob with President Reagan. One showed Bob and a teenaged Amanda with Ron and Nancy Reagan at an inaugural ball in 1981.

But the wall didn't just show Bob with Republicans. He clearly had spread his money around to Democrats, as well. There was a picture of him with former Governor Bob Graham, now one of the state's two senators. Another was more intriguing. It showed Bob and former Senator Lawton Chiles walking along a highway. Chiles, who everyone called Walkin' Lawton, won election by famously walking from one end of the state to the other. Looks like Bob was connected to him enough to make part of the walk with him.

Another wall offered photos of Bob from his Vietnam days. One had been taken by a news photographer who was embedded with the unit at Cu Chi. It shows Bob, his leg bloody from the gunshot wound, carrying a grimacing soldier away from a burning helicopter. Fitz was surprised Jonathan hadn't included that photo. It had to be the incident that earned Bob the Bronze Star with V device.

The credenza behind his desk offered a half dozen photos, all family. There was a wedding photo of him and Juliet. Bob's in his semi-formal Class A uniform. There also was a picture of Bob, Juliet and a young Amanda in Paris with the Eiffel Tower looming behind them. There were two other photos of Amanda. In one, she's in her cap and gown at her graduation from Brown. The other showed her standing at the Delta ticket counter at Tampa International with her pack on her back. It was probably the last picture Bob had taken of her.

"Welcome to Tampa, Mr. Fox."

"Please call me Fitz. Everyone does."

"Okay, Fitz. I've been curious as hell since Eileen said you asked that I clear my calendar for the rest of the day. What's up?" Bob said with a bit of a smile.

Fitz looked at him solemnly for a moment. Bob knew instantly. His face drooped and he appeared to stop breathing.

"Oh no. It's Amanda. Is she okay?"

Fitz had tears in his eyes as he looked at Bob.

"I'm afraid not."

"Oh God no. No. Please no."

He fell back into his chair and sobbed uncontrollably. Fitz remained seated across from him, knowing that there was nothing he could say or do right then to help.

After several minutes, Bob got some control of his anguish. His breaths, though, were still coming in gasps. Finally, he looked back to Fitz, said nothing for a bit, then stood and walked around the room. He sat in a formal seating area in the center of his office. Fitz rose and took a seat opposite him.

"Mr. Anderson, I can't begin to tell you how sorry I am. We found out yesterday at State. When we learned she was your daughter, we notified the president. He asked that I tell you that he and Nancy are holding you in their prayers."

"Was it some kind of accident?"

"No."

Bob was again silent for a bit.

"Not an accident? I don't understand. She was healthy. She called me just a few nights ago. She was someplace called Melaka."

"I'm going to be direct with you, Mr. Anderson." He took a breath. "Amanda was murdered."

"Oh Christ!" He began crying again. "My poor baby," he cried out through sobs. "God. Oh God."

Fitz let him sit with that piece of information before speaking again.

"Tell me, Fitz, what happened. And don't spare my feelings. I need to hear it all."

"It's not good, Mr. Anderson."

"Please stop calling me that. I'm Bob. Just Bob, okay? Now tell me!"

Fitz removed the police report – without the photos – from his briefcase then spent several minutes telling him what the report said. He didn't tell Bob that she was naked and appeared to have just had sex. If asked directly, he would be honest, but saw no reason to add to Bob's pain.

"It sounds like the police have leads. This guy she left the restaurant with. How long before they'll track him down? Do they think he's from, what's the name of the town?"

"Mersing. It's a fishing village that backpackers stop at to take a boat to Tioman Island.

"Bob," Fitz continued, "my guess is that they'll never find him. It's Malaysia, not America. The local police don't really deal with major crimes. They don't have the training or the resources. Neither does what passes for the national police. They focus on threats to the government. The murder of a foreign backpacker probably won't even be followed up on."

Bob stared at Fitz. It was easy to see the anger building, not just in his face, but his whole body.

"You're fucking kidding me, right," Bob seethed. "Some scumbag murders an American girl and no one will even try to find him?"

"I'm not going to lie to you, Bob. The odds of the authorities catching the guy who did this are between slim and none. I know you don't want to hear that, but it is what it is."

"How about you guys in State. Can't you do something?"

"We'll ask, of course. Maybe the president could write a personal note to Prime Minister Mohamad. Don't count on that making a difference, though. There isn't a lot of goodwill between the US and Malaysia right now."

"There has to be some way to find this guy. There are people who know what he looks like. How about a Malaysian private detective? I can afford pretty much anything."

"A Malaysian detective would probably be a waste of money. I'm sure there are good ones, but I don't think that's the way to go."

"So, what is?"

Fitz stood and walked to the window wall. He stared out as he thought through something.

"There is a guy that I know in Bangkok who might help, but he comes with baggage."

"I don't care about his fucking baggage. I don't care what it takes. The cocksucker who did this to my girl is going to die. I fucking mean it."

Fitz nodded solemnly. Bob's rage was front and center. He needed to acknowledge it. After a few moments, he told Bob about Mason Ray. He first met Mason in 1972 when both were stationed at Vientiane, the capital of Laos. Fitz was pure State Department. Mason was a covert operative for the CIA.

"He was really good," Fitz said. "Then something awful happened."

Fitz said that a bomb blast at Mason's home killed his fiancé, a beautiful young woman who also worked at the embassy. The North Vietnamese wanted to eliminate Mason for the trouble he was causing them along the Ho Chi Minh Trail. Not knowing that he had been called away unexpectedly, they blew up his house thinking he was in it. Sylvie, his fiancé, died instantly.

"Mason was never the same after that," Fitz continued, "but it was more than just not being the same. He had always enjoyed a drink, but he started enjoying them too much. He was probably a functioning alcoholic."

Fitz told Bob that what no one at the embassy knew after Sylvie's death was that Mason was plotting revenge.

"It was 1974," Fitz said. "The war, at least as far as the CIA was concerned, was still raging and Mason continued to do a kick-ass job disrupting NVA use of the Ho Chi Minh Trail. Nobody had a clue what he was doing on the side."

Mason had worked with Hmong fighters around the country, Fitz continued. He even learned to speak the language.

"Those CIA guys, you know, are pretty autonomous," Fitz said. "He put together a special team on the agency's dime. Their job was to find

63

out exactly who ordered the hit."

Fitz said it didn't take long for his guys to learn that General Tho Van Tho himself had ordered the hit. General Tho was the North Vietnamese Army general responsible for the Ho Chi Minh Trail in Laos. Mason was making him look bad. Really bad. Like his father, the infamous General Tho Nguyen Giap, Tho was a small man. Unlike his father, a brilliant military strategist, Tho was known for his brash, impulsive nature.

General Tho ran the Laos operations from the safety of Sam Neua. The city sits in the far northeast corner of the country. It's a short distance from the border with North Vietnam. The Pathet Lao controlled the surrounding countryside. Much like the Viet Cong in South Vietnam, the Pathet Lao had one goal. Both sought to overthrow the governments in their country so they could install communists.

Mason's team sneaked into Sam Neua and shadowed General Tho for weeks. They cataloged everything they could see him doing. A few patterns emerged after several weeks. One member of the team returned to Vientiane. He detailed three opportunities each week to kill the general.

At about eight o'clock every Saturday evening, General Tho walked with his family two blocks from his home to a restaurant for dinner. It would be easy to drive by on a motor scooter and shoot him at close range.

He also visited a tea market between five and six every Wednesday afternoon. The team had found a good sniper's roost about three-hundred yards away that had a clear view of the entrance to the market.

Finally, the general took his mistress to lunch every Tuesday. They sat at the same seats at the same table in the same restaurant each time. General Tho sat with his back to the wall and could watch people pass by the café. A bomb planted near him would certainly kill him and the two guards who were always close by.

The first two options were straight from the CIA playbook for assassinations. Mason chose option three. It was justice, Mason felt, to take him out with a bomb.

Mason returned to Sam Neua with his Hmong teammate. He wore a disguise that enabled him to not call attention to himself and his Hmong colleague did all the talking, when it was needed. Mid-afternoon Monday, he sat in a sidewalk café across the street from the general's Tuesday lunch spot. He watched as three members of his team entered the restaurant and sat at what would be the general's table the next day.

For the next hour, they dined on spring rolls and fried rice, washing it all down with modest amounts of beer. They also carefully and surreptitiously packed the underside of the table with C-4 explosives and a remote detonator.

Tuesday came. Mason again took a table at the café across the busy street and waited. He had a straight line of sight to the general's table. Right on time, the general and his mistress arrived and were seated at their usual table. Mason's pulse quickened as he stood and waited until he made brief eye contact with the general. It took a moment, but the sudden recognition on the general's face was what Mason needed to see. He then smiled and detonated the explosives.

The general and his mistress died instantly. So did fifty-four others. In the chaos and confusion, Mason and his accomplice were able to simply walk away. Once back to Vientiane, he reported his unsanctioned assassination to the Chief of Station. While the fact that he had taken out a high value target was commendable, to do so in such a rogue manner and with so much loss of civilian lives was not.

The Agency reassigned Mason to a desk job in Udon Thani. That was a huge air base in northeast Thailand where intelligence for Southeast Asia was analyzed and shared. That was his job for the next two years.

Meanwhile in Washington, DC, the CIA was coming under scrutiny for its tactics. Newly elected President Jimmy Carter was signaling that he opposed extreme measures. Langley asked its stations around the world to report any knowledge of its people doing things that Carter

THE NEXT BEST THING

would clearly object to.

Udon Thani sent Langley a report on the bloody off-book Sam Neua assassination. Langley's response was quick. They dispatched Mason to the embassy in Bangkok.

Upon arrival, the Bangkok Chief of Station told Mason he understood that Mason did what he felt he had to do. "The motherfucker got what he deserved," the COS told him. But, he continued, the heat was getting too intense on the Agency and Mason was now a potential liability. He had to go.

The Agency wasn't abandoning him, though. They were going to make it as easy for him as they could. Off-book, of course.

The Bangkok COS told Mason it wasn't a good idea for Mason to return to the States until things calmed down a bit. To help him, he had arranged with an American businessman in the region to retain Mason. Private security. Industrial stuff. Maybe even some covert work for friendly nations.

"That was twelve years ago," Fitz told Bob. "Mason still hasn't been back to the States, as far as I know. He's now a security 'consultant.'" He made quote marks in the air when he said consultant. "I haven't seen him in years, but Southeast Asia is my responsibility so I've kept tabs on him. Some. I don't know if he's still a big drinker, but I do know that I haven't heard any complaints. He definitely gets shit done."

"Connect me to him," Bob said.

Fitz used the phone on Bob's desk to call Jonathan. He told his aide to go to the Rolodex on his desk and get the info for Mason Ray in Bangkok. He held while Jonathan got the info off the card, then the young man read it to him. He wrote it down and handed it to Bob.

"We need to talk about what to do with Amanda's remains," Fitz said. "Right now they are being held at the embassy in Kuala Lumpur. I recommend, unless you have a religious objection, to have her cremated there. You can then have the embassy oversee sending her home. I know that money isn't an issue for you, but it really is best."

"I need to go to Malaysia myself and see her before anything like that happens," Bob said. "I'll fly out tomorrow."

"Bob, it's pretty gruesome. You sure you need to do that?"

"Absolutely. She's my little girl." Tears again rolled down his cheeks.

"I'll let the embassy know. We have a good man there, John Monjo. I know him well. He used to have my job."

"Thank you, Fitz, for your help. I should call Mason Ray to see if he'll take the job."

"Don't call him right now. We're eleven hours behind Bangkok. It's about two in the morning there. I'd call him at ten or eleven o'clock tonight your time. That'll give my assistant Jonathan a chance to send Mason the file so your call won't be completely out of the blue. And if you're doing this, you should fly through Bangkok and get him to meet you at the airport."

"I'll do that. And listen, if he can't help. I'd like to talk with you again about who else I can try."

"Actually, Mason would be a better person to ask than me. But I think he might do it, especially if you pay him enough."

"What will he cost?"

"No idea. He'll tell you, I'm sure. I don't think he's the kind of guy who will take advantage of you. I always liked Mason. I think you'll be fine with him."

Day 6

It was just past midnight in Tampa when Mason returned Bob's call.

"I'm so sorry for your loss," Mason said with a softness that hinted at his Georgia upbringing. He had worked for years to un-Georgia-fy the way he spoke, but his roots still seeped in at times, which wasn't necessarily a bad thing. "I know what it's like to lose someone to violence. It's plumb awful."

"Thank you, Mr. Ray. I haven't come to grips with it yet. I'm sure it'll take a long time."

"Please sir, call me Mason. Just sayin', comin' to grips is somethin' that never really happens. Havin' said that, you do learn to get through each day."

"I appreciate that, Mason. So, tell me how much do you know?"

"I had a fax waitin' for me this mornin' from an old bud, Fitz Fox at State. Fitz said he met with you yesterday about your daughter. The police report was part of the fax. Gruesome. Fitz also said there had been another young woman who was murdered earlier this year. He didn't know yet if the two were connected. He said he was going to get right on it."

"Another girl? Damn. Listen, Fitz told me that there's not a snowball's chance in hell that the Malaysian police will find the guy."

"Right as a rain, sir. Not a chance."

"So, what do I need to do to hire you? I want to track down the sonofabitch who did it and see that he gets what's coming to him. Money is no object. Whatever it takes. As long as it takes. I want that fucker to pay."

There was an awkward silence on the phone. Then Mason spoke again.

"You don't know, sir, how much I get how you feel. Fitz was right to send you to me. I will do everythin' I can to root out the asshole who took your sweet darlin' from you. When I find him – and I swear to God, if he can be found I will find him – when I do then we can figure out what to do with him. Agreed?"

"Yes. Thank you."

Bob told Mason that at Fitz' suggestion, he booked flights through Bangkok and on to Kuala Lumpur. His flight would arrive in Bangkok at about nine at night, too late for a connection. His flight on to KL would depart at eight the next morning, so he had reserved a room in the onsite airport hotel.

"There's a right nice bar in the hotel atrium," Mason said. "Why don't we meet up there at, say, half-past-ten? That will give you time to get into your room and get yourself cleaned up a bit, if you want. It's a long-ass flight. I'll wait at the bar till you get there, then we can move to a more private spot."

"Okay. One more thing." Bob paused briefly. "Should I bring you cash?"

"Why don't you bring, say, four thousand dollars. I'll give you the details when I see you for wirin' money to me down the road."

"Okay. See you tomorrow night then."

"Yep. Tomorrow night."

Bob hung up, walked to the safe in his bedroom, opened it and removed his passport and a stack of hundred-dollar bills. After the four thousand dollars for Mason, he would have six thousand left for his needs. It would be more than enough. He climbed into bed, hoping he could sleep at least a little. His plane to London, the first stop on his twenty-three-hour flight to Bangkok, would leave at ten in the morning.

———————

Big Willie knocked on Joey's second-floor apartment door. Joey's place was in a newer two-story, six-unit building nestled among trees a couple blocks back from the beach. It wasn't fancy, by US standards, but it was a nice place from a local perspective. It was well maintained and for Malaysians it was the kind of place normally occupied by the professional class. One thing was for sure, it was far better than the shithole that Joey had lived in when Big Willie first met him.

Joey answered the door with a broad smile.

"Hey! Come on in."

Big Willie removed his shoes and stepped in. The cool air from the window air-conditioner greeted him. The apartment was much as he remembered it.

It was modest in size with just three rooms. The main room that visitors entered stretched from the front of the apartment to the far wall. The front area was the living room, followed by the dining area and then the kitchen with a wrap-around counter.

The living room focused on a big TV sitting atop a sizeable TV stand that also housed Joey's VCR and sound system. Next to the television was a bookcase that held hundreds of videotapes – movies and TV shows – on the upper shelves, and albums and plastic cases filled with cassette tapes on the lower one.

"Few young Malaysian men know how to live this nicely, Joey," the fat Thai said to him. "How do you know how to do this?"

"Well, you know, I watch lots of American TV. I want my place to look like a single guy's apartment on a TV show. Even the kitchen. I cook mostly American foods. I wish there were more TV shows about cooking. I could watch cooking shows for hours."

Big Willie looked into the bedroom, which was just big enough to have a full-size bed, two nightstands and a dresser. One wall offered a walk-in closet. The bed was covered by a colorful bedspread. The room was filled with natural light thanks to a large window along one wall.

Big Willie then stuck his head in the bathroom. It was small, but clean. It had a tiled shower stall with both overhead and bidet showers, a vanity and a Western-style toilet.

"Is it always this clean?" Big Willie asked.

"Pretty much," Joey said. "I used to do chores with my American mom at the mission. She taught me to keep things clean and tidy. I guess it stuck."

"Get in the habit of always of just calling her mom. Same with the pastor. He's just dad."

"Okay. I used to do chores for mom."

Big Willie looked around some more before joining Joey in the kitchen.

"You could easily bring a lady here tomorrow," Big Willie said. "The only thought I have is that it might look a little too old for you. You're 26, not 46."

"I had been thinking about framing a poster I saw for the wall across from the TV. It was for Michael Jackson's Thriller album. What do you think?"

"Yes. Might be enough."

After an American dinner of meatloaf, mashed potatoes and green beans, Joey told Big Willie that he had thrown away most of his clothes.

"When you think about creating a new you, well, some of the stuff just isn't as appealing as it had seemed," Joey said.

Joey walked into his bedroom and came out a moment later with a pair of jeans, two pair of cargo shorts popular with backpackers and two casual shirts and three tee-shirts. The tee-shirts were all new and popular culture. His favorite was a solid black one of Prince with his picture and name in bright purple.

"These are all fine," Big Willie said.

Day 7

J oey woke up with a plan. He would head to the beach at lunch time to, as he thought of it, practice. He knew he had little trouble with younger women. He could have his pick of women in their early twenties. But he had never tried to woo a more mature woman, one in her thirties.

He figured he had a few things to work on. First, how would he approach an older woman? The younger girls just wanted to have fun. They were willing, maybe even eager to take risks. The hint of danger added to their excitement.

An older woman would probably be a lot more cautious but he had no personal experience to base this on. He'd never been with anyone older than twenty-four. No, he made this assumption based entirely on how older women behaved in movies.

He was sure a woman in her thirties would think twice or even three times before crawling into the sack with a stranger. He was equally sure they still liked a good romp but would likely want to take a slower route to bed. That was okay. His goal wasn't a quick night of passion and then the immediate payoff. The goal was to build trust. Trust takes time. He'd have to find a new rhythm.

Then there was the whole issue of qualifying them. The last thing that he wanted to do was waste days or even weeks winning over a woman only to find out she didn't have enough money in the bank to do what he needed.

With that in mind, he put on his cargo shorts and a Polo pullover that he had set aside with Big Willie's approval, laced up his new Nike's and headed to the outdoor café next to the Holiday Inn. He was in luck. Sitting by herself, reading a paperback, was a woman he guessed to be about thirty-four or thirty-five. Dark brown, shoulder length hair, glasses. Not a knock-out, but attractive enough.

There were few customers in the restaurant, so he was able to sit at a table near her.

Joey needed to find a reason to start a conversation with her. The best option would be to comment on the book she was reading, but she had the pages turned back so that he couldn't read the title. He was about to say, "What are you reading?" when the waiter brought her a cobb salad for lunch. She laid the book down on the table and he was able to see that it was The Handmaid's Tale.

"Is that a good book?" Joey asked her, and without giving her a chance to answer added, "I saw Oprah interview Margaret Atwood earlier this year and it sounded weirdly interesting."

She eyed him for a moment before answering.

"I saw that Oprah interview, too. It's why I packed the book for my trip."

"So, is it? Weird I mean"

"I don't think I'd say it's weird, but it is thought-provoking. You know the story, right?"

"Only what I picked up from the show. Let's see, America isn't America anymore. In its place is a totalitarian regime that faces the fact that fewer and fewer couples are able to have children. So they round up fertile young women and force them to be handmaids. Slaves basically. Their sole purpose in life is to be impregnated by the husband of a childless couple who would then raise the baby as their own."

"Wow! You really were paying attention to that interview!"

"Guilty. I love Oprah."

"She's great."

"Yes. I'm Joey, by the way."

"Andie."

"Nice to meet you, Andie. Where you from?"

"California. You?"

"North Carolina, but I moved here recently."

"Really? Work?"

"No." Joey got a pensive look and gazed out over the water. "I guess you could say I'm finding myself."

"Deep," Andie said, and they both laughed.

His BLT, fries and a Coke came. Before the waiter could sit it down, Andie invited him to move to her table. He did. After eating a fry, he told her the story of being born in Melaka to a Malaysian mother and a father who was a sailor on shore leave from a British frigate. He told Andie how his mom died and how he was adopted by a pastor and his wife from North Carolina.

"This might sound cold and heartless, but it worked out great for me," Joey said. "Here I was a half-breed only child of an ostracized single mother who could barely make ends meet. Next thing you know I'm living on a farm outside a small town in North Carolina. I have two loving parents and everything I need."

"Wow," she said, only this time her voice was soft and reflective. "And it sounds neither cold nor heartless."

He took a bite of his sandwich and told her he could eat a BLT every day and it would never grow old. Yes, it would, she said.

"So," he picked up the story, "after getting my degree I went to work for a company in Charlotte and tried to start my grown-up life. I woke up one day and realized that I wasn't happy. Not really happy, you know what I mean? I convinced myself that I wouldn't be until I came home. So, here I am."

"And are you?"

"Happy?"

She nodded.

"Well, hmmm, it didn't work out the way I expected, but I feel like I'm on the path. How about you?"

"Am I happy?"

"Yes, are you happy?"

"Not yet."

"So, I told you mine. You have to tell me yours."

Andie frowned a bit.

"I don't know if I'm as comfortable doing that as you are."

"Come on. Give it a try. I'm a complete stranger. It'll be like talking to a shrink. Hey, wait. Would you feel better about it if we went down to the beach, you recline in a lounger and I pull up a chair?"

She offered up a devilish smirk.

"Well, let's see. I got a degree in philosophy from UC Santa Clara."

"When was that?"

"'76. Anyway, I was done with school, but you know what a philosophy degree trains you for?" She made a zero with her fingers and thumb. "Nothing. Nada. And the country was coming out of the worst recession since World War Two. Companies were hiring again, but it was mostly the people who had lost their jobs. Those people had experience and training. I had a philosophy degree. I had to move back in with my mom. It sucked."

"I missed that recession and the one in 1980," Joey said.

She told Joey how living with her mother was driving her nuts and no jobs were coming her way. She heard from a college girlfriend that a law firm in "Mo-fucking-desto," where her friend lived, was hiring typists. She sent in a resume, got a call, drove over for an interview and got the job.

"I knew it was a mistake within a few weeks, but there I was," she said.

She stuck it out for two years, which, at least, qualified her to apply for law firm jobs in San Francisco. One of the bigger firms downtown hired her for an office support job.

"I sold my car and got an efficiency apartment in the Richmond district. My world was a lot better, even though I knew I would outgrow it. And then what? That question nagged at me."

It took eight years, she said, but she finally had enough of it.

"Lawyers can be lecherous douchebags," she said.

75

"Something happen?"

"Joey, not a week went by that some middle-aged dude didn't hit on me. I mean, I couldn't count the number of times a lawyer would touch me, not overtly sexual mind you, but close. And then several times a year one of the guys would literally grab my ass!

"The final straw for me," she continued, "happened when I went along with one of the attorneys to take notes during an interview with a potential client. When the potential client left, Howard, that was the prick's name, walked him to the door, said goodbye to the man, then locked the door. I thought, oh shit. Then he turned around and whipped out his a… you know! He said, I swear to God, 'This give you any ideas?'"

"What a slime ball."

"You think? I quit the next day."

She told him that she had saved a little and decided to use it to travel. She figured she had enough to spend about three months in Southeast Asia before she'd have to go back. She was thinking of working part time and going to law school.

The waiter brought their checks. She paid hers and he his. He told her that it was great to meet her, but that he had other commitments that he had to run off to.

"Maybe I'll bump into you again," he said politely. He wished her well. They hugged. Then he walked home.

He had to rate his first outing a total success. He was able to break the ice with a thirty-something American woman. That made him feel good. He was also able to steer the conversation in a way to find out that pursuing her would have been a waste of time because she didn't have enough money. That, he realized would be the biggest challenge. He had to find a woman good for at least fifty thousand dollars.

He was sure he could do it.

———————

Bob's flight from London landed in Bangkok a few minutes early. Being in first class, he was able to deplane quickly and head to the hotel.

Customs was a breeze. He followed the signs for nothing to declare, was stamped and out in no time. His checked bag would be held and forwarded to his next flight. Within fifteen minutes of landing, he was in his room with his carry-on, ready to shave and take a quick shower.

When he entered the atrium bar, it was easy to find Mason. He was the only white guy there. He made eye contact and Mason signaled with a nod. The two men shook hands.

"What's your poison?" Mason asked.

"Whatever you're having looks good."

Mason turned to the bartender and asked for a Jack Daniels on the rocks. "Water?" he asked Bob, who nodded yes. He told the bartender. They had small talk about the flight until the whiskey and side of water arrived, then moved over to a sofa and chair that was set off by itself to afford privacy.

"What's the plan? How will you begin?"

"I have a flight tomorrow mornin' to Penang," Mason said. "There was a murder two days after your daughter's. This one in George Town. Same MO. Pretty, young thing stayin' by herself in a low-cost hotel. They found her naked in her room with her throat slashed deep and wide. Everythin' of value taken. I'm headin' there first because an old buddy of mine is now chief homicide detective for the Penang police. The Penang police have a lot more going for them than the small force in Mersing. I expect Bo – that's what we called him back in our Laos days – will have some leads by the time I get there."

"What about the other girl who was killed earlier this year?"

"Yep, I heard back from Fitz. It's related. Exact same MO. That's three we know of. Fitz is gonna go back to see if there were others. I'm bettin' we find at least one more. He's also reachin' out to some of our close allies, the Brits, Australia, Germany, to see if they have had similar cases."

A bar girl came by and Mason smiled up at her. "Hey sweetheart, kindly bring my friend here and me another round."

"I'll head to Mersing after Penang. I suspect I'll learn somethin' from

77

the hotel manager and the bartender. I might then head to Tioman Island to see if I can find the three young people Amanda arrived with."

Mason explained that the nature of investigations is to simply follow down the most promising leads. "You know where you're startin', but from there you have to play it by ear. I'm startin' in Penang and then Mersing. Can't say for sure yet where it'll take me after those two places."

The two men let the conversation veer from the case. Bob told Mason he had served two tours of duty in Vietnam in the mid-sixties. He talked about how much the war had changed between his first tour and his second. He shared some medevac stories, including the one near Cu Chi.

"I don't know if Fitz told you what I was doin' when he and I worked together," he said. "He was on the ambassador's staff in Vientiane, that's the capital of Laos. You probably know that. Anyway, I was a newly minted CIA hotshot. This was in '72." He paused to think. "Fifteen years ago."

Mason said few Americans know much about the wars in Laos and Cambodia that were going on at the same time as the big one in Vietnam.

"The Pathet Lao – our version of the Viet Cong – they were backed by North Vietnam. On our side were the Hmong tribesmen. Fierce motherfuckers. Loyal, too. But greatly outnumbered and outgunned. My job when I first got to Laos was to work closely with the Hmong to try to turn the tide on the Pathet Lao."

Mason said that after the Paris peace treaty, the North Vietnamese Army stepped up the amount of stuff they were moving down the Ho Chi Minh Trail through eastern Laos.

"I was given marchin' order to fuck 'em up as much as I could. We couldn't bomb their asses from four miles up anymore, but we could sure as shit mess with 'em on the ground. And that's what me and my Hmong guys did. We made their lives a livin' hell. I gotta tell ya, it was fun!"

Mason then turned somber as he told the story about his unexpected trip to Udon Thani and the bombing of his home in Vientiane that killed his fiancé, Sylvie.

"I've been thinkin' about you goin' to identify your daughter's remains. I'm thankful I never had to do that with my Sylvie. There was nothin' left to identify."

"Can I give you some advice?" Mason continued.

"Sure."

"Have her cremated in KL You can take her back with you at your seat instead of in a fuckin' coffin in the belly of the plane."

The two men quietly sipped on their whiskeys for a bit.

"You know, Bob, when I told you on the phone that I could understand what it meant to you to find the asshole who kilt your little girl?" Bob nodded. "Well, that's because I've fuckin' been there myself. I tracked down the NVA general who gave the goddamn command that kilt my Sylvie. I found that sonofabitch and I blew his ass to kingdom come while he was havin' lunch with his girlfriend. I made sure it was his last day on earth. Blew up the entire fuckin' restaurant. Sure, I paid a price. It's what eventually got me booted out of the Company."

Mason paused, then raised his eyes from his glass to peer squarely at Bob.

"I was sittin' in a restaurant across the street. Lookin' straight at him. You should have seen the look on his when he saw me, smilin' like I'd just hit a Vegas jackpot. That look of recognition, then panic. That's when I pushed the goddamn button." Mason raised his hand and used his thumb to push a button on an imaginary detonator switch. "He disappeared like that." Mason snapped his fingers. "It felt so right, Bob. Revenge. It doesn't right wrongs, but fuck man if it's not the next best thing."

Bob took in the man he was trusting to exact his own revenge. After a moment, he raised his whiskey to clink it with Mason's.

"You are the right man," he told Mason as the two touched glasses. "That's what I want. I want the next best thing."

Before parting, Mason went over how they would work from opposite sides of the world.

"If you need to reach me," Mason said, "you need to work through Boonsri. She's my assistant. She's great and speaks English really well. I will check in with her most days, so she can get a message to me. Be patient, though, because with the time difference it can take a while. We'll let Boonsri set up when you and I will do a weekly progress call. I'll tell her when I know what day is gonna work. She'll call you to let you know I'll be callin'."

Mason told Bob that his fee would be one thousand dollars a week, plus another thousand in expenses. "Don't expect receipts for the expenses," Mason said. "I'll keep track in my notebook. You just have to trust me. If I don't spend the thousand, you'll get it back."

Mason gave him a sheet of paper with banking instructions for wiring the weekly fee. He suggested that Bob wire the money every Thursday so that it would show up in Mason's Bangkok account on Friday.

"When I find him," Mason said, "I'll be expectin' a bonus. The amount is entirely up to you."

———————

It was midnight when Mason returned to his small condo in Bangkok's Victory Monument neighborhood. It was on a quiet street, if such thing existed in this city that never sleeps, in a building of twelve units. Mason's one-bedroom apartment was on the third floor away from the street, overlooking a garden. The building was designed to appeal to Western business and professional types. It had a kitchen that would be right at home in Los Angeles and a bathroom that would, as well.

Mason was one of the original residents of the building. He moved in when it opened just four years earlier. He knew his neighbors enough to say hello using their names but wasn't really friends with any of them. He was happy with unit 3-C and saw no reason he would ever need to move.

The night didn't go well. At some point around two o'clock, Mason bolted upright in bed, uttering a scream. He never screamed. Ever. He was instantly awake. For the first time in his life, going back even to when he was a child growing up on the farm in Georgia, Mason experienced a full-on night terror. His dream flashed back to the day he killed General Tho. But while he had consciously recalled the moment of the general's death countless times, none of them had upset him. In fact, he had felt a calm sense of satisfaction every time he had thought about the look on the general's face when the realization of his imminent death flashed across it. This nightmare was different.

The image in Mason's mind was not of the general. It was the waiter who was serving him. The Laotian man, who appeared to be about thirty years old, was leaning over General Tho's left shoulder pouring tea.

In the nightmare, the waiter literally melted in slow-motion and then the dream jumped to a small living room with a photo of the man on the wall. An older woman, who Mason seemed to know was the waiter's mother, was sobbing, as were a younger woman and two children. It was clearly the waiter's family and they were in intense grief. The vision was painful. Excruciatingly, intensely, overwhelmingly painful.

Mason was sweating profusely and his breathing was shallow. He shook.

When he finally slowed his breathing and regained some control, he wondered what the fuck had just happened? What did it mean?

It had been fourteen years since he killed the general, but he had never thought about the waiter. He searched his conscious mind. Did he remember the man serving the general? He didn't. Had he made it up? No. The general would have had a waiter, for sure. In fact, there was probably another standing nearby. Mason then realized that he had seen the man darting about the restaurant, even talking with the general. He had just never truly noticed him.

So, Mason had locked away any thoughts of the man for fourteen years. Until tonight. He wondered if the waiter would replace General Tho whenever his mind drifted back to that day.

He got out of bed, went to his kitchen and got a bottle of water from his refrigerator. Sitting on the side of the bed, he tried to picture others at the scene, but no faces emerged. He knew there were others. Fifty-four people other than the general had died that day. In fourteen years, he'd never given them any thought. Why couldn't he recall their faces? Any of them? And why did the waiter suddenly appear to him?

Mason had thought that the bombing at Sam Neua was behind him. But there was no question that the images of his nightmare had opened something raw within him. As he tried fitfully to get back to sleep, his fear was that the dream was not a fluke. That the man and his family were real. He just knew it. As he tried to coax himself back to sleep, he wondered if this was a one-time thing. He hoped so, but his fear was real. He feared that he would meet the other fifty-three innocent victims of his anger in the days, weeks, months and years ahead.

God, he hoped not.

Day 8

"Hey Fitz. You caught me runnin' out the door. I have a flight to Penang. What's up?"

"This guy is a serial killer," Fitz said. "We should have caught this, but we didn't. Over the past two and a half years, there have been seven murders of young American women in Malaysia. The three you know about and four others. They all follow the same MO. Young, blonde, traveling alone. Knife to the front of the throat."

"Shit. I was afraid that we might find somethin' like this," Mason said. "But it's good for what I'm doin'. This guy probably has patterns that will lead us to him. Do you have files on all of them?"

"We're still pulling it together."

"Fax me what you have right now and I'll take it with me. Then as you get more, fax it to Boonsri and she'll find a way to get it to me."

"Okay. It's in the fax now."

Mason asked if they'd checked if there had been similar deaths in nearby countries. Fitz said they had but nothing had turned up.

"Anythin' else?" Mason asked.

"Yes. One of Amanda's credit cards was used several times in Penang over the past week and her traveler's checks were cashed there, too."

Mason asked that Fitz include those details in the fax.

"Listen," Fitz continued, "seven young American girls in two and a half years escalates this to a big fucking deal. Some of the people who've been read in are going ape-shit. I'm concerned some asshole is going to leak it to a buddy in the press. I met with the Secretary at the end of the day. I explained that Anderson had hired you and that we should let you take the lead and offer you whatever help you need. He hemmed and hawed, but finally agreed."

"Fuck man! Can you keep it out of the press?"

"I think so. Only a handful of people know right now. Believe me, everyone here knows how fragile our relationship with Prime Minister Mohamed is. I think it'll stay under wraps. I'll try to manage our end."

Mason asked about the American embassy in KL.

"That the sixty-four-thousand-dollar question, my friend. We have to tell the ambassador."

"What do you know about that guy? Will he muck it up?"

"John Monjo is a good one. Solid. He's only been at the post for a few months, but he's a career State guy. I like him. He and I are tight. Let me take care of him."

"Okay. And the Malaysian government itself? Can we keep 'em in the dark? I'd like to do this on my own."

"I talked with the Secretary. We're going to hold off telling them. I don't know how long we can do that, though, Mason. Seven goddamn murders of young American girls. It's dicey. Our position right now is that officially, the US government isn't doing anything. This is a matter between a private American citizen whose daughter was killed and a private detective he hired."

"One potential wrinkle that I see," Mason said, "is that I'm meetin' this afternoon with Bo. You remember him from Vientiane?"

"Yes. Why is he relevant?"

"Because he's now the chief homicide detective in Penang. He's on the Mary Higgins case."

"That's fucking great. Well, play it by ear. Bo always struck me as a guy who knew when to keep his mouth shut. Maybe you can convince him that this is such a time."

"Well, he only knows about the Higgins girl. I planned to tell him about Amanda Anderson. He's gonna have access to info that I need. I think I can still tell him about Amanda just not mention the others. At least, not yet. I think if he thinks it's just the two cases, he won't see any reason to report it up."

"Sounds solid to me."

Mason hung up, grabbed the fax, said goodbye to Boonsri and dashed to catch his flight.

————

Fitz called Ambassador Monjo after getting off the phone with Mason. He briefed him that Bob Anderson was well connected to the president. In fact, Fitz told him, the President and Mrs. Reagan had sent their personal condolences to Anderson. Monjo knew what that meant, to treat Bob almost as if he were a visiting head of state. He made sure that other key staff knew, as well. When Bob arrived shortly before lunch time, he was immediately escorted into Monjo's office.

"Mr. Anderson, I'm heartbroken about your daughter. I truly am," Monjo said.

"I appreciate that, Mr. Ambassador."

"Please call me John."

"Thanks John. And I'm just Bob."

"Bob, how do you want to handle today? My staff and I are here to make things go as well as they can, under the circumstances."

"I guess the first thing is that I need to see her."

"Of course."

Monjo walked to his desk and spoke on his phone softly to someone. "Yes, that's right. Mr. Anderson would like to come down now. Will that work?"

Hanging up the phone, Monjo looked back to Bob. "Dr. Simpson is our medical officer. He needs about five minutes and will meet us where, a..., well, where we are keeping her."

A few minutes later Bob entered a complex of rooms in the basement of the embassy that served as a medical wing. There were a couple of Malaysian men in white smocks who appeared to be some kind of lab techs. In the back room of the wing was a stark windowless room that was noticeably cooler. In the middle of the room was a table. A body, covered in a sheet, lay on top of it.

"Hello. I'm Dr. Simpson. If you have any questions, I'll do my best to answer them."

"Thank you, doctor."

"Bob, why don't the doctor and I give you some privacy. We'll just be outside the door. Take your time."

Bob nodded, then waited for the men to leave the room. He inched closed to the table until he was standing next to the upper torso. His hand shook as he reached out, took the top of the sheet and pulled it down to reveal Amanda's lifeless face.

He had thought about this moment throughout his journey to Kuala Lumpur. He was glad to be alone because he knew he would sob.

But he didn't.

All he felt was rage. A man had taken his beautiful daughter's life. He would find that bastard and he would fucking kill him.

He pulled the sheet back over her head, took a deep breath. "He won't get away with this, sweetie. I promise you. I will find him and I will make him pay." He paused, then added, "I will always love you."

Bob bent over and kissed her forehead through the sheet, then turned and left the room. He asked if she could be cremated.

"That's a wise choice," Dr. Simpson said. "There is a facility we use. Would you like for me to take care of it for you?"

"Yes. How long will it take? I want to take my girl home."

"They'll probably be able to do it sometime tomorrow. I think you are safe to fly back the next day."

The flight to Penang took about two and a half hours. Mason had called Bo before departing Bangkok. The two had agreed to meet at a George Town café where they often dined whenever Mason was in town.

Detective Jun Shan-Bo was already sitting at a booth when Mason walked in. He offered a small wave to Mason, who walked over to where Bo was sitting. Bo stood. The two men shook hands, looked at each other, then did a quick hug.

"Good to see you again, my friend," Bo said. "It's been too long this time."

"What?" Mason said. "It's only been about six months. I had some work back in Vientiane, so I used the trips there to renew my visa."

"How is Vientiane now that the communists run the place?"

"Like goin' to China under Mao. The commies sucked the life right out of it. You'd hate it, Bo. It's nothin' like it was. All I can say is at least it's not Cambodia."

The two men ordered lunch and continued to catch up for a bit. Bo told Mason the latest exploits about his two boys, ages six and eight. A scientist-to-be and a budding sports star. Eventually, though, the conversation turned serious.

"I've been hired by an American businessman," Mason said, "to track down the guy who killed his little girl in Mersing a week ago. Here's the thing, the MO is the same as your Mary Higgins case."

"You mean the slashed throat?"

"Yeah. It's not just that," Mason said. "They're like two peas in a pod. Both girls are about the same age. Both Americans. Both blonde. Both murdered in their hotel rooms after havin' sex. Both had everythin' they had of value taken, so same shit."

"Yes. Similarities," Bo said. "But Mersing is very far away. It could be nothing more than coincidence."

"With all due respect, bud, this is no fuckin' coincidence. I learned this mornin' that my girl's credit cards have been used right here in Penang several times in the past few days."

"Hmmm. That's different. I would say there is a good chance we're looking for the same guy."

"That's my thinkin', too. So, we should share info on the QT. I brought you a copy of the Mersing police report. Not up to your standards, but it is a good place to start. Can you share what you have on the Mary Higgins case?"

Bo slid a file folder over to him.

"When you called and said you wanted to meet to go over a mutual case, I figured it had to be Mary Higgins."

Both men studied the files before them.

"The knife wounds look identical," Bo said. "Same angle. He's left-handed. And this guy's precise."

"The girls are similar, too," added Mason. "Same ages. Blondies. My girl was five-foot-five. Yours five-four. Both left buck naked on their beds after havin' sex. Both Americans. Have you had other cases with young girls who aren't American?"

"No. Nothing like this at all."

Mason eyed the Mary Higgins' file.

"My girl was travelin' with some others who probably got a good look at our guy. They left town, though, before the police could talk with 'em. You spoke with one of your girl's friends?"

"Yes. We've interviewed a young Kiwi girl from the hotel," Bo said. "She saw Mary having dinner with a guy the night Mary was killed. She thinks he was an American. She said his name was something like Jimmy or Johnny or something like that. She wasn't sure. She said he seemed nice, though."

"Did she meet him at the hotel?"

"No. At a restaurant, the Rama-Rama. I spoke with a waiter there who remembered them," Bo said. "He said they both sounded like Americans, though he said he thought the guy might be Malaysian. When I pressed him why he thought that, he said he kind of had a Malaysian look. I pressed him a bit and he was basing it mostly on skin tone. But that was pretty much it. Kinda sorta. You can't take that to the bank."

"So, he could be an American, or at least another backpacker," Mason said, then got a slightly sour look on his face and added, "I don't know, man. Walkin' like a duck and talkin' like a duck doesn't make it a fuckin' duck."

"My friend, odds are it's a duck. The only thing that says otherwise is that his skin tone is not somehow right. But America is a big country and comes in many colors. Besides, I don't think I've ever met a local who could pull off being an American to Americans. My guess is that he's an American."

"You might be right," Mason said, then paused in thought for a moment. "We might be barkin' up the wrong tree, though, Bo. The American thing just doesn't seem to fit."

"How's that?"

"Backpackers don't strike me as the type to do somethin' like this. And for what? A little cash and maybe a camera? I'd be more likely to buy kinky sex crimes. I mean, think about it, Bo. Sure, the cash could go straight in his pocket, but what about everything else? Where is a backpacker gonna unload a passport, traveler's checks and credit cards, not to mention items like cameras or jewelry? Seems like a stretch for a backpacker. That dog don't bark. No, I think he knows people. He has a fence. Our boy's a local."

"Good points and explains why your girl's stuff showed up here," Bo said, "but I can also tell you that young American girls don't hang around much with Malaysian guys."

"I hear you, buddy. But maybe our guy's only part Malaysian. I mean, all we really know is that he apparently can pass himself off as an American. Maybe he went to college in the US. We just don't know yet. Let's keep an open mind. I'm headin' down to Mersing later today. Hopefully, I'll learn more there. I'll find a phone and call you tomorrow evenin.'"

Day 9

Mason had flown into Singapore after meeting with Bo. This morning found him in a rental car on a two-and-a-half-hour drive to Mersing. It was going to be a scorcher today, so he was glad he paid for a larger car with air-conditioning. It was late morning when he arrived at the Mersing police station, a small, single-story white building near the center of town.

He went in, introduced himself and asked to see the chief. He was led to a small office toward the back of the building.

"Good mornin', chief," Mason said, offering his hand to shake. "My name is Mason Ray. I work for the daddy of the American girl who was kilt here a week or so ago."

"Yes. Yes. Awful. Bloodiest mess I've ever seen. You say you work for her father?"

"Yes sir. He wants me to help authorities like yourself. Mr. Anderson knows how few resources might be available. I'm a trained investigator, so he sent me here to talk with witnesses. I know you've already spoken with lot of folks. I read your preliminary report."

While Mason was speaking, the chief was thinking he thought he was done with the Amanda Anderson case when he sent the report to KL. No one in Mersing cared about a loose young American woman being killed. It wasn't as if it had happened to someone they knew. And besides, nothing like Amanda's murder happens in Mersing. It just doesn't.

"Look, Mr. Ray, I'm happy to tell you everything I know, but I don't want to bother our folks here in Mersing. Why don't we start with. . ."

"Thank you kindly for the offer, chief. But I'll do my own talkin' with folks. It won't take long and I won't ruffle any feathers. I promise you that."

After a brief silence, the chief finally spoke again.

"Okay. Sure. Mr. Ray. Let me take care of a couple things and I'll walk you over to the hotel."

"Won't be necessary, chief. I'm just gonna walk around a bit to get a feel for the place. I stopped by to see you mostly to find out if there has been anythin' new since the report you filed with Kuala Lumpur."

"Not really. I didn't have the manpower to send one of my men to Tioman to track down the three other backpackers. I did talk with the captain of the fishing boat who took them to the island, but it didn't produce anything. He took them to the pier and dropped them off. He said the German fellow came up to the bridge once on the crossing, but they didn't talk about anything important."

"So chief," Mason said while pulling out a small map of Mersing. He had marked the police station on it. "It would be kind of you to show me on the map where the Happy Song and the Portside Café are."

The chief looked at the map, took a pen and marked two Xs on it. By one, he wrote "Hotel" and by the other "Café."

"Well, thank you, chief. I should be out of your hair tonight or first thing in the mornin'. Just doin' my job, you know. If I learn anything new at all, I'll swing back by and tell you."

With that, Mason rose, as did the chief. They shook hands and Mason left.

His first stop was the Happy Song Hotel. It looked as if it was at least fifty years old and perhaps was last painted shortly after World War II ended. It had a regular house door in front. He opened it and walked in.

"Hello, you want room?" a Chinese Malay man asked him in a clipped accent when he walked in.

"Is the manager here?" Mason asked.

"I manager. You want room?"

THE NEXT BEST THING

"No," Mason said. "I'm here about the girl who was kilt here last week."

"I already talk to police. You not need to know. Goodbye."

Mason reached into his pocket and pulled out an American twenty-dollar bill and placed it on the counter. That was ten times more than Amanda paid for her room. "I just wanna talk. If I learn somethin' new, I put another twenty dollars on the counter for you. Okay?"

"I talk. What you want?"

"Let's start with your name. I'm Mason. What should I call you?"

"I Pug. Everybody call me that."

"Okay Pug. Start from the beginnin' and tell me everythin' you remember about that night."

Pug said he saw the five backpackers get off the bus at the bus stop halfway down the street. They walked to the Happy Song, but only the four came in.

"What did the other one look like?"

"He backpacker," Pug said.

"Okay, but was he as tall as me? Did he have brown hair? Anything stand out about him?"

"He maybe tall as you. Hair like you, too. He not white like you and the others."

"Oh. That's interestin'. Was he black?"

"No. Just not white."

"Malaysian?"

"He backpacker!" Pug said. "He across street."

Mason asked to see the register from the night they all checked in. Pug opened to the page and turned around the book. Pug pointed to the four names. They matched the police report, but Mason also wrote down their names as spelled in the register and their passport numbers.

"They want to see rooms. Dead girl take room nine on second floor. Other alone girl take room twelve. Couple take bigger room on this floor, room three."

"I'd like to see Amanda's room."

Pug grabbed a key and walked up the stairs. Room nine was last one down the hall on the left.

"Where does this door go?" Mason asked about the door at the end of the hall when they reached Amanda's room.

Pug opened it to show Mason that it was a back exit.

"Was this door unlocked the night Amanda was killed?"

"Door always unlocked from inside. Fire escape."

Pug then took Mason into Amanda's room. It was small but had a private bathroom. Mason surveyed the setting. In his mind, he could see what likely happened. Amanda got up after the sex and went into the bathroom to pee and freshen up. The killer would have stood behind where the door would open. He'd have a knife in his dominant hand. When she came out the door, he would move up behind her swiftly. Undoubtedly, he would put his hand tightly over her mouth to stifle a scream, then quickly slice through the front of her neck. The whole thing would take maybe two seconds. The killer probably knew that if he cut deeply enough that she'd be unable to make any sounds. Mason could picture him easing her body onto the bed to let her bleed to death.

Her turned back to the hotel manager.

"What time do you go to bed, Pug?"

"Late."

"How late were you up that night."

"One in morning."

"So, they came back to the hotel after 1 a.m."

"No, they come earlier. Maybe midnight."

"Really. There was nothin' in the police report about you seein' them arrive."

"Police not ask. Police ask if I was at desk when they came in. I said no because I not at desk."

"Where were you?"

"My room behind desk. I look out when I hear door. I see it her, so not get up."

"So, you saw her. How about the guy?"

"Just peek. Same guy from bus."

"Did they say anything?"

"Whispers. I no hear words."

"Anything else you can tell me?"

"German guy come back a few days ago."

"You mean one of the backpackers?"

"Yes."

"What did he say?"

"He ask when other girl check out. Said she not come Tioman."

"What did you tell him?"

"I tell him she dead," Pug said while pulling his finger across his neck.

"What did he say when you told him?"

"He look sick. Then he cry a little."

"Did you tell the police he was back?"

"No one ask me to do that."

"Is he still here?"

"No. Leave next day."

Mason pulled a second twenty-dollar bill and handed it to Pug.

"Thank you, Pug. You've been a big help. I'm gonna head down the back exit."

Pug was wearing a big smile, already thinking what he might do with forty US dollars.

Mason opened the door and left. On the ground, he stopped and looked around. No windows faced the small backyard. This is how he left, Mason thought. It would be easy for someone to sneak away like this in the middle of the night.

It was too early to go to the Portside Café. The travelers and Amanda were there in the evening, so that's when he wanted to arrive. He walked about the town a bit. He strolled past the docks where the fishing boats were moored. He likely would need to take one to Tioman the next day to find the other travelers. They spent more time with the killer than anyone he could talk with in Mersing. They'd probably be able to give him a better description. Back outside the police station, he got in his rental car and drove to his hotel.

Boonsri had booked him one night at the Mersing Hotel, a far cry from a Hilton but several heads and shoulders above the Happy Song. His room was spacious with an air conditioner that pumped out refreshingly cool air from above the room's one window.

It was 2 p.m. The twelve-hour time difference between Malaysia and Washington, D.C. made it too early to call Fitz for an update on the other murders. He'd do that after the Portside. He did check in with Boonsri, but she had nothing new to tell him. So he closed his eyes and within minutes was asleep.

It happened again. He saw a young woman clearly. She was in the street between Mason and General Tho. She was attractive and looked to be about twenty. A baby, perhaps four or five months old, was in a strap on her back.

In the nightmare, both the woman and the baby were peering at him. The woman's face had a haunting quality. She knew, Mason realized, that her life and that of her little boy were about to end. Her eyes bore into him and seemed to beg to know why.

Then, in a sudden burst, she and the baby turned to smoke and blew away. Mason woke up and began to cry. In his heart, he knew she, like the waiter, were real. Had he really killed that little baby? Yes, he had. It took him a while to pull himself together.

What was most unnerving to him, though, was why now, after nearly fifteen years, was he having these visions? What did it mean? And the bigger question: Would they stop?

Mason took a bottle of Jack Daniels from his bag and poured a couple fingers into a glass. "Pull yourself together," he told himself again. He downed the whiskey, feeling the burning tingle as it traveled through his throat.

He walked into the bathroom, unrobed and took a long, hot shower, then shaved. Back in the main room, he tuned the TV to the English language station and caught up on the day's world news.

Why did the news always have to be so bad? Markets were crashing around the world and the mother of all typhoons had killed more than eight hundred people in the Philippines. President Reagan was in Berlin. He gave a speech at the Brandenburg gate between West and East Berlin. He used the speech to send a message to the Soviet leader, Mikhail Gorbachev, to "tear down this wall." "Fat chance," Mason said to the commentator on TV.

The shower and TV did what he needed done. They distracted him. Still, his mind would out of the blue flash on the young Laotian woman and her baby from his nightmare. Whenever it did, an icy cold would overtake him.

Mason walked into the Portside Café at a little after seven o'clock. About half the tables were filled, as well as several seats at the bar. Soccer, or football as it is called everywhere except America, was on the TV above the bar. Another TV in the dining room was airing an episode of *Cheers*.

TV was the way Mason stayed connected to America. He hadn't been back since he first arrived in Southeast Asia in early 1972, not even for his dad's funeral. He would have done that, but he was on a job when it happened and he didn't get the message until too late. He had since called his mom once a month. She wanted him to come home, but he couldn't bring himself to do it.

Mason didn't really know why. While he had been eager to get away from the small town where he grew up and away from the farm, he loved his mom and dad. He and Sylvie had planned to take a month back Stateside for the wedding. Mason had wanted to take Sylvie to meet them before heading on to her parents' place in Connecticut.

After Sylvie's death, the Vientiane chief of station suggested that maybe Mason should take a break and visit his folks. Mason, though, was too focused on his secret plan to get revenge to heed the advice.

Once he moved to Bangkok Mason became obsessed with American TV shows. It wasn't an easy obsession in Thailand. Pirated videotapes of movies could quickly be found, but TV shows took work and patience. He had a network of people who would sell him black market tapes of shows. That was how he came across *Cheers*. One of his sources said he would love it and he did. The current TV shows weren't on when he left the US in 1972. He loved some of those old shows. He could still find himself singing the theme song to *The Beverly Hillbillies* at the oddest time.

Come and listen to my story about a man named Jed,
A poor mountaineer, barely kept his family fed,
And then one day he was shootin' at some food,
And up through the ground come a bubblin' crude.

Oil that is. Black gold. Texas tea.

Maybe, he thought, he should start singing that song in his mind whenever he had flashbacks to the bombing.

But *Cheers* had become Mason's favorite series. He had all the shows on tape through the previous season. He wished Bangkok had an English language network like Malaysia so he wouldn't have to wait for shows to be available on videotape. Even on the black market, there was a major lag. He watched the show on the TV in the dining room for a bit, but it's not the same with the volume turned off. Then the bartender was standing in front of him.

"Good evening, mate. What will you have?"

"You're Australian?" Mason asked as he broke into a broad grin. "Didn't see that comin'."

"Yep. I'm a Sydney boy. I'm Michael. Can I pour you a freezer beer or would something else do for you?"

Mason ordered a Heineken and watched as Michael pulled one straight from a freezer behind the bar. He popped the lid, was about to set it on the bar, then paused.

"You a glass guy?"

Mason shook his head no, then reached and took the bottle from Michael.

"So, what brings you here? You're a wee bit older than my usual expat customer."

"Actually, I came to talk to you."

"Me?" the bartender asked, then without missing a beat added, "Oh. About the girl?"

Mason introduced himself, then told Michael that Amanda's father had hired him because he wanted the guy tracked down. He knew that it would never happen if he left it to the police.

"Got that right, mate. I'm not sure how much help I can be but give it a go. I'll have to dart around a bit, though."

With that, two fellows at the other end of the bar waved him over and he was off. When he returned, Mason didn't jump into the formal interview. Instead, he just chatted with Michael and how Michael ended up tending a bar in Mersing. Michael said he'd been a bartender at places like the Portside all over Malaysia, Thailand and even in Bali.

Mason switched to his preferred drink, Jack Daniels straight up. By half past eight, business at the Portside was slowing. Mason got to the reason he was there.

He laid a photo of Amanda on the bar.

"You recall her, right?"

"Yeah. Pretty girl. Had a great laugh. Had she come in here alone, I would have talked her up myself. It's one of the perks of the job. It's a bloody shame what happened to her. I hope you find the guy."

"Tell me what you remember."

"She was the last to arrive. The first were a couple – a German guy and his American girlfriend – and another single girl. A ginger, she was. And a looker, too. They had been here just a few minutes when the other guy showed up. They saw him when he came in and called his name."

"What did they call him?"

"Joey," Michael said. "Maybe five minutes later, the Amanda girl came in. The German bloke pulled another chair to their table between him and the Joey guy."

"Did they drink a lot?"

"No. Not a lot. The German guy had three or four beers. The others a couple. That's not much considering that they also were here to eat."

"Did you notice anythin' about how they acted," Mason asked, "or maybe what they talked about?"

"They acted completely normal, you know. They talked a bit about Tioman, I know that. The Joey guy had been there before and was telling them about it. They also talked about other places they had been. They bitched about the bus ride from Melaka. Sounded like they were in a non-air-con bus and it was hot and dusty."

"They didn't all leave together," Mason said, making it sound like a question.

"No. Joey and Amanda stayed, ordered another beer and asked if I'd tune the TV above the bar to TV3. It was time for *L.A. Law.* I don't know how they knew that, but they did. I figured as long as they were drinking beer, they could watch whatever they wanted. There were only about six or seven people left in here by then. When the show came on, I turned on the volume."

"Did they stay for the whole show?"

"Yeah."

"Did they appear attracted to one another?"

"Hard to say, mate. They weren't touching or anything like that."

"So, describe Joey to me."

"He's about five feet ten, give or take. I'd say about eighty kilos. He looked very fit. He had some muscles. You could see them under his tee-shirt. Oh, he had a nasty scar on his left forearm." Michael used his finger to trace a line about eight inches long on the top of his left forearm. It was clean, like a knife wound. I bet that sucker hurt when it happened."

"That's good info. How did he look, though? You know, eyes, hair, nose. That kind of stuff."

"He was a good-looking bloke. He was presenting himself as an American. I mean he sounded exactly like an American. But I'm not so sure."

"Why's that?"

"Well, working this job you meet a lot of people from everywhere. After a while, you can pretty much guess where someone is from before they say it. This Joey guy was not easy. It wasn't that he looked Malay. His facial features weren't right. But his skin color was spot on Malaysian."

"Couldn't he have been American with African or Hispanic blood in him?"

"No, I don't think so. Malaysians have a little yellow tint to their skin color. You don't see that in Americans, or other Westerners, for that matter. Wherever he is from, he's part Malaysian, or Indonesian. No matter what his eyes and nose looked like, he wears the skin of someone from here."

"I will say he had nice, soft features," Michael continued. "His face, you know eyes, mouth, nose, even his eyebrows could have been American, but that was the extent of it."

"What about eye and hair color? Did you notice those?"

"His hair is definitely Western. Kind of a light brown. Most Americans seem to have brown or blonde hair, don't you think? His was thick and wavy. It wasn't long, but a longer style than you see on locals. That's for sure. I have no idea about his eye color, but he had nice eyes. Like I said, he was a good-looking guy."

Before Mason headed back to his hotel, he asked Michael if he had an idea when he could take a boat to Tioman. Michael smiled and said anyone in Mersing could answer that question. "It all has to do with the tides," he said. "The fishing boats need a high tide to leave the docks. That would be around 9:30 the next morning."

Mason thanked him and was about to head back to the hotel when Michael thought of one other thing.

"He's left-handed," Michael said. He drank with his left hand. That's how I first saw the scar."

Mason thanked him again and left. When he got back to his room, he made a list of new information.

The likely killer went by the name Joey. He might be a biracial Malaysian American. He was a few inches taller than most Malaysians, about five feet ten inches tall. Maybe about one hundred eighty pounds. Was a good-looking guy. Muscles. He was left-handed and had a nasty long scar on his left forearm. He had arrived with Amanda and three others on a late afternoon bus from Melaka. Finally, the German fellow had returned to the Happy Song for one night a few days after Amanda's murder. He clearly didn't know about it.

———————

"Hey Fitz."

"Mason. Making any progress?"

"Does a fish swim?"

He shared what he had learned that day, then added that he was going to Tioman the next day to try to find the young women who were traveling with Amanda in Mersing.

"Let me tell you what we know about the other murders," Fitz said. "First, we're still not telling the Malaysian government. The time will come when we'll have to. But we want to give you as much time as we can before we do."

"Thank you, sir. I appreciate that."

"Except for the last one – that would be Mary Higgins in George Town – all the others happened at a place like Mersing," Fitz said. "So, not at a destination, but at a gathering point to go to the destination. We kicked that around here and think we know why."

"Okay. Why?"

"We think it's easier to spot a young woman traveling alone. Mary Higgins, for example, was apparently exploring George Town on her own when she met this guy."

"Wait, George Town is a destination not a jumpin' off point and Amanda was with three other friends," Mason interjected.

"Maybe, but was she really with friends? They all left without her."

"Good point," Mason conceded.

"I know George Town doesn't fit the theory. It doesn't jive with the usual timeline either. But hear me out.

"We think the other reason he chose those locations is because they are easy to flee from. We think he'd stash a car some place nearby but out of sight. After the murder and robbery, he'd dash to his car and speed back to Penang."

"Penang? Why Penang," Mason asked.

"About the only thing all seven victims have in common is that their credit cards were used in Penang in the days following their deaths. Certainly sounds like he takes his goodies to Penang to fence them. Maybe you should share this info with Bo and see if he can identify possible fences."

"Yeah. Good idea. I plan to call him tomorrow mornin'. If I had my druthers, I wouldn't share the other murders yet, but now that we know they're all connected, I might have to. I just hope I can talk him out of passin' the info on up the chain."

"Ask him not to and see what he says," Fitz added. "Tell him that you need him to let you know if he decides to do it. We'd need to make sure we reach out through the embassy to the government, if it comes to that. Do you think you can convince him to sit on it for a bit?"

"Yeah. Me and Bo go back a long way. We shared some shit in Laos, you know. He'll try to give me what I need. At least a few more days. I trust him, Fitz."

Day 10

Today was Joey's third day practicing on older women. He was able to do two yesterday. One at lunch. Another at dinner. No problems making the connection. Both women were in their early to mid-thirties. Neither, though, struck Joey as having money back in the States. He told himself to be patient. It was early. He was just practicing. And, it was a numbers game. If he met with enough women, one with a good bank account would turn up.

He was back at the Holiday Inn today, having gone to other places yesterday. An attractive redhead walked in after he had been sitting for just a few minutes. She took a nearby table. He gave her a slight nod and smile, then refocused on his menu. Not that he needed a menu. It was part of the act. He had eaten in this café scores of times.

Joey glanced over at her again. She was pretty, but not in a Miss America kind of way. Her red hair intrigued him. He had never known anyone himself with red hair, though that girl – what was her name? – on the bus to Mersing had red hair. Suzy, that was it.

Red hair is certainly not a Malaysian trait. Her hair fell to just below her shoulders in soft waves. It paired nicely with her pale skin.

He found himself oddly hoping that she'd be the one. He was attracted to her in a basic, primal way. That was something he didn't expect. Now, though, he understood that it made sense. If he were going to have to spend weeks winning her trust, he'd hope it would be with someone he was drawn to.

If she had noticed him, she didn't show it. She was sitting at her table, just two away from him, reading a yellow paperback guidebook. When the waiter handed her the menu, she had set the book on the table. It gave him something to say.

"Great book," he said to her.

"Pardon me," she responded.

"Your Lonely Planet guide. It's been my Bible."

"Oh. Yeah. I find it really helpful." She looked back at her menu.

"So, how did you end up in Batu Ferringhi? Lonely Planet doesn't really recommend it."

The waiter came and took her order, then his.

"Honestly?" she said. Joey nodded. "I wanted a hot shower."

Joey laughed. "Been there. Done that," he said.

"I'm Joey, by the way."

"Jessica."

"I picked up my Lonely Planet book right after I read a review in the Charlotte Observer."

"Seattle Times."

"What?"

"I got mine after reading about it in a story in the Sunday travel section of the Seattle Times."

"Is that where you're from?

"Yes. You?"

Her first question back to him. Not in the door yet, but he had successfully broken the ice.

"Believe me, you've never heard of it. I'm from a tiny town in North Carolina called Bentonville."

"Explains Charlotte."

"I moved there after college for work."

This is where he would expect her to ask him what kind of work he did or if he liked Charlotte, but she didn't. She seemed shy, nervous or something. He needed to get her talking.

"I've never been to Seattle. Does it really rain there all the time?"

"Not really. We have the most spectacular summers. Long, sunny days. Warm but not hot, at least most of the time. Certainly nothing like this heat. It rains in the winter, probably when you were dealing with snow in the mountains."

"Mountains! We don't have no stinking mountains!" Joey said like the bandit in the old Humphrey Bogart movie *The Treasure of Sierra Madre*. Jessica frowned. "I know people think of the Great Smoky Mountains when they think of North Carolina, but the mountains are at the far western part of the state. I'm from the other side. Has a few hills. Mainly farmland."

The waiter brought their lunches at the same time.

"Mind if I join you? It's okay if not. I just enjoy talking with someone from home, you know."

"No. It's alright. Have you been on the road long?"

He moved his plate and soda to her table and sat.

"Well, that's not a question with a simple one-sentence answer for me."

"Why's that?" she said, taking her first bite of a spinach salad.

"Okay. Let me give you the simple answer first. I've been here, in Malaysia, for about six months."

"Really? Isn't that's a long time to stay in one country? Why?"

"And that, dear Jessica, is where the story gets complicated."

Joey had revised his backstory a little from the one he had used for the past two and a half years. In the new version, his mother, who worked in the laundry at the Port of Melaka, had a one-night stand with a British sailor. She knew him only as Reggie and didn't even know which ship he arrived on. In any case, he was long gone back out to sea when she found out she was pregnant.

"She gave it her best shot," Joey said, "but it was just too much for her. When I was three years old, she left me at an orphanage. She pinned a note saying she was an unwed mother and couldn't take care of me anymore. She said my name was Yusof and added the stuff about my dad being a long-gone British sailor and all. She signed the note with just her first name, Zara. That was her name."

Joey then said that a childless American couple was vacationing in

Malaysia and visited the orphanage. The woman, Helen, apparently fell in love with him right away.

"They hadn't planned on adopting me or anyone else," Joey said. "The only reason they were there was for church work. My folks took their faith very seriously. Long story short, they took me back to Bentonville as their son. You could say I lucked out."

"That's quite a story, Joey. So, let me guess. You came back to find your birth mother?"

"That's what got me here. I tried hard for two or three months to find her. But it had been too long. I did find a birth record at a hospital in Melaka for a Zara Zainya giving birth to an unnamed baby boy. I'd bet that was me. When I found it, I was sure I'd be able to find her. Didn't work out that way.

"I stayed in Melaka for a month," Joey continued. "But nothing. And I mean nothing. I found someone who worked with her at the Port and remembered her from when I was a baby, but she had no idea where my mother was. She said my mom left twenty or so years ago. I figured she must have left town. So, I went looking elsewhere. Kuala Lumpur first, then Penang. Dead ends. It was when I fully realized that this isn't America. I'm sure I would have been able to find her in America. Just wasn't going to happen here. Maybe if she had been a man it would have been different."

She asked him why he had stayed in Malaysia once he knew he wouldn't be able to find his mom.

"That's a good question, isn't it," Joey said. "To be honest, I'm still trying to figure that out. Mom and dad, the ones in North Carolina, died in a car crash last year. . ."

"Oh, I so sorry," she interrupted him.

"It was awful. Still is," he said. "But I don't have a pressing need to go home, so it seems important and timely to explore this side of who I am right now. They left me a small insurance policy. That's how I'm paying for being here."

Neither spoke while the waiter cleared their dishes.

106

"Hey," he said. "Enough of this sad stuff. You want to do something that I've wanted to do since I moved to the beach?"

Jessica looked at him but didn't say anything.

"There is a butterfly sanctuary on the island. They have tens of thousands of butterflies there. It's supposed to be awesome. Want to go?"

Going off with someone she just met sounded impulsive and maybe even risky. It's certainly something she wouldn't have done when she first left Seattle a couple months before. But this trip was about getting out of her rut. That meant doing things she wouldn't normally do. Besides, she liked Joey. He seemed nice. He was clearly younger than her, but not a lot. It didn't matter. That was the old her thinking. She had waited long enough. Time for a fling?

"Sure," she said.

They shared a taxi to the butterfly sanctuary. It was everything it had been said to be. Beautiful. Gentle. Colorful. There were few people there. Joey told her that it was probably because it was a weekday and it was quite a drive from George Town. They meandered the grounds for about ninety minutes.

Joey even grabbed her camera and took a photo of her with butterflies all over her. Turns out butterflies are drawn to sweat. And on a hot day, pale, redheaded girls from Seattle do sweat. Two perched on her hair, a third on her nose. More on her bare shoulders. It's hard to be stressed when butterflies are landing on you and their wings are slowly moving up and down literally drinking you in. When they were finally ready to leave, Jessica was surprised to see the same taxi waiting for them.

"That was absolutely great!" she told him in the taxi on the way back to the Holiday Inn. "Thank you for suggesting it. And to think I hesitated. I hope that picture of me with the butterflies all over me comes out okay."

As they approached the hotel, Joey suggested they get together the next day. He said he had an engagement that evening and again in the morning, but if she were up to it, they could meet about noon.

She tried not to show that she was a little disappointed that she wouldn't see him for dinner. He was fun and she needed fun. But tomorrow sounded great. She asked what he wanted to do.

"Your turn to choose," he said. "I thought maybe we should head into George Town, but I'll leave it up to you. Pick, like, three places."

"Want to meet in the café for lunch first?"

"No. Let's find a place in George Town. Got to mix things up."

They arrived at the Holiday Inn and both got out. She insisted on splitting the cost of the taxi.

He walked her to the entrance to the hotel lobby.

"Thank you for a great time today," Joey told her. "I'll meet you in the lobby at noon tomorrow."

He smiled and she returned it. He then turned and left. No kiss on the cheek. Not even a friendly hug.

There was a bounce in his step, though, as he walked back to his apartment. It had been a good day. He still had no idea if she qualified, but her offering to pay half the taxi fare and the fact that she could afford to stay in the Holiday Inn were promising. Maybe tomorrow he'd learn more. He wasn't going to rule her out too quickly.

————

Mason was at the docks at 8 a.m. His plan was to catch the Merlin launch. It costs nearly twice as much as a fishing boat. Still, it would only total about ten dollars and would be well worth it. The Merlin boat could make the crossing in two and a half hours. The fishing boats took four to five. It would also be far more comfortable.

The oft-told story was that Tioman Island was the setting for the famous Hollywood film, *South Pacific*. Mason had seen that movie countless times growing up. Whenever it would come on TV, his mom would insist the family watch it. His mom loved musicals; his dad not so much.

Some great songs came out of *South Pacific*. Of course, that was to be expected since it was a runaway Rodgers and Hammerstein hit on

Broadway. Probably the best-known song was *Some Enchanted Evening*. Mason was partial to *Bali Ha'i*.

It was mid-morning when the Merlin boat pulled alongside the dock at Tioman. Mason disembarked. A ways down the beach to his right was the Merlin Hotel, the only actual resort on the island. On the way to the island he learned that it had a small grass airstrip and had a daily flight to and from Mersing and Kuala Lumpur. Once he heard that, he decided that he'd fly back.

To the left, small clusters of accommodations designed for backpackers dotted the beach. Each place offered huts around an open-air restaurant. Some of the huts were like bungalows. Others were simple as A-frames built atop a small wooden platform. The platform was there to keep occupants and their gear off the ground during a heavy rain.

He wandered north. Stopping at each gathering of huts to search for anyone who looked like the two travelers. At each place, he would ask about them. It would have been easier if he had photos.
His fourth stop was a place called Happy Bungalow. Rock music blared from speakers. On the beach, he saw a redhead who fit the description of Suzanne.

"Hey, miss, are you by any chance, Suzanne Harper?"

She looked at him suspiciously. "Yeah," she said with obvious unease.

"Sorry darlin', I didn't mean to alarm you. I'm tryin' to find Amanda Anderson. There was a family emergency and her daddy needs to find her. I know that she was with y'all when you checked in at the Happy Song Hotel in Mersing. I was hopin' she was here with you."

"No. She didn't come," Suzanne said. "We thought she was coming, but she didn't show up for the boat. Listen, there was this guy who boarded the bus with us in Melaka. I think she's with him. We all met up at the Portside Café that night for dinner and a few beers. When the rest of us left, she stayed to watch *L.A. Law* on the TV with Joey. That was his name."

"Do you know where Joey was stayin'?"

"No. He just said he was trying a different place that he had heard about."

"Do you think he might have told Martin or Crystal?"

"Maybe. We were at the restaurant for more than two hours. Lots of side conversations."

Mason asked Suzanne if she knew where Martin and Crystal were staying, not letting on that he knew Martin had left. She told him they'd had a big fight. She moved in with a guy named Thomas over at the next set of bungalows. Martin left the island that day. Now he knew why Martin showed up at the hotel by himself. Suzanne said Crystal would be hard to miss. Big blonde hair on a petite body and a Southern accent so thick you could cut it with a knife.

"Way more than yours," Suzanne said with a smile.

Mason asked her if she they had taken any photos of the group. She said they had, but she didn't think Joey was in any of them.

"He offered to take the pictures but said he didn't like to be in them. Struck me as strange because Joey was, mmmm, how do I say this? Joey was a hunk. Those kind of people usually love being photographed."

Mason then asked her for a description of Joey.

"At first, he said he was an American," Suzanne said, "but Martin called him out, said he looked like he was Malaysian. Joey said something about being of Malaysian descent but that he was hundred percent American. He certainly talked and acted like he was American. But you know, I think I could see a little Malaysian in him once Martin mentioned it. Anyway, I'd bet that Amanda took off with Joey. She told me on the bus that she wanted to, mmm, date a local. He was probably close enough. I will say this" Suzanne added with a big grin, "Joey had immensely kissable lips."

Mason thanked her and continued down the beach to find Crystal. It was easy. He heard her first.

"I'm plumb tired of sittin' here in the sun, darlin'. I'm gonna meander back to the hut and have myself a cold drank. You comin'?"

Mason caught up with her at the tree line.

"Pardon me, Miss. Are you Crystal Erickson?"

She looked at him, smiled and said, "Well, yes I am. Who might you be, sugar?"

He told the story that there had been an emergency in Amanda's family and he was trying to find her. She hadn't seen her, she said, since the night at the restaurant before they left Mersing.

"I think she's with that Joey fellow. He's a hunk, you know. And part Malaysian."

Mason asked if she had any idea where they might have gone?

"Not a clue, darlin'. They sure as shit didn't come here."

He asked her to tell him about how they met Joey. She hadn't seen him before he got on the bus after them in Melaka. By the time they got to Mersing, though, they were all friends.

He asked her to describe him and got a repeat of what he had heard before. She did add one piece of new information. Joey had said he was from North Carolina.

Mason headed back toward the Merlin. He didn't know what time the flight to Mersing was and hoped he'd get there in time. On the walk there, he did a mental inventory of the case.

The suspect goes by the name Joey. Likely biracial; mix of Malaysian and Caucasian. He boarded a bus to Mersing in Melaka the day before Amanda's body was found, where he joined a group of backpackers who boarded ahead of him. He was a charming guy with "kissable lips." The women thought him to be very attractive. Five feet ten inches tall. About one hundred eighty pounds. Obvious muscles. Skin tone darker than Caucasian, but not likely mixed with African, probably Malaysian. Light brown wavy hair. Clean-shaven. Soft features. Scar on his left forearm. Left-handed.

When he arrived at the Merlin, he learned that the flight to Mersing was scheduled to take off in ninety minutes. That would get him into Mersing by 4 p.m. He'd grab snacks and water for the car and head to Melaka.

He called Boonsri from a radio phone at the Merlin. He asked that she make him a hotel reservation for the night in Melaka. She should tell the hotel that he would be arriving late. If he didn't call before she left the office, she should leave the hotel info with the answering service to pass along to him.

Boonsri told him that a long fax had come in from Fitz. Police reports and photos for the other murders. He asked that she fax them to him at the hotel he had stayed at in Mersing, but to do it a few minutes after 4 p.m. He would swing by to pick them up on his way out of town.

"One more thing," he told her. "Send a fax to Mr. Anderson's confidential fax number. Tell him that I will call him between ten and eleven his time tomorrow morning with an update." That would give him enough time to settle into his hotel tonight before making the call.

Mason landed back at the small airstrip outside Mersing right at 4 p.m. He took a taxi to the hotel, where he had left the rental car. He popped inside. The first page of the fax was printing as he watched. That was good. No one would be able to send a copy to the police chief. He wouldn't know about the other murders.

While the fax was printing, he used a hotel phone to call Boonsri again. She gave him the info on the hotel and confirmed that she had sent the fax to Mr. Anderson. When the fax was finished, he put it in a file folder and left, stopping before leaving town at a market. He bought three bottles of water, peanut butter, bread, fruit, a pack of gum and two Snickers' bars. They gave him a plastic spoon for the peanut butter.

Mason was on the road out of town by 5 p.m. He parked opposite the entrance of the Hotel Puri in Melaka at 9:30. He loved these old, heritage hotels. This one did not disappoint. It was elegant in an old-world kind of way. Yet, it was inexpensive by American standards. His room for the night was about twenty dollars US.

He checked in and they directed him a short distance down Heeren Street to the hotel's secluded parking lot. He parked the car then went to his room. He had some time to kill before the call to Bob Anderson.

He showered, then headed down to the restaurant only to discover it did not serve the burger he was craving nor the Jack Daniels that he wanted even more.

Fortunately, there was a pub just a block away that served both. He ordered an American-styled hamburger and his Jack. The burger was so-so but satisfied him. The Jack Daniels was Jack Daniels. He didn't touch the Coca Cola that came every time he ordered the whiskey in this country. Must be a Malaysian thing, he thought to himself.

Mason used the time to write out his key points to pass along to Bob and to think about what he wanted from the phone call. It was simple, he wanted Bob to know that he was making good progress, but that they had a lot of work left to do. He wanted Bob to hang up thinking he had made the right choice to hire him.

He then decided to take the can of Coke and return to his room. He settled in a chair at the ornate desk with inlaid stone in his room and called his client. Bob answered after the first ring. Mason was deferential to Bob's feelings. It had been just a week since the man had learned of his daughter's death. Within a couple minutes, though, he told Bob he had a lot to report.

"It's been a dang good week," Mason said. "Jump right in with questions anytime somethin' pops in your mind."

Bob said okay.

"First, Amanda was the sixth victim of a serial killer."

"Oh my God."

"And the fucker killed someone else a couple days later."

"How do you know all of this?"

Mason told him that the State Department had gone back through its files looking for similar deaths of young women over the past few years. They didn't limit it to Malaysia, but added in Thailand and Indonesia, as well. There had been two murders in Thailand and one in Indonesia during that time, but the only thing they had in common were that the victims were Americans.

Malaysia, though, Mason said, was different. Since early 1985, there has been a young American girl killed in her hotel room about every five or six months.

"State really dropped the goddamn ball," Mason said. "That shit just isn't supposed to happen. That many murders of similar victims should have yelled out to someone."

"Why didn't it?"

"Beats the hell out of me. But hold your horses, there's more. Each girl was between nineteen and twenty-three years old with blonde hair. Each died naked in her hotel room by havin' her throat slashed. You don't have to be Albert fuckin' Einstein to see that this is all the doin' of one sick-as-shit asshole."

"Wait, someone at the local police must have put this together and saw it was just like a case they'd had before."

"The guy never kilt in the same place twice. I'll give him this much: He has to be a pretty smart cookie."

"Jesus. I can't believe they didn't know this at State?"

"Fitz admits they should have caught it at State but didn't," Mason continued. "At this point, none of that shit matters. We're on to this guy and we'll find him."

Mason told Bob everything he had learned to date. Bob was impressed.

"I'm in Melaka now. Got here a short while ago," Mason said. "This Joey guy boarded a bus here with Amanda and the others. I'll start in the mornin' callin' on hotels and restaurants near the bus station. He had to stay somewhere and since he wasn't killin' in Melaka, he might have been less careful to cover his steps.

"The other thing I'm gonna do tomorrow," Mason said, "is get a roll of film developed that I got from one of the other girls. She doesn't think this Joey guy's on it, but I gave her a hundred dollars to let me take it to get it developed. If I think he's on it, I'll fly back to Tioman and have her ID him. If he's not on it, I'll just mail the photos to her home address."

Bob asked what was next.

"We have descriptions of him, but I'd really like to get a picture. That's probably a long shot. Hell, there's no probably about it. Don't get your hopes up. But it would be a huge if we can find one. Maybe we'll get lucky with the film from Suzanne.

"And I want to find out his name. I really don't think he's an American, as he claims. If he's not, the Joey moniker doesn't mean a lot. We do know that he has used it at least twice – Amanda and the Mary Higgins girl last week in George Town – so knowin' helps. I'd bet the fuckin' bank he has a Malaysian name. That's what I want."

"That sounds like a long shot, too."

"You think? It'll take more than a little luck. But that's what this kind of work is all about. Just sayin' that if I keep at it, I will find his name and him. It might be slower than molasses, but I'm good at this stuff, Bob. I'm like a hound dog on a scent. I don't stop."

"I believe you, Mason. I'm glad Fitz connected me to you. Call me in another week. Or sooner if you have a breakthrough."

"I will. Listen, I'm like one-hundred-and-four percent tired. I need to try to get some sleep."

"Good night, Mason."

Sleep had never been a problem for him. He'd close him eyes and after a few minutes would drift off and then awaken seven or eight hours later, well rested and ready to take on the day. He wasn't usually much of a dreamer, or at least he didn't often remember his dreams.

All that had changed in the past several days. He had had two dreams so powerfully disturbing that he awoke in near panic. As he prepared for bed, he wondered what kind of night it would be tonight. Would he wake rested in the morning or face a middle-of-the-night vivid image of an innocent person whose blood was on his hands?

It would, unfortunately, be the latter.

In the dream, the restaurant was bustling. He could see General Tho and his mistress at their special table, but across the room his mind focused on a different table. A family was sitting there. There were two older women and an older man. Mason knew they had to be

115

grandparents. Four children also sat at the table. They ranged in age from about six to a boy who appeared to be about sixteen. Then, of course, there was the children's mother and father. They looked proud and Mason could tell this lunch was for the oldest boy. They appeared to be a close family. Laughter and smiles surrounded them.

They died in an instant. It happened so quickly that they all wore smiles as they took their last breaths. Mason watched in horror, though, as those smiles were ripped from their faces. All of them. Even the six-year-old.

Mason was sobbing as he woke up. He couldn't stop. Those happy faces replaced in his mind's eye by ragged, bloody ones. He got up and washed his face, hoping the cold water would push him to a new place. He grabbed his bottle of Jack and took a healthy swig. It was nearly three hours before he was able to sleep again.

Day 11

Mason had second thoughts about his day when the alarm went off. But he had a job to do, so he cleaned himself up and went down for breakfast. The Hotel Puri put out a grand buffet for breakfast, both Malay and Western styled. He had a plate of fresh fruit, ordered a fluffy omelet from the egg station, then added two pieces of toast with butter and fresh jam. He had three cups of coffee with thick, sweet milk.

After breakfast, he drove to the old bus station on the outskirts of town. Suzanne had told him that they had all boarded at the same terminal in Batu Berendam. There wasn't a lot in Batu Berendam, which was a good thing for Mason.

It took him about half an hour to drive there. The first thing he did was cruise around the neighborhood near the old terminal. He wanted to get a feel for the place. It was, though, uninviting. Mostly industrial. A little dirty or at least unkempt. Why, he found himself wondering, would they have departed from here when there was a much nicer, newer terminal near the center of the city.

After parking the car, he was surprised to find a couple dozen western backpackers waiting for their buses in the station. He approached a small group of two guys and three girls who he heard speaking English.

"Pardon me," Mason said glancing around the group. "Can I ask you a question?" They nodded yes. "Why are you using this terminal? There's a better one in town."

"It's cheaper here," one of the fellows said. "The downtown buses are all fancy air-conditioned ones with TVs and all. This terminal is for the older buses. They're about half the price."

"Do folks like you stay near here then or did you come up from the city this mornin'?"

"We stayed near here last night," one of the girls said. "Rooms are cheaper here, too. If you are leaving Melaka anyway, why pay more for one more night in the city? You're just sleeping."

She gave him directions to the nearby hotel district.

Mason drove to where he saw the first hotel. He parked the car and headed out on foot. Same routine, hotel after hotel. He'd go in, ask for the manager, show the picture of Amanda and ask about Joey.

Nothing. Meanwhile, the wear and tear on his sleep-deprived body was taking a toll. The mid-day sun was making the walks from hotel to hotel miserable. By noon, the temperature already had reached ninety-four degrees. By one-thirty, he was exhausted, thirsty and hungry.

He wanted desperately to cool off. He passed a few cafes that had windows wide open and knew they'd offer little relief. When he finally saw a decent looking café with air conditioning, he walked right in. The Arzed Restaurant had about twelve tables. He took the one closest to the window air conditioner.

The first thing he noticed was that he was the only westerner in the place. That didn't bother him. When you have lived in Southeast Asia as long as Mason had, you get used to it.

A young man who Mason guessed to be in his early thirties came over to offer him a menu.

"Thanks. I would like something cold to drink."

"No alcohol. Just Coke, Fanta, water or juice," the young man said in reasonably good English.

"A Coke sounds great, and a bottle of cold water, too."

The man left and returned shortly with a can of Coke, a capped liter of water straight from the cooler and a glass. Mason had spread a few items from his file on his table. Included was the photo of Amanda.

"She's a pretty girl. She was here last week. Why do you have her picture?"

"This girl? Are you sure? Look closely."

"Yes. Yes. Same girl. She was going to catch bus. Very nice girl. Smile and talk. Very friendly. I remember her name. Ermanda."

"Yes. Amanda. Was she with anyone?"

"No. Alone."

"Did she talk with anyone else?"

"No. Just me. There was just one other person here that spoke English, but he not speak."

"The other person who spoke English. Man or woman?"

"Man."

"Do you know him?"

"Not so much. He comes in every few months. But my little sister knows him. He had been in before when she was here."

"How would your sister know him?"

"School. They both went to the mission school before it close."

"Could you tell me what this fellow looks like?"

"Like a Malaysian but not. It hard to say. My sister said his father was an English."

Mason's pulse quickened. So far, this sounded like Joey.

"How tall is he?"

"About like you. He muscle man," the waiter said, flexing his biceps. "You can tell."

"Do you know his name?"

"I not remember. My sister she know."

Mason couldn't believe his luck. Then again, Amanda and Joey – he was sure it had to be Joey – might have chosen this café for the same reason he did. The big air conditioner above the front window.

"Can I talk with your sister?"

"She work. Not be bothered."

"Could I maybe talk with her after her work?"

The waiter didn't respond for a bit, then said, "No. Not right."

Mason realized what the young man was thinking.

"Is she married with a family?" The waiter nodded yes. "How about

119

if she brings the family here for dinner this evening? I will pay for everything."

"I don't know. You a stranger."

"Listen, what's your name?"

"Haziq."

"Listen, Haziq. This is important. That nice girl is missing. She got on the bus with the fellow described. They went to Mersing. He was the last person seen with her. Her daddy is worried about her."

He took out a small roll of bills and pulled a hundred-dollar bill from the roll.

"Here, Haziq, this is for your helping me. I know it's a lot of money, but we have to find her. And if your sister and her family meet me, I'll give them one hundred US dollars, too."

At the sight of the first hundred-dollar bill, Haziq stood rigidly and his eyes widened. That was more money that he earned in a month. He could only imagine how his sister would react.

"Who are you?" he asked Mason.

"Mason Ray. I work for Amanda's daddy. She has a health problem and he's very worried about her. That's why he sent me."

Haziq gave it some thought.

"Okay. You come back at seven. My sister and her family will be here."

Mason finished his meal, took his bottle of water and left. He saw Haziq as he was walking out the door.

"Tonight at seven o'clock. See you then."

Haziq, still looking a little frightened, just nodded his head.

Mason returned to the hotel. Even though he had checked out that morning, he asked if he could stay another night. Of course he could, he was told at reception. He could even have the same room. He took the key and climbed one flight to his room.

He wanted to call someone, but it was two-thirty in the morning in Tampa and D.C. He tried to call Bo, but the detective was out of the office. He left a message for him to call back at the hotel.

He called room service. He asked if it would be possible to get an ice-cold beer. He was told they kept bottles of Tiger in the freezer. He said he'd like one sent to his room immediately. Two minutes later, a young man knocked on his door. He carried a silver tray with a single bottle of Tiger, sweating from being pulled from the freezer, and a chilled glass.

Mason took off his shoes and sat on the sofa in his room. He poured the Tiger and took a sip. It was exactly what he wanted. He took several bigger sips, then turned on the TV. He was in luck. Oprah was on. He fought the idea to take a nap, though he could certainly use one. He didn't want to risk another vision before meeting Haziq's family.

It was a little before seven when Mason arrived back at the Arzed Restaurant. Haziq met him at the door.

"Mr. Ray, please come in," the young man said while ushering him to a big table that he hadn't noticed when he was there at lunchtime. "Please to introduce you."

Mason smiled at everyone, trying to project that he was a friend. Everyone, though, looked like Haziq did earlier in the day. Frightened.

"This is our mother. You call her Mrs. Adelia. Her English okay but not good. I will help."

"Good evening, Mrs. Adelia, ma'am" Mason said to the short, stout woman with piercing eyes. "It is an honor to meet you."

Haziq translated and his mother offered a small smile but didn't speak.

"And this is my sister, Aishah. It is okay to call her Aishah. She speaks English as well as I speak it."

Aishah appeared to be in her mid-twenties. She was taller than her mother but seemed to inherit her inquiring eyes. Mason noticed that she was dressed in a more Western style that you normally see in Muslim women who are married. He wondered for a moment what that might mean.

"Thank you so much, Aishah," he said, "for meetin' me tonight. And please call me Mason. Whatever you can tell me I'm sure will be very helpful."

Aishah looked anxious and glanced back to Haziq.

"And this is her husband, Abdul."

Mason offered his hand to shake. Abdul took it in a simple shake, but never took his eyes off Mason. He was wearing some type of work uniform and Mason guessed that the man did some kind of physical labor. He was broad-shouldered and his upper arms revealed well-toned muscles.

"This is most unusual," Abdul said.

"I know," Mason answered. "But it is important."

"Is the boy in trouble?"

"Honestly?" Mason said. "I don't know. We're just tryin' to find a young woman who was last seen with him. I suspect they went off somewhere together. I mean him no ill. Her daddy is just worried about her because she is not well and she didn't call him for her usual weekly call."

Mason turned to Haziq.

"Haziq. I promised dinner. Perhaps we could begin?"

"Yes. Yes. Of course."

Haziq returned to the kitchen and soon two waiters emerged carrying trays of food, teapots with brewing tea and cans of Coke.

Everyone was seated. Haziq placed his mother at the head of the table, with Mason to her right. Aishah and Abdul sat to her mother's left. Haziq took the seat next to Mason. The children, there were four, filled the other seats.

Aishah asked Mason where he was from. He told them that he grew up in Georgia, a state in the American south, but that he moved to Bangkok many years ago for work. His work, he said, takes him all over Southeast Asia.

"Do you have a Thai wife?" Abdul asked.

"No sir. I'm not married. I almost married an American girl shortly after I moved to Asia, but she died. I never really got over her."

"Have you ever been to Bangkok?" Mason asked Abdul.

"No, but Haziq has."

"Is that so, Haziq. When were you there?"

"Three years ago. I was working for a big company then and I had to go for a meeting."

"What did you think?"

"Too big. Too noisy. Too dirty."

"You got that right. That's Bangkok. Big, dirty and loud!"

They continued to make small talk until dinner was over. Mason then turned to Aishah.

"So, Aishah, Haziq says you went to school with the man I know as Joey."

"Yes. Joey. Pastor Johnny give him that name. Real name is Yusof. Pastor Johnny said Yusof was Malaysian for Joseph and in America kids named Joseph are called Joey."

"That's right. Do you know Yusof's full name?"

Mrs. Adelia spoke up. "His father British sailor. Not know family name."

"That's right," Aishah said. "He was an English. Do you understand how Malaysians are named?" Mason used his hand to wiggle back and forth to indicate that he knew a little.

"We have a first name and then our last name is our father's name," she said. "So, my husband is Abdul bin Masonyan. That means Abdul son of Masonyan. Now we just say Abdul Masonyan.

"All Yusof's mother knew about his father," Aishah continued, "was that he said to call him Reggie. Isn't that right mother?" Mrs. Adelia nodded yes. "She couldn't name him Yusof Reggie, though. Reggie is not a Muslim name. So, she gave him her name. Very unusual. He became Yusof Zaina."

"Yes. Yes. That's right," Mrs. Adelia said.

Mason asked if Yusof's mother was still around. Mrs. Adelia said she died when he was a young boy. She was hit by a car. Not too long after that, he was taken in by Pastor Johnny and his wife, Mrs. Helen. The pastor and his wife ran a mission school, but that it had closed about

123

ten years ago.

"Mrs. Helen got sick and returned to America," Aishah said. "Pastor Johnny left about a month later. Yusof had lived with them like a son. But they left him here."

"Lord have mercy, that must have been hard on him," Mason said.

Aishah said that Yusof had lived at the mission by himself for a bit, but then had to leave when the rent wasn't paid. He became a petty thief.

"No one blamed him," she said. "He had to. He not steal from anyone here. He went into the city for that."

"Do you have a picture of Yusof?"

"No," Aishah said.

"Yes, picture," Mrs. Adelia added quickly. She said something to Haziq and as she was saying it Aishah started shaking her head yes. Mason looked to Haziq.

"My mother said that a year before the school closed, Pastor Johnny had a school photo taken," Haziq said. "Everybody in the class was in the picture. She's sure that Yusof is in it."

"Can I see it?"

The family spoke in Malaysian again and Abdul got up to leave.

"It's at their house," Haziq said. "Abdul will go get it. Mother told him where it is."

They chatted while waiting for Abdul to get back with the photo. Mason learned that Haziq was the manager of the restaurant and that the owner had promised to sell it to him if he could come up with the money. Mason asked how much he needed. Haziq said ten-thousand ringgits, or about four thousand US dollars.

"My family is trying to save the money, but it is not easy. Ten-thousand ringgits is a lot of money for simple working people."

"If this thing I'm helpin' Amanda's daddy on works out, he might be able to help you," Mason said. "He's a rich man."

Haziq looked at his sister and mother. "That would be . . ." He paused to try to find the right word, then settled on "helpful."

Mason then asked if they knew Pastor Johnny's last name or where he was from. No one knew.

"Everyone just called them Pastor Johnny and Mrs. Helen," Aishah said. She turned to her mother and said something. Her mother shook her head no.

"Mother doesn't know."

"How about where they were from?"

"America."

"Yes, but where in America?"

Again, no one knew.

"You said it was a mission school. Do you know what faith?"

"Christian," Aishah said.

"Yes, I figured that. But what type of Christian? Like Baptist, or Methodist."

"Christian," Aishah said again. "Jesus church."

This wasn't going anywhere, so he dropped it.

"Did your mother save any documents from the school?" Aishah asked her mother.

"Photo," Mrs. Adelia replied.

"But anything else? Did you get a report card or a certificate?" Aishah shook her head no. Again, she looked to her mother at the head of the table. The older woman also shook her head that they had nothing else.

Then Abdul returned with the class photo. He set it on the table in front of Mason. Aishah pointed to a boy clearly visible standing next to Pastor Johnny in the second row. "That's Yusof," she said.

Mason couldn't believe it. He stared down at a boy of about 16, but with the unmistaken features that had been described to him.

"I have a big favor to ask," Mason said. "Can I borrow this here photo long enough to have a copy made. One or two days."

They all looked to Mrs. Adelia. Haziq translated to her just in case she didn't understand what Mason had asked. She frowned and gave a small shake of her head side to side. She said something to Haziq.

"My mother said this photo is very important to our family," Haziq said for her. "She doesn't want to lose it."

"She won't lose it. Tell her that you or Abdul or Aishah can go with me tomorrow to get it reproduced, if you wish. It won't take long. I'm so sure that I'll get it back to her that I will give her five-hundred US dollars to hold until I bring it back. That's a lot of money, but proof that I will bring it back."

Haziq spoke to his mother again. When he said the amount in ringgits, she flinched, and studied Mason more intently. She then responded to Haziq in Bahasa Malay, then looked at Mason.

"My mother says she would not feel good with that much of someone else's money," Haziq said. "She has decided that I should go with you in the morning to get the photo reproduced. She doesn't want you to give her five hundred US dollars."

Mrs. Adelia smiled. Mason smiled. "Tell her I said I am honored by her trust." He looked to Mrs. Adelia. "Thank you, ma'am, very much."

"You're be welcome," Mrs. Adelia said in broken English.

Mason returned to the hotel. He was excited about what happened. Not only did he learn Joey's real name, but he also would have an old photo of him. Even though it was late, he called Bo but was unable to reach him. He left a message with the police operator to tell Detective Jun that he should expect a photo the next day of a person of interest in a case he was working on.

It was morning in D.C., so Mason figured Fitz would be at his desk. Mason called to bring Fitz up to date.

"Dumb fucking luck, my friend," Fitz said.

"Like my mama liked to say, don't look no gift horse in the mouth," Mason answered.

"But I've always believed that luck is only part serendipity," Fitz said. "The rest is doing what is needed to be in the right place at the right time. You deserved this good fortune, Mason. Have you told Anderson yet?"

"Next call."

Mason said he'd fax the photo the next day. They said their goodbyes and hung up.

Bob answered on the second ring.

"This isn't our check-in day," Bob said, "so I'm guessing you either have something great or awful to tell me."

"Great actually," Mason said. "I know his real name and I'm gettin' a ten-year-old photo of him in the mornin'."

"Holy fuck, man!" Bob exclaimed. "How did you do that?"

Mason told him the story. When he hung up, he was feeling pumped but his sleep issues were catching up with him. God, he said to himself, I just hope I can get a good night's sleep tonight.

God apparently was listening – a little. Mason fell asleep at about 11 p.m. and the nightmare didn't jolt him awake until almost six the following morning. Seven wonderful hours of sleep, even if it did end abruptly. This time he saw a young woman arrive for lunch with a young man who was already at the café. He was clearly her boyfriend. In his dream, the blast ripped their limbs from their bodies. It was a bloody, awful mess.

––––––––

"You're soaked," Jessica said as Joey dashed into the lobby of the Holiday Inn. A torrential rainstorm had moved ashore in Batu Ferringhi as Joey was making his way to the hotel.

Rainstorms in this part of Malaysia could blow through in less than an hour, or they could linger.

"It's hard to tell how long this will last," he told her. "Could be over in a few minutes or could stick around for most of the day."

Jessica said she was fine hanging out at the hotel for a bit. They could grab lunch and wait it out.

"I'm a girl who likes to chill," she said. "And there's something about a good tropical rainstorm that gets my blood pumping. The smell. The sudden bolt of lightning. The thunder claps. We never get this in Seattle."

They walked to a table at the edge of the café. A sudden gust might actually get them wet, or in Joey's case, wetter, but it put Jessica on the edge of the torrent. It was more exciting. A waiter approached.

"Do you think you could find a towel for my friend?" Jessica asked the man, pointing to Joey. The waiter took one look at Joey, shook his head yes and darted off.

They glanced at the menu and decided on what to order.

"I told you my story yesterday," Joey said. "Why don't you tell me a little more about you?"

She gave him the Cliff Notes version with few details. She grew up in Edmonds, a small town just north of Seattle. She went to Western Washington University in Bellingham. She could tell it didn't register.

"A little more than an hour's drive up I-5 from home," she said. "Close enough to visit the folks anytime I wanted, but far enough to not be expected to."

He nodded.

"What was your major?"

"Human biology. I had figured out that I wanted to be a nurse."

"Oh," Joey said. He realized that perhaps the disappointment was obvious in his voice. Nurses didn't make that much. At least, he didn't think they did. She didn't appear to pick up on it. "Did you become one?"

"Eventually. After grad school at the University of Washington."

Jessica was moving on with her story.

"I was working at a hospital in north Seattle before I left on my trip."

Joey thought about that. Hospital nurses probably make more than other nurses. Maybe. He wasn't sure, but he wasn't ready to rule her out.

The waiter returned with a warm towel. Joey used it to dry himself while they gave the waiter their order. Dryer, Joey handed the towel back to the man and offered his thanks.

Jessica resumed her story but was done talking about nursing. She told him that she had played soccer and basketball growing up. She was a walk-on for the soccer team at Western but found it too demanding.

"It was hard to do it and keep up my grades," she said. "I've always been a bookworm. I wasn't in college to play sports. You know what I mean?"

Joey nodded yes.

"I played pick-up games, though. Lots of three-on-three basketball. I was decent. Great jump shot." She pantomimed shooting a ball with her hands.

They chatted some more about a variety of topics and spent a good ten minutes talking about *The Princess Bride*, a movie both had recently seen and both professed to have loved. They'd both also had seen the latest Bond film, *The Living Daylights*.

"I don't know," Jessica said. "I just never bought into Timothy Dalton as Bond. I can't imagine anyone measuring up to Sean Connery."

"I didn't like Dalton either," Joey said. "But I kind of like Roger Moore as Bond. Did you see *The Spy Who Loved Me*? He was great in that. I thought it really set him up as the new Bond."

"Ehh. Doesn't hold a candle to Sean Connery. That man exudes Bond."

They had killed nearly two hours and it was still raining.

"Listen," Joey said. "Why don't we turn tomorrow into today? The rain will be gone by then, I promise. I'll swing by and we'll do the sightseeing we were going to do today."

Jessica said that would be great, but he could tell she was a little disappointed that he was ending their day. If he had to admit it, he was a little disappointed, too. But he was feeling more like Jessica might be the one. Maybe hospital nurses made enough. He found himself hoping that would be the case. If so, he knew the importance of taking things slow and easy.

129

Day 12

Mason drove his Toyota rental car to the restaurant to pick up Haziq and the photo at 8 a.m. He had asked at the hotel about a place in town to get a photo reproduced quickly. The manager gave him instructions to Melaka Photo and Supply in the old part of the city.

Mason and Haziq made small talk as he drove them back into town. Mason learned that Haziq had worked for KFC in Malaysia. He had started working the front counter, then became an assistant manager and then the manager. A couple years later, KFC promoted him to the regional office. It was KFC that sent him to Bangkok for the meeting, which was training on how to use a personal computer to track and predict inventory needs.

He told Mason that KFC wanted to move him to Kuala Lumpur, but he didn't want to leave his family, so he turned them down. Shortly after that, the owner of the Arzed Restaurant got ill. An old family friend, he asked Haziq to take over while he got better. Haziq turned out to be a natural at running the restaurant. The man decided to let Haziq stay in charge and simply pay him a weekly salary.

"The arrangement was working," Haziq said, "but now he wants me to buy him out. The bank says I have to put up more money than I have. I don't know if I'll be able to. Our family is not rich."

"How much time you got?"

"I have some time. A few months?" Haziq answered as if a question. "I'm sure something will work out. If not, it is Allah's will."

Melaka Photo and Supply was just off a main street in the heart of the old city. Mason showed the gentleman at the counter the photo and that he was most interested in an image of the boy with biracial features, pointing toward Joey. Mason said he could also do a separate photo of the American couple standing next to the boy, as well as one of the entire class.

"When can I get the copies?" Mason asked.

"Tomorrow," the clerk responded.

"I need 'em today, as soon as possible. I can pay a rush charge."

The clerk looked around, then whispered to Mason, "How much rush charge?"

"You tell me," Mason answered.

"You American?"

"As American as apple pie."

The clerk looked confused.

"Yes sir. I'm an American."

"I can do for you for twenty American dollars. Two hours."

"Thank you kindly, sir."

Mason gave the man twenty dollars, then added, "If the copies are available at 11 a.m., I'll give you another twenty dollars. If they take longer, then I won't."

"I need one other thing," Mason said. He handed the man the roll of film Suzanne gave him the day before on Tioman. "I need you to develop and print this roll of film. Same deal. Get it done by eleven and I'll give you another twenty US dollars."

"Yes. Yes. Everything will be ready, my friend. Just from me. No one else. Okay?"

"Yep. Just you." He looked at the nametag, "Raahim. I'll see you at eleven."

Mason and Haziq left the store. Mason asked Haziq if he had time to wait or did he need to go back to the restaurant.

"I must go back," Haziq said. "You will bring me the original photo today?"

"Yes sir," Mason said.

Mason was back at Melaka Photo and Supply at eleven. The clerk welcomed him with a big smile, then quickly glanced around to make sure they were alone. They were. He handed Mason two envelopes. The bigger one contained the original school photo and the three copies. The developed film and three by five prints of all the shots were in the other envelope.

Mason opened the bigger envelope first and examined the copies. Excellent. He then opened the other package and looked through the prints.

As he thumbed through them, it appeared that Suzanne was right. Joey had managed to avoid all the photos. Then he got to the very last one in the stack. It was the first shot on the roll. It was taken on the bus of Amanda standing in the aisle. Behind her was an out-of-focus three-quarter profile of someone who had to be Joey. Sadly, though, it was just too blurry to use.

"These are sweet as my mama's pecan pie," Mason said, then gave the clerk the promised two twenty-dollar bills. The clerk beamed, looked around and quickly stuck the bills into his pocket.

Mason couldn't believe his luck.

Mason returned to his hotel and told the manager that he needed to send four faxes. Two to the US, one to Bangkok and one to Penang. The manager told him the charge. Mason then sat and wrote cover notes to Fitz, Bob, Bo and Boonsri.

He told the manager he wanted to personally send the faxes. The manager, though, said hotel policy forbid it. But another twenty dollars saw Mason was standing at the fax machine. He started with Bo.

"Bo, this is a photo of our guy. At least, I'm pretty sure it is. Joey, a.k.a. Yusof Zaina. It was taken ten years ago. I singled him out from a group shot of a mission school he was attending here in Melaka. I'm flying to Tioman later today to show it to the two women who saw him the night Amanda Anderson was murdered to make absolutely sure it's him. Later. . ."

He signed it Mason and sent the cover sheet and photo to Bo.

He then sent a copy of the Joey photo, the one of Pastor Johnny and

Mrs. Helen to Boonsri, as well as the class photo. She'd know to add them to the case file.

Next up were Fitz and Bob. It was about midnight in the US eastern time zone. They wouldn't see the photos till the morning. He faxed the photo of Joey, as well as the one of Pastor Johnny and his wife to Fitz. He sent Bob simply the picture of Joey, with this note:

"Bob, I knew you'd want to see this as soon as possible. This is the ass-wipe who murdered your girl. His real name is Yusof Zaina. It was taken from a group photo shot about ten years ago when he was a student at a mission school in Melaka. I'm flying back to Tioman later today to show it to the girls who were traveling with Amanda for a positive ID. But I'm all but certain it's him. Bob, it's not going to be easy, but we are going to find this asshole. I promise you. – Mason"

When the last fax was sent, Mason packed up, checked out of the hotel, then drove to the restaurant to give the photo back to Haziq. He had a quick lunch then drove to the airport. He needed to find someone with a small plane to fly him to Tioman. It didn't take long before he was airborne.

———————

Joey walked into Big Willie's shop at 9 a.m.

"Joey!" the Thai said. "I have lots for you today. First, let's put you in a fine suit."

Joey had never worn a business suit in his life. He didn't quite know what to make of the man he saw looking back at him as he stood on the little raised platform in front of the three angled mirrors. He looked, well, dignified. He tried on the other pieces of clothing that Big Willie had made with the same result. Everything fit him perfectly and he looked great.

"Here are your new papers," Big Willie said, handing him an envelope that Joey emptied onto the counter.

The first thing he saw was what appeared to be a US passport with entry and exit stamps from Thailand, Malaysia and Singapore. It showed Joey arriving in Bangkok from the US about six months ago.

He had left Thailand shortly thereafter and entered Malaysia. He also had a three-day visit to Singapore and another three-week sojourn back to Thailand. The passport looked so real.

He set the passport down and picked up a colorful small card that Big Willie said was meant to be a North Carolina driver's license.

"This license is better than your last one," Big Willie said. "It will look real to anyone not from North Carolina, but I wouldn't show it to someone from there. We couldn't find an actual North Carolina license to copy, so we had to get creative."

The final item in the envelope was a bogus Mastercard.

"This is for show," Big Willie said. "Don't use it. Just say you're at your limit. Anybody with a credit card knows what that means." He saw that Joey didn't know. "Each credit card has a total amount that you're allowed to charge. Once you hit that total, you can't use it again until you pay off some of the card."

Big Willie wasn't done.

"My family in Singapore can get your business going without you having to go down. They faxed up some pages for your signature. He handed them to him. "Remember to sign as Joseph T. Jackson. Here. Here. And here." He said handing Joey a pen and pointing to lines on the document.

"I need to practice first," Joey said. Big Willie handed him a piece of paper and Joey made several attempts to sign his name. "This isn't easy."

"You're trying too hard. Don't try to make it so neat. Most signatures aren't readable. You just have to do it the same way each time." The Thai took the pen and showed him what he meant. He wrote Joseph by making a J then a squiggled line to what might have been a h at the end. "You can skip the T, then do something similar for the Jackson."

Joey tried a few more times and started to get the hang of it. Big Willie told him that his last few efforts were good and to just use them whenever he needed to sign something. Joey pulled the documents back to in front of him and added his new signatures. With those signatures,

Joey created a Singapore company called Bungalow Paradise Holdings.

"My cousin said that we should wire him five hundred dollars for creating the company and another thousand dollars to open the bank account. They can do that for you, too. Here's the form from the bank. My cousin filled in the company name and a post office address. Just sign here," he said and pointed to another line. "Can you bring me the money later today?"

"No. I have a date," Joey said with a big grin. "I'll bring it in the morning."

"I'll fax these things back and tell my cousin that we'll wire the money in the morning."

Joey rushed back to his apartment, put things away, then walked to the Holiday Inn. He was waiting in the lobby when Jessica got off the elevator. She saw him and smiled.

"Hey, you," she said, as she walked over to give him a gentle hug.

"Ready to see some sights?" Joey asked her.

"I figure you're better at choosing than me, so lead on."

They got into a taxi in front of the hotel and Joey told the driver to head to the Chew Jetty. On the way, he gave Jessica a little history lesson.

"There are more Chinese in Penang than anywhere else in Malaysia," he said. "It's because the British turned this into a free port. When that happened, lots of seafaring Chinese immigrated here. That started in the early eighteen-hundreds. To be close to the water, they built what amounted to villages on stilts over the mudflats."

He explained that there were eight jetties built by the Chinese, each representing one family clan. The Chew Jetty remains the biggest.

"All the people living there today and all those running the businesses there are descendants of the original Chew clan. Pretty impressive when you stop to think about how long it's been and it's still all in the family."

"So, there have been generations of Chews living in the same houses?"

"You'll see they're not exactly houses like you and I think of houses.

135

But yes, some of these homes date back in the first half of the 1800s."

Jessica watched the city pass by as they made the drive to Chew Jetty. As they rode on, Joey explained that the Chinese came to Malaysia in two waves. The first wave started in the fifteenth century, but the big wave began in the early nineteenth century when the English colonized Malaysia.

"Like I said, when the British turned Penang into a free port, merchant Chinese came by the thousands," Joey told her. "And they continued to come for a hundred years."

"I like the history lesson, but I'm getting hungry," she said eventually. "Do you have a place in mind?"

"The best food in Penang is not in the restaurants, but from food stalls. So, we'll follow our noses!"

The aromas filled the air the moment they got out of the taxi. Following their noses would prove difficult. Joey took her hand and said for her to follow him. He knew just the place.

They walked a couple hundred feet along the wooden sidewalk over the water to a small stall with three little round tables on the side.

"Is there anything you won't eat?" Joey asked her.

"Of course," Jessica answered, "but this looks pretty safe. I think."

"Great! Mind if I order for both of us?"

"Go for it," Jessica said.

Joey ordered char kway teow for two and two Tiger beers. They found seats at one of the small tables. Soon, a young man brought them their beers and the same fellow delivered their food a couple minutes later.

"So, Joey, what am I getting into?" Jessica asked. "Any weird stuff in this dish?"

"You're going to love it. Char kway teow is like a national dish. The name literally means flat fried rice noodles, but there is a lot more to it than that. It's been a staple here in Penang since, well, since the Chinese first arrived."

Joey explained that char kway teow has a full, rich flavor that comes from the combination of ingredients and the skill of the person wielding the wok. This one, he said, will have prawns, cockles…"

"Wait," she interrupted. "Cockles? What are cockles?"

"Clams," Joey said. He went on to say that the dish also includes bean sprouts, eggs, onions, sausage, chilis, fish cakes and two types of soy sauce.

"The key to a great char kway teow is the skill of the cook. A good cook gives the dish what the locals call 'wok hei.' Everything is fried at a high temperature in pork lard and the soy sauces in such a way that the food gets a smoky sweetness. You're in for a treat! Every place tends to make it a little differently, but it's almost always yummy."

Jessica fiddled with her chopsticks and ladled some into her mouth. She smiled and then her eyes watered from the chilis. The smile returned.

"You get to pick out all the food from now on," she said. "How did I spend thirty-three years of life without ever eating this? What's it called again?"

"Char kway teow."

After lunch, they continued to explore the jetty. It's a special experience to walk over wooden planks, but it also took some getting used to. Some of the planks were weathered and creaking from decades of use.

"Did you grow up in Seattle?" Joey asked as they meandered along the wooden sidewalk.

"Yep. We lived in a town just north of the city called Edmonds. My dad just retired after thirty years working for Boeing. He was an engineer."

"How about your mom?"

"Teacher. High school English. She's still at it. I think she'll probably retire in the next year or two. She and dad want to travel and I think he's going stir-crazy at home. I have an older brother, Peter. He lives in L.A. Has a wife and two little ones."

"So, you're a nurse?"

"Guilty."

"Was becoming a nurse a lot of work? Is it like getting a college degree?"

She looked at him a little surprised. Jessica had told him she had graduated from Western and then got a masters from UW. But a lot of people have no idea what it takes to become a nurse. She cut him a break and gave him a short lesson.

"There are a lot of levels of nursing," she told him. "You can become what's called a licensed practical nurse by going to a junior college for a couple years. Most hospital nurses are registered nurses," she said, emphasizing the registered part. "You don't have to have a bachelor's degree in nursing, but most do, at least in Seattle. I'm what's called a certified registered nurse anesthetist. I have a shitload of education. It's a master's degree and then some."

"Wow. I had no idea."

"Yeah."

"So, are you like a surgical nurse?"

"Yes. It's a little more complicated than that, but yeah. That's me."

Joey absorbed that for a while. He was impressed. He also realized that she probably had a bank account with more than enough in it to meet his needs.

"You just quit? Walked away? That kind of job must pay a lot."

"It pays great. But I needed a break."

Jessica looked away, then murmured, "Let's talk about something else."

Joey let it drop. There was more to her story. It might not affect him at all. She'd probably tell him at some point anyway.

Before them facing toward the Strait was the Chew ancestral temple, a relatively small space ablaze in red and gold with ornate carvings. Small altars with incense burners provided a sweet scent to visitors. Plaques honored the clan's ancestors.

"The ancestral temple can be a fairly low-key place like this one. It serves mostly as a house of remembrance," Joey said. "Or it can be a lot more than that. We're only a few minutes' walk from the biggest and most famous clan temple in Malaysia. It's worth the walk. The place is incredible. Want to see it?"

She looked at him with a smirk. "How could I not after that build up?"

They took the easy walk to Khoo Kongsi. It was as Joey said it would be. Ornate. Colorful. Teeming. And where the Chew Shrine was quiet and contemplative, Khoo Kongsi was bustling with activity. And tourists.

"This is different than the Chew Ancestral Temple," Joey said. He explained that kongsi is a term to describe an organization. This one was established to make life better for the Khoo clan. The building houses the temple, but the organization provides for schooling, social customs, celebrations and anything else that the leaders feel is important. "The Khoo Kongsi is the biggest and most influential in all of Penang."

After touring the temple and the grounds, Jessica said she was hot and ready for a break.

"I've been on this trip for two months and I'm still not used to the heat," she said. "We don't get this in Seattle. Ever. Here it's an everyday thing."

Joey said most people try to get out of the mid-day sun, if they can, then said, with a tad of excitement, "Hey, I know just the thing." He walked her to a nearby cendol stand.

Joey flashed two fingers to the man working the stand with an assistant. The helper added shaved ice to two deep bowls, then the two of them together started adding toppings. It got doused with coconut milk and gula melaka, a palm sugar syrup, sweet fermented kidney beans and green jelly noodles. It's the noodles that give the treat its signature look. Mixed into the concoction were chunks of glutinous rice and then the whole thing was topped with chopped nuts.

"Oh sweet Jesus," Jessica said as she slurped her first spoonful. She quickly went back for a second spoonful. "This must be at least a thousand calories."

"Don't think about the calories. You're on vacation!" Joey said.

After they finished the desserts, Jessica said she was ready to head back to the hotel. They flagged a taxi.

"Do you think you might want to go to dinner this evening?" Joey asked her on the ride to the Holiday Inn.

"I'd love to, Joey, but if we're going to hang out, I need to pay my way," she said. "I can afford it and I'd feel better if we were splitting costs fifty-fifty."

"That's thoughtful of you, Jessica," he responded. "But it's not necessary."

"Yes, it is."

He looked at her. She smiled and then he did, too.

"Okay. Fifty-fifty."

She really could afford it and it struck her as the right thing to do. Besides, Jessica just knew that she had more money than he'd probably see in a lifetime. She wasn't about to take advantage of him. Well, not financially, at least.

He left her at the hotel and they agreed he'd come back at five o'clock. He said they should take the funicular to the top of Penang Hill to watch the sunset and the lights come on across George Town. After that, he said, they could go to dinner. As he headed back to his apartment, he felt that he'd found the right woman for his plan. He wasn't sure how much she made in her job, but it was clearly a lot. And she had made a point of telling him that she could afford to pay her own way.

That evening they took a taxi to the base of the railway up the hill. She said they should take turns paying for the taxis and it was her turn. They each bought tickets for the funicular and ascended to the top of the hill.

The view from the top, she admitted, was spectacular. To the west, the sun was sinking behind the last hill separating them from the sea. To the east, George Town was coming alive with lights. White lights, red lights, blue lights, yellow lights. Lights that blinked and moved and others that didn't. It all happened in an eerie quiet that was completely devoid of the ever-present sounds of the city below.

Jessica leaned into Joey. "Thank you for bringing me here," she said as she looked out at the city and a much more sedate Butterworth across the Strait.

They dined that night at a regular sit-down restaurant. The food was good and the surroundings mellow. As they stepped outside, she hooked her arm into his as they walked down the street.

"How old are you, Joey?" she asked him.

"Old enough," he said.

"Seriously," she said, "how old are you?"

He looked into her eyes. "A part of me wants to lie, but I won't. I'm twenty-six. You?"

"Thirty-three."

"Close enough," he said.

"Close enough," she repeated. A younger man, she thought. When was the last time that happened. Had it ever happened. She thought about it. No, it hadn't. Have fun and go for it, she told herself.

He knew that he needed to keep things moving forward, but not too fast. The goal was not to get her into bed quickly, but to nurture trust. Back at the Holiday Inn, he gave her a hug and a gentle kiss on the cheek.

"Same time tomorrow?" she asked.

He smiled. "I'm looking forward to it."

———————

The Cessna carrying Mason back to Tioman landed a little after four o'clock. Mason gave the pilot money to have a nice dinner at the Merlin. He thought it would take him a couple hours, but if it took longer Mason would pay for a room for the night.

He set off for Suzanne's bungalow, about a thirty-minute walk up the beach. She saw him approaching, stood and called him over. He waived back and approached.

"Hey honey, can we go someplace a little more private," he asked her.

She eyed him with a smirk.

"You dog, you," she said.

"No. Forgive me. It's not that," he said. "You're a little too young for me. It's somethin' else and we need some privacy."

She immediately looked more serious. "Sure," she said. "Let's go to my hut."

A few moments later they were sitting in her hut. "So, what brought you back and why all the secrecy?"

First, he gave her the developed film she had given him. He decided not to mail it to her home, but to simply give it to her here. He told her that there was one image of Joey, but that that he was in the background and it was too blurry.

"I have another picture that I think is of him taken ten years ago. I wanna show it to you and you tell me if it is him."

He removed the image that had been pulled from the school photo and showed it to her.

"That's him," she said instantly.

"You're sure?"

"One hundred percent. That's Joey. Where was that taken?"

"At a church school in Melaka."

"He would have been living in North Carolina then. Are you sure?"

"Listen, Suzanne," Mason said, looking for a moment out at the sea before looking back to her. "I didn't tell you the truth when I was here a couple days ago. It's not good."

"Oh no," she said. "Something happened to Amanda, didn't it?"

Mason looked at her with a resigned expression.

"She didn't meet you at the boat that mornin' because," he paused briefly to take a breath, "well, because she was dead."

"Oh God," Suzanne whimpered, as tears welled in her eyes. "God. Did Joey kill her?"

"It looks that way. They found her in her room that afternoon. She died of a knife wound."

Suzanne grabbed a shirt laying nearby and used it to wipe the tears trickling down her face.

"There's more," he said.

"What? How could there be more. Amanda's dead. That asshole killed her. I can't believe it. He seemed so nice."

"By more, I mean Amanda wasn't his first victim. Over the past two and a half years, it looks like Joey has kilt a half dozen young American women travelin' alone. Kilt 'em all in their rooms the same way."

"Wha...what?"

"He's a thief. He targets girls travelin' alone. He charms 'em and gets 'em back to their rooms. They have sex. Everythin' is fine at that point. Then he kills 'em with a knife across their throats. He might be charmin' but he's a heartless motherfucker. He watches 'em die. Then he takes everythin' they have of value. Cash. Credit cards. Traveler's checks. Passport. Anything he thinks he can pawn. He takes it all. He kills these girls for a couple thousand bucks."

"Oh my God." She shuddered with the sudden realization that she had been hanging out with a serial killer. And then another thought struck her and she went rigid.

"My God. It could have been me," she said barely above a whisper.

"Not likely," Mason said. "All his victims have been blondes."

They talked some more. This was a lot for her to process. She told him that she had been thinking about when she might wrap up her trip and go home. She hadn't thought it would be now, but maybe it was time. She didn't know.

"I only knew her for a day," she said. "I probably shouldn't be taking this so hard."

"Cut yourself some slack, Suzanne. With these kinds of things, a day, a month. It doesn't matter. The pain and the shock are the same."

Mason told her that, if she wanted, she could fly back to Melaka with him. From there, it would be easy to head on to either Singapore or KL to fly back to the States. She stared away at the crowd starting to gather in the restaurant area for dinner. After a bit, she took a noticeable breath and said she wasn't ready to decide on what to do. She had lots of new friends here, she told him. For the next several days, at least, she needed friends. That made her think of Crystal in the huts next door.

"I have to go tell Crystal," she said, looking at Mason. "Thank you for finding me and offering to help. I'm going to find Crystal. Goodbye, Mason."

They stood and hugged. No more words were said. Mason walked back to the Merlin, glad that she took the job of telling Crystal. He found the pilot in the dining room finishing off a big piece of chocolate cake.

"I'm ready to fly back," Mason said. "Can we leave?"

"I don't think so, Mr. Mason. Melaka airport closes at nine. Not enough time. We leave early tomorrow. Yes?"

"I'll get us rooms."

In his room at the Merlin, Mason called Fitz. The State Department lifer had arrived early to his office.

"You get them pictures I sent you?"

"Yes. I wasn't sure if there were something you wanted me to do with them, though."

"No sir. At least not yet. I just wanted you to have 'em. I'm hopin' you can track down Pastor Johnny and his wife, Helen. She might have passed. I don't know if the picture will help, but you might be able to match it to a passport photo on file."

"Last name?"

"Not a clue. Here's what I know. The wife got sick. She left Melaka and returned to the States in November 1978. The prognosis must've been bad. Pastor Johnny packed up quickly, closed the church school, then left about a month later."

Fitz asked if Mason knew what state they were from. Mason said no, but if Joey learned English from them that he'd bet on the Midwest somewhere. "He apparently has no accent. My guess is that the pastor and his wife didn't either. Says Midwest to me."

Fitz told Mason that he'd assign a couple assistants to start going through passport control records for November and December 1978.

"That's a lot of records," Fitz said. "It's going to take a while. They started converting those records to computer files a couple years ago, but I'm sure that 1978 will still be paper."

Fitz said it would help if they could focus on one coast. Would they arrive in L.A. or San Francisco, or would it more likely be New York?

"I don't think we can rule either coast out. If they're from one side of the country, they'd fly through an Asian gateway city which would bring them into a California airport. If, on the other hand, if they're from east of the Mississippi, they'd probably come through some place in Europe, like London. That would likely take them into New York."

Mason asked if there was any more info on the victims' stolen passports and credit cards. Fitz said they'd only just started gathering those records, but that it looked like the credit cards were being consistently used in Penang. The passports were a different story. Most appeared to be first used in Bangkok. Fitz said he was still waiting for a response for the traveler's checks.

"Hey Mason," Fitz said before the two ended the call. "I recommended you to Anderson and all, but to tell you the truth, I really didn't think that you'd ever be able to identify this guy. Nothing against you. I just thought it was a nearly impossible job. To have identified him and even have a photo is incredible. And in one week! Kudos to you, my friend. Great work."

"Thank you kindly, Fitz, but like we said last night, I was incredibly lucky. Can't count on stayin' lucky. It's going to get hard."

"Still, my friend, incredible work."

Mason then called Bob on the special line Bob had set up just for the two of them. It rang several times, then went to an answering machine.

"Hi Mason," the recording of Bob's voice said. "I'm not around this phone right now, so I couldn't answer it. I have one of those new cellular phones for when I'm out and about. You can try me on it. That number is (813) 988-3081. But also leave me a message here in case I've just stepped away briefly. Tell me where I can call you back."

Mason left a message saying that he was able to confirm that the ten-year-old photo was definitely Joey.

"I have my contact at the Penang police trackin' down people who go by the name Yusof Zaina. Maybe our luck'll hold. I went back to Tioman to get a positive ID on the photo from one of the girls. One-hundred percent certain it's him. Flyin' back to Melaka in the mornin' to pick up my rental car. The plan is to check out the area around the mission, then drive back to Penang. Should be there around dinner time tomorrow."

Mason told Bob the number for the Merlin but told him that he didn't need to call back unless there was something pressing. He was going to grab dinner in the hotel restaurant and try to get a good night's sleep.

Finally, Mason called Bo, who picked up on the second ring.

"Detective Jun."

"Bo, this is Mason."

"A picture and a name! Goddamn! How did you pull that off?"

"Long story, but the short answer is I was one lucky motherfucker. I'll tell you later. Anythin' on the name?"

Maybe, the detective said.

"There are twelve people named Yusof Zaina according to our people in KL. No real details yet, but I should have more tomorrow. I'm checking on passports because they'll have a photo on file. I'm also checking on driver's licenses for the same reason. Finally, I have a buddy checking records at the Army. I figured this guy is the right age that he might have served. Nothing yet though."

"I'm on Tioman right now, but I have a plane flyin' me back to Melaka in the mornin'. My rental car is there. My plan is to be back in Penang by dinner time tomorrow. Can we meet?"

"Yes."

"I'm gonna have Boonsri book me a room at the Straits Hotel. Why don't we meet in the lobby at eight. We can go to that little bar I like down the street."

"Sounds good."

"I have a lot more to tell you, Bo. Not over the phone, though."

"Don't tease me like that!"

"I'll give you the details tomorrow night. But listen, buddy, you gotta keep this to yourself for now. Okay?

"Jesus Mason. Yeah. Sure. My lips are sealed.

"Amanda wasn't his first victim."

"Fuck me."

"You got that right."

His last call was to Boonsri. She had gone for the day, but he left her a message on the office answering machine with what he needed.

Day 13

Joey got up early and took the cash that he kept in a hidden safe in his apartment to Big Willie.

"Jessica's the one," he told the fat Thai. "She quit a high-paying job and told me that she insists on paying her share because she can afford it."

"That doesn't mean she has fifty-thousand dollars," Big Willie said. "It means she has pride."

"No. She has the money. And she's starting to trust me."

"Have you fucked her yet?"

"That'll come. I'd like to. Believe me. But it's the long play. I have to be patient."

"Don't be so patient that she starts to think you're not interested in her that way."

"You know, Big Willie," Joey said with a grin. "This is a big difference between you and me. I know women. And you're celibate."

"I'm not fucking celibate."

"Okay. You're not celibate. You just aren't getting any."

"Fuck you, Joey."

Joey handed Big Willie an envelope with fifteen-hundred dollars in it.

"Here you go. As promised."

Joey told him that it might be awhile before he's back. He said he planned to suggest to Jessica that afternoon that they take a small trip to Langkawi. If she agreed, they'd leave tonight or tomorrow. Depending on how that goes, Joey said he was going to say he should show her around Malaysia.

Joey was back at the Holiday Inn and waiting for Jessica at noon. Another day of sightseeing. She came down wearing a sexy sundress.

"You look. . ." he wanted to find the right not-to-suggestive word and then it came to him, "great!"

She smiled. "I hoped you'd like it."

"I do."

"What's the plan for today?"

"Temples and monkeys."

"Odd combo. So, there are temples with monkeys?"

"No. We're going to visit some temples, then take in the Botanical Gardens. That's where the monkeys are."

"I vote for fewer temples and more monkeys. I'm getting kind of templed-out."

"Okay. Then we'll focus on the monkeys first, then see if we want to take in a temple or two."

Jessica smiled. He took her hand as they walked out of the lobby to hail a taxi.

Jessica loved walking the Botanical Gardens, though she was a little intimidated by the monkeys. There are two kinds of monkeys at the Gardens. When people arrive, they often are set upon by long tail macaques. The novelty wore off quickly and there was little cute about the buggers. The creatures long ago lost any fear of people. They want treats. They'd snatch them right out of your pocket, if you let them.

The dusky leaf monkeys were a different story. They're black but with white circles around their eyes. Jessica said they should be called panda monkeys. They're smaller than the macaques and more reserved.

The Botanical Gardens is more popular with locals than with tourists. The air is so fresh and it feels cooler. There are also waterfalls that add to the beauty of the surroundings, but it is a grueling hike. At one of many stands at a small food court near the main entrance, Joey and Jessica picked up some things for a picnic. They found a shady, private space. Joey removed a small, thin blanket from his pack, spread it on the ground and they enjoyed lunch.

"I want to propose something to you," Joey said as they reclined on the blanket, breathing in the lush scent of the abundant jasmine and other flowering plants.

"What might that be?"

"It's okay if this idea is too out there. I won't be hurt if you say no."

"Come on, Joey, spill it out."

"There's a small group of islands just north of Penang called Langkawi. They're beautiful and still, well, undiscovered. I know a guy who runs a place on one of the islands with a few huts. It's nothing like Penang. Just endless white sand beach and jungle. I'd like to show it to you."

"Hmmm. How long does it take to get there?"

"A few hours."

"How long did you think we'd stay?"

"Two or three days."

Jessica starred at two birds in a tree nearby. Their wings, back and tail were a bright turquoise blue. Their heads, chests and legs were a chestnut brown with a long reddish beak. While she was watching they swooped down out of sight, then returned to the limb. One had what appeared to be a small mouse in its beak.

"Is there anything dangerous about it?" she asked him.

"I'd never take you anywhere truly dangerous."

"When would we go?"

"I was thinking tomorrow."

She thought some more. When she left Seattle she hoped for adventure. Surely adventure could include South Seas sex with a good-looking younger man. Hell yeah, she thought to herself! Besides, Joey seemed harmless enough. Sweet actually.

Still, she wouldn't abandon all caution. She'd not check out of the Holiday Inn. She would tell the manager where she was going and that she would only be gone a few days. She'd also write a letter to a friend back in Seattle. She'd catch her up on her journey, especially her past few days in Penang with Joey, then slip in the trip details about

Langkawi. She had a flash that she was being paranoid, but it was what she needed to do to convince herself to go.

"Okay," she said, looking back at him with a huge smile. "Let's do it!"

Joey explained that they had a choice of two ferry routes. He said he'd always ridden his motorcycle up to Kuala Perlis for the two-hour crossing. There also was a ferry directly from Penang. It departed every night at 11 p.m. and arrived at Kuah on the main island at seven the next morning. He told her the Penang ferry was more costly and not especially comfortable for an eight-hour trip.

"Wait. Back up. You have a motorcycle?"

"Yeah."

"And we've been taking taxis?"

"I didn't know what you might think about touring around on the back of a motorcycle."

"Well now you know," she said smiling.

Joey said the cycle really wouldn't work for this trip. It would be impossible to load more than one bag. She joked that women don't share their bags.

They stopped at the ferry terminal on the way back to Batu Ferringhi and bought tickets for the eleven o'clock departure. The fare was about fourteen US dollars each.

The ferry departed right on time. By midnight, Joey and Jessica were huddled under a blanket sharing a chaise lounge in the open sea. The moon had yet to rise and the sky was filled with thousands and thousands of stars.

"This isn't half bad," she said looking up. She snuggled a little closer to him and closed her eyes. Amid the balmy salt air, she fell asleep to the gentle rocking of the ship.

— — — — —

Mason and the pilot were up, fed and at the Cessna by eight. As the only plane at the airstrip, they were airborne within minutes. Less than three hours later they were taxiing to a stop in Melaka. Mason paid the pilot, got in his rental car and headed to Arzed Restaurant.

Over lunch, he had Haziq show him on a map where the old mission school was.

By noon, he had pulled up to the old building that housed the school. It sat vacant and appeared to have been unoccupied for years. He asked around and eventually was directed to an older man, Mohamed bin Ali, who had rented the property to the pastor and his wife.

"Yes. Yes. I remember Pastor Johnny and Mrs. Helen well," Mohamed said. "Very nice and always pay rent on time."

"That's great to know, Mohamed. Can you tell me their surname?"

"Oh. Let me think." He paused for an extended time. "I don't remember. Everyone just called him Pastor Johnny."

"Perhaps you could check a copy of the lease he signed."

"Too long ago. I don't keep papers for more than a couple years after someone leaves."

Mason looked clearly frustrated. He decided to take a different approach.

"Did Pastor Johnny ever tell you about his home back in the States?"

"Oh yes. He had many stories about growing up."

"Did he ever mention a place?"

"I'm sure he did,"

"And. . ."

"I don't really know. I'm sorry."

Mason thought some more for a new angle.

"Did he ever talk about anything that happened back home?"

"I remember a story. He said that every year they'd have a celebration for some battle. Lots of flags and banners. They would fix up the school for it, too."

"US flags?"

"No. Some other flag."

"Was it bright red with a blue X that ran from corner to corner with white stars in the blue?"

"Yes. Yes. That was the flag. 'The south will rise again.' That's what Pastor Johnny would say. 'The south will rise again!'"

"Do you recall anything about the celebration? Anything about the battle?"

Mohamed closed his eyes and seemed to be trying to remember the celebration at the school.

"I believe it started with a B. There was a banner that said 'Battle of B something. Bennervul? That's not right. Sorry."

Mason was getting enough for Fitz to piece it together.

"Do you recall when during the year they'd have the celebration?"

"I don't know. Maybe the first part of the year." It was more of a question than a statement.

Mason tallied it up in his mind. A small town in the south with a big battle that they celebrate every year, probably in the early part of the year. Battle likely starts with a B. Might be close to Bennervul, or more likely Bennerville. He thanked Mohamed and returned to the restaurant. He needed to use a phone to call Boonsri.

He dictated a fax to send Fitz:

Fitz, found out a little more about Pastor Johnny and Helen. They're from the South, not the Midwest. They held a celebration every year at the school for a Civil War battle. I imagine they have the same celebration in their hometown. Their former landlord said they'd put up a banner that said Battle of Bennerville. Or something like that. He said it started with a B.

Then he hit the road for the long drive to meet Bo in George Town.

————

Mason and Bo took a booth at Best Bar and Grill. Mason liked this place because they made a real cheeseburger with bacon and nice, crispy French fries. The waiter took their orders. For Mason, that included a Jack Daniels. Bo had a beer.

"Mason, you look like shit man," Bo said as they settled into the booth.

"I know. I haven't been sleepin' well."

Mason wasn't ready to talk about his nightmares. Bo knew the backstory. He was in Vientiane when Mason assassinated the general. They had never spoken of it, though.

"Listen, Bo," he said, changing the subject. "We have a lot to go over."

Before we do, though, I need your word that you and I will agree before we share any of it with your government. You'll see why in a minute. Okay?"

"Oh shit. My government's involved?"

"No. It's just gonna cause a diplomatic row. My guys need to be ready to keep it from gettin' out of hand."

"This doesn't sound good, Mason. Just tell me. I can keep it secret, at least for a bit."

Mason told Bo that Joey had killed six young, blonde American girls, seven counting Mary Higgins. He started about two and a half years ago. Same MO in each case.

Except for Mary, the murders had been spread out by time and distance. He explained how each happened on the mainland but where travelers would catch a ferry or boat to an island. Each of the girls had been traveling alone. The killer had sex, apparently consensual, with each, then slashed their necks severing their carotid arteries.

Like Amanda and Mary, the motive was robbery. For each girl, he took all their valuables. The credit cards were then used in Penang and that he suspected that the traveler's checks were, too. The passports had mostly been used out of Bangkok.

"This will be ugly if it goes public," Bo said. "I agree that we should try to keep it quiet."

"You got that right, bud. The good news is that we have a name and an old photo."

"I have some news on Yusof Zaina," Bo said. "As I said last night, there are twelve showing up in national records. Five have passports, but none of those match our guy. Seven have a driver's license, but again none fits our guy."

Bo then looked at Mason and got a devilish look in his eyes.

"What?" Mason asked.

"Late today, I got motor vehicle records," Bo continued. "Five cars registered to people named Yusof Zaina, but they all match up to one of the driver's licenses. But there was one motorcycle registered four years ago to a Yusof Zaina. The address is in George Town. It doesn't match any of the other addresses we have. I thought you and I could check it out in the morning."

"Motorcycle would fit," Mason said. "He stashes it near where he expects to make a hit. Then after he kills the girl, he gets back to the motorcycle, cranks that sucker up and makes a beeline for George Town. By the time anyone finds the girl's body, he's probably at least a couple hundred miles away."

Mason took the last sip of his Jack Daniels and signaled the waiter for another.

"What's happenin' with the Mary Higgins case?" Mason asked.

Bo laid out the evidence.

"She graduated from Boston College earlier this year," Bo said. "It looks like she hit the road a month or so later. Flew into Bangkok and used every day of her sixty-day tourist visa before crossing into Malaysia on the upper east coast. Worked her way down to Tioman, then headed up to Taman Negara. She then stopped briefly in KL, then came here on a bus the day before they found her body. I pieced most of this together after talking with her mother by phone this morning. Mary planned to take a year and go around the world."

Bo said she had rented the single room at the Lum Fong that she was found in.

"The manager said she hung out with another young woman, a Kiwi named Samantha Watson," Bo said. She was the one who asked the manager to open the door to Mary's room when Mary didn't show up for breakfast, as they had planned."

Bo looked at his notes. Everything inside the room was the same as the Amanda Anderson case. He paused and looked at Mason. "My guess is that all the victims' rooms were the same," he said. The body was found naked on the bed with a deep slash across the front of the neck.

"Cause of death was blood loss from the wound," Bo said. "No other injuries. Coroner puts the time of death between midnight and 4 a.m."

"The coroner confirmed she had sex shortly before she died," Bo continued. "Nothing to indicate it was forced. But our guy, Joey, left nothing behind. No semen on her or in her. None on the bed. We think he was wearing a rubber."

Bo said the guests in the surrounding rooms had not yet checked out when she was found, so his team had a chance to interview them.

"The guy next door said he could hear them going at it about two in the morning," Bo said.

"What did he hear?"

"The guy said it was just her moaning like she was really enjoying it. No sounds from the guy. He said he could hear the bed thumping a little against the wall, at least that's what he thought it was. They were definitely doing the nasty."

Mason asked if anyone of the front desk saw them come in.

"The desk isn't staffed after ten o'clock," Bo said. "If someone comes in after ten, they have to ring the bell to summon the night manager or be there at the same time as someone leaving." No one remembered seeing them come in.

"When he kilt Amanda, I think he slipped out a back door," Mason said.

"Probably same here, I think," Bo said. "Mary's room was close to the back stairs. Highly unlikely that anyone would see him leave that way."

Bo said he personally had interviewed the friend, Samantha, yesterday. She had run into Mary briefly the evening of the murder. She and her boyfriend were walking past a restaurant on Chulia and Mary called to her. They went over and spoke with her briefly, then Samantha and Mary arranged to meet for breakfast.

Mary introduced the fellow she was having dinner with, but Samantha couldn't recall his name. She said it was something like Jimmy or Johnny."

"Or Joey."

"Yeah. My thought, too. I asked her if it could have been Joey. She said maybe, but she wasn't sure. She gave a decent description, though.

Sounded like our guy."

"When I got the photo you faxed, I went back to the hotel to show it to her," Mason said, "but she had already checked out."

Bo said they tried to find her, but they think she left Penang. "We've asked a contact at the New Zealand foreign office in KL to contact her family to have her contact me when they next hear from her," he said. "Nothing yet, but it's only been one day. I'd like to show her the photo."

"Should we head to the George Town address tonight?" Mason asked.

"I don't think so," Bo said. "If he gets away at night, we'll never find him and we will have tipped our hand. I think we should do it tomorrow and bring back-up just in case he's there. I have a guy watching the place tonight. Had to get overtime authorized. I think we're okay for tonight."

Bo suggested that he swing by Mason's hotel at eight in the morning to pick him up with a couple uniformed officers. Sounded good, Mason said.

Bo said goodnight, then added that he hoped Mason could get a full night's sleep. Mason stayed to finish his drink. He was nervous about not moving on Joey's apartment right away, but Bo had made a good point and the place was staked out. About ten minutes later, Mason walked back to the hotel, went up to his room and was sound asleep within minutes.

It happened again at about three in the morning. This time it was an old man, walking with a cane. There was a bright flash, then the old man's body was crumpled in the street. Mason's heart was racing, as was his mind. Was his brain going to dish up every innocent victim of his bomb blast? He didn't even recall seeing any of these people. How was he seeing them now?

Were they even real? Did it matter, he asked himself? If they were figments of his imagination it didn't change the fact that he had killed fifty-four innocent people that day. And they all had private stories. He might not have thought about their lives before, but now they were about all he could think of. One thing he knew for sure was that all fifty-four of those he killed that day had their own lives that had nothing to do with the general.

Yet, he killed them. Gripped by revenge, he had taken their lives along with General Tho's without a moment's thought of what it might all mean. One word came to mind: terrorist.

Day 14

The overnight ferry from Penang docked at Kuah, the only real town in Langkawi, a little after seven in the morning. Kuah wasn't much to look at. No one would ever confuse it with Penang. Joey had called it undiscovered. As she looked at the old, weather-beaten buildings, she wondered why Joey had been so excited about this place.

"Don't worry. We're not staying here," he told her. "We're going to a smaller island south of here called Pulau Bumbon. I know a place there that rents very basic bungalows and serves great meals."

To get there, Joey said, they need to find Omar among the boats near the ferry dock.

"Won't be hard," Joey said. "Look for a bright yellow boat with the word 'Bumbon' painted on the side."

"There it is!" Jessica said, pointing to a boat about one hundred feet offshore.

"Omar!" Joey called out and waved to get the man's attention. Omar waved back then moved the boat toward them, eventually running it up on the beach.

"Welcome, Yusof and lady," Omar said, securing the boat on shore. "You go to Bisaam's?"

Yep, Joey said, as Omar helped Jessica into the boat. Joey climbed in and sat next to her, then Omar pushed the boat back from the beach, turned it to face the sea, then jumped in himself.

The trip to the bungalows took about thirty minutes over calm seas. They circled about halfway around what appeared to be an uninhabited island when Omar steered the boat to the left toward the beach. Jessica could see, nestled in the trees, three bungalows and a small house next to an outdoor eating area and kitchen under a thatched roof. The setting was spectacular. A thick jungle appeared to begin a few short feet behind the buildings.

A Malaysian man walked toward the beach from the kitchen area. He was older than Joey, perhaps in his mid- to late-thirties.

"Yusof! Welcome my friend," Bisaam called out.

"Bisaam, I couldn't stay away," Joey said as the two men shook hands and helped Jessica from the boat. "This is my friend, Jessica," Joey continued as they walked toward the bungalows. "We need two bungalows for two nights. Is that possible?"

Bisaam stopped and faced Joey.

"I'm sorry my friend, but two of my three are taken."

"Jessica and I are," Joey paused, "friends, Bisaam. Perhaps there is a hammock for me?"

"It's ok, Joey," Jessica said. "We can share the bungalow."

"Very good!" exclaimed Bisaam, smiling broadly at Jessica.

"Are you sure?" Joey asked Jessica. She looked at him, and said, "Yes," then turned back to see Omar carrying their packs from the boat while a gentle breeze swept across her face. No turning back now, she thought. She was sure that her Southeast Asian adventure was going to get a punctuation mark tonight. It better, she thought as a small smile spread on her face.

The bungalow was the very definition of basic. It was an unpainted wooden structure elevated about three feet off the ground. A small porch with two chairs adorned the front of the cabin looking out at the sea. Omar set their packs on the porch, then headed back to his boat. Jessica said, "Thank you, Omar," and the man kindly nodded his head in response.

The bungalow's one room was a tight eight feet by eight feet. In the middle against one wall was a double mattress on a platform. A mosquito net hung over it. A small wooden table sat next to the bed. A single light bulb hung at arm's height on a wire in the middle of the room.

The bungalow had a small bathroom at the rear. Jammed in a space of about three feet wide behind the back wall was a hand sink, a toilet and a handheld shower. The back wall of the bathroom rose about four feet with just a screen extending the rest of the way to the roof.

"So, Jessica, this is rustic," Joey said, "but that's why I love it here."

"Joey, this place is incredible. It's so beautiful and," she paused to think of the right word, "primitive."

"Wait till evening when you start to hear the creatures in the jungle," he said. "The cicadas and other insects go nuts. And the birds and the monkeys. Bisaam says there might be a tiger in there somewhere, but I don't think anyone has ever seen one. It's just a story he likes to tell."

"Oh, God, tigers? You said it wouldn't be dangerous."

"No, no, no. I've been here a half dozen times. There is no tiger. Every time Bisaam tells the tiger story there is a twinkle in his eyes. He likes telling it. That's all. You're safe here.

"The biggest danger," he continued, putting air quotes around the word danger, "is that you'll catch a cold from the shower.

"There is no hot – or even warm – water. The water comes straight from a spring-fed stream Bisaam piped into a couple hundred feet back in the jungle. Brace yourself when you turn on the shower. It never warms up. In fact, it gets colder! You'll get used to it, though."

They dropped their packs on the bed. Joey suggested they walk the beach.

The beach was not wide but consisted of pure white sand. The surf was gentle and there was an ever-present light breeze. The jungle was just twenty to thirty feet to their left as they strode up the beach. She could hear the occasional sounds of what she took to be birds.

"What an awesome place," she said, taking his hand. "It's so untamed. And no people! This is exactly what I had hoped I would get to experience on my trip. Nothing came close to this in Thailand, though. Thank you, Joey, for bringing me here. I love it."

He smiled. "You're welcome."

They walked in silence a little farther. "Bisaam and Omar called you what sounded like maybe Joseph. Was that your name in Malaysian?"

"My parents named me after my Uncle Joe, but Joseph is a Christian name. The Malays call me Yusof. It's a Muslim name. It's fine with me. The Chinese just call me Joey, though."

They walked back to the bungalow. Jessica took a new paperback, sat on the porch and started to read. Joey grabbed his Walkman and a couple cassettes, sat in the other chair and listened to his music. He glanced over to see what she was reading and was momentarily startled. The title was *Murder in Georgetown*. He had a fleeting thought that she was reading about Mary Higgins, then realized that was a stupid thought. He had killed Mary barely more than a week before. There could be no book already.

A little later they noticed another couple at the communal table and decided to go introduce themselves. John and Melinda were from Australia. They had been on Bumbon for a week.

"The snorkeling here is bloody gorgeous, mate," John said. "Undisturbed, you know. Lots of color. And the fish. Thousands and thousands of them."

"Do you snorkel?" Melinda asked, looking from Joey to Jessica.

"I never have, but it sounds like this might be the place to try it," Jessica said.

"Bisaam has some gear we could use," Joey said. "Want to do it tomorrow?"

John offered to take them to the sites he and Melinda liked. They'd take Bisaam's inflatable raft.

Two other guests joined them at the table. Ibrahim and Mo were from KL. Jessica noticed that when they spoke by themselves, they spoke Bahasa Malay, but both spoke English well and only spoke English with the group. They had no problem joining the chat.

"You going snorkeling tomorrow?" Ibrahim asked, looking at Joey and Jessica. It was a way to ease into the conversation. "Mo and I like the reef around the south tip of the island. It starts at about two or three meters and most of it is less than ten meters. I'm Ibrahim."

They introduced themselves.

"The fish are magnificent," Mo added. "And sea turtles, too."

"John and I have been there," Melinda added. "We love that spot." She turned to Jessica. "You'll love this, Jess."

Jessica smiled. Her dad called her Jess.

"Were you snorkeling today?" Joey asked the fellows from KL.

"Fishing," Ibrahim said. "We caught dinner!"

They had, indeed, caught a half dozen highly prized red groupers. Bisaam had kept two to prepare for dinner and gave the others to Omar to sell at the jetty in Kuah. The hotel restaurant usually would buy any freshly caught red grouper offered. Bisaam and Omar would then split the money paid for the fish.

Bisaam, who was working on dinner nearby in the kitchen, called over to the group that he was steaming the red grouper with ginger and onions.

After dinner, Joey and Jessica returned to their bungalow. They turned on the overhead light. It was harsh, so they lit a couple candles. The bed was shrouded in a mosquito net. In the flickering candlelight, Jessica thought it looked romantic. She was glad she was still taking her birth control pills even though it had been a long time since she needed them. She knew that she would need them tonight. She felt it was going to be a special night.

And, my God, it was.

It was going to be different kind of night for Joey. He was, much to his surprise, a little anxious. Every woman he had ever bedded had been a one-night stand. Every one. He had never once even thought about how what he did or didn't do might have an effect on his relationship with the woman. He didn't have relationships. He wondered what he should do after the sex. And for the first time with a woman, he wasn't so cock-sure about what to do.

"I'm going to take a quick shower," Jessica told him and headed into the bathroom. He heard the water come on, then her gasp as she stepped into the cold shower. "That's wakes you up," she called from the bath.

To calm his nerves, Joey did what he had done in other situations: He came up with a plan. He knew he was good at pleasing a woman but was clueless about how or even if pleasing her would build trust. Maybe, he thought, if she felt more in charge at times, it would give her a sense of control. Her being more in control had to help build trust.

He decided that he would go slowly. Show initiative, but also defer to Jessica. He would try to tune in to those moments. Then, he realized, he had never needed to read a woman that way. Would he be any good at it?

The shower ended. A moment later Jessica stepped back into the room. Her red hair, which she had tied back in a ponytail all day, was framing her face. She was wearing just a tee-shirt and panties.

He felt himself getting aroused but urged himself to slow down. Jessica was a long play, he kept telling himself. He had to win her over, to get her to trust him far more than sexually. She had to fall in love with him. Not suddenly, not tonight. But soon.

He wanted her to wake one day three or four weeks from now and at least thinking about the possibility of spending the rest of her life with him. That's what it would take, he knew. Only then would she willingly give him the money he needed.

He thought back through all the love stories he had seen in the movies. There had been some good ones, but he hadn't really studied them for tips on making a woman fall in love with you. He loved Top Gun but couldn't see himself as Maverick to Jessica's Charlie. Maybe Out of Africa? The love story between Karen and Denys built slowly, but it wasn't he and Jessica either.

His mind played with other love stories that he had watched mostly on video in his apartment. While no one film showed him what to do, he did find a lesson in how the good love stories developed. They shared a gentleness, an openness. The men could still be bold and daring, but with the women they had to be gentle and deliberate. Yes, he would let Jessica set the tone. The pace would be her pace.

"The shower was great," she said to him. "You should take a quick one, too."

"Okay."

"Notice I said quick." He saw that she had a big smile. It was a strange role reversal. Wasn't she supposed to be the one who was feeling the butterflies and maybe even doubting what she was about to do? He liked it that she was a strong woman character in the movie about to play in his mind.

A few minutes later, he emerged from the small bathroom wrapped in his towel. He saw her, in the flickering candlelight inside the netting, lying on the bed. The only noises were the soft lapping of the surf nearby and the cacophony of sounds coming from the jungle behind them.

"Drop the towel and come to bed," she told him, clearly taking charge. He was self-consciously aroused again. He approached the bed, then turned his back as he dropped the towel, opened the gap in the mosquito net and sat back on the bed. He turned his head and looked at her. She wasn't exactly smiling, but she did look ready. "Come here."

She kept her eyes on his as he moved up to lie next to her.

"Just so you know, I haven't done this in a while," she said. "Really. No one since my husband."

"It's okay," he said softly. "We can do whatever you want. If it doesn't feel right to you, just say stop. I'll understand." They lay looking in each other's eyes. "You're beautiful, Jessica. Really beautiful."

And he meant it. Every word.

She smiled. "If you say so." She loved the compliment. "But you are truly the most handsome man I've ever dated – and I think we're about to do more than date." She put an emphasis on the word date. He chuckled.

"Maybe."

"What do you mean, 'maybe?'" She leaned in and kissed him on the lips. He kissed her back, but didn't move in. Instead, he traced a line on her cheek, while continuing to look deeply into her green eyes. It was sweet and all, but Jessica had known what she wanted from this evening the moment she said yes to taking this trip. She reached down between his legs and touched him. It was unexpected and caused Joey to catch his breath.

This whole experience amused her. She had always been a self-confident woman, but not sexually aggressive. Taking hold of Joey like that was new. It was a side of herself that she wanted to explore.

He was more than ready, of course, but he wanted, he kept telling himself like a mantra, he needed to – take – his – time. But he also knew he couldn't just lie there. He had to respond. He brought his hand down and cupped her face. He leaned in to kiss her again. Gently at first, his tongue outlining her lips. Even though he kept telling himself to go slowly, he couldn't deny the passion that was building. When he thought he might be losing control, he broke away again.

Outside the cicadas were chirping. Jessica and Joey could also hear John and Melinda still talking with Bisaam. The net surrounding the bed moved in the breeze and then Joey and Jessica could smell a coming rain. She started to stroke him but also seemed to move her chest toward him. When she did, he moved his hand under her tee-shirt to her breasts. They fit in his palm and he moved her nipple between his index and middle finger. He felt it stiffen slightly.

She sat up and pulled the shirt over her head. She pushed him onto his back and started kissing his chest. His hands were all over her now. She moved up, her hair hanging from her face around his, and kissed him, deeply this time. Her tongue met his. Their breathing was gathering speed.

Joey rolled her over and slipped his lips down to her breasts. He sucked on them wetly, then drew a line with his tongue down to her navel. Her hands were in his hair and gently pushed him further down. Between her legs now, he pulled her panties off, bent down and with his lip and tongue caressed her. Oh, she liked that! She liked it a lot. He got the message, so he kept at it. Then she told him, "Now, Joey. I want it now."

He moved up and kissed her lips. He was about to reach down to guide himself in, when she did it for him. She moaned softly. She wrapped her arms around his neck and her legs around his hips. Together, they found a rhythm. Like a slow dance at the prom, they felt the movement of the other and matched it to their own.

This felt differently to Joey than before. There was a connection to it that made it feel far more personal than anything he had experienced. It dawned on him that this was the way sex was supposed to feel. More than physical. Complete.

Jessica was just thinking that it felt good.

Within a couple minutes, they were increasing the pace of the thrusts. A little sound was coming from Jessica's throat with each push. "Uh…Uh…Uh…Uh," The sounds grew more resonant. To his surprise, the moans of her pleasure turned him on. He realized he had never really listened before.

The pace picked up again and he found himself angling for deeper thrusts. As he did, Jessica's sounds turned more to muffled cries. "Oh God, yes. Joey. Yes, that's right! There! Please yes! There! Yes!" And then it was welling up inside him, too. He was about to release a torrent.

The pace quickened again for both of them. Jessica started to cry out, not scream but cry out with abandon. She was at that ultimate peak. Joey was right behind her.

As they lie there, spent, they both overheard Bisaam tell the Aussies, "They actually asked for separate bungalows."

"Really? What was that about?" John asked, rhetorically.

"He said they were just friends."

"I want friends like that," Melinda said.

Inside the bungalow, Jessica and Joey could hear them laughing. They both giggled. He stayed inside her for a bit, lying on top of her. Then he rolled to the side and out.

"My God," she whispered, as if to herself. It had been, she was quite certain, the most intense sex she had ever had.

Joey just laid there thinking about how different that was than all the other times he had sex. Different didn't do it justice. He had never felt so alive. Sure, he had orgasmed before. But never like this. Why was that, he wondered?

Soon, he realized that what was different was that he was totally focused on Jessica. Not like he had been with the other girls. With them, he just wanted their last orgasm to be a good one. He knew how to do that. But with Jessica, he wanted her to feel more than physical pleasure. He wanted her to love the way it lifted her up. In that moment, he realized that he had never really cared before. Sure, the others all enjoyed their last time, but then they would die and it made no difference to him whatsoever.

This time it wasn't about taking his knife to her neck. All those thoughts had been completely out of his mind. As he lie there, he could still taste her on his lips and it tasted good. He realized in a flash that he really wanted her to love it because he wanted desperately to do it again. And again.

A totally new experience for him.

Then his mind did turn to business. He had no doubt that if he played his cards right, she would grow to trust him. She would give him what he needed. And then he would kill her.

And then an unsettling thought struck him. What if when the time came, he didn't want to do it?

Of course, he would. He had done it seven times and he could do it once more. He had a solid plan. Just stick to the plan, he told himself.

She rolled over to face him and brought him back to the moment. "Let's tell each other one secret."

"Really? Okay."

"The first time I had sex was in the back seat of Tommy West's Chevy after the senior prom. I was eighteen and maybe a little drunk. I didn't like it that much. It definitely wasn't like tonight."

Joey's mind raced. He didn't tell secrets, except to Big Willie, but that was different. What could he say? It had to be good. And none of his real secrets could he possibly tell her, so he winged it.

"My dad was a preacher."

"That's your secret? You already told me that your dad was a preacher."

"No. That's not my secret," he said with a slight laugh. "That's part of the set up," he paused. "I was rebellious. I was dating a girl named Annie. We were both seventeen. She was on the wild side. Really. I definitely wasn't her first. One night, we snuck into the church and we did it on the first pew."

"That's twisted."

"That's why it's been a secret." It was more than a secret, of course. It was total fiction.

They lie quietly for a while, then she rolled over and gently bit his nipple. Round two had begun.

———————

Mason was finishing breakfast in the hotel dining room. It was a decent American-style breakfast of sunny side up eggs, chicken sausage because pork is forbidden in Muslim establishments and buttered toast with jam. But Mason had a hard hankering for grits. Christ, he missed grits. He had found an international market in Bangkok that sometimes carried instant grits. No self-respecting Georgia boy would eat instant grits back home, but he looked every single time he was in the store. Bo walked in a few minutes before eight.

"Good morning, partner," Bo said, eyeing a tired-looking Mason. "Rough night?"

"I'll be fine."

Mason downed the last of his coffee, had the waiter bring the check and charged it to his room. Then they headed to Joey's last known address.

They parked a half block from the run-down apartment building. A plainclothes cop walked over and leaned in Bo's window. Before he spoke, he took in the American sitting next to the detective. Unusual, he thought, but then refocused on Bo.

"Good morning, Detective Jun," the man said. "I've seen no one who fits the description of the suspect. And I couldn't find a motorcycle that matched the registration, either."

"Has anyone come and gone?"

"Yes sir. Between six-thirty and a few minutes ago, I saw seven people leave the building," he said, checking his notes. "One couple who I would put in their thirties, a woman who I'd say was early twenties. And four single men of various ages. Not our guy, though."

"Thank you, sergeant. Please stay with the team a little while longer in case we need help."

The sergeant nodded.

Bo had one of his men go to the back of the building, then stationed the sergeant and the other officer near the front door.

"Let's go, Mason," Bo said. They rang the buzzer for the apartment manager.

"No vacancy," a voice squawked back at them through an old intercom.

"Sorry to bother you, sir. I'm Chief Detective Jun Shan-Bo of the Penang Police. We need to speak with you about a tenant."

The door buzzed and Bo and Mason entered the building. The inside looked no better than the outside. The hallway was dimly lighted by a single overhead exposed bulb. There was a musty smell about the place. The walls hadn't seen fresh paint in many years and what paint was there was peeling. The floor creaked with every step. A man in a white undershirt opened a door and stepped out.

"What tenant you want?"

"Can we step inside for privacy," Bo asked, showing the man his police identification.

The manager, a Chinese Malay, said his name was Daniel Heah. He had been manager for more than ten years.

"Does a young man live in the building named Yusof Zaina?"

"No more. He move maybe three year ago."

"Do you know where he moved to?"

"Beach."

"Do you know what beach?"

"No. Maybe Batu Ferringhi. He said he like Batu Ferringhi."

"When was the last time you saw him?" Bo asked.

"I see him on motorcycle in town maybe one month ago. He not see me."

"How about before that. Has he been back to visit?"

"No."

"Mr. Heah, you saw him a month ago on a motorcycle. Was it the same one he owned when he lived here?"

"Yes. Red Honda. He got it right before he move. He pay me to let him keep it in the hall."

Bo told the manager that they had a photo of the Yusof they were looking for, but that the picture was about ten years old. He showed it to Mr. Heah.

"Yeah. That Yusof. He not look Malay but is. He look more like you," Heah said nodding to Mason, "but darker. Nice hair. He very nice. Yusof in trouble?" he asked.

"We're just trying to find him to ask him some questions," Bo answered.

"He was good tenant," Heah said. "Always pay rent on time. Friendly. Not loud. Best thing – he put satellite tv on roof! He said if I let him do it, he would run cable to me, too. When he leave, he let me keep it! Said he wouldn't need it where he was going."

Bo asked if Yusof had a job.

"I don't think so. He was around days and nights. But he pay rent on time every month, so I not ask questions."

"How about friends? Did he have any friends?"

"He nice guy. But I not see any friends. He quiet. No visitors. Good tenant."

Heah said that Yusof told him an uncle in the US had died and left him some money.

"I thought maybe he move to America."

Bo thanked Mr. Heah and they walked back outside. Bo told the other officers they could go, that the suspect no longer lived there.

Mason and Bo returned to Bo's car. They sat there for a bit, then Mason raised a question.

"So, he started killin' American girls two and a half years ago, but he didn't have a job before that, accordin' to his landlord. Yet, he paid his rent on time and bought a motorcycle. How was he supportin' himself?"

"We're thinking of him as a serial killer," Bo said. "But maybe we should be thinking of him as a thief first."

"Okay," Mason said. "What does that get us?"

"Actually, maybe a lot," Bo said. "The most common thing that young thieves do is snatch purses from tourists. My guess is that he was living off the cash and anything that he could pawn from the purses. Then, one day he realized that maybe the credit cards and other stuff might have value, too. He just didn't know how to convert it to cash. He might have asked around and eventually found the right kind of fence. The number of fences in Penang who can move passports, credit cards and the like is a small number."

"So, if we find the fence, he'll lead us to our guy."

"Maybe. Worth a shot."

Bo drove Mason back to the hotel. He said he was going to talk with detectives in the robbery unit.

"I want to see if any of the purse-snatching victims gave descriptions that could have been Yusof," he said. "Then we can see what was stolen and that might point us to specific fences. I know little about who fences what, but I'd bet some of the robbery guys do."

"I'm gonna go cruise around Batu Ferringhi," Mason said. "In all my trips here, I've never been to the beach. I wanna get a feel for it. My bet is that Joey or Yusof is still livin' there."

The two parted at Mason's hotel. Mason told Bo he'd call him later in the day to see if either of them had turned anything up.

Mason got in his rental car and headed to Batu Ferringhi. He had little of a plan. He needed to soak it in and then try to think as Joey might. If he could see the place through Joey's eyes, he might be able to narrow down where Joey might be living, Mason thought. He knew it was a long shot, but so was stopping in that one restaurant and getting his first real lead.

The first things Mason noticed about Batu Ferringhi were that it was cleaner and quieter than George Town. The palm trees were swaying gently, revealing a cooling breeze off the water. There were a few high-rise resorts along the beach itself. A scattering of various shops and cafes lined the one main road that paralleled the beach.

Back from the main road opposite the beach were residential areas. There were modest individual houses, which you never saw in George Town, and apartment buildings. The apartments were mostly newer construction, but also the occasional older, wooden structure.

He had hoped that he could find Joey by looking for satellite dishes. But Batu Ferringhi was a much nicer place than Joey's old George Town neighborhood. Satellite dishes adorned the roofs of most of the apartment buildings. His back-up plan was to look for a red Honda motorcycle. Again, though, motorcycles were fairly common.

Mason debated with himself what he should do. He had no easy options. Was it worth parking the car and going door to door? He wished he had taken the time to learn to speak Bahasa Malay. As languages go, it's a simple one to pick up. But he never had reason to learn it. If he were going to knock on doors, he had to hope that most would be answered by English-speakers.

He developed a plan. The first thing he would do is look at the mailboxes at each apartment building he approached. Some offered tenants names, but just as many were just mailbox numbers. If there were a way to get behind the boxes, he would do that because sometimes a mail carrier would put a tenant's name on the opening. Unfortunately, that access to the back side of the mailboxes didn't happen often.

The buildings themselves were mostly two- and three-story structures. He decided that he would only knock on ground floor doors, unless he was not able to reach anyone in a ground-floor unit. In that case, he'd go to the next floor. He'd continue until he'd spoken with at least one person in each building.

Mason would always smile and say he was looking for a friend he'd met on the beach. He called him Yusof, not Joey, because he felt certain that the young man would be going by his Malaysian name here. He wouldn't show the old photo of Yusof but would tell the person that Yosef looked a little white but was a Malay. Then he'd add that the fellow he was looking for spoke English like an American and had a red Honda motorcycle.

It was a long, tiring task. Even in the slightly cooler climate, he was sweating and could feel himself growing frustrated. By mid-afternoon, he decided to take a break and grab a late lunch. Afterwards, he'd call Bo to see if the Penang detective had made any progress.

He found a nice little café on the beach with a distinctively Western menu. After he finished his spinach salad with roasted chicken on top and a cold beer, he walked to a nearby hotel. He gave the desk clerk ten ringgits to use a house phone. He called Bo and told him what he had been doing.

"Has to be done," Bo said. "We know that he probably lives there somewhere. Someone is bound to recognize him. He doesn't speak or look like they do. And we know that as recently as a month ago he still had the red Honda."

"So, have you found out anything?" Mason asked.

"One of the guys said there were descriptions of a purse-snatcher a few years ago that could have been Yusof. He said I should speak with Detective Dahari. I'm waiting for him to come back in. Why don't I call you at the hotel later."

"Okay. I'll talk with you later, then. Maybe we can grab a drink."

"I can't tonight. I have to get home. We have a school thing. But I can tell you what I find out over the phone and we can talk about what we should do tomorrow."

Mason hung up, walked out to his car and drove back to his hotel.

"I got some good info from Dahari," Bo told Mason over the phone later that evening. "Tourists always report it to police when their purse is stolen. Dahari said there were many that appeared to be done by a fellow, right age, and victims couldn't say, for sure, that he was a Malaysian."

"With a good sketch you'd think they would have snagged his butt. Why didn't they?"

"He slowed down," Bo said. "He'd been doing a grab every week or two that they knew of, then less than one a month. Here's the kicker, though, about the time you and I know to be the first murder, he stopped completely."

"Our guy, for sure."

"Yeah. And here's a useful piece. Dahari said that early on a good Samaritan would usually find the purse and turn it in along with passports and credit cards and stuff. Then when he started slowing down it stopped."

"That's when Joey found out those things were worth a lot."

"Probably. Dahari said it was probably when our guy connected with a fence who could move financial and identity items."

"Did he have names?"

"Yeah. He said there are maybe five fences that could do it. He said they're smart guys. Rarely screw up."

"Names?"

"Yes. Four Malays and a Thai Malay."

"It's the Thai," Mason said. "The passports went to Bangkok."

"Could be. He's a good place to start. I'll call on him in the morning. Do you want to come with me?"

"I'd like to, but I'm gonna head back to Batu Ferringhi to knock on apartment doors."

"I'll be back at the station by one," Bo said. "Call me then and I'll tell you what I find out. If anything."

"Will do."

"And Mason, maybe you should take something to help you sleep. You look really tired, man."

"I know."

"Something going on? I've never seen you look like this, my friend. The investigation is going so well. It just doesn't make sense."

"Yeah. It's not the investigation."

"I'm here for you, buddy, if you want to talk about it. You and I go back a long way."

"Thanks, Bo. I'm not there yet."

Day 15

Mason slept through the night. It felt great, Maybe, just maybe, the nightmares were behind him.

By 9 a.m., he was back in Batu Ferringhi. He picked up where he left off, reading names when they were available on mailboxes and knocking on doors.

Knock. Nothing. Knock knock. Nothing. He just kept telling himself that as much as he hated canvassing this way, there was a decent chance he'd come across someone who knew Joey. At about ten-forty-five, he got a break.

"Pardon me, ma'am. I'm tryin' to find a friend I met on the beach the other day," he said with a smile to a middle-aged woman who answered what felt like the hundredth door he had knocked on that morning. "Perhaps you know where he lives. He's Malay but looks kind of white. He speaks English like me, an American. Do you know him?"

"Yusof?"

"Yes ma'am, Yusof!" he said with a broad smile.

"He drive red motorcycle."

"Yes, that's right! Do you know where he lives?"

"No."

Mason looked confused. "But you know him. Right?"

"He eat at my husband's restaurant."

She told him where the restaurant was located and that her husband's name was Malik.

"You go ask Malik," she said. "Yusof regular customer."

Mason hurried back to his car. It was too early to call Bo, so he drove straight to the restaurant. When he got there, it was well before anyone would have shown up for lunch. He walked in and saw a middle-aged man in the kitchen.

"Pardon me, sir. Are you Malik?" Mason asked.

"Yes. I am Malik. Who are you?"

"My name is Mason. I'm lookin' for a friend and your wife told me that he eats here often. His name is Yusof."

"Yes. Yusof is a customer. You say you are a friend?"

"Yes sir. Do you know where he is?"

"No. He comes here three or four times a week, but not for more than a week now. He travels every few months and I don't see him then."

"Do you know where he lives?"

"No. Nearby, but not so close that he walks here. He always comes on his motorcycle."

"Would anyone else know where he lives?"

"You say you are a friend? If you are a friend, why don't you know where he lives. Yusof never comes here with a friend."

"Yes sir. Sorry I didn't make it clear. I'm a friend from the beach. When he rides up or leaves, do you know which direction he goes on the highway?"

"He always comes and goes from the west."

"Thank you kindly, Malik. If you see him before me, tell him Mason said hello."

He didn't mean it, of course. But it didn't matter because Malik would certainly tell Joey the next time he walked in anyway. He'd know, then, that someone was on to him.

Mason got back in his car and headed west. He figured that Joey might walk at most a half mile. But he always came on his motorcycle, so he was likely at least that far away. The more he headed west, the less density he saw. At a little under a half mile, he turned left off the main road. The street that paralleled the main road was lined with apartments. He drove it looking for a red Honda.

He continued on for about a mile more, then headed back to the main highway and then turned back toward the center of Batu Ferringhi. He decided, though, to go straight to the police station to talk with Bo face to face.

Bo was sitting at his desk waiting for Mason to call when his intercom told him that there was a Mason Ray in the lobby to see him. He grabbed a file and headed out to meet Mason.

"Let's go get lunch," Bo told Mason as he approached him. As he got closer, he said in a softer voice, "I don't want to talk about this here."

Mason's car was parked right outside, so they jumped in and Bo directed him to a place that served barbecue brisket. In the car, Mason started the conversation.

"I found someone who knows him. The fellow runs a restaurant. Joey comes in three or four times a week when he is around. Hasn't seen him, though, in nearly a week."

"Do you think that means he's away?"

"Likely."

"Damn. You think he's going to kill another girl."

"Damned if I know. It doesn't fit, though? He spaces the murders five or six months apart and then slam, bam, thank ya ma'am does two in one week, then heads out for a third right away? I'm not buyin' it. He's changin' things. He has somethin' new in mind."

"Or he's just taking a trip."

"Maybe. But it feels different. Did you find out anything in your meetin' with that Thai guy?"

"I think he knows Yusof," Bo said. "Claims he doesn't, but when I pulled out the sketch and mentioned Yusof's name an assistant standing a few feet away nearly shit a brick. He literally flinched. Not the fence, though. Cool as can be."

"Did you say why you were lookin' for Joey?"

"I was vague. I said it was part of an ongoing investigation."

Bo shared some of the background information he had gathered on the fence. His name is William Chirathivat. Everyone calls him

179

Big Willie. "The guy is huge," Bo said. "He must weigh four hundred pounds." Officially, he runs a tailor shop in George Town. Three generations of Chirathivats at that location.

"But guess what?" Bo asked, then answered himself. "Descendants of a crime family in Bangkok."

"Hot damn! That would explain how the passports ended up bein' used in Bangkok."

"The Chirathivats are a shadow of what they once were. Dahari said they used to have family operations in cities throughout Southeast Asia, but only a few remain. They were suspected of trafficking rare art and antiquities, but nothing could ever be proved."

"What's next with him?"

"I have one of my best men sitting on the shop. His instruction is to tail Big Willie whenever he leaves."

"I'll tell you what I think," Mason said, "He's gonna tell Joey to get out while the gettin's good. He won't wait. He'll try to do it today."

"Almost certainly."

"I'll be at the hotel. Call me the moment anythin' happens."

The phone in Mason's room rang at three-ten. "He's on the move," Bo said. "Looks like he might be on his way to Batu Ferringhi."

"Let's go," Mason said. "Pick me up lickety split."

The plainclothes officer Bo had following Big Willie radioed that he was entering Batu Ferringhi. Bo told him not to lose the Thai. They needed to find the apartment.

"Try to get pictures, but don't let him see you," Bo added.

Twenty minutes later, the radio squawked again.

"Detective Jun, the subject has stopped outside an apartment building on the western outskirts of town. He's approaching a unit on the ground floor."

"Pictures," Bo said.

"Yes. I'm getting them," the sergeant said. "He's knocking. Knocking again. Looks like no one is home. He's pulling an envelope from his pocket. Looking around now. He's sliding the envelope under the door.

180

Walking away now. I need to slide down in the seat to make sure he doesn't see me."

"Good job, sergeant. You can let him leave. Meet us on the main road. We're about ten minutes away."

When they arrived, the sergeant led them back to the apartment.

"How do we do this?" Mason asked. "In America we'd need a search warrant."

"This isn't America, my friend. Let's find the manager."

It took them about five minutes to find the manager, Mr. Chew. He said he hadn't seen Yusof in a couple days but added that he couldn't say for sure that Yusof wasn't home.

"Let's go check," Bo said.

The manager balked. "I don't know if I should do that," he said.

"Listen, you either let us in or face the prospect of impeding an investigation of an international fugitive. Why do you think this gentleman from the American Central Intelligence Agency is here?"

The manager looked startled. He stared briefly at Mason with newfound recognition, then grabbed his master key and led them to Joey's door.

"Unlock it but stay outside. This might be a crime scene and we don't want you contaminating it."

He did as he was told.

"Sergeant, please stay here with Mr. Chew," Bo said. "Mr. Chew," he continued looking at the manager. "Not a word."

The first thing they saw when they opened the door was the red Honda parked against the wall next to the door. Otherwise, it was a tasteful apartment that could easily belong to a professional employee of a major company.

"The kid lives well," Bo said.

On the floor just inside the door was the envelope that Big Willie had left earlier. Mason bent to pick it up, but Bo stopped him.

"Just a minute, Mason." He pulled a small camera from a pocket and took photos of the envelope on the floor. He then turned to snap some establishing photos of the main room of the apartment. He made sure to show the motorcycle. He then pulled two pair of latex gloves from a back pocket and handed a pair to Mason.

"Put these on," he told Mason, as he put the other pair on himself. He then reached down and took the envelope. Mason handed him a knife and Bo carefully slit the envelope open. Inside was a hand-penned note.

Joey,

The police are on to you. A detective came to my shop today asking about you. I said I didn't know you, of course, but this changes everything. You need to get away right now. I know you are probably off with the Jessica woman. Drop that plan and leave as soon as you get this note. And don't contact me again. Sorry my friend. I had hoped this day would never come. Please burn this note in your sink before you leave. But leave quickly.

Willie

Bo placed the note on the dining room table, turned on a light, and photographed it. He then looked at Mason.

"It's only a matter of time," Bo said. "We're going to get this asshole."

"Who's Jessica?" Mason responded.

———————

Joey and Jessica joined John and Melinda near the coral reef they had discussed over dinner the previous night. Joey lathered her back and legs with sunscreen – "the most important part of the day" – and then gave Jessica a short lesson in how to use the mask and snorkel. He practiced with her in shallow water.

"There are really just two things you need to learn to do to enjoy snorkeling," he told her as they sat in shallow water near the beach. "The first thing is that you have to make sure your mask fits snugly on your face. If it doesn't, you're going to be leaking water inside the mask."

He took her mask and put it against her face.

"Breathe in through your nose," he said. She did. He took his hand down and the mask stayed suctioned to her face. "Great! No air leaks here means no water leaks there," he said pointing to the water. He broke the seal and took the mask away.

"The other thing is to take easy, slow, steady breaths," he continued, "in and out of your mouth. The nose doesn't work. That takes a little getting used to, but it's not hard. That gives you so much more control. Even if water gets in the snorkel you can easily blow it out. We're going to practice here in the shallow water, so you can get the hang of it."

He helped her put her mask on, made sure the strap was behind the widest part of the top back of her head. He then showed her how to keep the mouthpiece almost loose in her mouth. "Don't bite it hard," he said. "Just let it sit between your teeth."

He had her float face down in the water and take those slow, easy breaths. She got it quickly. Then, staying in the shallow water, he had her add in slow, rhythmic kicks with her fins. Finally, he told her to dive down just enough to fill her snorkel tube with water. "When you break the surface coming up, give a quick blow of air through the mouthpiece." She did it and squirted water several feet into the air when she surfaced.

"You're ready," he said. "We're going to swim out to where it is deeper. Trust me. I'll be next to you the whole time. Go at your own pace. If you find yourself getting nervous, just stop and stick your head up. The fins will make it easy to keep your head above water. Steady kicks. But you'll do great. You ready?"

"I'm ready."

With that they headed out to the deeper water where John and Melinda already were swimming next to a small inflatable boat.

They spent the better part of the next hour swimming among thousands of brightly colored fish of all shapes and sizes. They swam slowly next to a sea turtle and then another. The entire experience was amazing.

"I'm ready for lunch," John called out. "Me, too," Jessica answered. They pulled the raft onto the beach, took out a picnic basket Bisaam had made for them and went up under the trees for lunch. The four of them sat there on the edge of the beach blanket chatting and eating, then John and Melinda said they were going to explore the beach.

Jessica stretched out and laid her head in Joey's lap. "This is heaven," she said, eyes closed. He played with her hair.

"Hey Joey?" she said.

"Yes?"

"There are a lot of places in Malaysia that I'd like to see."

"There are some great spots. And not just beaches," he responded.

"I was thinking that maybe you could be my personal guide."

He was quiet for a minute and she wondered if she had misread him.

Finally, he spoke. "That sounds like you want to hire me." There was what sounded like hurt in his voice. She sat up abruptly.

"No. Not like that. I want to travel with you. That's what I meant. I feel good around you. Jeez Joey! I feel great around you. Besides, I want more nights like last night."

A broad smile spread across his face and his eyes twinkled.

"Oh. Yeah. I like that idea. I could take you to places around the country that I've been to, then after we've done that, who knows. I wouldn't mind going to Bali."

She stretched back out on the blanket and put her head back in his lap. She looked happy. This was turning into the adventure she had wanted when she left Seattle. And with a young stud, no less.

"When do you want to start?" he asked her.

"Right away. I've seen all of Penang I care to see. When we get back, I'll check out of the Holiday Inn and we can take off."

"Sounds like a plan," he told her.

————

Bo radioed headquarters. He assigned a plainclothes officer in an unmarked car to stake-out the apartment from four to 10 p.m. and another officer to do the day shift the next day. Because of budget cuts, he couldn't assign anyone to after 10 p.m. without approval from the chief himself. He couldn't do that after what he went through the last time he requested overnight OT. Bo told Mason that if he had to go to the chief, he'd have to tell him the full story. They agreed that the odds of Joey rolling in and leaving in the wee hours were small, so they'd risk it.

Before they left, they pulled the manager, Mr. Chew, aside.

"Listen," Bo told him, "not a word of this to anyone. You understand? No one. If you so much as tell one soul, I'll personally see to it that you are prosecuted for aiding and abetting a known criminal."

Mr. Chew said nothing but looked terrified as he nodded his head that he understood.

'What do you think our next step should be?" Bo asked Mason as they drove back toward his hotel.

"I think we go knockin' on the man's door right now," Mason said. "The last thin' that guy wants is to get his fat ass thrown in a Malaysian prison. Let's make it easy for him to roll. An easy way out."

"I'm listening."

"I'm thinkin' we stroll right in. Just you and me. He'll see you and know somethin' is up. I mean, a visit from the chief of homicides twice in one day? He'll try to play it cool, and that's when you show him the envelope. He'll shit a brick. He's a smart guy. He'll see that the gig is up."

"Do we cuff him then?"

"Maybe take 'em out and set them in plain sight. Let him sweat in silence for a bit."

"Yeah, I can then let him know that we're not really interested in his fat ass. If he tells us what we need, we'll walk out the door and he can go on being the worthless piece of shit he is. I'll spell it out for him. Right now, you and I are the only ones who know about the note. The note clearly links him to a serial killer."

"Don't they hang fuckin' murderers in this country?"

"Yeah. Not a lot of due process. Arrested. Quick trial. Guilty verdict. The noose. He'll get the picture. He could be dead this time next year."

"Right as rain, buddy. He'll flip his fat ass so fast it'll feel like a fresh breeze is rushin' in."

185

"So, what do we want from him exactly?"

"Who the Jessica woman is? Where they are? And every little scrap of info he can tell us about Joey that will make it easier to find him."

They drove straight to the tailor shop. It was closed.

"What do you think?" Mason asked. "In the wind?"

"Doesn't make sense. He's got a going business and nothing that he thinks that makes him part of the murders. Here's my guess. Either he's stopped off some place to have a few drinks or he's gone to a safe house he has somewhere to cool his jets. In either case, he'll be back. The question is when."

"Let's grab dinner, then come back to see if he's showed up."

Over dinner, Bo again asked Mason what was going on.

"I've been havin' nightmares. I wake up in a cold sweat and breathin' like I just ran a fuckin' marathon."

"People have nightmares. Although, now that I think about it, I haven't had one in years. Why do you think you're having them?"

"How much do you know about my takin' out General Tho?"

"A little. I know it was off-book. You found out that he ordered the bombing of your place that killed Sylvie. And you took him out. An eye for an eye."

"Well, yeah, but there's more to it than that. I didn't limit my killin' to the general. We packed so much C4 under his table that when I pushed the button it took down the entire fuckin' buildin' and kilt fifty-four innocent people."

"Yeah. I had heard that. Collateral damage."

"Well, yes. I guess. Here's the thing. I've been fine with it for all these years. Really, I've given it little thought. Then about a week ago, I started havin' the visions of individual people and sometimes their families who I kilt with that bomb. It's horrible. The things I see.

"It happens most nights, though it didn't last night. I'm hopin' I'm done with it. I get really nervous before fallin' asleep, so I don't sleep so well and then bam! I have the nightmare and I'm wide awake. Then, unless I stay really busy my mind keeps revisitin' it throughout the day."

"You need to get help, man."

"I know, but I can't right now. Timin' sucks. I gotta finish this case. You know how it is. Single-minded."

Bo asked if Mason thought there were any connection between the case and the nightmares.

"Maybe. They did start when I took the case. I do really get Bob Anderson's pain and need for revenge. I've taken it very personally, you know what I mean. I wanna find this Joey guy and string 'im up by his balls. Maybe my subconscious is forcin' me to deal with what I did. But that sounds so fuckin' touchy-feely. It's embarrassin'."

"This kind of shit happens, man. I bet the two are connected. Maybe if you can figure out how, the nightmares will go away."

"Yeah. Maybe. In the meantime, I need some sleepin' pills. Do I need a prescription here?"

"Afraid so. But I have a friend who's a doctor. I'll call him and see if he'll call you in a prescription."

"Thanks, Bo."

They finished dinner and headed back to the tailor shop. Two hours had passed and he was still not there.

"Goddamnit," Mason cursed. "We should have stayed on 'im."

"Should we put out a BOLO for his car?" Bo asked.

"Let's give it till tomorrow. I don't want us to have to explain all this shit to anyone."

Day 16

Jessica and Joey were up and in the boat with Omar at 10 a.m. to catch the noon ferry back to George Town. Joey had gotten everything he wanted from the Langkawi getaway. Jessica liked him and trusted him enough to travel alone with him. More than that, though. She adored spending time with him. And, he had to admit, he enjoyed her, as well.

The ride back to Penang was faster but felt longer. They'd slept most of the way to Langkawi. The trip back was in the sun and heat of the middle of the day. They spent much of the return trip trying to find and stay in the shade. There was seating below deck, but it was stifling down there. Eventually, they settled into a spot near the stern on the port side of the boat, shielded from the direct rays of the sun. It was bearable.

They napped when they could and took turns walking the deck. They didn't want to leave their spot because someone else would likely take it. And they weren't about to leave their packs unattended.

It was mostly a quiet time. They had plenty of time to plan their tour of Malaysia and just chat.

"There's something I want to tell you," Jessica said. "I was married before."

"Yeah. I picked up on that when you said you hadn't been with a man since your husband. So, you're divorced?"

"No. He died. Had a massive heart attack. Wallace – that was his name, Wallace Jamison – he was only 42."

"I'm sorry," he said, then after a long pause asked, "Were you married long?"

"Six years, but it felt longer." He didn't know how to react to that and she could see it in his face. "We had problems. We were both really focused on our careers. He was a big-time attorney."

She looked at him, debating how much more to say, but she kept talking.

"It was easier for him. He was screwing his secretary. It had been going on for at least two years. Wallace didn't know I knew, though."

"He was cheating on you? That's really hard to believe. You're beautiful, Jessica. Why would he do that?"

"Happiness needs more than looks. I guess he wasn't getting what he needed from me."

"I'm sorry, Jessica. But I don't see how this could have been your fault. He was the one sneaking around. Besides, if he wasn't getting what he needed from you, he wasn't trying very hard. You are. . ." he paused to ask himself if this was okay to say, then decided it was, "You are great in bed." A small smile crossed her face. She was, she thought to herself. Then, he definitely was, too. She could go with this for at least a couple weeks.

They sat quietly for a bit.

"Forty-two is awfully young for a heart attack, isn't it?" he asked.

Jessica told him about Wallace. He had become really fat and a chain smoker. When they met a decade before, he had taken better care of himself. He had never been skinny, but there is a huge difference between being a little overweight and being rotund. He had become rotund.

The smoking seemed to grow with Wallace's waistline. It was a disgusting habit, but as Wallace's career took off, he seemed to crave the nicotine.

"No doubt that he was addicted to it," she said. "As a nurse, I knew how that could happen, but it didn't make his doing it any easier to take. God, he reeked of cigarette smoke the last couple years. Disgusting."

She said she had stopped being sexually attracted to him a few years back.

"That's probably what drove him to her," she confessed.

"Hey, he made choices that drove you away," Joey said, showing the forced empathy that psychopaths can gin up when the occasion calls for it. "Don't take it on yourself."

She knew he was right, but it was hard to let go that had she been a better wife that maybe Wallace wouldn't have strayed. Then, and perhaps this was the new adventurous Jessica thinking, what difference would that have made? As unhappy in her marriage as she had become, she would never have cheated on him. Why hadn't she just left him?

That was, she knew now, the old Jessica. The new Jessica was far more willing to take risks.

They sat there in silence for a minute.

"Still, just forty-two," Joey said.

"Yeah. I buried him about eight months ago. It's been a strange time since."

"In what way?"

"So many. I knew I was supposed to feel remorse, but I really didn't. His death did what I had been unwilling to do. He was gone from my life. One minute he was part of it and the next not. But I no longer had to live with his lying and cheating. It was like a great weight was lifted."

"I can understand that."

"And you know what made it even better?"

"What?"

"His secretary, Judy – the one he was having the affair with – she was left high and dry. He had been giving that bitch jewelry and all kinds of nice gifts. He was paying for her apartment and taking her on so called business trips. That gravy train ended. She got nothing. I got it all. Every last dime."

"It was all I could do not to rub her nose in it," Jessica continued. "At the funeral, she was dressed in black and all crying and stuff. I figured most of her tears was from all the goodies that ended like that," she said, snapping her fingers. "And then there I was. Well provided for. I mean, who names their mistress in their will? I had to act somber on the outside, but inside I was – oh God, this is going to sound awful of me – but on the inside I was dancing."

They sat in silence for a few more minutes. Joey's mind darted around. He heard her, of course, when she said that Wallace had provided for her. A part of him wondered just how much Wallace had left her. But another part of him was truly moved by her story and her willingness to share it with him. How does someone share a secret that big, he wondered?

"Thank you for telling me about Wallace," Joey said finally.

"It just felt like I needed to tell you. I'm not sure why. I'm glad I did, though." She snuggled up to him and before long was napping.

They were about an hour from Penang when Jessica woke up.

"You're still here," she said with a smile.

He hugged her a little tighter. "I'm not going anywhere without you."

"Speaking of which, any thoughts on our next stop?"

"I was thinking we might take in the Cameron Highlands first," Joey said. "You up for that?"

"You're the captain of this expedition. I go where you go. What are the Cameron Highlands?"

"I think you'll like it. Totally different experience than the beach. It's about a mile above sea level so it's a lot cooler, but it also gets a lot of rain. It's beautiful up there. Good hiking. Lot of scenic vistas that match your green eyes."

The ferry docked a little after seven o'clock. Jessica suggested they head back to the Holiday Inn for a hot bath and a night in a nice room. Joey pulled her closer and said it was a great plan. They had a leisurely dinner in the hotel dining room before heading up to her room. She started a bath.

"Listen, Jess, I'm going to run over to my place and pack for being away for a while," he said through the bathroom door.

She noticed that he called her Jess, not Jessica. Her dad calls her Jess

191

THE NEXT BEST THING

and it always makes her feel special. Joey had heard Melinda call her that and she seemed to like it, but he wasn't sure why. He decided on the crossing that he'd work it in and see how she reacted.

It was about ten-thirty when he arrived at his apartment. He walked in and was surprised to find the light on over his dining table. He was pretty sure he had turned it off. He looked around. Everything seemed the same, otherwise. But he couldn't shake the feeling that someone had been in his apartment.

It didn't take him long to pack. The last thing he did before leaving was to open a small safe he had secreted away in his closet. He removed twenty hundred-dollar bills, two hundred Malaysian ringgits and his Joseph Thomas Jackson passport and credit card. He debated bringing the drivers' license. He didn't think he'd need it, so left it. He stuck the ringgits in his pocket then added everything else to a money belt that he had taken from one of the girls. For a moment he tried to recall which one but couldn't.

He took an additional three hundred dollars from the safe before locking it and securing it out of sight back in the closet. He walked to the kitchen where he had a drawer with paper and envelopes. He pulled a pen, a sheet of paper and an envelope, moved to the table and wrote a note to Mr. Chew telling him that he was taking a trip. The envelope, he wrote, contained the rent for the next two months. He signed it Yusof Zaina, Apartment 3.

Mr. Chew was in Apartment 7. Joey knocked on the door and Mr. Chew answered. He looked startled. His eyes darted around, looking up and down the street. He was frightened, no question. Joey had never seen him this way. He handed the manager the envelope.

"I didn't know if I'd catch you, so I wrote you a note," Joey said. Again he noticed that Mr. Chew looked increasingly nervous and was taking shallow breaths. "You okay? You don't look well."

"I fine," Mr. Chew said. "Everything fine."

"Okay. Well, I'm going to be gone a couple months. The envelope contains my rent for while I'm away."

"Okay. Fine. Goodbye." Mr. Chew closed the door.

That was weird, Joey thought, and left.

Inside his apartment, Mr. Chew picked up the card Bo had given him from his kitchen counter. He debated if he should call the policeman, then remembered the CIA was involved. His hand was shaking as he dialed the number on the card. The front desk rang Detective Jun's phone. No answer.

After a half-dozen rings, the operator came back on the line. "Detective Jun is gone for the day. Can I take a message?"

"Yes. Yes. Important. Tell him that Yusof Zaina come home tonight but said he is leaving on a trip. Detective Jun will want to know right away, I think. Right away." He left his contact details and hung up.

Five minutes later, Chew's phone rang.

"Chew? Detective Jun here. He's there?"

"No. He left. Was here a little bit. Where your man? I look but not see him anywhere."

"No one there overnight. Listen, are you sure he left?"

"He walk away. I saw him."

"Did he say where he was going?"

"No. He said he was going to be away. He paid me rent for next two months."

"I'm on my way."

Bo called Mason.

"I'll be out front in five minutes," Bo said. "Be there."

They put the flasher on the roof and sped to Batu Ferringhi. Bo had mobilized the force at the small Batu Ferringhi precinct. Three cars of uniformed officers were already at the apartments when Bo and Mason rolled up. They went straight to Chew. He let them back in Joey's apartment.

An hour had passed since Joey stood in Mr. Chew's doorway.

"Fuck! Fuck! Fuck! He's long gone," Mason said in a muffled yell. "If he were leavin' in the mornin', he'd stayed here for the night."

"We need to put people on the bus and train stations. Airport, too.

He didn't take his motorcycle, so he's going to need a way to get out of town."

Bo went to his car to radio headquarters. They needed all available officers at the terminals with Joey's description.

Mason started going through everything. Soon, Bo returned and joined him. They didn't know what they were looking for. Anything that would shed more light on who he was, where he was going and maybe what he was up to. Clearly, he was up to something new.

The living room and kitchen turned up nothing. Mason moved to the bedroom. He flipped the mattress off the bed, then turned the box springs over. Nothing. The nightstand and the dresser also revealed nothing. He opened the closet doors and started pulling stuff out. A new suit still in the bag with the Chirathivat name on it. Other new items, too. Even a new pair of wingtips shoes.

When the closet was nearly empty, Mason noticed what might be a false wall to the far left. He studied it closely and saw how to open it. Inside was a lockbox portable safe. Mason yanked it out and took it to the dining table.

"Bo," he called. "A lockbox."

Bo joined him and they discussed how to open it.

"I bet I can do it with a crowbar," Bo said. "Got one in the car."

He dashed out and was back in a minute. It took some prying, but they had it open in a minute. Inside was a stack of hundred-dollar bills with a rubber band around them, the registration for the Honda and a North Carolina driver's license issued to Joseph T. Jackson with an address in Bentonville, NC. Like driver's licenses everywhere, it included a nice color photo.

"I'll be damned," Bo said. "There's our guy."

"Sure as shit," Mason said, "but where the hell is he goin'?"

Little did they know that he had just showered less than a half mile away. At that moment, Joey was wrapped in a white towel, having just stepped from the shower in room twelve-thirty-one of the Holiday Inn. He approached the room's queen size bed. Jessica, just Jess now, was lying there with her red hair spread across the pillow. She held out her arms and pulled him to her.

After they made love, Jess quickly fell asleep. Joey's mind, though, kept going back to his strange encounter with Mr. Chew. He and the manager had a fun, easy-going relationship. Joey pondered what might have caused the man to be so spooked. And why was he looking up and down the street so anxiously? What had Mr. Chew gotten himself mixed up in? Or, did it have something to do with Joey himself? No, Joey told himself. Only he and Big Willie knew his story. Chew had somehow gotten himself in a jam. Too bad for him, Joey thought. He liked Chew. Joey was finally able to roll over and snuggle up to Jess. Soon, he, too, was sleeping.

Day 17

J oey and Jess were up early. They had a big, American-style breakfast of steak, scrambled eggs, hash browns and toast with coffee in the hotel restaurant. Over breakfast, Jess suggested that they rent a car.

"I don't think I can," he told her. "My driver's license is expired. I didn't even bring it."

"I can do it," she told him, "We can put it on one of my cards. And I can do the driving. Or we can both drive, as long as you don't get pulled over for speeding or anything."

He gave her a smirky grin.

After breakfast, Jess arranged to get a Toyota coupe from Hertz through the concierge desk. When asked how long she would need the car, she looked to Joey. "How long?"

"I don't know. I paid my rent two months in advance last night."

She turned back to the concierge. "Two months."

The concierge said someone from Hertz would be there with the car in about thirty minutes. They'd have to go back to the Hertz office to finish the paperwork and pay, but it shouldn't take long.

Jess then stopped at the front desk and said she would be checking out within the hour and would they please prepare her bill. They returned to the room and finished packing.

It did go quickly at Hertz. By ten o'clock, Jess was driving across the new bridge toward the mainland. They had stopped at a market for snacks and bottles of water. The drive to Cameron Highlands would take about five or six hours. Jess drove while Joey fished through his backpack for cassette tapes.

"Okay. We have some choices here," Joey said. "If I'd known we were driving I'd have brought more. Let's see, I have Madonna, U2, Huey Lewis, Prince, Genesis, oh yeah, some Smokey Robinson, Ben E. King. What are you in the mood for?"

"You came prepared. How about a little soul."

"Ben E. King it is. *Stand by Me.*" He loaded the cassette into the player in the car's dashboard and they sang along with the master.

When the night has come
And the land is dark
And the moon is the only light we'll see
No I won't be afraid, no I won't be afraid
Just as long as you stand, stand by me

"I loved that movie," Joey said, as Jess drove on. Next up, *Save the Last Dance for Me*, had them both crooning the chorus. *So darlin, save the last dance for me.*

————————

It had been another bad night for Mason. He was up for about two hours after his latest nightmare. This time it was of the husband of the young girl with the baby. The unsettling thing about this dream was that, for the first time, it didn't start at the scene of the bombing. He knew, though, the connection.

He was in a small room somewhere. There were pictures of the man, the woman and baby on the walls. The man was sobbing uncontrollably, then he raised a pistol to his head. Mason's mind watched as the man pulled the trigger and blew the top of his head away.

Mason awoke to overwhelming grief. He felt dead inside but knew that feeling dead inside was not the same as being dead. If he could just sleep through it. He never remembered dreams. But there was no sleeping though these night terrors.

God, he hoped Bo's doctor friend would come through today with the sleeping pills and that they would knock him out. He knew that was a big if.

But he was on a case, so by eight in the morning he was up faxing copies of the driver's license and note to Boonsri and told her he'd check in later in the day. He also put together a more detailed fax to Fitz.

Fitz,

We now have a full American-sounding name for Joey to go with his Malaysian birth name. I also have an address in Bentonville, NC on what I'm sure is a fake driver's license. The address might be as bogus as the license, but it might actually be the address for Pastor Johnny. I'm betting that you find out that Pastor Johnny's last name is Jackson.

I'd like for you to see if you can find the pastor based on this information. It aligns with the last info I sent you about him being in North Carolina. Here's the info (copy of driver's license attached).

Joseph Thomas Jackson
Rural Route 3, Box 17
Bentonville, NC 27524

DOB: 3/15/1961
5' 9"; 175 lbs
Brown hair; brown eyes

If you find the pastor, find out the last time they spoke or even exchanged letters. Get as much as you can about Joey's background. It's your call how much you want to share with him.

I'm pretty much in my room at the Straits Hotel in George Town today. We don't know where he is. Hopefully, if we can find his fence again, he'll have more info. Try to call me when you get this fax. I'd like to bring you up to speed. I'm getting ready to call Bob Anderson for my weekly check-in.

Mason

Mason thought through his upcoming chat with Amanda's dad. He had a lot of good news to provide, but also wondered how he would tell him about the current – current what? Clusterfuck? Situation. There was nothing he could do today except wait. He didn't want to say that. At the designated time, Mason picked up the phone in his room and called Bob in Tampa.

"Hi Mason," Bob answered. "You know it is hard for me to get through the last day when I know you're going to call with an update that night."

"I bet it is," Mason said.

"So, what's new with the case? Are you closer to finding that motherfucker?"

"Yes, we are." Mason gave Bob everything they had learned in the past day or two. They now know who he is and where he lives. They have a current photo of Joey and last night came within an hour of catching him.

"Holy fuck!" Bob said. "That's incredible. Could today be the day?"

"Fat chance. As great as all that is," Mason continued, "today is a day for sittin' on our keisters and hopin' for a break. It could come from one of two places. One of Bo's officers might catch him at a terminal Joey would use to get out of town. To be honest with you, I'm not holdin' much hope for that outcome. Besides, if that happens, you and I won't be able to personally make him pay the price for what he did to your sweet girl. If I had my druthers, I'd like for us to find the Thai who slid the note under the door."

"You think that Thai guy knows where Joey's going?"

"He might. But I'd bet dollars to donuts that he knows who this Jessica woman is. If we find her, I bet we find him."

"What are the odds?"

"I don't like to do that, Bob. These kinds of investigations can be so fuckin' unpredictable. Like when I was havin' lunch in a random restaurant and the waiter takes a gander over my shoulder and recognizes Amanda's picture. I mean, really. What were the odds of that happenin'?"

"Trust me, Bob," Mason continued. "We will find this guy. It might seem slow as molasses. It could take a few days or it might take weeks. But we know too much about him now. Besides, he left his prized motorcycle and a few thousand dollars in his apartment. You know he'll be back for the bike and the money."

Mason said he would call the same time next week. Before they disconnected, Bob told him how much he appreciated what Mason was doing.

"I know I'm paying you for this work," Bob said. "I can tell, though, that it's personal for you. I just want you to know I appreciate it."

They hung up.

It is personal for me, Mason thought, as he lay back across his bed. Why is that, he wondered. Was it all related to Sylvie?

The nightmares were screwing him up and they started after he took this job. Mason didn't believe in coincidence. That means, he reasoned, that the two events – the case and the nightmares – were likely related. But how?

He thought back to Sylvie's death. It had changed the trajectory of his life forever. The senseless brutality of her death pushed him to a moment of extreme revenge. He knew how compelling the need for payback could be. He understood Bob's motivation as only someone who had been there himself could.

But with these gruesome flashbacks in his dreams, he was questioning for the first time if he had done the right thing those many years ago. Now he was on a course for revenge again. Not his own revenge. But a revenge that he had bought into, lock, stock and barrel. Did hearing the story of Amanda's murder and seeing the bloody crime scene photos of Amanda prompt the nightmares? Was his subconscious mounting an attack on the whole notion of revenge?

Mason had learned in the past week that revenge is only sweet in the moment. In that instant, revenge plants a seed of regret. That seed took years to blossom in his case. How could he now not regret what he had done to avenge sweet Sylvie? How this might play out for Bob, though, escaped him. What he had figured out was that his pursuit of Joey had somehow become a stage for his own demons.

Mason hated thinking about it.

If he were to be honest with himself, though, Mason's deepest agony was no longer on Sylvie not being in his life. Yes, that still hurt. He felt – would always feel – cheated. If he thought about it, a sadness would sweep over him.

No, the deeper pain today was on how he had responded to her death. Sylvie no longer graced his thoughts and the few dreams he remembered. She had been pushed aside by the lingering, violent images of others. When his sleeping mind would wander there now, it served up the faces of the innocent victims of his extreme moment of payback.

Could he live with those images? It was getting hard.

He knew the one that troubled him the most was the young woman and her baby. Their deaths were so senseless. His heart ached to think about how, with no thought whatsoever, he snatched them from life. He did that. Not the general. Him.

He recounted the scene for the hundredth time. When he was about to detonate the bomb, he stood so that the general could see him. He held the detonator in his right hand, raising it to get the general's attention. But raising his hand also caught the woman's attention. She was looking directly at him the instant the explosives went off. She knew. Her lost hopes were written all over her face. And the worst part of all was the baby strapped to her back.

Everything about that day now weighed on him. He didn't have an issue with taking life on the battlefield. A soldier knows when they become a soldier that death might be part of the deal. His own and his enemies. What kept him awake at night or snatched him violently from sleep was that he had killed so many innocents that day.

In his gut, Mason was sure that his fervent quest to find Amanda's killer was caught up somehow in his own story. He didn't know how. But he just knew it was true. And he didn't have a clue whether he would ever again find peace.

Day 18

The phone on the nightstand next to Mason's bed rang. The clock said it was 10:15 in the morning. He couldn't sleep the night before. Yet another flashback to Sam Neua. It had been fourteen years. Would the flashbacks ever end? The last time he looked at the clock it had said 4:10 a.m.

"Hello," he mumbled into the receiver.

"We found Big Willie's car. It's parked outside a house in a residential neighborhood on the southeast end of town. I dispatched one of my guys to watch it. I'm going to go knock on the door. Want to come with me?"

He was instantly awake and swung his legs off the side of the bed. "Like white on rice," Mason said, already standing. "Wouldn't miss it."

Forty-five minutes later they climbed into the back seat of an unmarked car parked down the block from Big Willie's Mercedes. No movement, Sergeant Aziz reported. Another team of four officers pulled up and parked at the other end of the street. Bo took the radio and gave instructions. Two were to go to the back of the house. The other two were to flank the property on the street out front. Bo, Mason and Sergeant Aziz, the plainclothes officer, would approach the door.

They waited for the other cops to get into position, then walked up the front steps to the ornate door. Bo knocked loudly. All three men drew their weapons.

"Willie Chirathivat. This is Detective Jun. The house is surrounded. Open the front door and come out now."

They could hear movement inside and a muffled "Coming."

The door opened to reveal Big Willie, still in pajamas and a bathrobe. "What can I do for you, Detective Jun?"

"We need to talk with you about the murder of Mary Higgins."

Willie glanced over to Mason, who had not seen before. An American. He didn't know what that might mean.

"Certainly," Big Willie said. "Please come in. Would you like some coffee or tea?"

Mason looked at Bo and shrugged. Bo told Aziz to let the others know to hold their positions and for Aziz to stand sentry outside the front door.

They followed Big Willie into a grand drawing room that might have been bigger than Mason's entire apartment in Bangkok. The furnishing looked to be antique French provincial. Several pieces of original art adorned the walls, including one piece that Mason was almost certain was an original Van Gogh. Big Willie led them to a seating area off to one side of the room.

"I've made a pot of coffee," Big Willie said. Mason said he would take a cup with cream. Bo passed.

"Rudy," Big Willie called out. A man, dressed in a crisply ironed white shirt and black slacks, appeared almost instantly in the passage to the room. "Please bring coffee and cream for my American friend and myself." Rudy nodded and left.

"Anyone else here?" Bo asked Big Willie.

"No. Just my assistant and me."

"What's the story with this place? It doesn't show up on any list of properties you own."

"Belongs to a friend who's away at the moment. London, I believe."

Rudy returned with a silver tray with two fine china cups of coffee and a small carafe of cream. He offered the tray to Mason first, who chose one of the cups, then added cream and stirred the mixture. Rudy then did the same with Big Willie.

"That will be all, Rudy. Thank you."

"We tailed you three days ago to Yusof Zaina's apartment in Batu

Ferringhi. We have a photo of you sticking an envelope under his door." The Thai showed no emotion. "After you left, we entered the apartment, found your note and read it. At the very least, we can charge you with aiding and abetting. I suspect it will be easy to link you to Mary Higgins passport, traveler's checks and credit cards. Probably Amanda Anderson's, as well, and perhaps five other murdered young American women over the past three years."

Big Willie sat silently, looking away from the men. He chewed subtly on the inside of his left cheek. He inhaled deeply, then sipped his coffee.

"When we do that," Bo continued, "you could be charged along with Zaina in the murder of seven women. The penalty for that, as I'm sure you know, is death by hanging."

Silence filled the room. But Bo wasn't done.

"The evidence against you has not yet been cataloged," Bo said. Big Willie immediately turned his head to look at the detective. He knew immediately what this meant. The detective might be about to offer him a way out. Finally, he spoke.

"Detective Jun. Please tell me what you are suggesting."

"What I'm suggesting, you fat piece of shit, is that you help us find Zaina. If you do, my friend here and I can make your note disappear. I can limit your exposure to trafficking in stolen items. You might even be able to bribe your way out of jail time. But this is a one-time, right-now offer. Otherwise, I will haul your fat ass down to the station and lock you away."

The Thai looked at Bo, then over to Mason. Big Willie led a lonely life. Joey was more like family to him than anyone else. He had taken a young Joey under his wing years before and guided him. Yes, he had profited off Joey. But it was never about the money. Besides, Big Willie could make more on one piece of stolen art than he'd ever made off Joey.

He mind raced back to the first day he and Joey had met in the restaurant. He liked Joey from the start, but he also had warned him. The number one rule was never to lead the police to Big Willie. The consequences, he had told the young man, would be dire for him. And now, here Big Willie found himself in exactly that predicament. He was sitting across from a homicide detective and an unnamed American whose eyes revealed a willingness to do whatever was needed.

"How can I help you, detective?"

It was Mason's turn to speak.

"Who is Jessica?"

Big Willie revealed Joey's plan. All of it. Jessica – no, he didn't know her last name – was going to be Joey's last victim. He was going to woo her romantically and win her trust. The plan was to have her willingly transfer fifty thousand dollars to a company Joey had established in Singapore.

"Why fifty thousand?" Mason asked.

The money, Big Willie said, was how much Joey needed to build a bungalow village for backpackers, most likely on Langkawi. He planned to call it Bungalow Paradise. He'd spend the rest of his life as a legitimate businessman. Once he had the money, Big Willie continued, he'd kill her in a way that would look like an accident. Before he did that, though, he'd take the money from the business account and close the bank account.

Mason asked how Joey would ever convince her to give him that kind of money.

"Women love him," Big Willie said. The Thai told the men how Joey had selected her then spent a few days showing her around Penang, gaining more of her trust every day.

"He won her trust enough to suggest a brief getaway to Langkawi," Big Willie continued. "His plan was for them to become lovers on that trip. He wanted her to be open to him showing her around Malaysia. I haven't seen him since before they headed for Langkawi. He told me before he left that if everything went as he hoped, he wouldn't see me till it was done. He planned for the Langkawi trip to be just a couple days. I imagine they're back. Maybe at her hotel?"

"What hotel?" Mason asked.

"The Holiday Inn. It's about a kilometer or so from his place. He met her in the beachside café there."

Mason asked Big Willie to describe Jessica.

"I never met her."

"I'm sure Joey told you about her. Why did he think she'd have that kind of money to just give him?"

"She was older. In her thirties. That was part of the plan – an older woman. He said she had a very good job back in the States. I think Joey said she was some kind of nurse."

"Nurses don't make a whole heap of money," Mason interjected.

"Apparently, she did. She was a special kind of nurse. What was it? Oh, yes, she was a surgical nurse. Joey said she insisted on paying for her share of everything when they were sightseeing. He told me that she said she could afford it."

"What did Joey tell you about her how she looked? Describe her."

"Again, I never saw her, but he did talk a little about how she looks. She has red hair. Pale complexion. Even some freckles. Joey said she was – how did he put it – easy on the eyes. Knowing Joey, that probably means she's quite a pretty girl."

"How tall?"

"A little shorter than him."

"And that would be. . ."

"He's about five-ten."

Bo said the information was a good start.

"Where are they going?" Bo asked.

"I don't know, but Joey has been to beaches and islands all over the country over the past few years. They could be heading to any of them. I suspect he'll let her choose."

Bo seemed to be satisfied with what he had heard. He caught Mason's eye and gave him a shrug and got a nod back. Bo and Mason stood, followed by Big Willie.

"We're good for now," Bo said. "But let me make something very clear." He took a step toward the Thai and used his finger to tap on the man's chest to emphasize what he was saying.

"If you try to run, our deal is off. And my friend here," he motioned to Mason, "is a former CIA operative who works outside the law." He paused for effect. "Outside the law," he repeated.

"It took him just two weeks to find Joey starting with nothing. If you think you can hide from him, you're fucking crazy. He will track you down and mete out whatever justice he thinks you deserve. Do you understand what I'm telling you?"

"I understand," Big Willie said, looking back at Mason.

As they left, Bo told the officer to keep the lookout on Big Willie and to follow him if he left the house.

Bo and Mason climbed into Bo's car.

"You think he's still there or already high-tailed it out of town?" Mason asked as they headed toward the Holiday Inn.

"He doesn't know we're on to him yet, so maybe," Bo said. "If they've left, though, we have the main ways out of town covered and they haven't turned up so far. Maybe we'll be lucky."

The drive to Batu Ferringhi took longer than usual because of heavy afternoon traffic. They drove up to the driveway in front of the lobby. A valet rushed out to take the car, but Bo flashed his badge. "Leave it." The valet bowed his head slightly and backed away.

Inside, they walked to the front desk. Bo showed his badge again. "We need the manager," he said.

One minute later, an older man, wearing an impeccable light grey two-piece suit, a starched white shirt and a blue and gold striped tie, approached them. His posture was ramrod straight and he held his head in a way that he appeared to be looking down at those around him.

"Hello gentlemen. I'm Arnold Hoffman. I'm the manager of this property. How might I help you?"

Bo filled him in on why they were there. Hoffman paused briefly to consider the request, then led them back to the front desk.

"Daniel, do we have a guest, an American woman with red hair, first name is Jessica?"

"She and her friend checked out yesterday, sir," Daniel said.

Bo picked up the interview.

"Show me her registration."

The clerk looked to the manager who nodded yes. A new computer sat on the counter of the registration desk. Daniel stepped to it and entered some information and waited as her reservation appeared on the screen.

"Yes, here it is. Jessica Stone."

Bo asked Daniel if he could print it out for them. Daniel did so.

"Thank you kindly, Daniel. You said they," Mason said. "Who was she with?"

"A young man. He might have been Malaysian, but I don't think so."

Bo pulled out a grainy enlarged copy of Joey's driver's license photo and showed it to the clerk.

"Yes. That's him."

"When did they leave?" Mason asked.

"About 10 a.m.," Daniel answered.

"Damn it! They skedaddled more than a day ago! You catch where they were headin'?"

"No."

"Would your man out front have flagged 'em a taxi?"

"I think they had a car."

"What?"

"Hertz. I overheard her arranging it through the concierge."

"Does the hotel have record of that?" Bo asked.

"No. We just connect the guest with Hertz."

Hertz had an office nearby to serve the Batu Ferringhi hotels. Bo and Mason took printouts of Jessica Stone's reservation. It included her passport data and the credit card she charged everything to. They then drove straight to the Hertz office. A man and a young woman were working the counter. Bo moved past two couples waiting in line to the counter. He flashed his badge.

"I need you to pull up some information for me," Bo said.

"I'll do it as soon as I finish with this customer," the young woman said with a smile.

"You'll do it right now," Bo said firmly.

The clerk looked at him as if he were being incredibly rude.

"Two minutes," she said, "while I finish up this gentleman's paper-work."

"Now," Bo insisted.

The clerk turned to the customer.

"I'm so sorry. I have to take care of this," she paused and stared at Bo, "police officer."

"What do you need?" she asked Bo.

"Yesterday morning, this office delivered a car to a Jessica Stone at the Holiday Inn. I need all the details of that rental."

The clerk walked over to a stack of papers and thumbed through them. She pulled one from the stack.

"Here we are."

Bo took the form from the clerk and glanced over it.

"Two months?" he asked incredulously.

"That's what it says."

"She wants the car for two months. Is that unusual?"

"Yes, but it happens. Usually means the customer is going to tour the country."

"She would have had to put this on a credit card. Do you have her credit card form?" Bo asked.

The clerk pulled it out and handed it to him.

"Her driver's license?"

"Last page."

"Make me a Xerox of all this," he told her, handing back the reservation form, her license and the credit card receipt.

She hesitated. "Now," he insisted.

Back in the car, Bo radioed in to pull all the officers from the terminals. That had been a waste of manpower. As he drove, Mason read through the info about Jessica Stone.

"She lookin' good in her driver's license photo," Mason said, holding the black and white photocopy over for Bo to look at. "How often does that happen? Never."

Mason summarized the info for Bo. Jessica Stone had a Seattle address, either an apartment or a condo since it listed a unit number. She was five feet seven inches tall and weighed one hundred and thirty pounds. Red hair and green eyes. Date of birth was March 18, 1954 in Seattle. That made her thirty-three years old.

"She charged the car rental to an American Express gold card," Mason said. "That tells us she's probably not hurtin' for money. She put the hotel bill on a Mastercard."

"Drop me at my hotel," Mason continued. "I'll fax this stuff to Fitz so he can get to work on it first thing in the mornin'. He'll be able to get us a better photo from her passport. Maybe he can get American Express to track her charges when he tells them she is unknowingly travelin' with a serial killer. Same with Mastercard. We'll be able to chart their movements by her charges."

"The problem, my friend, is that you'll always be a couple days or more behind them."

"I know," Mason said, "but I bet we'll see a pattern. If she makes a charge in a town with a ferry to an island, we put two and two together and figure out where they're headin'. Islands are good for several days. Maybe even a week or more. It's our best shot at catchin' up with 'em."

"I just hope there's time," Bo said. "He's going to kill that woman, Mason. It's only a question of when."

Mason was flagged by the front desk when he entered the hotel.

"There is a fax for you, Mr. Ray," the desk clerk said, handing Mason an envelope with the fax inside. Mason opened it as he headed to the elevator. It was from Fitz.

Mason,

We found the pastor in Bentonville. The address on the driver's license was indeed bogus, but it seems everyone in Bentonville knows Pastor Johnny. I

spoke with him briefly by phone and will interview him in-person tomorrow.
I'll try to call you after I meet with him.

   Fitz

Back in his room, Mason wrote new faxes to Boonsri and Fitz. He
was glad Fitz had found the pastor but now wished Fitz could focus
on Jessica Stone and the credit card tracking. He wasn't sure what, if
anything, of value could now be gained from Pastor Johnny.

   Fitz,

There is new vital info that requires your focus. Maybe you can delay the
pastor, if you haven't already left. I can't believe I don't have your home
phone number. I don't even know if you live in the District or one of the
adjoining states.

We know his next victim and his plan. Her name is Jessica Stone. A
surgical nurse from Seattle. I need her photo off her passport. We have a
Xerox copy of a Xerox copy.

Joey intends for Jessica Stone to be his last victim, so he's going big. He
plans to charm her over time until she's willing to invest fifty thousand
dollars in a business venture of his. Once the money is moved, he's going to
kill her in a way that looks like an accident.

Bo and I got these details from his fence, who rolled on him to avoid murder
charges. They have the death penalty here and aren't reluctant to use it. Bo,
by the way, hasn't told anyone about Joey being a serial killer of American
girls. I knew we could trust him.

You might have to get one of your friends at the Bureau to help for what we
need next. To catch up with Joey, I need American Express and Mastercard
to let us know whenever anything is posted to Jessica's cards. They're driving,
so there will be gas charges, for sure. Bo and I both think they are likely to
stay in hotels that are notches above what Joey is used to. Likely charges
there, too.

The card companies might balk about how urgently we need the info. They
need to know that a young woman is traveling with a serial killer but doesn't
know it. Unless we can catch up with them, she will surely die. If that
happens and they haven't been cooperating, it will fall on their shoulders for

not helping.

We should also start monitoring her bank accounts. We don't know where she banks, but I'm sure someone in the Hoover Building can get that info pretty quickly. Someone high up at her bank should flag her accounts. They need to call you the moment, day or night, that a big wire transfer is attempted.

Send me your goddamn home phone number.

Mason

He called down to the front desk. Where, he asked, could he get a road map for all of Malaysia? The front desk connected him with the gift shop. They had one that unfolded into a three-foot square. The gift shop agreed to send one up to his room along with a pack of Post-It notes and a yellow highlighter.

When the map arrived, Mason found a place on one wall where it would fit. He took a roll of tape from the desk in his room and used it to adhere the map to the wall. He sat opposite the map and studied it. Joey and Jessica, he figured, most likely went to one of two places.

They might have headed east. The east coast facing the South China Sea was known for its beautiful beaches. On the other hand, they might have headed south to Pangkor Island, the only other real beach destination on the west coast.

Mason placed Post-Its on each beach where Joey had killed girls before. Would he take Jessica to one of them? Why not, he reasoned? Little risk for him there now. Of the locations, Lumut, the jumping off spot for Pangkor was the closest. That's where Joey killed Sally Simpson. He and Ms. Stone could be there in four or five hours and they left yesterday.

Kota Bharu would be a little longer drive. He studied the map and guessed six or seven hours. From there, it is a short drive down the coast to Kuala Besut, where you catch the ferry to the Perhentian Islands. Joey killed his first victim in Kuala Besut, a marine biology graduate student named Annie Smith.

Mason felt the sudden urge for a guidebook. He knew little about the places on the map. How might Joey choose where to take her? He dashed out in search of a bookstore. An hour later, he was back in his room with three paperback books. First was *South-East Asia on a Shoestring*, the Lonely Planet guide. The bookstore clerk said it was most popular guidebook among backpackers. He also picked up one called the *South-East Asia Handbook*, as well as a *Fodor's Guide to Malaysia*. He guessed that Ms. Stone might be more of a Fodor woman than a Lonely Planet one.

If Mason left right now, he could be at either location by evening. But, if he chose wrong, he would be farther away from them. And, he really wanted to speak with Fitz. That would be easier from here.

Then he got an idea. There was a chance that Fitz had given Bob his home number. One of those "call me anytime" things people do hoping the person never really calls them. He looked at the clock. It was still too early to make the call. He'd do it at 6 p.m. That would be 6 a.m. in Tampa. If Bob had Fitz's number, Mason might then reach Fitz before he headed out on the long drive to meet with Pastor Johnny.

Mason made the call at six. A groggy Bob Anderson answered.

"Mason, what's up?" Then he realized that the unusual call might be important, so he sat upright quickly in bed and forced himself awake. "News?"

"I'm terribly sorry to have called you so early, but I'm hopin' you have something that I need."

"It's fine. Sure. What do you need?"

"Did Fitz give you his home phone number, by any chance? I need to call him ASAP."

"Give me a minute to see if he wrote it on his card. Where did I put the card? Hmmm. Of shit! It's at the office."

"It was a long shot. Don't pay it any mind."

"Listen, I'm heading into the office a little early today. I'll check first thing and let you know. Probably seven-thirty or eight. Will that work for you?"

"Sure." He gave Bob the hotel number and his room number. He added he would wait for Bob's call. "Call me either way."

Bob called at 7:35 a.m. "I have it. He wrote a number on the back. Are you ready?"

Bob read off the phone number. Mason thanked him and hung up. Then he put through the international call to what should be Fitz' home number. Except it wasn't. It was a messaging service for senior State Department employees. He stressed to the operator that it was urgent and to please reach out to Fitz. Don't wait for him to call in. She told Mason that she would ping his pager. If he were near a phone, he'd likely call in within minutes.

Mason thanked her, then waited. He was about to give up at eight-thirty and grab some dinner when the phone rang.

"Hi Mason. Sorry it took a while to call you back. I'm on the road. What's so urgent?"

Mason told Fitz everything he had put in the fax.

"Jesus. I'll call the pastor and tell him I have to reschedule. I can be back in the office ten-thirty or eleven. I'll get right on it. In fact, I'll call Bill Spears at the Bureau right now. He's the Bureau liaison for Southeast Asia. He usually can make things happen. I'll either call or fax you an update at the end of the day. I'll also have Jonathan grab her passport photo and get it to you by courier tomorrow, if possible. Next day at the latest."

"Call me. I'll still stayin' at the Straits Hotel."

———————

Joey and Jess – that's what he was calling her now - had arrived at Tanah Rata in the Cameron Highlands late the afternoon before. They had stopped to enjoy a leisurely lunch in Ipoh, the gateway to the highlands. Mountains loomed on the horizon east of Ipoh. Indeed, the two-hour drive from Ipoh to Tanah Rata climbs, climbs and climbs. Where Ipoh is just seventy feet above sea level, the fifty-five miles between the two cities saw an elevation gain of nearly five-thousand feet.

Some people called Ipoh the city of millionaires because of all the fortunes that had been made nearby mining tin. It also had a seedier persona. Every street seemed to offer a strip club or a massage parlor – or both.

But all that money gave the city another asset. It offered an array of fine restaurants. Joey and Jess settled on The Rahman, an exquisite Indian restaurant in the heart of the city. They ate a light curry and finished the meal with a banana roti. Jess had enjoyed the dish before at a food stand in Bangkok, but the one she shared with Joey seemed lighter and sweeter. Maybe it was the quality of the bananas, or perhaps the sweetness of the condensed milk and chocolate topping.

They chatted a good part of the way to Tanah Rata.

"On this trip," Jess told him, "I want the final say on where we stay. I'm not interested in staying someplace – unless we have to, of course – with no hot water. I know you're probably more adventurous than me. But I'm not a twenty-something girl. I like feeling the kind of clean that comes from a long, slow, hot bath. And while we're at it, I also like comfortable beds with clean sheets." Then, with a smile to try to take some of the weight off, she added, "Maid service is always a plus."

Joey didn't echo her smile. He sat stoically, pondering his response, just not for the reason she thought.

"Jess, I don't know if I can afford my half of that for two months," he finally said. "I can't burn through all my money. I'm working on a business plan."

She had thought about his balking at the cost before bringing it up, but this was the first she'd heard of a business plan. She decided against pressing him on it right then. It might have just been something he said to deflect attention from his lack of funds.

"Listen, Joey," she said, glancing over at him as the winding road would allow, "if you had come into a decent amount of money, would you want me to pay half the costs of our trip?"

"I don't know. Maybe not."

"Well, maybe I shouldn't tell you this, but I got a good insurance settlement when Wallace died. I can afford to pay for nice rooms. It's why I was at the Holiday Inn and not some budget place in George Town."

She paused to let that sink in. His mind, she could tell, was trying to take it all in. He looked confused.

"Listen Joey, I love being with you. You're fun, good looking, a great guide and incredible in bed. Let me burn through some of my money with you. Please. Don't you worry about what things cost. I'm not going to worry about them. Okay?"

"It's not the way I was raised, Jess. I understand what you're saying. I just need to think about how I feel about it."

It was all an act, of course. She had just confirmed that she had more than enough money for his fifty-thousand dollars. He felt elated on the inside but had to put on a different face.

He paused and stared out the car window. They continued in silence for a bit before Joey spoke again.

"I guess it's not like I'll be taking your money. You and I together will be spending Wallace's instead of his secretary. Payback. Serves him right!"

Jess looked over at him and beamed.

"We are going to have so much fun," she said.

Joey looked over at her and felt enveloped in her smile. "Yes, we are," he said. And he meant it.

When they arrived in Tanah Rata, they were exhausted from the drive through more switchbacks than they could count. All they wanted was to find a nice hotel and crash.

The first thing that struck Jess was that while the name of the town, Tanah Rata, was all Malaysian, the architecture was distinctively British. During the colonial period, the Brits would come here, sometimes for extended stays, to escape the heat of the rest of the country. And they were drawn, as well, by the perfect climate and terrain for growing tea. The Brits do love their tea.

Tea plantations stretched as far as the eye could see in and around Tanah Rata. Pure, lush green. The first glimpse of the plantations happened as they completed one switchback on the drive. They came around a bend to reveal the first of the sprawling plantations.

"On my God! Jess exclaimed. "This is breathtaking. I've never seen anything like it. Did you say it's all tea?"

"What you see here is tea," Joey said. He explained that the area was also well known for its strawberries. "Wait till you taste one. Picked ripe and served the same day. It'll spoil you."

Out of the blue, Joey told her to take the next left. She did.

"How about some strawberry short cake right now?" he said.

"What? Before we even get a place to stay?"

"The hotels aren't going any place."

He directed Jess to the KHM Strawberry Farm. They were able to park right in front.

"Come on!" he said, jumping out of the car. They climbed the curved stone walkway to the entrance. When they got to the top, Jess was hanging on Joey like a schoolgirl.

"I like this impulsive side of you," she said, beaming at him.

They had the little open-air restaurant to themselves and grabbed a table overlooking the valley. They ordered one strawberry short cake, a half-dozen chocolate dipped strawberries and two cups of coffee with warm milk.

The shortcake was a freshly made scone that came with a generous service of just-whipped cream and KHM's own strawberry jam. The strawberries were medium-sized and brilliant red. They were dipped halfway in chocolate.

"On my God, Joey," she said as she took another bite of the shortcake they were sharing.

"Yeah, well taste this." He took one of the dipped berries and teased her lips with it.

"Stop it," she said with a giggle, then opened her mouth and took a bite. Her body relaxed in a pleasure response. She leaned in and kissed him. He beamed.

"This was such a great idea," she said. "Thank you, Joey." She kissed him again.

They were at the farm for about thirty minutes.

"Let's go find a hotel," she told him. "I want to, ahhh, rest."

They drove past a place called The Smokehouse Hotel, a Tudor inn nestled in an English garden.

"That's the place," she said, pulling over then doing a U turn to drive back to the small street the inn faced. "Let's have a peek," she said.

The inside of the hotel was as British as the outside. The fifty-year-old inn, which was built by colonists between the two world wars, could have just as well been in the English countryside. They asked to see a room and the rate. They liked what they saw, so Jess registered and paid with American Express.

The room was lovely. Spacious with a poster bed with white canopy that set against a deep red wall. A colorful Turkish rug covered a portion of the polished hardwood floor. Wingback chairs flanked one of the two windows that filled the space with natural light. A fireplace was nestled into the wall next to the bed. Jess walked over and peered out through one of the windows to a sweeping view over a golf course to the hills covered with lush green tea plants.

A big clawfoot tub took up one end of the bathroom. Jess filled it with hot water, climbed in and soaked away the tension from the drive. When she came out of the bathroom, Joey was asleep on the bed. He really likes his naps, she said to herself, prompting a smile. She gently crawled in next to him, still wearing the hotel bathrobe. Soon, she, too, was snoozing. It was five o'clock.

Joey woke at eight. The room, which had been filled with rays of the late afternoon sun at five, only had the faintest glint of moonlight coming in the two windows. Joey looked over at the outline of Jess. He found himself taken by the thought of how pretty she was.

In the darkness of the room, only his mind could see her features. He liked her dainty nose. It dawned on him that he had never noticed a beautiful woman's nose before.

As he lay there in the darkness, his mind conjured how she looked earlier that day driving the Toyota in the mountains. She was beautiful. He liked the hint of freckles on that cute nose and her cheeks. You don't particularly notice them at first. As you drink her in, though, you see them. Freckles were a new thing for him. Maybe the freckles were because of her red hair. No experience there, either.

She had more freckles on her shoulders and they slipped down her arms, as well. He had become aware of them in Langkawi. Her hands, though, were mostly freckle-free. He liked her hands. They were feminine, yet she wore no rings, nor did she polish her nails. Most of the younger girls he had seduced wore rings – sometimes several – and usually wore richly colored polish. Jess was different that way.

He could see more now that his eyes had adjusted to the low light in the room. Her chest was gently rising and falling along with the soft sounds of her breathing.

Should he wake her? He wanted her. He needed to wake her. But how should he do it? Should he reach over and cup her breast? Or should he do something subtler?

He reached over and with the back of his fingers on his left hand, he gently stroked her right cheek. She twitched with the second stroke. On the fourth pass, she opened her eyes and turned her head slightly toward him.

"Hi," she said.

He said nothing but moved his hand to the other cheek and gently traced over it to her lips. She edged her tongue out to greet them.

"You are so beautiful to me," he whispered.

"Please don't make that Joe Cocker face," she said. They giggled.

The laugh, though, was short-lived. She rolled over and started kissing his chest, then between the kisses sang another Joe Cocker lyric with a twist.

I'm just a girl whose intentions are good
Oh Lord, please don't let me be misunderstood.

And then she slid lower and took care of business.

They sauntered into the dining room at nine to eat.

Day 19

An unusual early morning thunderstorm swept through the highlands waking Joey and Jess abruptly. The weather yesterday had been beautiful, but today's downpour shouldn't come as a surprise. One reason the highlands are so lushly green is that the rainy season pretty much extends for all twelve months. Even in a supposedly dry month, it rains half the days. Today was going to be one of those days.

Jess loved the rain, though. There was something about the ferocity of it here. It was loud and wild. For some reason, it felt life affirming.

It never poured like this in Seattle. What most people don't know is that Seattle's reputation about it raining all the time is largely a myth. To begin with, the summers are dry. It can go for two, three, even four weeks without a drop of rain. Rain in Seattle is a winter thing. But even that is misleading. Except for six to eight weeks from Thanksgiving into January, the rain falls as a fine mist.

Jess got up and crossed to the window.

"Wow. It's really coming down," she said. "Sucks for sightseeing."

"Not really," Joey answered. "These storms blow through. The sun will probably be out mid- to late-morning. The only real problem will be the mud. When it rains like this, some of the dirt roads and trails get too muddy or slippery to use."

Joey said it was okay if they took it easier today. He explained that most people need a couple days to adjust to the altitude.

"It's so much cooler here that you think you should be able to go and go," he said. "But there's less oxygen in the air, so you can get winded.

Some people get a slight headache. Don't worry. You get used to it."

Joey told her that, for the most part, daytime temperatures top out in the mid-seventies. In Penang, the same day could see a temperature in the mid-nineties.

"Why don't we go down and have breakfast," Joey suggested.

The sun was breaking through the clouds by 10 a.m., just as Joey's predicted. It was clear that the rain was over, at least for now. Joey said that if she had pants and a long-sleeved shirt, she should wear them. Mosquitos can be bad, at times, he said. He dug in his bag and came up with a small green plastic bottle of Deet.

"Here," he said, handing it to her. "Put some wherever you have exposed skin. And make sure you put it around your ankles."

The rain had introduced a freshness to the air. They got in the Toyota and headed to nearby Bharat Tea Plantation. Without question, tea plantations were the defining visual element of the Cameron Highlands. As far as the eye could see, carpets of tea created endless green stripes across the rolling hills.

They joined a tour at Bharat that walked them through the process of making tea. It starts with withering, where freshly picked tea leaves are exposed to hot air. It reduces their moisture content by sixty-five percent. The drier leaves are then put into machines that break the leaves to expose their juices. That allows them to ferment. It's during this fermentation stage where the flavor is formed.

The crushed leaves sit exposed to the air. That's when they change color from green to copper. Then comes three-hundred-degree temperatures to further dry them out. Finally, they are sorted by quality.

After a cup of tea, they headed to the nearby Big Red Strawberry Farm, where they picked a batch of the juiciest, sweetest strawberries Jess had ever tasted.

It was past time for lunch, so they headed back toward the center of town. Along the way, they passed the Orchid Food Corner. Jess insisted they stop.

The place had no walls. Joey said they should go to an actual restaurant, but the aroma of the Orchid pulled Jess in. Joey relented. They shared a large order of chicken skewers, murtabak with minced beef and fried rice.

"You up for a hike?" Joey asked as they finished lunch. "There is a network of trails around here. We could hike to Robinson Falls – believe me, it's worth it. The whole thing should take three, maybe three and a half hours. What do you say?"

And so they did. It was a little harder than either expected. The morning rainstorm made parts of the path perilously slippery and other sections terribly muddy. Each of them slipped and fell more than once, so they were quickly covered in mud.

It was exhilarating to Jessica. She had never been in an actual jungle. Langkawi certainly didn't measure up to this experience. They hadn't actually hiked into the jungle there.

The path was enveloped in the dense jungle. There were no views, but that mattered little. When rays of sunshine would cut through the canopy above, the shafts of light produced a magical sense to their surroundings. They were surrounded by an explosion of green. Moss covered every inch of wood. So much green that Jessica began to think that perhaps she would sweat it out her pores. And sweat she did.

They saw no fierce jungle animals, though the sounds of what might lay just out of sight were ever-present. What she did see were giant millipedes. They were so huge that she knew no one back home would ever believe her. They left a trail behind them as they inched across the soil. The first one frightened her, but Joey insisted there was nothing to fear from them.

"Just try not to step on them," he said to her. "Getting that stuff off your shoes would be disgusting."

They were dog-tired when they arrived back at the hotel. Briefly taken aback by their appearance, the desk clerk recovered and asked if he could take their shoes and have them cleaned.

Getting all the mud that off their bodies was a two-person job.

"This is nice," Jess said. They were sitting in a big tub, her back facing him. Joey used a soapy sponge to rub off her mud stains.

"Yeah," he said. "I've never done anything like this?"

"You've never bathed with a woman?"

"No. First time."

If he had thought about what giving a woman a sponge bath would be like, he would have gone straight to it being sexual. But this strangely was not sexual. He didn't feel aroused. He felt content. It was a good feeling. A new feeling for him.

Later, over dinner in the hotel dining room, Jess said she wanted to just hang out at the hotel the next day.

"If the weather is nice," she said, "I'd like to spend the entire day in one of those chaise lounge chairs in the garden reading my book. Would you be okay with that?"

"Maybe you have one packed away that I could read?"

"I bet I do. I brought four. One is a spy thriller that I think you'd like."

———————

Fitz called Mason at 7:30 in the morning.

"Spears came through. Both American Express and Mastercard are on board. And some more good news. Some hotels are connected electronically to the credit card companies. If she uses the card at one of those hotels, we should know about it within a few hours."

"Getting' it right away would help," Mason said in a monotone way that Fitz paused a moment to think about the response.

"Don't get too excited," Fitz said after the slight pause. "There aren't too many hotels in Asia doing it yet, but if she stays at one of the big chains, the account gets pinged the moment the reservations people enter the data from the card. She chose a big chain hotel in Batu Ferringhi. Maybe she will at other places."

Mason asked how much lag there would be if the hotel wasn't connected to the card company electronically.

"Best case? Three or four days. And that's from when they pay the bill. Some hotels will charge a deposit to the card on arrival, but not everyone does. Most just take an imprint of the card."

"Damn. So, we'd find out that they'd just left a place. That's diddly squat."

"Not necessarily. Like you said earlier, if the charge happens in a town where they can catch a ferry to an island, you can just go straight to the island."

Mason asked if they'd tracked down where she banked yet. Fitz said they should have that info tomorrow.

"Listen, Mason, I'm keeping all this very close to the vest. Makes me nervous. I haven't even told my boss the full extent of it all. And I'm all but sure that the Secretary doesn't know more than the barest facts. If I say something about Joey zeroing in on a new victim and we know who it is, people are going to go apeshit."

"You got that right."

"Normally, we'd inform the parents. I haven't done that, but the time will come when I have to."

"I know. Thank you, buddy, for sittin' on it for now."

"The way I see it, we don't have much choice."

"No sir, we don't. Once they find out her folks will move heaven and earth to get her to safety."

"And you know they'd tell her the next time she calls them. If Joey got any wind of it, he'd kill her right then and there. She knows too much. Hell, I bet she has even taken pictures of him."

"We have to sit on it a little longer. I'm basically off-book. That gives you and Spears a little cover."

"Not much."

"No. But we're makin' progress and I'd hate to give this guy a do-over."

"Agreed."

Fitz said the Bureau had done a quick records check on her.

"Some interesting stuff. She had a high-paying job but came into a shitload of money last year."

"Inheritance?"

"Yes and no. She was married to a hot-shot plaintiffs' attorney who had a heart attack, died and left her millions."

"No shit. I wonder if Joey knows."

"You think it would change anything if he does?"

"He might wanna try to get more out of her. In the end, though, he only has one exit strategy."

Fitz told him about Jessica's job as a nurse anesthetist at a big hospital.

"So that's a big deal kind of nurse?" Mason asked.

"Yep. About as high as a nurse can get. Not as much training as a doctor, but damn close. Spears told me it's a high salary job."

"So she's a smart young woman. Let's hope that comes in handy."

"I suspect she's traveling to try to get over the tragedy of losing her husband. No idea what their relationship was like. They were both workaholics. Her husband – name was Wallace Jamison..."

"Christ! Is that really his name?"

"Yeah."

"Sounds totally like a lily-white Ivy League lawyer's name, if I ever heard one."

"The cracker in you is showing, Mason."

"Oh shit, man. I forgot I was talkin' to Mr. Blair Fitzgerald Fox, the Yale man."

"Ha."

Fitz got back to his notes. "Jamison was well enough known that the Seattle Times did a story about him when he had a heart attack at age forty-two and died."

The story, he said, focused first on Jamison's professional accomplishments. He had made a name for himself – and apparently tens of millions of dollars – in asbestos cases. The second half of the story, though, was about the odds of having a heart attack in your early forties.

"Jamison was a good seventy or eighty pounds overweight and smoked like it was going out of style. Two or three packs a day," Fitz said. "The story quoted some public health people saying tobacco use and obesity are major contributors to heart disease. It was made worse in his case by long hours in a high-stress job."

Mason asked if the story said anything about Jessica.

"Only that he was survived by his wife of six years, Jessica Stone. She kept her maiden name. No kids."

Fitz asked if Mason wanted to have the Bureau do a broader background check on her.

"Not yet. Hard for guys in black suits askin' questions to be subtle. We can't risk word gettin' back to her that the Feds are snoopin' around, askin' people questions about her."

Mason turned the conversation to his immediate plans. He shared his thoughts about Joey's two likely initial destinations. Mason said he thought Joey would either go to Pangkor Island off the lower southwest coast, or the Perhentian Islands, off the upper northeast coast. He'd read about both.

"No comparison, really," Mason said. "Accordin' to the guidebooks, Pangkor is okay, but not spectacular. The Perhentians are spectacular."

"So, you're going to head to the Perhentians?"

"Actually, I'm thinkin' Pangkor."

"You lost me. Why?"

"If I were this guy, I'd be wantin' the trip to get better and better. You know – save the best for last. If they do the east coast first and then Pangkor, it will be a big letdown. I'm thinkin' they do Pangkor first, then they maybe could visit Melaka – risky as that might be. From Melaka it's an easy drive to Mersing and on to Tioman for their first east coast stop. Then just meander up the coast and end at the Perhentians."

"I see your thinking, but it's a big gamble. If you're wrong, you are literally on the opposite side of the country."

"Damn, boy, don't you have any faith in my special powers? If I'm right, then I right there with 'em."

"I know you hate sitting and waiting, Mason, but I'd give it one more day. There's a good chance we'll have a credit card hit."

"One day is good."

Mason thought about what Fitz had told him about Jessica Stone. She's a widow. Like him, she lost someone at the center of her life. People cope with loss in different ways. Maybe she tried to get on with her life, but just couldn't. After nearly a year of trying, she probably thought that she needed to put geographic space between her pain and her life.

Had that worked for him, Mason wondered? Not really, but then he had moved quickly to revenge. He didn't give the buffer of time a chance to work. And until last week, he would have said that the revenge thing worked for him. Now? Maybe not.

Mason was trying to figure out how to get through the nightmarish nights and the days that followed. Increasingly, he found himself recalling the images of the dead from his nightmares during his wide-awake days. He feared it would soon undermine his sanity.

He was drinking more, which he knew wasn't good. He had bought a silver flask back in Penang and filled it with Jack Daniels every morning before heading out. If he didn't keep busy focused on his work, the images would throw themselves into his thoughts. Whenever that happened, he pulled out the flask and took a swig. Maybe two.

It was a good day if he could get through the day and back to his hotel without emptying the container in his pocket. He was more likely to drain it by the end of lunch. The alcohol didn't make him forget. No. It just deadened the intensity of his feelings. The amazing thing was that he was still able to focus and get work done.

Of course, one of the things he had to figure out was where, in a Muslim country, could he buy a bottle of Jack Daniels. Muslims not only are prohibited from drinking alcohol, they can't serve or sell it either.

Fortunately, while Muslims make up a majority of the population, more than a third of Malaysians are of Chinese descent and another ten percent are Indian. No restrictions on those folks when it came to booze.

The Indians and Chinese run a lot of businesses. Most towns will have at least one small market owned by one or the other. Walk into an Indian or Chinese convenience store and you'll find a decent liquor selection, often behind the counter or near the back of the store. And while they might not carry much American whiskey, a fifth of Jack seemed to always have a place on the shelf.

As he thought back on his life since Sylvie's death, he acknowledged that he wasn't the outgoing, good-natured man he used to be. He wasn't a recluse, but virtually every night would find him sitting in his favorite chair in front of his TV watching pirated tapes of American TV shows. Alone. Always alone. His only companion was the bottle of Jack on the side table and the glass he poured it into. Had he become an alcoholic? He didn't think so. He wasn't a drunk. But he'd down three glasses of Jack a night. He figured he just had a high tolerance.

Drinking during the daytime was something new for him. He told himself it was to cope with the nightmares. But he knew it was a lie. He wasn't coping. He was masking. He needed help. When this case was over maybe he'd get it.

At 7 p.m. – that would be seven in the morning in D.C. – Mason called Fitz at his home. He knew Fitz would be up and getting ready for work by then. He told him that he had gotten a pager and how to send him a message. Mason stressed to Fitz that he should page him anytime day or night if they got a hit on one of Jessica's credit cards.

Day 20

The clock next to Mason's bed said it was 3:35 in the morning when the phone jarred him awake. He clicked on the light, scooted up in the bed and answered the call.

"Hello," he mumbled into the phone.

"Mason, it's Fitz. We got a hit on the American Express card. She used it to fill up at a Shell station in Ipoh three days ago. Looks like they're heading south."

Mason tried to recall where Ipoh was, but couldn't. Still half-asleep, he turned on the light next to his bed, then fumbled with the phone to put it on speaker.

"Hold on. I put a map on the wall. Let me get my bearin's." He approached the map, followed the main highways south out of Penang. After a bit, he found Ipoh.

"Doesn't make a lot of sense," he said to Fitz. "Yeah, he's headin' south, but it's way out of the way if he's gonna take her to Pangkor."

"Maybe he's taking her to one of the highlands," Fitz said. "I visited the Genting Highlands a few years ago. Really beautiful place. It's a mile above sea level."

Mason studied the map some more. It was a direct route south from Ipoh to the Genting Highlands. The route did make sense for Genting. It also made sense for Kuala Lumpur, but there was no reason he'd want to take her there.

Genting would all but rule out Pangkor. Where would he go from Genting? Melaka was pretty much due south.

"Do you think he'd risk takin' her to Melaka?" Mason asked Fitz.

"I don't know. Can't rule it out, but people know him there. I think he'd want to avoid that, don't you?"

He backed up to Ipoh again, then used his finger to trace routes out of town. Where else might Ipoh be on the road to, he wondered.

"Hmm, looks like it's where you head into the mountains if you are goin' to the Cameron Highlands. What's that like? Do you think he might take her there?"

"Yeah," Fitz said. "Maybe. I don't know a lot about it, but a lot of tourists go there. It's big on tea plantations and nature walks. A lot cooler up there. And green. It's probably less crowded than Genting. Genting is only about an hour from KL. It's why I went to Genting. I was visiting the embassy and had a day to kill."

"I'm lookin' at the map. I wonder if I should head to the Cameron Highlands. From there I could still head to Pangkor or drive east across the country to the east coast."

Mason asked Fitz to fax him the location of the Shell station. He'd stop and see if anyone remembered Joey and Jessica and perhaps – a long shot, for sure – where they were heading. He told Fitz he was going to try to get a little more sleep. His alarm was set for seven-thirty. He hadn't had a nightmare yet and wondered if he would be spared this night. His mind was racing, so he used a meditation technique that Sylvie had taught him years before. It always helped him clear his mind. It took a while, but eventually he was again asleep.

———————

Jess and Joey slept in until almost nine o'clock. After breakfast, they stepped outside and discovered there was still a chill in the air. Back in the room, Jess pulled *Murder in Georgetown* from her backpack, then turned to Joey.

"Book time for me," she said. "Did you decide if you want to read one of my paperbacks?"

"Yes. I thought I'd try *A Matter of Honor.*"

Jess dug into her pack again, found the book and pulled it out.

"Here you go. Jeffrey Archer. I haven't read anything of his before, but this one sounded good. It was a bestseller."

He plopped down on the bed next to her. They lay side by side for the next hour, reading quietly before she broke the silence.

"I was thinking that maybe we could head out tomorrow."

"I'm good with that. You have a place in mind?"

"No, not really. The east coast sounds good. I wouldn't mind doing some more snorkeling."

"Then we should definitely go to the Perhentian Islands. The coral and sea life there are even better than Langkawi."

Jess nodded her head in quiet agreement.

"Is it a long drive?"

"It'll take the better part of a day to get to Kota Bharu. It's only about two-hundred miles, but a lot of it is on a narrow road through the mountains. That's why it will take so long. It's a pretty easy drive from there down to Kuala Besut where we catch the ferry."

"So we're staying in Kuala Besut tomorrow night?"

"No. Kota Bharu. Hotels with hot water," he said with a grin. "It's pretty close to Kuala Besut, though. We'll drive down the next morning."

They read some more then Jessica told Joey she needed to go downstairs to use the house phone to call her parents. It would be a little after eight in the evening in Seattle.

"They expect me to check in with them every week or so," she said. "I'm past due."

"You going to tell them about me?"

"If they ask. My dad won't but my mom might."

"You could tell her I'm a good lay," Joey joked.

"Yeah, right. 'Mom, I met this guy. He really knows how to pleasure me.'"

"That's definitely what your mom would want to hear."

She grinned, punched him lightly on the arm and headed downstairs.

Her dad answered the phone on the third ring. He was happy to hear her voice, he said, but it had been too long since her last call.

"Your mother and I worry about you, Jess. It's not safe for a young woman to travel by herself. I still don't understand why you're doing it. You should have taken Patty with you. You can afford it."

"It's not about affording it, dad. It's about having some time to sort things out."

They chatted some more, then he handed the phone to her mother.

"Hi sweetie. You having fun?"

"I really am mom. I'm in the Cameron Highlands right now. It's beautiful. A mile above sea level."

Jessica gave her a rundown on the tea plantations and the strawberry farms and let slip that "we" took a hike to a waterfall and how incredible the jungle was. Her mom, being a mom, picked up on the plural.

"So, you're making friends?"

"Yeah."

"That's good. I feel better knowing there's someone around to keep an eye on you."

Here we go again, Jessica thought.

"Mom, I'm thirty-three, not nineteen. What's that even supposed to mean?"

"You know, sweetie. Girls look out for one another."

"How about guys, mom? Would you like it if a guy was looking out for me?"

"Is a guy looking out for you?"

"As a matter of fact, yes, a guy is looking out for me. He's giving me a private tour of Malaysia."

Her mom was silent.

"You know, mom, I'm past being deflowered. I've been married, for Christ's sake!"

"I know, honey. It's just that it hasn't even been a year since Wallace died. You're still grieving. That kind of thing can affect your judgment."

"My judgment is fine. Can we drop it?"

"Okay. . . Wait. What's his name?"

"Joey."

"An American?"

"North Carolina."

"That's good, honey. I'm sure he's a nice boy."

Jessica said she needed to get off the phone. They said their "I love yous" and "goodbyes." Jessica hung up and let out an exasperated sigh.

Her dad had mentioned that she should have brought Patty with her. She had thought about it. She and Patty had been best friends since nursing school. Patty was even maid of honor at her wedding to Wallace. When Jessica found out that Wallace was cheating on her, Patty was the only one she told.

While Patty didn't make the trip with her, Jessica, now being rich, had convinced her friend to let her pay for a first-class roundtrip ticket to Singapore. The two were supposed to meet there at the end of the month. Those plans were made long before Jessica met Joey. She hadn't told Joey that she was supposed to meet up with Patty.

Things were heating up, though, between her and Joey. As much as she wanted to see Patty, the timing sucked. She decided to call her friend and ask her to delay the trip.

Patty was thrilled to hear Jessica's voice.

"I'm so excited about my trip" were the first words out of her mouth.

"Well, that's one reason I'm calling."

"Oh. What's up?"

Jessica could hear the disappointment in Patty's voice. It made her feel awful.

"I met a guy. I wrote you about him. I think I'll need more time before I want to take a break from him."

"Wow! Really? Spill the beans, girl."

Jessica told her all about Joey and how totally fucking great he was in bed. That he was only twenty-six. She explained how they met, their weekend getaway to Langkawi and how it led to Joey showing her around Malaysia. She brought Patty up to speed on Joey being born in Malaysia, half British and half Malaysian, but that when he was little, he was adopted by a preacher and his wife from North Carolina.

"Wait! He's a preacher's son?"

"Yeah. Praise the lord and all."

"Seriously, you know what they say about preachers' sons?"

"No, but I think you're going to tell me, right?"

"Of course!"

"So, what do they," she placed emphasis on the word they, "say about preachers' sons."

"Hellions! They're never what they appear to be."

"Well, Joey is a sweet, gentle guy."

"There you go! Danger, Will Robinson," Patty said, repeating the line from the Sixties' TV show.

"Patty, I'm not lost in space."

"And I'm only kidding. . .Kind of. . .Be careful."

They agreed to push her trip back a month. Jessica was sure she'd be ready to move on from Joey by then.

Jessica returned to the room and found Joey sitting in one of the wingback chairs reading. He looked up and smiled.

"I take it you told your mom that you're getting laid every night," he said.

"Yeah. I said you had a little dick but that it still felt okay."

"Touché!"

———————

Mason stopped at the Shell station. One of the workers remembered the woman with the red hair, but nothing that shed light on where they might be going. He didn't really expect that anyone would have heard anything useful, but you have to ask. Mason filled his tank, crossed the street to a KFC for lunch, then headed on to a town at the heart of the Cameron Highlands called Tanah Rata. The driving kept him occupied enough that he never once went to his flask.

He got there about two-thirty in the afternoon. It was bigger than he had hoped. And more spread out. He wasn't even sure that they had come here.

He considered what he should do first. On one hand, he could start

234

visiting hotels. He figured there were at least a dozen that were nice enough to appeal to Jessica if she was going to stay with a Holiday Inn-level place. Scores more if they would settle with a lower-cost, fewer amenities option. Given what he now knew about her finances, he couldn't see her going with a budget hotel unless Joey insisted. He didn't think that would happen. Still, a dozen properties spread all over the local map were a lot to cover.

Maybe, instead of checking the hotels, he should check some of the bigger tourist attractions. A handful that were close in. Tea plantations, a couple of big strawberry farms, a temple, an outdoor market and a few other landmarks. He figured that no one would come here without visiting at least one tea plantation and probably a strawberry farm. He decided to check into those first. He'd re-evaluate after that.

The biggest and best known of the plantations was BOH. It was farther out from the main part of town, but its reputation attracted more visitors. Mason went in with his photos, but no one recognized either Joey or Jessica.

Next stop was the Big Red Strawberry Farm. Again, no luck, though he did grab some big, ripe juicy strawberries to snack on. The next stop, KHM Strawberries, bore fruit.

"Yes, yes. Girl with red hair. Very pretty. I remember her," said a young woman whose nametag identified her as Sophia.

"When might that have been, darlin'?"

"Two days ago."

"Was she by herself?" Mason asked.

"No. With a young man. Very much in love," Sophia softly giggled. "They kissed a lot and stared into each other's eyes. Very romantic."

"Did they happen to say where they were stayin'?"

"No."

He thanked her. His hunch had been right. But were they still there?

His next stop was another big tea plantation. Bharat Tea Plantation was a little farther out of the main part of town to the south, but closer than BOH was to the north.

235

He showed the photos to several workers before one of the fellows remembered them. Again, it was Jessica's red hair that Ifran recalled. He remembered that she was with someone but didn't recall whom. When did he see them? Yesterday, Ifran said. He, too, had no idea where the red-haired woman might be staying.

Mason thought through what he knew. They would have passed BOH and the Big Red Strawberry Farm on the drive in from Ipoh but didn't stop. He guessed that meant they got a room first, then headed out for some nearby sightseeing.

He also figured that they likely found a place farther south, making them closer to the Bharat plantation and KHM Strawberries. That limited the hotels some, but there were still at least eight, according to his guidebook, and probably others.

It was getting dark, so he decided to find himself a room and then check out some restaurants where they might have dinner, if they were still in town.

He drove to the biggest hotel in the area, the Victoria. He'd check in and start showing the photos to staff. It was a nice hotel and expensive by Malaysian standards. It was a homage to Queen Victoria, whose portrait as a young woman, all four feet eleven inches of her, hung over the reception desk.

By all accounts, Queen Victoria was a remarkable woman. She became queen at just eighteen when her uncle William IV died. She would rule Britain for sixty years.

Her legacy stretched far beyond the United Kingdom. She and her husband, Prince Albert, had nine children in a span of just seventeen years. Quite a feat when one considers that Queen Victoria hated being pregnant and refused to nurse any of her children.

She allowed herself to be almost constantly pregnant for a simple, but dynastic reason. Of her nine children, eight married into foreign royal families. Her children produced royal heirs throughout Europe.

Mason settled into his room, dug out his guidebooks and plotted his stops. First, he would focus on the Victoria itself, then visit as many restaurants as he could. He pocketed a roll of twenty-dollar bills and set out to do the Q and A of staff and others.

At 10 p.m., he returned to his room. No one had recognized the people in his photos or seen anyone with red hair.

The next morning, he would drive from hotel to hotel. That wasn't what was on his mind, though. Another night brought the prospect – no, the likelihood – of a nightmare of someone else he had killed in the Sam Neua blast. He faced the fear with a glass of Jack. Sometimes two. He didn't sip them. He gulped them wanting to quickly flood the whiskey's effects throughout his body.

Maybe it was the whiskey. Or it could have been the sleeping pills he'd picked up at the pharmacy before leaving Penang. More likely, it was the combination of the two. But he slept straight through until his alarm buzzed at seven the next morning.

———————

Jess and Joey decided to keep dinner simple their last night in the Camerons, so they walked to a nearby commercial district. They found a sidewalk table along the main drag and ordered fried mee goreng and a plate of spring rolls.

Sometimes, it's just a small world. Joey and Jess were finishing up when he locked eyes with someone from his not-too-distant past. Martin, the German he had met on the bus to Mersing with the girls, was walking straight toward him. Martin was one of the few people who could connect him to Amanda.

Joey's heart raced. What did Martin, who Joey didn't like that night in Mersing and even less now, know? There was a glint of recognition in Martin's eyes. Not a smile, exactly. More a curiosity.

"Joey!" he said when he reached the table. There was an empty chair at the adjacent table. Martin pulled it out and sat. "I doubted I'd ever see you again."

Martin looked at Jessica. "Hello. I'm Martin."

Jess reached her hand across the table to shake Martin's hand. "I'm Jessica. How do you two know one another."

"We took a bus from Melaka to Mersing together a couple weeks ago, then hung out in a bar that night."

"Is Crystal with you?" Joey asked.

"Nah. We split on Tioman."

"Have you been here in the Cameron Highlands for long?" Jessica asked.

"Arrived yesterday. I'd been on Perhentian Kecil diving for the past week. Thought I'd head here for a few days to take in the cool mountain air, then make my way to Penang."

"We just came from there and we're headed to Perhentian Kecil from here," Jessica offered.

"Kecil is awesome. You'll love it. Beautiful coral. Sea Turtles. Blacktip sharks – they're friendly, by the way."

Joey didn't like bumping into Martin. He could spoil things with Jessica if the conversation turned to Amanda. And Joey's years of not being caught rested somewhat on his never running into anyone who could link him to a murder. But now here was Martin. Perhaps, though, Martin didn't know.

That proved wrong with Martin's next statement.

"Hey man, did the police talk to you about Amanda?"

"No. Why would they?"

"Of fuck, man. You don't know?"

"Don't know what?"

"Amanda's dead. Someone murdered her in her bed that very night."

"What? Wait. Who's Amanda?" Jessica asked.

"A girl we all met on the bus to Mersing a couple weeks ago," Joey said. "We hung out that night. You're saying someone killed her?"

"Slit her neck," Martin answered. "Pug told me when I stopped back at the hotel after Tioman. Looked like a robbery, except she was naked, so maybe some kinky stuff first. What kind of fuckwad does that? Get's all romantic, does the nasty with her, then when she's basking in that afterglow, he slits her goddamn throat so deeply that she bleeds to death. Then and only then, he robs her? I can tell you who does that, a sicko."

"Oh my God," Jessica whispered. "You and she were friends?" she asked Joey.

"Not really," he said. "We had just met that day."

"True, but you two clearly liked each other."

"I don't know why you'd say that."

"Because it was so obvious, man. Amanda was a looker. And Suzy told us on the boat that she had the hots for you. We all kind of laughed when neither of you showed up to cross to Tioman. We figured you stayed at the bar after the rest of us left for a reason."

"To watch *L.A. Law*. We watched the show and I walked her back to the hotel, said goodbye and that was that." Joey realized he was sounding defensive.

"Well, you were probably the last person to see her alive. I bet the police want to talk to you."

"God, Joey, you could be a suspect."

"That's crazy."

"I know," she said, "but if you were the last person seen with her you can bet the police have their sights on you."

"We'll be in Mersing in a couple weeks. I'll stop in to the police station then. I'm sure I can clear everything up."

Martin, though, wasn't about to drop it. His eyes became beady as he bore in on Joey.

"I thought you and Amanda were going to Tioman?"

"That was the plan, but something came up. I had to leave. I walked her to her hotel after the TV show, said good night and that was the last time I saw her."

Before Martin could answer, Jessica turned to Joey.

"And you didn't see her the next day to say goodbye? Doesn't sound like the thoughtful, considerate Joey I know."

"Listen Jess. Me and Amanda had just met. It wasn't like we were a couple or even good friends. When I got back to my room, I had a message. I had to leave. Simple as that."

239

Jess turned back to Martin. "So, what did the police ask you?"

"Nothing. They never came to Tioman. I guess I could have stopped by the police station when I was back in Mersing, but I didn't."

Martin said Suzy and Crystal might know more. They might have been interviewed.

"I'm supposed to meet up with Suzy in Penang in a couple weeks," he said. "Maybe she and I can compare notes."

Joey desperately wanted to change the subject.

"Where you staying?" Joey asked Martin.

"At the hostel on the street behind us here. Happy Traveler Hostel. Original name," Martin said with a smirk.

"Is it nice?" Jessica asked.

"Well, it's a hostel. But it's fine. I've stayed in worse."

"Do you have your own room?" she asked.

"No, but I was the only guy in the room last night. There were a couple girls in the girl's room."

Jess was going to tell Martin that they had a room at the Smokehouse, but it was so much nicer than a dorm room in a hostel that she chose not to.

"How about you guys? Staying nearby?"

"Not too close. We have a room in an inn up the street," Joey offered.

The conversation lulled. Before long, Martin said his goodbyes but not before staring blankly at Joey. Joey could practically see the German's mind trying to figure if Joey might have been the one to slash Amanda's throat. Then, in the same non-committal way he had walked up, Martin stood and left.

"That was disturbing," Jess said when Martin was safely away.

"Yeah," Joey said, trying to act like he would if he had just found out. "That poor girl. Martin was right. I did like her. She was fun. I can't believe someone killed her. Why would they do that?"

"Apparently to steal her stuff."

They paid their bill and headed back to the Smokehouse. Joey's mind was playing out different scenarios. What awful luck to run into Martin on their last night in town. Should he do something about it? Joey hated loose ends, but what could he do?

He and Jess made love in their four-poster bed. He tried to make it good for her, but he feared he was too distracted. After they finished, she went to the bathroom, then crawled in next to him again.

"Goodnight, Joey."

"Goodnight, Jess."

Day 21

Always the one for a plan, Joey hatched one as Jess slept. At about two in the morning, he eased himself out of bed, quietly dressed, grabbed what he needed and crept down the stairs to a back door. It was too far to walk and not be seen. He'd be too exposed with no place to hide. He drove to within a few hundred yards of Martin's hostel, then walked in the shadows the rest of the way. Hopefully, Martin would still be the only one in the room. He knew what he needed to do.

Getting into the Happy Traveler was easy. The door was unlocked! There was a dim bulb illuminating the hallway. The men's and women's dorm rooms were clearly marked. The other doors, Joey figured, were for travelers on a more generous budget who could afford a private room.

He gently pushed open the door to Martin's room, stepped inside and closed the door behind him. He stood motionless to let his eyes adjust to the darkness. After a couple minutes, he could see the dark shapes of four single beds. Looking more closely, he could see that only one was occupied.

Quiet as he could, Joey moved to Martin's bedside. The German was on his back, snoring softly and clearly in a deep sleep. Joey removed his pearl-handled knife and opened the blade. He bent over Martin and then, in a swift move, cupped his hand over Martin's mouth as his blade sliced deeply through the young man's neck. Martin's body buckled, but only once. His windpipe and jugular severed, he was unable to push air to yell out. But Joey continued to hold his hand over

Martin's mouth and settle the weight of his body over Martin's.

It didn't take long. When Joey was sure that Martin was gone, he got up and started the second phase of his plan. He made it look like a robbery.

He found Martin's money belt. It contained nine-hundred German marks. Joey had no idea what they were worth. The belt also held four-hundred-eighty US dollars and five-hundred ringgits. A thin piece of fabric separated the cash from Martin's passport and credit card. He took both, though he didn't intend to keep them. He wanted nothing that would tie him to the dead German.

He threw the now-empty money belt on the bed to make it obvious Martin was robbed. He was sure Martin had other things of value, but he had taken the most prized items and all the police would need to call it a robbery. Before he left, he thought like a thief and found Martin's pants. In his pockets were another forty ringgits. Joey left the pockets turned inside out and the pants on the floor next to the bed.

Done with Martin, Joey moved back to the door. He put his ear against it to listen for noises. The last thing he needed was to run into a young lady on the way to the common toilet. There were no sounds, so he cracked open the door and glanced into the hallway. Clear. He moved quickly to the front door and out.

Joey found a trash can a couple blocks away. He opened it, saw a discarded food bag, and added Martin's passport and credit card to the bag. He put the lid back on the can, then jumped in the Toyota and headed back to the hotel.

He only had one problem. There was blood on the front of his shirt. He could throw it away, but would Jess notice it was gone? He had only packed four shirts. A decision loomed. Should he toss the shirt?

If he kept the bloody skirt on and then returned to the Smokehouse, where someone would be at work all night, it would raise all kinds of questions. And of course, the fellow on the front desk would share the story. He could envision someone hearing about the bloody murder, putting two and two together and calling the police.

He was about to toss the shirt when he realized that a bloody shirt might draw attention in the trash. Was he far enough away from the murder scene? He had to risk it. He drove around and found a bulging garbage can, stripped the shirt off and buried it as best he could. He was probably safe, he thought to himself. The police wouldn't even know to look for a bloody shirt. He was being paranoid.

When he arrived back at the hotel, he strode in through the front door. He decided that he was going to tell the clerk that he had to run out to the car for something. To his amazement, no one was at the desk. He moved quickly and quietly up the wooden stairs back to their room. He stripped down and climbed into bed.

Jess rolled over to him.

"Where were you?" she asked in a sleepy voice.

"Couldn't sleep, so I went for a walk. I feel more relaxed now."

"Hmmm," she said and feel back asleep.

————

After a breakfast of ham and farm-fresh eggs, Jess used her American Express card to check out of The Smokehouse Hotel. The sun shone brightly and with luck, they'd be through the mountains and perhaps all the way to their next hotel before the rain came. It would be drier heading east this time of year, so their odds were good. Joey convinced her to let him drive.

They loaded the Toyota and headed north along Route 59 toward Kota Bharu. About an hour later, they had connected to Route 185. The constant switchbacks on Route 59 gave way to gentle ups and downs and curves. Route 185 reminded Jess of an interstate highway, except there was little traffic. Cutting across the heart of Malaysia revealed a largely undeveloped country. There were no real towns in more than an hour. Just jungle-covered mountains.

"Tell me about the business," Jess said as he drove east.

"What?" Joey responded.

"A couple days ago you said something about needing to save money for a business. What's the business?"

Joey had prepared for this moment. He knew exactly where to start.

"So, remember when you were on Koh Samui and you stayed at Joy Bungalow on Chaweng Beach?"

"Yeah. I loved that place."

"Places like Koh Samui," Joey continued, "have bungalow village after bungalow village along the beach. It can be like every hundred feet or so in some places."

"There was like this daily ritual on Koh Samui," Jess said. "People would start strolling up the beach in the afternoon to see what movies were playing that evening at which restaurants. Each little bungalow village had its own restaurant and they all showed movies on TVs. Some of the movies were almost new."

"Counterfeit," Joey offered.

"I'm sure. But every place had them. It wasn't the movies so much that I liked, though. I liked how open the people were. During the day, people did their own thing. They'd lay on the beach tanning, or in a hammock reading. The more adventurous ones might go snorkeling or fishing or even hiking. But in the evening, the whole environment would change. It became super-friendly. Even if you were alone, you made friends."

"Exactly. Thailand is a lot further along on those kinds of places than Malaysia."

"Why do you think that is?"

"I don't know. Maybe it has something to do with the fact that Thailand was never a colony, not counting the Japanese, of course. Malaysia had the Portuguese, then Dutch, then the English, then for a bit the Japanese, then the Brits again."

"So you want to build a bungalow village somewhere in Malaysia?"

"One for starters. There is a beautiful beach area on the west coast of Langkawi that reminds me of Koh Samui. Beautiful. Right now, though, there's no place to stay. Someday I expect that beach to be a backpacker mecca. I'd like to open the first bungalow village there. Market it to backpackers, get the guidebooks to visit. Build the Bungalow Paradise brand. Then add new ones in other beach locations around Malaysia."

"Ambitious! A side of you I haven't seen before. I like it!"

They chatted some more. Jess asked him a load of questions about everything from the name to how he planned to build a brand. He had answers for most of her questions.

"So, what's keeping you from doing it?"

"I want to be able to build it without partnering with some unscrupulous money guy. I've put my folks' house up for sale back home. I should have more than enough to buy the land and build it once the house sells. It doesn't take that much really.

"The problem is that the real estate market in Bentonville sucks. It's not Atlanta or even Charlotte. If I reduce the price to sell it, I might not have enough to do what I want to do. If I keep the price where it is, though, it sits there unsold. I just keep telling myself to be patient. It's a nice enough place. It'll sell."

"How much do you need?"

"I can get the first one going for about fifty-thousand dollars. Of course, that's just to get it open. It will take time to build up business. I figure I'll need enough to keep it and me afloat for at least a year, maybe two. Once it is self-supporting, I'll build the second one. I'm thinking maybe on Tioman Island. But once I have at least fifty thousand I'll buy the land and get started."

"Fifty-thousand isn't a lot in the grand scope of things," she said.

"It is if you don't have it."

They drove on. After a few minutes, Jess spoke again.

"You're an impressive young man, Joey Jackson."

———————

Mason bought a Cameron Highlands map of the area in the hotel shop. The clerk was a delightful young woman who spoke English very well. It turned out that she had spent a year in London with an uncle.

He gave her the usual not-quite-true story that a young woman's father had hired him to find her. She hadn't checked in for weeks and he was worried about her. Mason said he had tracked her and a traveling companion to Tanah Rata, but didn't know where here they were staying. His plan for this day was to visit all the nicer hotels in the area and see if they were there or if anyone had seen them.

"Maybe I can help you," she said, "at least a little."

The young lady then had him open the map. "We are here," she said, circling the Victoria on the map. It was one of only four hotels shown because of the historical significance, at least that's what she told him. Using a pen, she marked locations for ten other of what she called the better hotels, offering a little commentary about each. He thanked her and headed for the Victoria's main dining room for breakfast.

Over fresh fruit, cheese, sausage, an omelet and toast, served with a pot of tea, he mapped his day. He would start with the hotels closest to the Victoria, then work his way farther south. He chose to ignore four hotels north of the Victoria. He would do them last, if he hadn't had any success with the others.

It was a frustrating morning. At each hotel, he would ask around and show the photos. No luck. He decided to make one more stop before lunch.

He drove up to The Smokehouse Hotel, a well maintained, very British-looking place. He got a whiff of grilled meat, perhaps lamb. He walked past a few guests who were milling around the English garden that surrounded the inn. Maybe he'd have lunch here after asking around.

"Hey!" he said to a smiling young man behind the reception desk. "Perhaps you can help me. I'm lookin' for an American couple who might be stayin' here."

He showed the photos to the man at the desk. The man looked at the photos, then back to Mason.

"One moment, sir," he said and walked to a nearby office, knocked twice, then entered. A minute later he re-emerged with an older man.

"Good afternoon," the man said. "I'm Lionel Hawthorne. I'm the manager. May I help you?"

Mason repeated the story about trying to find the young woman for her father. The manager took him in before finally speaking.

"I'm afraid they checked out this morning."

"Dang! Did they say where they were headin'?"

"Not exactly. No."

"Not exactly? What did they say?"

"I overheard the gentleman tell the lady that they would be on Route 59 with all the switchbacks for about an hour. He then told her the highway would become more like a freeway and they'd make better time."

"You know this area far better than me. Where do you think they were goin'?"

"North obviously. Either Penang or the upper east coast."

"I came from Penang and the highway was narrow and windin' all the way from Ipoh."

"Exactly. I believe they would be heading to the east coast. He was describing Route 185."

Mason wanted to punch this guy. Why not just say that in the beginning?

"How long ago did they leave?" Mason asked.

"They checked out this morning. They've been gone at least four hours."

Mason pondered the situation.

"Would you mind showin' me their room?"

"Most certainly not," Hawthorne said with a haughty attitude and a noticeably stiffer spine. Mason saw that the reception clerk rolled his eyes. "The Smokehouse respects the privacy of our guests."

"I just wanna see if they left anything that might say where they were headin'. Sometimes people write itineraries or names of hotels on pieces of paper that they leave in the room."

"Absolutely not," Hawthorne said. He turned and walked back to his office.

Mason watched him leave, then turned back to the clerk.

"I would have been happy to make it worth his while," Mason said and pulled a hundred-dollar bill from his pocket to show the clerk. The clerk's eyes widened. "I'll be in the dinin' room havin' lunch, should the manager change his mind."

Mason had ordered and was waiting for his food – it was roast lamb that he smelled on arrival - when the clerk walked into the dining room. He surreptitiously handed Mason a room key. On it in place of a number it simply said Glenlee Suite.

"Go now before the room is made," the clerk said. "Second floor. I'll tell the kitchen that you had to step away for a minute but will be back."

The clerk walked toward the kitchen. Mason stood and headed toward the stairs, being careful to avoid the manager's office.

There was little in the room, which didn't surprise Mason. There was a notepad on one of the nightstands. Mason examined it. Something had been written and torn away. He looked around and found a pencil in a drawer and lightly moved the point back and forth across the pad. Soon he saw what had been written on the sheet above, but it made no sense to him.

"How much do I say?" It was underlined three times for emphasis. Had to be Jessica who wrote it. Say about what. He wondered? Maybe she hasn't told him yet how rich she is.

He removed the paper from the pad, stuck it in his pocket and headed back toward the dining room. He saw the clerk at the front desk and surreptitiously handed him the hundred-dollar bill. "Thank you kindly," he mouthed and continued to the dining room for lunch.

He kept asking himself what it could possibly mean?

———————

Much of the drive was in silence. The scenery, as nice as it was, grew monotonous. They'd feed a new cassette into the in-dash player every forty-five minutes or so. Jess read for a bit, then napped.

It all left Joey alone with his thoughts. His situation troubled him. On one hand, she had more than enough money to finance Bungalow Paradise, but he strangely found that when he thought of what it would be like, she was there with him. Needless to say, that wasn't the plan. Besides, would she even want to do that? He couldn't imagine it.

He looked over at her, sleeping softly with her head resting against a small pillow on the door window. Even in her twisted, unflattering pose, she took his breath away. A woman had never affected him this way before. He was so very drawn to her.

He looked back over at her. His mind played with the thought that perhaps he could get her fifty-thousand dollars and have her stay with him as part of Bungalow Paradise. But he soon put that fantasy to rest. She would never settle for him, he told himself. She could have anyone. Did he say that out loud? No. He just said it with conviction in his mind.

She didn't budge. He focused on the road ahead.

"Hey you," she said to him some time later. He looked over at her, now awake and looking content. "A penny for your thoughts."

He looked back at the road, then back to her.

"Jess, I. . ." but he was at a loss for words.

She smiled. "Yeah. I know. I love spending time with you, too."

It was four o'clock when Joey pulled into the driveway at the Palace Hotel in Kota Bharu. This was a place he would never stay at. It wouldn't be that he wouldn't want to. No. He'd want to. But he could never have afforded such a place. Jess, though, had insisted as they drove past.

"Are you sure you want to spend this much money? It's just a room," Joey asked.

"Trust me, Joey. It has my name written all over it. It'll be nice."

They pulled up and a uniformed attendant rushed to the car, first opening Jess' door then dashing around to open Joey's.

"Will you be staying with us tonight, sir?" the attendant asked. Joey nodded they were. Almost instantly a similarly uniformed bellman pushed a cart toward them.

Joey tipped the first attendant five ringgits and followed Jess into the hotel. They approached the front desk where a sharply dressed middle-aged man addressed him in flawless English.

"Will you be checking in?"

Jess responded, which seemed to surprise the clerk.

"Yes. We'll be staying one night," she said, handing the man her American Express card and both their passports. "We'd prefer a non-smoking room," she looked at his name tag, "Adam. Is that possible?"

"Yes ma'am."

She completed the registration. The clerk photocopied the passports, then handed them back.

"Dinner is served in the Garden Room from five to ten this evening. Breakfast tomorrow will be in the Riverside View Room from six to ten."

Jess thanked him as he signaled the bellman over. He handed the man their keys and they followed him to the elevator and on to their room on the sixth floor. It was spacious. The bellman opened the drapes to reveal a view of the river and the town that hugged it. He then stepped into the bathroom. Switching on the light, he gave the room a quick visual inspection. The bellman then re-entered the main room, handed the keys to Joey and asked if they required anything else. Joey said no, then handed the man another five-ringgit tip.

"You know," Joey said once the bellman had closed door. "Those ten ringgits I've just given in tips would pay for our bungalow on Perhentian."

"Hey, stop thinking about money."

———————

Mason rushed back to the Victoria and checked out. He had the kitchen make him a basket of food for the road. The staff provided a couple sandwiches, a small selection of cheeses, fruit and strawberries, as well as two liter bottles of water. He was out the door headed north by three, which meant he'd be well through the mountains before dark.

He knew Joey and Jessica were not returning to Penang. They were on an adventure around Malaysia. They were, and of this he felt quick certain, heading to the Perhentian Islands. The Perhentian Islands were made up of a small cluster of islands in the South China Sea off the coast of northern Malaysia. The jumping off point was Kuala Besut, a small town that offered little more than fishing boats and a ferry to the islands.

Five of the Perhentian Islands are tiny and uninhabited. The other two were where the action was, which is saying more than it's worth. Perhentian Besar is the larger island and the most developed of the two. But again, to call it developed would be an overstatement.

There are no services on the islands. None. No common electricity. Certainly no phones. No roads. There is a small general store at the jetty that serves the small island, but it only accepts cash for items that are markedly more costly than they are back on the mainland.

What the Perhentians offer are beautiful powdery white sand and crushed shell beaches and pristine turquoise waters. Big green sea turtles and blacktip reef sharks that can measure up to six or seven feet casually swim the waters. The sharks, which frighten away many swimmers, are timid creatures that avoid humans. People snorkel and dive among them every day in peaceful co-existence.

The undersea world also offers abundant color in crystal clear waters. Unlike so many dive spots throughout Southeast Asia and the rest of the world, the coral surrounding the Perhentian Islands is largely undisturbed. It's vibrant and thriving. It attracts an amazing array of clown fish, blue-spotted masons, trigger fish, puffer fish, and so many more.

The families and others who like to stay on Perhentian Besar might call it primitive. Perhentian Kecil, literally Small Perhentian, is even more so. It is less developed, though slightly nearer the mainland. Many believe, though, that the snorkeling is better than on the big island. Kecil even boasts what amounts to a small fishing village. Backpackers prefer it, if for no other reason than it provides cheaper accommodations. To be honest, though, cheaper in this case doesn't mean inferior. Basic is basic, whether it costs two dollars a night or ten.

As Mason drove north on Route 8, he was again alone with his thoughts. Again, he asked himself why now, after so many years, was he seeing things that he had been oblivious to? Again, he questioned if the faces he was seeing in his nightmares were real. They could simply be grotesque images his mind was conjuring up.

But did it matter? Either way, they felt very real to him.

He now, for the first time really, was confronting the magnitude of what he had done. In any context, he was a terrorist. That it got him bounced from the CIA was no consolation. In a just world, they would have executed him. But all he got was a quiet discharge. They even set him up with his first client, for Christ's sake. No wonder he was having horrendous flashbacks. The only question was why it had taken so long.

Mason took the turnoff at Route 3 to Kuala Besut. He figured that Joey and Jessica likely were already on one of the islands, given their head start. Night had fallen an hour earlier, so he would have missed the last ferry of the day. That was okay, though. He would board an early morning crossing and be there on their first full day.

He hadn't planned on the scarcity of places to stay. He thought there would be at least one or two decent guest houses or inexpensive Chinese hotels. After all, everyone wanting to visit the Perhentians had to go through Kuala Besut. He was wrong. He should have figured it out when his *South-East Asia Handbook* gave no recommendations for places to stay in Kuala Besut. His Lonely Planet guide offered only one guest house, called simply Rest House. That's where he stayed.

The Rest House was spartan, but it did have a pay phone in the common area. After getting settled, Mason waited patiently while a French couple called home. He then made four calls of his own. He figured he'd be out of reach for several days, perhaps even a week or more. He needed to update everyone.

First up was Bo. He wanted to give him a status report before it got any later in the evening. Bo, after all, was a family man. His next call was to the office. Boonsri wouldn't be there, but she needed to know his whereabouts and that he was going to be unable to check in for quite some time. He left a message with the service and had them read it back to him to make sure it was right.

Fitz was next. The two men had a brief but fruitful chat. Fitz had finally connected with Pastor Johnny. The reverend, Fitz said, was protective of Joey. He said he was a good boy. Joey was very loving, especially toward his wife, Mrs. Helen.

Joey, he said, would act out from time to time, like all kids do, but he never saw him do anything mean or violent. In fact, he said Joey was the opposite of impulsive. He was a plotter and planner. If there were something he wanted or needed, he'd figure out how to get it. But, the pastor said, it was always things Joey could do. He said Joey never hurt anyone. He didn't see any way possible that Joey would have killed anyone.

Fitz was able to clear up the mystery about Mrs. Helen's sudden departure and the pastor's following on. Mrs. Helen had developed an aggressive form of breast cancer, Fitz said. That's why she left abruptly. And it was why Pastor Johnny followed her a month later. He wanted to be with her through all her treatments. She fought for months, but eventually the cancer killed her.

"I asked him why they didn't take Joey with them or at least tell him what was happening," Fitz said. It turns out that they had raised him, but never actually adopted him. Getting him released to them would be difficult and time consuming.

"Joey was a catch twenty-two kid," Fitz said. "Authorities insisted he was a Muslim while at the same time denying that he was a Muslim because he didn't have a Muslim father."

Pastor Johnny and his sick wife felt they didn't have the emotional strength or time to fight that battle, Fitz said. Mrs. Helen was dying and trying to save her sucked them dry.

"Pastor Johnny said their big mistake was not telling Joey what was going on," Fitz said. "All the pastor said to him the day he left was that he'd be back. When months passed, though, without word, Joey felt he was on his own. He had no idea that the pastor had learned that once Joey turned eighteen, less than a year away at the time, he'd be free to travel on his own.

The pastor planned to send him a ticket. Once he was in the states, they'd legally adopt him. None of that happened, of course, because they never told him it was their plan. To Joey, they just deserted him.

"Pastor Johnny eventually went back to Melaka to find Joey, but it had been months and Joey was no longer there. No one knew where he had gone," Fitz said. "He hired a private investigator, but the PI got nowhere. Pastor Johnny said it had troubled him ever since."

"Did you tell him why you were askin' about Joey?"

"Pretty much had to. When I told him, the poor man started to cry. He kept saying it couldn't be Joey because he was such a sweet boy. But a part of him knew or at least feared it was all true. He blamed himself for not taking Joey with him, or at least not letting him know what was happening. Joey was seventeen. He was old enough by then to handle it."

No argument from me on that, Mason thought. There's a good chance none of this killing would have happened if they'd simply told Joey what was going on.

Mason then called Bob. Bob was always excited to take Mason's call.

"Mason!" he answered enthusiastically. "What's happening?"

Mason told Bob that he had tracked them to the Perhentian Islands, off the northeast coast of Malaysia.

"There are two islands where people, mostly backpackers and serious marine biologists, visit," Mason said. "The islands are primitive. Only a handful of places to stay. You can't really hide there. I'll find them tomorrow or the next day at the latest."

Mason told Bob a little about the islands, about how basic everything there was, but also about how the snorkeling and diving were supposed to be among the best in the world.

"The reefs are pristine, but it's only a matter of time before the tourists discover the place."

255

Mason told Bob not to be surprised if he didn't hear from him for a week or more. "There is no communications there," he said. "Not even a radio phone. It's a remote place."

Bob asked how long Mason thought Joey and Jessica would stay.

"I really don't know. Backpackers will sometimes find a place and just not fuckin' leave. I mean, sometimes, they'll stay on an island for a month. I don't think that'll be the case with these two. My guess is that it might be a week or so. But I wanted you to know, in case you don't hear from me. Once I find 'em, I ain't gonna head back to the mainland just to make a phone call. I'll stay on 'em like white on rice."

"So, what's the plan?"

"He won't do anythin' to her there. He wants the money and he ain't gonna get it on the Perhentians. I'm gonna play it by ear. I might move on him there. I might wait till they're back on the mainland. I'm toyin' with the idea of findin' a way to talk to the girl. She's a smart cookie and might listen to facts. I don't know yet."

"I want to be there!" Bob said. There was gravitas in his voice. "This is the part where we decide together what to do. We can't do that if I'm on the other side of the world and not even reachable by phone."

"I know it's what you want, Bob, but I don't know if it's a good idea. The thing you want most is justice for your girl…"

"Justice is only part of it," Bob broke in. "And I'm not so sure I trust 'justice.' I want what you had. I want revenge. You called it the next best thing. I want to be there and watch the life leave his body. I want to see the fear dance across his eyes knowing that it's over. I can't do that if I not there."

"I hear you, Bob. But when we started, he wasn't targetin' a new girl. Plan A puts this Jessica girl at risk. If he gets the sense someone is closin' in on him, he could kill her. That troubles the hell out of me. Her folks don't even know yet. You should find it pretty damn easy to put yourself in their place. Nothin' would be more important than keepin' her safe. That should be our goal, too."

"I don't see anything you'd do differently if I were there," Bob said.

"Maybe. Maybe not. But I work alone. I'm concerned that if you were here there might be things I'd not do to avoid the risks. I gotta keep my options open. We've made a lot of progress doin' it my way. Give me a little more time."

"I hear you, Mason. You want me to stay out of your hair until you wrap things up. I'm not going to make any promises, though. I'll think about it."

"That's all I ask, Bob. If you think about it and how close we are, you won't wanna get in the way."

Calls completed, Mason returned to his room. He had his two glasses of Jack and popped two sleeping pills. Would he avoid the nightmares tonight? God, he hoped so.

The images woke him at four. At least he got six hours of sleep.

Day 22

Joey awoke to the smell of fresh brewed coffee from the in-room coffeemaker. He could hear Jess in the shower. He rose from the bed, opened the curtains and looked out at Kota Bharu. It wasn't much to see, but he knew it was an important city just south of the Thai border. It even had an airport.

He poured his coffee, then added one of the little tubs of half and half. He put on one of the plush white bathrobes and saw that there was a newspaper on the table. Did someone enter their room? Unlikely, he surmised. Jessica must have picked it up. It didn't matter. He had zero interest in the news.

He sipped his coffee, then tapped on the door to the bathroom, opened it and entered. He let the robe slide to the floor, opened the door to the shower and joined her. She smiled at him.

"This is a great shower," she said. He nuzzled her from the rear and playfully nibbled her neck.

"What are you doing?" she asked.

"I need a little breakfast."

"Is that so?"

"Uh-huh."

She turned to face him. They kissed while his hands caressed her butt. He was already aroused. She smiled and took the soap from the dish, rubbed it in her hands to work up a lather, then moved to his groin. She lathered him up, turned him around and did the same to his backside. Still behind him, she reached around and took him in her hand and began to stroke him.

She turned him back around to face her. The shower rinsed the soap away.

"I want you in me," she said, standing and pointing down to a bench along the back wall of the shower. He sat, his back against the wall. She put one foot on the bench then lowered herself on him. She was in control. Slowly at first, she moved up and down. She moaned softly.

"This is what I want," she said. The pace quickened. She looked at his face and saw his eyes closed. He was feeling the moment just as she was. She stepped it up again, driving him deep with every thrust. He started making those little noises that he did when getting close, but she could no longer think about him. She felt her own orgasm rising inside of her, rushing to her pelvis. Then, in a burst of release, she cried out, "Yes! Yes! Yes!" Three thrusts later, he, too, released.

She stayed there with him inside her for a moment, reveling in the satisfaction. Then she pulled her head back, looked him in the eyes, smiled and said, "I'm up for an omelet. How about you?"

They finished their shower, dressed and went to breakfast. At ten, they had checked out and were making the short drive down the coast to the jetty at Kuala Besut. They loaded up on some supplies along the way.

"Everything on the island costs twice what it does on the mainland, if you can even get it," Joey told her as they looked for a market on the way out of Kota Bharu. They grabbed two six-packs of Tiger beer, a bag of Oreos and even two apples. Then they added a few rolls of film for her camera and two of the new Fujifilm disposable cameras in waterproof plastic cases for snorkeling. They found parking near the jetty and were able to grab the last two seats on the noon crossing.

The hour and a half ferry ride was uneventful on a placid sea. Joey and Jessica disembarked at the fishing village on Perhentian Kecil, the ferry's first stop. To call it a village was a stretch. It consisted of a few small wood-frame buildings with tin roofs. One housed a one-room store, another a restaurant. The other structures had no markings. There was no road; just a meandering path. That gave the buildings a non-linear arrangement. The sound of fuel-powered generators could be heard behind the store and the restaurant buildings. There was no electricity provided anywhere in the Perhentians.

"We're going to head up to Long Beach," Joey told her.

"Is it far?" Jess asked.

"Not really. About twenty or thirty minutes. We could try to find a water taxi. Would be quicker and cooler."

"I like that idea," Jess said.

They walked back down to the water.

"Wait here," he told her. "Let me see what I can arrange. I'll use what little Bahasa skills I have."

A minute later he flagged her to join him.

"This is Mat. He'll take us to the Majestic Turtle for two ringgits."

"Hello Mat. I'm Jessica," she said sticking out her hand to shake, but Mat just turned and walked to his boat.

"Not the chatty type," Jess said.

The boat ride was an experience. The ferry had been a big, lumbering vessel that cut a smooth path across the sea between Kuala Besut and the island. Mat's boat was more like a small fishing boat you'd find on rivers and lakes back in the States. Maybe four feet at its widest point and perhaps sixteen feet long. Mat revved the outboard motor and almost immediately tore northward. As soon as he was away from the beach, the little boat picked up speed and splashed through the rolling waves, at times swaying back and forth.

The wind and splashes of the waves blew through Jessica's red hair as she death-gripped the sides of the boat with both hands.

"Holy shit!" she exclaimed to Joey. "Next time we're walking."

"Trust me. You get used to it."

After five minutes that felt to Jessica more like an hour, Mat steered the boat up to the beach. A sign announced they were at Majestic Turtle Chalets.

"This is a great place," Joey said. "Right in the heart of Long Beach. Nice huts, each with their own shower and toilet."

"Hot water?"

He looked at her with a scrunched-up face. "What do you think?"

"All I'm saying is you saw this morning what a good hot shower does for this city girl."

"I'll just have to find a different way to meet your needs."

"I'm sure you will," she said as they climbed out of the boat. Joey gave Mat two one-ringgit notes. They hefted their backpacks and stood at the water's edge while Jessica took in the great arc of the beach.

It was everything Joey had said it would be. Pure, white sand with pieces of shells underfoot. Crystal clear water lapped at the feet and Jessica instantly knew that the snorkeling would be great. The jungle hung back forty or fifty yards and then was resplendent with a variety of palms and other shade trees. Colorful flowers perfumed the air.

Long Beach formed a large crescent as it arcs into the island and then out again. At each end were magnificent rock outcroppings that towered above the water. The Majestic Turtle occupied a prime space at the middle of the crescent. Nestled among the trees overlooking the sea, eight bungalows fanned around a central covered dining area and kitchen.

The owner, Umar, a Malaysian man in his thirties, and Umar's wife, Laila, plus their two children, lived in two-room cabin behind the semi-circle of bungalows. Two generators sat behind that cabin to meet their simple power needs.

A small, fairly quiet one ran round the clock to power the refrigerator, pump and dining area lights at night. The second one ran at Umar's whim in the evenings for the bungalows. He cranked it up at dusk. When he turned it off was another thing. Some nights he would shut it down by nine, others around ten and on rare occasions eleven. Killing the power came with no warning to the guests. One minute they might be reading a book and an instant later the generator went quiet and the lights would flicker out. Guests who were at an exciting part of their books either finished by flashlight or candle.

Joey and Jess got bungalow Number 6. There was nothing fancy about it, but even from the outside it gave Jess a cozy feeling. She liked it immediately.

All the bungalows were raised well off the ground to accommodate the water that rushed past during the rainy season and the occasional typhoon. Number 6 was nestled among shade trees that keep it cooler during the heat of the afternoon.

The cabin was unpainted inside and out. It measured about eight feet square with a small room at the back for a toilet and shower. A mosquito net covered the platform bed, but mosquitos didn't seem to be a problem most of the time. A single light bulb with a pull-string switch hung in the center of the room under the tightly thatched roof.

Jess was taken by the hut's front porch. About three feet wide and the width of the cabin itself, it offered two wooden chairs with padded seats that were akin to Adirondack chairs. She plopped into one, threw her legs up on the wooden rail and gazed out at the sea.

"This works for me," she said.

———————

Mason tried to go back to sleep, but since he wanted to take the first ferry anyway, gave up. He took a shower and shaved. As he stood there looking into the mirror, the face he saw staring back looked haggard and pale. No one would believe he was just thirty-seven years old.

The nights of waking up in terror were taking a toll on him. Dark bags had formed under his eyes and he looked puffy. He looked more closely at his eyes. They were dull and streaked with red. Old man's eyes, he thought to himself. Then a more apt description came to mind: Jack Daniels eyes.

He was at the jetty before the first ferry run of the day at eight o'clock. The ferry made just two roundtrips a day, at eight, then at noon. He had expected it to be packed, but fewer than half of the fifteen seats were taken. The boat, though, was loaded with supplies for the islands.

The crossing on the flat, tranquil sea took about ninety minutes. He chatted briefly with the captain, mostly to ask if he'd seen a red-haired American woman in the past day. No, he hadn't. The captain said the sea can turn rough at times, so he's not always paying attention to the passengers. In fact, the ferries completely shut down service during the rainy season because the crossing is just too dangerous.

The ferry made two stops. First was the jetty at Perhentian Kecil, the smaller island, Mason got off at the second stop, the jetty on the big island of Perhentian Besar. There were no actual hotels on either of the Perhentians. He quickly learned that there were only a handful of very rustic places to stay on both the islands. He spent the next few hours trudging from one group of bungalows to the next asking if anyone had seen an American woman in her early thirties with red hair. No one had. People remember red hair, so he felt confident by mid-afternoon that he could move to Perhentian Kecil, the smaller island.

He took a boat for the short ride from the Besar jetty to the one at Kecil and walked into the village. He was in luck. He asked a waiter standing outside the village's sole restaurant and the man said that a red-headed American woman and a man had gotten off the second ferry just a couple hours earlier.

"You know where they are headin'?"

"Only two places," the waiter responded.

"Is that the trail up ahead?" Mason asked.

"You take boat. Just two ringgit."

Mason thanked the man and walked back down to the beach, secured a boat and was soon pulling ashore at Long Beach. The sign in front of him said Majestic Turtle. He hefted his backpack and strode up toward a small open-air restaurant with six simple tables. He saw her red hair before he was even half-way there.

Mason plopped down at a table near Jessica and Joey. Umar approached him to take his order.

"Good afternoon, sir," Mason said. "I'm lookin' for a place to stay. You got a cabin I can take?"

Umar gave him the specifics for bungalow Number 4 and asked if he would like to see it. Mason said it wasn't necessary. He'd take it. He then ordered lunch and tried to tune in to Joey and Jessica's conversation.

From his seat, Mason could watch them without appearing to stare. He was taken by how Joey doted on her. If it's an act, Mason thought, it's Oscar worthy. He's gentle. He speaks softly. He smiles and his eyes light up. This guy was good. If he didn't know better, Mason would swear they were a couple in love, just like the giggling girl said at the strawberry farm.

Now that's an interesting thought, Mason mused. Could Joey have fallen in love with her? If he did love her, would he kill her? Maybe a better question isn't would he kill her, but could he? If he had fallen in love, how did it change his big plan? Then again, Mason was pretty sure that the cold-blooded killer in Joey wasn't capable of love when lots of money was on the line.

Mason wondered how Jessica truly felt about Joey. If first impressions meant anything, the woman had feelings for him, too. At the very least, she greatly enjoyed his company. You could see it in her body language, especially when they got up to leave and walked back to their cabin. She was draped around him. They looked like a couple of high-school sweethearts.

What, if anything, did it all mean to what Mason should do? What exactly was his next play now that he had caught up with them? His promise to Bob that they would decide together what to do with Joey was less practical now that Jessica was in the picture. From his last conversation with Bob, he knew what his client would want: to kill the sonofabitch. There was even a chance that Bob was already on his way to the island to do it himself.

Then there was Bo, his old friend and Penang homicide detective. Did he need to give Bo a chance to weigh in? That could pose a problem. What if Bo insisted that he come to Perhentian Kecil, arrest Joey and take him back to stand trial? That would take the decision out of his hands.

Worse, it would cause a diplomatic incident. Seven young, innocent

American girls savagely murdered. Relations between the US and Malaysia already were strained. He might be able to convince Bo that everything about the case should end on Perhentian Kecil. That would make Bob happy.

Here's something Mason knew with absolute certainty: Fitz would never want to see Joey stand trial for murdering seven young American girls. Diplomatically, it might be a death blow for US-Malaysia relations. But even more significant, Mason realized, was that heads would roll at State. How do seven young American women all suffer the same brutal death in the same country in a relatively short period of time and no one notice? Fitz, a career State Department man and long-time friend, would certainly be among the first to go. Mason wasn't willing to sacrifice his friend if there were another way.

It weighed on him, but he knew what he had to do. He would not alert Bo and there just wasn't time to loop in Bob, as he had promised to do. He wished he had told Bob to come over when he called him from Kuala Besut instead of arguing for him to stay in Tampa. Well, he didn't and there was nothing he could do about it now. Bob might come anyway. If not, Bob might be pissed at him for taking Joey out on his own, but the bottom line would be that the asshole who murdered Bob's daughter would get what was coming to him. Bob would get over it.

Yes, he would just have to do it himself. And here on the island.

It would be easy if not for one big problem: Jessica.

He had to get her out of harm's way. That would be tough. His guess was that Joey and Jessica were almost never apart. As he thought through options, he realized it wouldn't be enough to simply get her out of the way. She needed to know why. Otherwise, she'd run to the authorities to say that this American guy killed her boyfriend. One thing would lead to another and the whole sordid tale would come out.

No, he had to find a way to talk with her and hope her brain would put the pieces together for her. She was smart enough. But was it already too late for reason? Had she crossed the bridge? Did she love him?

Mason realized that he didn't really have a choice. He had to find a way to talk with her. To lay it all out there and hope the scientist in her who lived in a world of facts would overcome her inner poet. It was a risk, but he had to do it.

How would she react? That was a no-brainer. Without knowing the full story about Joey, she'd be devastated and furious at the same time. He needed enough time to tell it all to her all at once. He was counting on her being able to separate her feelings from the facts. That's a tall order. Something, though, told him she could do it.

The second big concern is that she would confront Joey with it herself. He'd tell her not to, of course. Still, almost anyone would want to hear the story from the person he or she trusted. She might kid herself into thinking she could tell if he were lying. Mason knew, though, that people who have been duped hear and believe what they want to hear and believe. And Joey could make it easy for her. Psychopaths are great liars.

Mason knew he had to be convincing. He had to find the words to win her over. But would she remain silent after Joey was, well, put down? In America, everyone is entitled to a fair trial. For what was about to happen, Mason would be the arresting officer, the prosecutor, the judge and ultimately the executioner. And it was likely to give new meaning to the saying that justice is swift. Confrontation to execution might take but seconds. How would she handle that?

What could he possibly say to her to win her over? Damn! This just might be the most difficult thing he's ever had to do.

Win her over. He considered those words. A dispassionate third party would easily be swayed by the evidence. But Jessica wasn't a dispassionate third party. She appeared to genuinely care for Joey. Was it love? Hmmm, Mason pondered that question again.

Did she love him? She had known him for less than two weeks. She was old enough to be cautious with her heart. She was also less than a year out from her husband's death. She might be adventurous, but, Mason reasoned, she wasn't likely to have allowed herself to be anything more than infatuated with Joey. No, she didn't love him.

Not yet anyway.

And Jessica was smart. In fact, incredibly smart. That was good, though smart people do stupid things all the time. Her training as a highly specialized nurse was to quickly assess facts regardless of how grim they might be, then figure out what she needed to do and do it. These would be the grimmest facts she had ever faced. But her ability to distance herself from the emotions of a situation and focus on the facts would bode well. That, he thought, might be the most important thing about her.

He should find a time when she was alone and tell her the entire truth about Joey. Then, when she would most likely want to run away, he would have to convince her to stay, to act as if nothing had changed. If she tried to flee, Joey might kill her. No loose ends.

He wasn't sure he could pull it off. He knew, though, he had to try.

Mason spent the afternoon on his porch, two bungalows away from Joey and Jessica. She sat part of her time on her porch, too, reading a paperback. They made eye contact at one point and he gave her a small subtle wave and a simple nod of the head. She nodded back and returned to her book.

It was clear they were there to stay, so Mason decided he should try to take a nap. If he kept it short enough, he could probably avoid a nightmare. He set the alarm on his wristwatch to four-thirty and laid down. He left the door to his bungalow open to enjoy the cooling breeze that wafted up off the beach. His body was exhausted, so it didn't take long for him to fall asleep. The alarm woke him as planned. He cleaned himself up, then kept an eye on Number 6.

Joey and Jessica headed to the dining area about an hour later. He was about a minute behind them. They were sitting at a table for two and he took one close by. They were the only ones there.

"Hey!" Mason said. "I just got here today. You guys been here long?"

"Today, too," Jessica said. "I'm Jessica. This is Joey."

"Mason," he said, shaking their hands. "You guys Americans, too?"

"Yes," she answered. "Seattle for me and Joey is from North Carolina."

"I grew up in Georgia. Woof, woof, Georgia Bulldog here."

"Not a lot of us Yanks in this part of Malaysia. Any part of Malaysia for that matter," she said.

"What brings you to the Perhentians?" Mason asked. "It's not what I'd call one of the big destinations."

"The snorkeling here is supposed to be great, at least that's what Joey says."

"You've been here before?" Mason asked Joey directly, hoping to get him to engage in the conversation.

"Yeah. Before the last rainy season. It's spectacular. That's how I knew about this place," he said gesturing to the Majestic Turtle. "I saw it last time I was here. I knew Jess would like it."

"Private bathroom," she interjected with a big smile.

"I've heard the coral is truly awesome," Mason continued, making small talk.

"Yeah. Wait till you see it," Joey said. "And thousands of fish. Have you ever swum some place where there are so many fish you can't see beyond them?"

"No sir, I haven't."

"You will here. It's mind-boggling. And sea turtles, too."

"What about sharks?" Mason asked.

"What about them?"

"Well dang, aren't there a lot of 'em around here? Over on Besar they even got a place called Shark Point."

"Yeah, but the ones around here are blacktip reef sharks. They won't hurt you if you leave them alone. They're timid creatures really."

"Sharks? Timid? That's a stretch."

"Not really. Sharks have gotten a bad name. There are a few hundred species of sharks and only about a dozen are dangerous."

"Well that's fine unless they're swimmin' in the water with you."

"Not going to happen here," Joey said.

"That'll be good news to my partner Bob. The whole idea of sharks scares him shitless!"

"Hey Mason," Jessica chimed in, "we're going snorkeling tomorrow. You ought to come with us."

Mason noticed that Joey stiffened slightly when she invited him but then recovered himself.

"Yeah. That'd be cool," Joey added.

"Sure as shit!" Mason exclaimed. "Who wants to go snorkelin' by themselves? And I'm not sure if Bob will even show up. He's a workaholic. Thanks guys!"

They continued to chat and eventually Jessica suggested that Mason pull the adjacent table up to theirs and join them. Joey seemed okay with it, so Mason did it.

After dinner, Joey and Jessica said they were going for a walk on the beach. It was a beautiful night. They planned to have breakfast about nine and go to the little dive shack at ten to rent equipment and hire someone to boat them around.

Mason said goodnight and headed to his bungalow. The first meeting with Joey didn't go as he had thought it would. Except for that one instant when Jessica invited him to join them tomorrow, Joey struck him as a happy, laid back guy. Hard to picture him as a cold-blooded killer. Then he smirked to himself because he knew there was no question that Joey was just that.

Back in his cabin, Mason poured his glass of Jack and made notes in his journal. With the second glass of whiskey, he popped two of the sleeping pills and curled up on the bed. Maybe it was the sea breeze or the sounds of the cicadas and other night creatures, but Mason fell into a sound sleep and didn't have a single bad dream.

Day 23

Through the window, Mason saw Joey and Jessica walk toward the dining area. He threw on a tee-shirt and shorts and joined them.

"Hey y'all," he said as they took the same seats they had the night before. "Best night's sleep I've had in a month of Sundays. I'm ready to chow down."

"Great!" Jessica answered. "But are you ready to swim with the sharks?"

"I'd be lyin' if I said I wasn't still a little scared about that – sharks bein' sharks and all. I figure, though, that if it were that dangerous this place wouldn't be the snorkelin' capital of the known fuckin' world!"

Mason turned to Joey. "I don't suppose you did much divin' growin' up in Carolina," he said.

"Nah. Just regular old swimming. All my diving and snorkeling have been done in this part of the world."

"Pretty much the same for me, though I did do some spring divin' in north Florida a few times when I was in college."

"What's that like?" Jessica asked.

Spring divin'? Fuckin' cool, actually. The water is crystal clear, colder and fairly deep in places. It's fresh water, so it's easier to stay down. One of the spots where I learnt how to do it was about eighty-five feet deep and with caves at the bottom."

"Caves? At the bottom? Not for me," Joey said. "I have no interest in going someplace I can't see my way out of."

"You got that right, hoss," Mason said with a laugh. "I didn't go nowhere I couldn't see out the other side. I'll tell ya what was great about fresh water divin', though. The manatees."

Joey clearly didn't know what manatees were.

"People call them sea cows. They're big ass lumberin' creatures. I mean, several hundred pounds big. But tame as a fat dog sittin' on the porch. Wouldn't hurt a fly. They just glide along mindin' their own business." Mason used both hands to show gentle up and down forward movement.

After breakfast, they had a few minutes to get ready to go to the dive shack. Back in his hut, Mason pulled on his trunks, grabbed a water bottle and a tube of sunscreen. It was too easy to burn your back snorkeling.

The three of them headed up the beach the short walk to the dive shack that was in front of the other set of bungalows. It truly was a shack sitting about thirty feet from where the gentle waves petered out. They rented snorkeling gear and an innertube with a mesh inner-lining to throw their stuff into, then headed to the beach. Joey said there was a great spot near the point at the north end of the beach.

"Lead on," Mason said. Joey used the rope to pull the tube along in the edge of the surf while the threesome walked toward the far end of the beach. Once there, they threw their stuff in the center area of the tube, put on their gear and headed into the water for the slow swim around the point to a place locals called D'Lagoon.

Joey was right. It was a great spot. The depth of the water varied from about ten feet to maybe twenty or twenty-five. The coral was spectacular. Mason found himself wondering how long it would stay that way if the tourists ever discovered this place the way they had so many islands in Thailand.

The sheer number of fish swimming nearby was staggering. Multi-colored tropical fish, like you would see in an aquarium back in the States, but bigger and quite literally in the thousands. The fish paid absolutely no attention to the swimmers, which meant the three of them could swim within feet of a school.

Same with the turtles. They were less colorful and fewer, of course. He could see maybe a half-dozen in his field of view as he snorkeled the point. But they glided along as if they didn't have a care in the world. Because they didn't.

The first shark caused Mason's pulse to quicken. It was swimming near the bottom and he quickly saw two others near it. They were big enough, maybe five feet, to do damage if they wanted, but like the sea turtles, they didn't appear to have any interest in the swimmers. Still, Mason found himself keeping a watchful eye out. Same with the barracuda that seemed to want to circle him, showing their long mouthful of teeth.

It's easy to get separated while snorkeling. Swimmers spend their time looking down at the coral and the abundant sea life, not over at their friends. Joey raised his head while treading water at one point and it took him awhile to see Jessica. She was fifty feet or so away. Mason was even farther from him.

That's when the thought popped into his mind that a snorkeling accident could be the best way to get rid of Jessica when the time came. They could be snorkeling by themselves at a remote location and he could drown her. There'd be no way it would look like murder.

As quickly as that idea had entered his mind, he jumped to a bigger question that had been gnawing at him. Should he kill her? He didn't know how much she was worth, but knew it had to be a lot more than fifty-thousand dollars.

He thought back to all those purses he had dumped because he didn't know enough to keep them. He had convinced himself that Wallace had left Jess a million dollars in life insurance. If she stayed with him, he was sure he'd end up with a big hunk of that money.

Get real, Joey, he told himself. It was a pipe dream. She would never stick around with him. Look at her, he heard himself say. She's beautiful, smart and rich. She wouldn't settle for him. Not in a million years.

Then, as if on cue, he remembered one of Big Willie's rules: Don't get greedy. He had set out to get fifty-thousand dollars to build Bungalow Paradise. It was within his reach. He could feel it. Stick to your plan, Joey told himself. Besides, there would be other Jessicas.

Joey watched her swim. She popped up her head and looked around in a small panic, then saw him and immediately smiled. He waved to her and she waved back, then put her head down and began kicking toward him.

"I should keep her around longer," Joey thought to himself, "but when the time comes, drowning is the way to go."

The three of them swam for a couple hours. The noon sun on their backs and the growling in their stomachs said it was time to take a break. "The fish aren't going anywhere," Joey said. "Let's go eat. We can snorkel some more later today, if we feel like it. Or tomorrow."

They swam back to the shore, pulling their tube behind them, then made the walk back to the Majestic Turtle.

They went straight to their seats at Umar's little restaurant. They shared a big platter of mee goreng, a spicy-sweet fried noodle dish that contained fresh prawns and an array of vegetables. It was both flavorful and filling. While they were waiting for the food, Joey got up, went into the kitchen area and returned with three cans of cold Tiger beer.

"We brought the beer from an Indian store on the mainland," Jessica said. "Muslims are prohibited from drinking or even serving alcohol. We could have kept it in our bungalow, but what good is warm beer, right?" Mason nodded. "Joey struck a deal with Umar. For a couple ringgits a day, Umar would let us keep the beer in his refrigerator, but we would have to get it ourselves."

After lunch, Joey said he wanted to take a nap.

"You going to join me?" he asked Jessica.

"I'll lie with you for a bit, but I'm not sleepy."

Joey smiled. He took her hand and they left the table.

"See you later, Mason," Jessica said as they walked away.

"You bet, darlin'," he said. "And thanks again you two for this mornin'."

273

Mason finished his beer and walked back to his cabin. He thought about napping himself, but he had slept so well the night before that he just wasn't that tired. Instead, he sat on his porch reading a book.

Jessica came out of her hut about twenty minutes later, saw him and walked over and sat in the chair next to him on his porch.

"Out like a log," she said.

"Does he take short naps or is he out for a while?"

"Probably a couple hours."

"So, Jessica, tell me about you and Joey. Have you been together long?"

"Not really. I met Joey in my hotel café in Batu Ferringhi about two weeks or so ago. We just hit it off. He's really a sweet guy."

"He would seem that way. What do you really know about him?"

She took a moment and looked more directly at Mason. The question struck her as, well, odd.

"What do you mean?"

"Well, you know. What has he told you about his background and all?"

She stared at him again, an inquisitive look on her face.

"What are you getting at, Mason? Do you think you know something about him that I don't? How would that even be possible? You two just met."

Now it was Mason's turn to stare. He would need to tell her at some point. Now was as good a time as any."

He took in a big breath and exhaled it through his nose. He looked at her. Clearly, his mind was working.

"Let's take a walk up the beach. You're not gonna like what I have to say."

She continued to stare at him. Her heart was racing. This was weird. Finally, she stood and said, "Okay. Sure. Let's go."

They walked north up Long Beach and on toward D'Lagoon at the far end of the island.

"So, what's this about, Mason?" Jessica said as they left the Majestic

Turtle.

"It's a long story and like I said, you're not gonna like it, but I swear to you, darlin', it's true."

"Just tell me."

He could hear the exasperation and anger in her voice.

He told her he was a former CIA officer who now did contract security and investigative work from an office in Bangkok. About two weeks ago, he said, a friend at the State Department in Washington referred a father to him whose daughter had been murdered in Mersing. "Do you know where that is?" he asked her.

"Yes. Does this have something to do with that Amanda girl?"

That took Mason by surprise. He stopped walking and turned to her.

"Yes. How do you know about Amanda?"

"When we were in the Cameron Highlands, Joey ran into a German fellow. They'd all been traveling together. Martin, that was his name. Martin said Amanda had been murdered that night in Mersing."

"What did Joey say?"

"That he had walked her back to her hotel, said goodnight, then had a message when he got back to his hotel and had to leave. He said he never saw her again."

"The police checked all the hotels in town and he hadn't checked into any of them."

Jessica said nothing, trying to figure out what to make of the info.

"The next day, Joey unloaded everythin' of Amanda's that had value to a fence he uses in George Town. Passport. Traveler's checks. Credit cards. A fancy camera. Even a locket her daddy had given her. The fence, Willie Chirathivat, family originally from Thailand, gave us a full statement to avoid being charged as an accessory to murder."

"This is bullshit," Jessica said. "Joey and I didn't just meet yesterday. We've been together awhile. I've really gotten to know him. He's the kindest, sweetest guy. You want me to believe he savagely killed this girl? Nope. Not the same Joey. You've wasting your time."

Mason looked into her eyes and could see she was fighting to regain control.

"I know this sounds crazy, Jessica. But you're a smart young woman. You let facts shape what you think. There is no place for emotions in an operating room, right?" That statement surprised her. How did he know she was that kind of nurse? Or any kind of nurse, for that matter?

"Same here. Here's what I'm askin' of you, darlin'. Let me tell you everythin' we know. You try to hear it as someone comin' to it fresh. I know that'll be hard, but I know you can do it. Let me lay it all out for you and then you decide if I'm crazy or if Joey has bamboozled you."

Jessica peered at him for a long time, then subtly nodded her head yes. And with that, he touched her elbow and they resumed their walk up the beach. Mason took her back to the beginning and walked her step by step through why he was certain that her Joey was the serial killer and that she was his next target.

He told her the whole story. He started with Joey's early life as Yusof Zaina in Melaka. How his mother, only eighteen at the time, had sex with a British sailor named Reggie. The next day, Reggie was back on his ship heading to its next port.

"She didn't even know she was pregnant for several weeks," Mason said.

This wasn't new to Jessica. She'd heard it straight from Joey, so she had no reason to doubt it. But it also served to vouch, at least some, for Mason's credibility.

Mason then spoke about Joey's formative years with Pastor Johnny and Mrs. Helen. She was thinking yada-yada-yada. Joey had told her about how the American couple had adopted him and taken him back to North Carolina. Then she realized that wasn't what Mason was now saying happened.

"Wait," Jessica said. "I've heard most of this story before from Joey. But they adopted him and took him back to America. He never said anything about staying in Malaysia or a church school. If he stayed in Malaysia, how come he speaks perfect English like an American? Have you heard how Malaysians speak English? It's nothing like Joey."

"The Jacksons loved him like a son," Mason said. "Mrs. Helen tutored him ever' day. A schoolmate told me that Mrs. Helen and Joey would play a game where they watch a TV show or a movie and he had to try to say lines exactly like the actor."

"How long did they live in Melaka before moving back to the US?" she asked.

"Joey has never lived in the US," Mason said. She gave him a disbelieving look. "Really. Never. I have a school photo in my cabin that was taken when he was sixteen. It's clearly taken at the mission. I'll show it to you later.

"They all lived at the mission for about ten years. Then one day, without warnin', Mrs. Helen packed up and left. Pastor Johnny followed her the next month. Turns out she was fightin' breast cancer. She died about six months later."

Jessica needed a moment. She walked the few feet to where the waves were gently lapping the shore and let the water ripple across her sandals. After a bit, she rejoined him.

"What you're saying," Jessica said, "is that he was abandoned by the only two people in his life and they didn't tell him why?"

Mason simply nodded yes.

Jessica asked why they didn't just take Joey with them. Mason said they couldn't. It is practically impossible for a Christian to adopt a Muslim in Malaysia and Joey wouldn't be able to travel on his own until he was eighteen.

Mason told her that Fitz had interviewed Pastor Johnny earlier that week. The Pastor said the plan all along was that they would keep the mission going until Joey turned legal age. He'd then fly back to North Carolina with them on a tourist visa. Once there, they'd adopt him as an adult.

"Then Mrs. Helen got the cancer."

"So, the woman dies and the pastor doesn't head back to get Joey?"

"No. He did. He searched for Joey, but too much time had passed.

Mrs. Helen held on for months. Joey had moved away."

Mason said Joey lived in the mission for a couple months, but the pastor, thinking he'd be back sooner than later, had only paid the rent two months in advance. Joey was forced out. He had nowhere to go. The money the pastor gave him was gone soon, too.

"I imagine it was a plumb awful time for Joey," Mason said. "He was no longer a boy yet not quite a man. With his looks, I'm sure he didn't easily fit in. You know that picture I mentioned. It was a class photo. He's standin' next to the other kids. His looks stick out like a sore thumb."

Mason said Joey turned to petty crimes, just not from people in his neighborhood.

"He told his buddy, the fence, that he took a bus to KL but that he hated it, so he moved on to George Town."

"This is all interesting, Mason, but it doesn't make him a killer," Jessica said.

"I'm gonna give it all to ya, darlin'. Hear me out."

He then told her how Joey became a skilled purse snatcher in George Town. He explained how Joey targeted older white tourists and how he came to work with his fence, whose nickname is Big Willie.

Mason said Big Willie helped Joey refine his talent at snatching purses. Joey became quite good at it. Good enough, in fact, that he was able to buy a nice motorcycle and move into an upscale apartment in Batu Ferringhi.

"So, he was a purse-snatcher. Not sure I'm believing it, but that's still a long shot from killing that girl in Mersing."

"This is going to be hard for you to hear," Mason said.

"Of, for Christ's sake, stop treating me like a child. Just say what you intend to say."

"Big Willie told us Joey came to him one day with a plan to use his skills as a fake American to woo young women travelin' alone," Mason said. "The girls he had in mind, they all shared two traits. They were in their very early twenties, well, one was nineteen, and every one of them was a blonde."

Joey had observed, Mason said, that some young Western girls didn't have hang-ups about sex with guys they had just met.

"He counted on it never takin' more than a day before he'd end up in the sack with 'em. They'd have sex; their guard would be down with just the two of 'em in the girl's hotel room. That's when he'd use a knife to slash across the front of their necks severin' their carotid arteries. He'd just let 'em bleed out. Once they did, he'd gather all their valuables, sneak off to his hidden red Honda motorcycle and hightail it back to Penang."

Jessica smirked and gave her head a little side-to-side shake.

"You're saying 'them,' as in he did this more than once?" Jessica said, in a voice that showed she was not convinced.

"I'm sorry, honey. Joey did this exact same thing seven times that we know of over two-and-a-half years."

"This is such horseshit," Jessica said matter-of-factly. "You're saying that a boy lovingly raised by missionaries becomes a cold-blooded murderer?"

"That's exactly what I'm sayin'."

She walked on, saying nothing, just staring up the beach.

"Even if I believed you, which I don't," she said after a good minute of silence, "none of what you said describes the Joey I know or Joey's relationship with me. I'm not a young blonde bimbo. I'm a thirty-three-year-old redhead. He didn't rush me into the sack. It took days and I'm the one who started it. Joey and I have been together nearly every minute of every day for two weeks. He's never made a single threatening gesture toward me. He dotes on me, caresses me. If what you say is true, I should have been dead a couple weeks ago."

They continued up the beach. Mason looked at her, then stopped again and faced her. They stared at each other in silence for a moment before Mason spoke again.

"His fence told us that Joey decided on a new plan. He had come to realize that he couldn't keep wooin' and romancin' pretty young things.

He told Big Willie that he would get too old for 'em. Then what would he do? It worried the bejesus out of him."

The new plan, Mason told her, was to target a slightly older, richer American woman. He'd win her trust and probably her love. Once he had, he'd get her to invest at least fifty thousand dollars in his business. The business idea, Mason said, was real. Joey did want to build a bungalow village.

"He was gonna call it Bungalow Paradise," Mason said and saw her react to the name. "Once he had the money, he would find a way to kill her so that it looked like an accident. No one would be the wiser. We got all this from Big Willie."

Jessica turned away toward the sea. Mason let her have a quiet moment. He knew she had to be reeling.

"I know this is overwhelmin', honey," he said softly. "I really do. The way he looks at you and treats you tells me that he might actually care for you. Hell, he might be fallin' in love with you. Who knows, he might ditch the plan to kill you. Maybe. But the fact is," Mason paused until she looked at him, "even if he doesn't kill you, Joey is a serial killer. Is that someone you wanna be with?"

She didn't answer, but her mind was racing. This was supposed to be a goddamn fling, not a death-do-us-part love affair. Why was she so conflicted?

If it were true, Jessica knew she should be repulsed by what Joey had done to those girls. But in that instant, she was close enough to Joey to give him the benefit of doubt. And she felt 100 percent certain that Joey would never hurt her. As she thought about their time together, she grew convinced that he had fallen in love with her. She didn't think she loved him, but she did feel she should give him the benefit of doubt. Something inside her told her she owed him that much.

She knew what she had to do.

"I just don't know," she finally told Mason. "This is a lot to process. I need some time."

"Sure, darlin'. You're safe here," Mason paused, then added, "at least as long as he doesn't know you know. Don't say a word about this to Joey."

She stared at him. She surely was going to talk with Joey. But she also realized, that if by some chance it were all true, Joey might feel trapped. Would he fear her? If so, what would he do about it?

She turned back toward the Majestic Turtle.

"We should head back," she said. "Joey will be waking up soon."

As they walked back, Mason said he did have another question for her.

"I was in your room yesterday at The Smokehouse," he said, evoking a condescending look from her. "You had checked out earlier in the day. I found a notepad where you had written 'how much do I say' on it. The original wasn't there, but I was able to pull it from the top sheet of the pad. What did that mean?"

"I have no idea what you're talking about. I didn't write a note. Joey might have. He's always writing stuff down. I think it's how he figures things out."

"Huh," Mason grunted, clearly not knowing what to make of it. Was Joey going to confess to her? He just didn't see any way Joey would do that. Maybe he was debating if he should tell her how he felt.

When Jessica arrived back at the bungalow, Joey was still napping. She looked at him lying there. It was so hard to believe what Mason had said. As compelling as Mason's argument had been, she knew Joey, she told herself. At least she thought she knew him.

She had to talk with Joey. Mason would be pissed, she knew. And it could be dangerous for her. Still, she owed it to him to hear what he had to say. And if he said it was all true, what then? Would she just up and leave him?

Of course she would.

Then a more ominous question pushed its way into her thoughts: Would he let her?

She didn't know the answer. A shiver ran through her.

Joey must have felt her presence because he stirred then opened his eyes. He smiled at seeing her, then saw that something was wrong.

"What is it, Jess?" he asked with genuine concern.

She sat on the bed.

"We have to talk. I care you, Joey. A lot."

His mind was trying to figure out where this conversation was heading.

"I just heard something," she said, "and I need to hear what you have to say about it."

Joey immediately sat up in the bed.

"Of course. What did you hear?"

"Mason's not exactly who he said he was."

"No? Who is he then?"

"He's a former CIA guy who was hired by the father of that young American woman who was murdered in Mersing, you know, the one Martin mentioned. Amanda."

Joey fought to keep the sudden panic from showing on his face.

"Okay. So?"

"So, he's been tracking down the guy who murdered her." She looked him directly in the eyes. "He says it's you."

"What?" he nearly shouted.

She began to cry. Joey stood and held her. She let him. There was comfort and a feeling of safety in his arms. And yet, fear, too, had crept in. Doubts.

"You don't believe him, do you?"

"Joey, he has details. He knows so much about you. Your name, your Malaysian name, Joey."

Her head was resting on his shoulder. He breathed in the scent of her hair while he rubbed her back in his embrace. She had heard the truth about him but hadn't fled. She was here. With him. That had to be a good thing. Maybe he could plant enough doubt that she wouldn't believe what Mason had said.

"Having my name means nothing. He could have gotten it from my adoption papers. I ask you, Jess, do you think there is a chance I could kill someone?"

"I told Mason he had the wrong guy. That you're a gentle soul. He insisted that he was certain. And there's more."

"Seriously?"

"He said you've never lived in America."

"That's absurd. How does he explain my passport?"

"He didn't."

"And then there's my accent. I don't have one. How could I possibly sound so American if I didn't grow up there?"

"He said your American mom at the mission tutored you every day watching American movies and TV shows."

Joey was stunned that Mason knew this but had to keep up the act.

"Jess, really, how crazy does that sound? I learned to speak this way the same way you did. At home. In America. This is just unreal."

"It gets worse, Joey. He said you had killed seven young women. . ."

". . .No way!" Joey exclaimed, pulling back from her. She gazed at him. There was a pleading look in her eyes. Christ, she wanted to believe him.

"He also said," she was whispering now, "you planned to get me to trust you, so I'd invest in Bungalow Paradise. He actually knew the name of the business you're starting and how much money you need."

Inside, Joey was feeling like a small boat in a bad storm. How could Mason had known that? There was only one way. Big Willie.

But Big Willie wouldn't rat him out – or would he? Maybe the police had tracked fenced items back to the fat Thai and it was either roll on Joey or go to jail. Big Willie had made it clear that under no circumstances was Joey to lead the police to him. Joey felt a twinge of guilt that he might have let Big Willie down, but at the same time, Big Willie let him down too. In any case, that didn't solve the question of how Mason tracked him down. Big Willie had no idea where he and Jess were.

He sat on the bed.

"Jesus, Jess. I don't know what to say. It's such an outlandish story.

I'm not surprised, though, that he knew a few details about my business. I talked it up to people. Any number of people could have told him."

He sat back on the bed, his mind appeared to be a thousand miles away. She sat next to him and he looked over at her. She saw what she felt was pain in his eyes.

"What are you going to do?" he asked her.

"I don't know, Joey. I don't want to believe it. I told Mason I needed time. He said I was safe if I didn't tell you. Am I safe, Joey?"

"God yes, Jess. I could never hurt you. You know that."

He got up and walked to the little sink in the bathroom. He needed to buy some time to think.

Joey's world just turned upside down. He had to focus on one thing now. Survival. How in the world had Mason tracked him down? Who else knew?

He turned on the spigot and splashed water on his face. An idea came to him. He walked back into the room and opened his bag and appeared to grab a ball cap. He used the cap to hide that he also had picked up his pearl-handled knife.

"Listen, Jess. My mind is racing. I need to think this through. I'm going to take a walk. I need some time. I'm sure you understand. I have to figure out how to talk with Mason about it. Maybe I can convince him that he has the wrong guy."

She said that he had time. Mason told her that nothing would happen until they were back on the mainland.

"When he gets back to Kuala Besut," she told him, "he plans to call a homicide detective in Penang who will come arrest you."

"Geez." That told Joey that at least one other person knew. The fact that it was a homicide detective in Penang meant that they had probably linked him to Mary Higgins. He could hang if he couldn't escape.

She was sitting on the bed. He reached down, cupped his hand on her cheek, then bent and kissed her.

"Why don't you rest while I walk," he said. "I'm not sure how long I'll be. If you see Mason, don't tell him you told me. I need to figure this out."

He turned and walked out the door. He needed to make sure that Mason saw him, so he walked to the dining area to get a fresh bottle of water. He struck up a conversation with Umar about what was for dinner. Out of the corner of his eye, he saw Mason standing in the doorway of his cabin. He gave a small wave and Mason waved back. That was good. He needed to get Mason to follow him.

Mason was a lone operator. At least, that's what he told Jessica. Joey needed to make Mason disappear. He couldn't kill the man in his room, though. That would summon the authorities. He needed to lure him away first and then kill him. That way he could leave Mason's body in a place it would not likely be found.

Joey left the Majestic Turtle and started walking toward the north tip of the island.

There was a risk, Mason realized, that Jessica had just told Joey and the man was about to flee the island. Mason threw on a shirt and hurried to the edge of the bungalow grounds in order to keep Joey in view. He waited till Joey was well up the beach then followed him. There was enough distance between the two men that unless Joey turned around and peered closely at him, he wouldn't recognize Mason.

Joey wanted Mason to follow him, though. This little gambit would be worthless if he didn't. Part way up the beach, Joey stepped down to where the surf washed up on the shore. It was a natural movement, but also turned him so he could glance back toward the Majestic Turtle. Sure enough, Mason was just leaving in his direction. Joey smiled, then continued up the beach.

They had been walking for about half an hour when Joey slowed a bit. He glanced back down the beach and saw Mason still following him. Joey needed Mason to see where he would leave the beach.

Joey knew there was a seldom-used trail that headed back into the jungle. After a short way, the trail would fork. The left fork would

285

continue up and over the mountain to Turtle Beach on the other side of the island. The more-often-taken right fork continued to D'Lagoon.

Mason saw Joey disappear into the Jungle. He picked up his pace. He couldn't let Joey get away. He had tracked Joey to the island largely by relying on Jessica using her credit cards. If Joey were to leave her behind and run, he could vanish. Mason wouldn't let that happen.

Trying to go faster in the beach sand, though, was taking a toll on Mason. The nights of little sleep, he realized, were catching up with him. He was laboring.

Mason saw the trail that Joey had followed and took it. The jungle was dense and this trail narrow. Mason could tell it wasn't much used. The oppressive heat and humidity, along with the climb up the steep hill wore him down even more. Still, he pushed on.

He didn't want to come upon Joey unexpectedly, so he tried to listen for the man ahead of him on the trail. But the jungle here is loud. A creepy feeling came over him and he felt very alone.

Up ahead, Joey came to the fork. He knew that the cross-island trail was used even less than the one to D'Lagoon, so he took it. But he needed to make sure than Mason didn't take the wrong path. About ten yards up the trail, he dropped his hat as if by accident. Mason would see it and make the right choice.

Mason knew Joey was ahead of him, but no idea how far. The trail grew steeper. His breaths more pronounced. A thought flashed in his mind about what he would do if the trail forked. He'd have to guess. All he could do was hope that when he got to the other side of the island that he'd see Joey walking on the beach. After all, he didn't want to catch him, just not let him get away. He picked up his pace to try to close the gap, but that caused him to grow even more winded. He had to see someone about the nightmares, he told himself. He couldn't go on much longer this way.

Further up the path, Joey has found a good hiding spot in thick jungle just off the side of the trail. The trail had been climbing over the rise in the center of the island. Joey had time to catch his breath. Before too long, though, he could hear Mason approaching. The man was breathing heavily.

The moment Mason passed him, Joey lunged. He took Mason sprawling to the ground. With a well-practiced move, Joey brought the knife to Mason's neck. But he did not cut him.

"I want some answers, Mason," he said. Mason didn't move or say a word. Joey had a knee between Mason's shoulder blades. He held Mason's head up to expose his neck with his right hand and had the knife in his left hand touching his pursuer's neck. A small trickle of blood dripped to the ground.

"Did Amanda's dad really hire you?"

"Yeah," Mason wheezed out. "He's a rich guy. Political connections. Got to me through the State Department."

Mason decided there was no reason to hold back the information. He didn't want to anger Joey because the man might simply cut his throat like he had the girls. He wasn't a fool, though. He knew Joey would never purposefully let him live. Mason had to figure how to get out of this deadly predicament.

"How did you find out who I am?"

"Good old-fashioned detective work. Hey, bud," Mason added with gasps, "I'm havin' a hard time breathin' here. Can you take some of the weight off my back?"

"Not going to happen."

"I talked," Mason continued, struggling to breathe, "to people who had seen you," he said pausing again for short breaths, "then I found out about the mission and Pastor Johnny and Mrs. Helen." Another pause and an effort to breathe. "She left because she had the cancer, by the way. She died the next year." Mason felt the knife momentarily drop away from his neck and the weight lift ever so lightly from his back. It's now or never, he thought.

With a singleness of mind and body, Mason threw himself upwards. The move caught Joey off-guard, causing him to slide just enough off Mason that the older man was able to roll away and stand.

They faced each other on the trail. Joey still held his knife.

"I should have just killed you," he hissed.

"Missed your chance, good buddy." Mason crouched in a defensive posture. "You are so fucked up. I actually feel sorry for you. Well, actually, I fuckin' don't."

Joey glared at him. Mason decided to rock Joey's world a little more.

"You really blew it, you know. You should have found a way to hold on in Melaka," Mason said. Joey didn't respond. "Pastor Johnny came back for you just like he said he would. That man loved you. Now that he knows you're a fuckin' psychopath he probably is havin' second thoughts."

"I did stay. He didn't come back. You're lying to me."

"I'm not fuckin' lyin', you piece of shit. Mrs. Helen hung on for several months. Once your ma died and he had her buried, he hauled his butt straight to Melaka."

Mason could see Joey's mind working. Mason almost knew what the young man was thinking. How much different his life would have been. Yeah, Mason thought as he stared at Joey, there's that look of recognition that he totally fucked up. Then Joey seemed to snap out of it and peered back at Mason with a new resolve.

"How did you find out about my business?"

"The fat Thai rolled on you. He was facin' a murder charge. He gave your sorry ass up like that." Mason clicked his thumb and middle finger.

Joey nodded slightly and pursed his lips a little. He had known it had to have been Big Willie. He wasn't done with the questions.

"How did you find me?"

"This is great, Joey. You think we're playin' twenty fuckin' questions! But hey, dickwad, I'll play along a bit. I didn't find you. You fucked up, man. You were so goddamn cock-sure that you never thought anyone might be on to you."

Joey clearly didn't get where Mason was heading.

"I found Jessica, nimrod. We tracked her credit cards. Ever' time she used one, we knew where you were. Then put two and two together to figure out where you were headin' next. Fuck man, I got to the Perhentians before you did! Isn't that a goddamn hoot!"

Joey had heard all he could stand to hear. He lunged at Mason. The two tumbled to the ground. Mason's focus was on getting the knife out of Joey's hand. They rolled and then rolled again.

Joey, though, was younger, bigger and stronger. Almost as quickly as it had begun, he had Mason pinned to the ground once more. The older man wiggled fiercely and tried to throw his legs up with force to dislodge Joey.

"Enough of this, old man," Joey said, barely above a whisper. The two men locked eyes, which gave Joey a moment's pause. He had never engaged the girls straight on this way. But that moment was fleeting. With the single-mindedness of the psychopathic killer he was, he brought his pearl-handled knife to Mason's throat. In one powerful move, Joey sliced the blade through Mason's neck.

Mason knew it was over. He could see his own blood squirting skyward during his last moments of consciousness.

There was no fight left in him. He was ready.

His mind drifted to Sylvie. If there were an afterlife, he hoped he'd be with her soon. But would God forgive him those fifty-four innocent lives? He would soon know the answers.

Then, Sylvie was there. He could see her. Clearly. Sylvie was saying something. "It's okay. I'm here." She reached out. All his doubts evaporated. He felt a peace that he hadn't felt in, well, ever. And with Sylvie's beautiful smiling face beckoning him, Mason Ray, the boy from a little farm on the other side of the world, died.

Joey waited until he was certain that Mason was gone, then dragged his body well off the trail. He pulled it through the jungle vegetation before dumping it next to a tree. Before he left, though, he went through Mason's pockets to remove his wallet. That way, even if his body were found one day, identifying him would be hard. He'd throw the wallet away in a different part of the jungle. He also took the man's watch. Once a thief, always a thief.

Joey headed back toward the trail. There was a good chance, he thought, that the wild animals that call the jungle home would pick Mason's bones clean. But even if not, the odds were small that Mason would be found soon.

Back on the trail, Joey worked to cover the blood with leaves and other jungle debris. But there was a lot of blood. "Good enough," he said, finally. He figured that a rainstorm would wash away the residual blood in the next day or so anyway.

————————

Bob Anderson wanted to be there when Mason captured Joey. He wanted to watch as Mason ended the man's life, perhaps the same way Joey had ended Amanda's. That would be justice.

When Mason had called him from the mainland, it was clear that he'd find Joey in the next day or two. It took Bob less than thirty minutes of thinking about it after the phone call to book the next flight to Kuala Lumpur. From KL, he took a local carrier to Kota Bharu, then hired a taxi to take him to the jetty in Kota Besut. He was exhausted, yet excited. He had missed the last ferry to the islands, so he found a room in the one fleabag hotel he saw.

The next morning Bob was on Perhentian Besar, not knowing that he was literally retracing Mason's steps from the day before. He spent until mid-afternoon looking for them on the big island. He had the faxes of Joey and Jessica's photos, but decided it would look too official to show them. Instead, he noticed that nearly everyone was in their twenties with few of those he met being Americans.

He didn't even ask about Joey. Instead, he said he was looking for his niece, a red-haired American woman in her early thirties. One couple eyed him suspiciously and said that another American had been asking a red-headed girl the day before. He soon exhausted the few places to stay on Besar. He took a boat to Kecil.

It didn't take long. A backpacker he asked at the jetty had seen her on Long Beach. "Don't see many gingers here, mate," the young man said in an English accent. "Especially on such a pretty bird." The fellow said Bob could either take the trail or go by boat. "I think she's at the Majestic Turtle. There are only two places. If she's not there, she'll be at the other."

Bob headed back down to the water and hired a young man with a boat to take him to the Majestic Turtle. Bob was walking up from the beach in front of the Majestic Turtle a few minutes later.

As he approached, he stopped in his tracks and turned around to keep from staring. Jessica was sitting at a table in the dining area of the little complex. No sign of Mason or Joey. He composed himself, turned back around and continued. A Malaysian man was working in the kitchen, saw him and came over and greeted him with a smile.

"Welcome, my friend. Would you like a bungalow?" Umar asked.

"Yes. Hi," he said. "I'm Bob Anderson. I'm looking for a friend who would have gotten here in the last day or two. Maybe you've seen him. His name is Mason. He's an American. About forty years old."

"Yes," Umar said. "Mason here. He in bungalow 4, but he's not there now. I saw him walk up the beach a little while ago. You want to wait? Want food? Drink?"

"Sure. Do you have a bungalow I can take?"

"Yes. Number 5 is next to Mason. Ten ringgit."

Bob pulled out some cash and gave the man twenty ringgits for two nights. "I might stay longer. It's up to my friend."

He ordered a Coca Cola and a chicken and vegetables stir-fry, then headed over to bungalow 5, a basic one-room wooden cabin with a platform bed and built-in nightstand. There was a small toilet area behind a wall with a hose that could be used to fill the toilet tank or be used as a shower. He threw his pack on the bed, then headed back to the dining area. Jessica was no longer there.

"I'm Umar," the Malaysian man said as he brought Bob his food and Coke. "I'm the manager."

"Nice to meet you, Umar."

He sat there, devouring his lunch. The stir-fry came with a small bowl of chili flakes to sprinkle on his food if he wished it to be spicier. Damn, it had been too long since breakfast, he was hungry, and it was good.

Bob looked up from his lunch and saw Joey approaching from a trail down the beach.

Every inch of him wanted to jump up and beat the living daylights out of the man. He so wanted to hurt him. Hell, he wanted to beat him to death. But he talked himself down while forcing himself not to stare at the man. Mason would have a plan. Besides, Mason was the hired killer. He should let Mason do what Mason does.He would just like to watch it happen. When he heard himself say that in his mind, that he wanted to watch, he told himself it was a sick thought. Then, just as quickly, said he didn't care.

Joey passed within four feet of him as he strode through the dining area to bungalow 6. Not only was Joey here. He was in the very next hut.

He had half-expected to see Mason tracking behind Joey. But thirty minutes passed and no Mason.

———————

After throwing leaves on the bloody path, Joey had continued on the trail. He descended the mountain to the other side of the island. He stopped to wash the blood off his hands in the surf. Then he headed south to a different trail head that would connect him back to the island's east shore just below the Majestic Turtle. As he approached the bungalow village, he saw Jessica standing on the front porch of their cabin.

"I needed that," he said with a smile as he approached her. "Let's talk. There's something I need to tell you. Then I think I should talk to Mason. Clear the air. I'm sure he'll see that he has the wrong guy."

They went back inside their cabin.

"I think I figured out what's going on," he said as they sat on the bed. "There is a sliver of truth to what Mason told you. I should have told you myself back in the Highlands."

"What about that awful story could be true?"

"When I got the idea for Bungalow Paradise, I decided I needed to look the part of a businessman. I would need a potential investor to take me seriously. All I had was backpacker stuff. I found a tailor in George Town to make me some professional-looking clothes. You know, a suit, dress slacks, a few shirts. The guy asked me why I was doing it?

"I told him all about my idea and how I needed another fifty thousand dollars and that meant finding an investor."

"Was his name Big Willie?"

"Yeah. That's him. When I went back for my first fitting, this Big Willie guy says that with my looks I should be able to get the money out of a woman traveling alone. He said women in their thirties and forties – your age – traveling alone usually have money in the bank back home. I should have cut him off, right then, but I kept listening."

Joey told her how his tailor walked him through a scheme to romance a woman, get her to trust him enough to put the fifty thousand in his business, then let her catch him in bed with another woman. He said she'd want out, but that he had associates in Singapore who could set up the transaction to make it virtually impossible for her to get her money back.

"I'm ashamed of all this, Jess." He took a deep breath and looked directly in her eyes. "I didn't meet you by accident. I targeted you. . ."

"What?! Fuck, Joey!"

"It wasn't like me, Jess. Then something happened that I just didn't see coming. You took my heart and made it your own. I love you, Jess, with every shred of my being."

She let the love comment pass.

"So, the difference between your story and Mason's is that you weren't going to kill me, but cheat on me so I'd leave you."

"Yeah."

They sat in silence for a bit.

"There came a point when we were in the Highlands," Joey continued, "that I realized I could never cheat on you. I struggled with whether I should tell you. I made the wrong decision. I decided that there was no reason why I had to tell you because, apart from choosing you on purpose, I never did anything else that I regretted. I've been honest with you since."

"Christ, Joey. I don't know what to make of this."

She stared at him and he kept her locked in his gaze. Finally, she asked him about the seven murdered girls.

"Why did this Big Willie guy tell Mason you killed them?" she asked.

"I can only guess," he said. "I think Big Willie is covering for someone. I mean I only knew the guy a short time, but it was clear to me that he wasn't just a tailor. He even connected me to the people in Singapore to draw up my business papers and come up with the way to shield the money. The guy was clearly in some kind of underworld crime ring or something.

"Here's what I think. The real killer is someone he's protecting for some reason. It was easy to give me up and make me look guilty."

Jess look at him softened. It seemed to make sense. At least it was plausible.

"I need to talk with Mason," Joey said. "I'm sure if I spell it all out to him, he'll see that what I'm saying is true. The only thing I'm guilty of is deceiving you. While I'm ashamed of doing that, it's not illegal. I never actually did it. He'll see I'm not his man."

They sat quietly for a minute. Then Jessica broke the silence.

"What now?" she asked.

"We have to talk with Mason. Is he around?"

"I haven't seen him since he and I spoke earlier today."

They walked together to Mason's bungalow and knocked. Of course, Joey knew there would be no answer.

"We'll catch him at dinner," Joey told her.

"Unless he's in Kuala Besut calling the detective."

"That wouldn't be good," Joey answered. "The law here isn't like it is in the US. Once you're arrested, it can be a fast track to being convicted.

If what Mason told you is what they think, I could be convicted and hung before you could blink an eye."

———————

Bob was about to head to his bungalow when he heard Joey and Jessica coming out of their cabin. They walked to Mason's cabin and knocked on the door. There was no answer, so they headed toward the restaurant.

Umar approached them, but Joey dismissed him. "We're just going to grab a couple of our beers, Umar. Okay?"

"Yes. Okay," Umar said and retreated to the kitchen. Joey followed him there and returned moments later with two frosty cold Tiger beers.

Jessica was indeed striking, Bob thought to himself as he watched she and Joey sipping their beers. It wasn't just her red hair. Yes, the hair was the first thing anyone would notice about her. What drew him in was her shimmering green eyes. The color would be at home in the jungle that engulfed them. They say that eyes are the windows to the soul and looking, even briefly, at Jessica's eyes he felt he knew the truth behind the cliché.

In her eyes Bob caught a glimpse not of a successful, self-assured woman. He saw a young girl torn between two bad choices. He remembered seeing that same vulnerable look in his Amanda. She was maybe twelve at the time. She was holding a secret about her best friend, Cari.

Cari had sworn her to not tell a soul that her cousin, an older boy of fifteen, was sneaking into her room every night and molesting her. Amanda had known it was wrong, that Cari needed to get help. But she found it agonizingly painful to even think about betraying a sacred trust. Bob knew his little girl well enough to know that something was seriously wrong.

He began a slow, loving chat with her. Amanda opened up. Together, Bob and Amanda chose to speak first to the school counselor. It felt easier to do that to go straight to the police. The counselor knew exactly what to do.

Cari didn't speak to Amanda for months. Eventually, though, the two found the special bond between them again. Cari remains to this day…well, remained to the end, one of Amanda's dearest friends.

That look wasn't anything he expected to see in Jessica. She was struggling with something. What, he wondered? Had Mason told her about who Joey really is?

Shit. He was staring. He had to remind himself to try not to look directly at her. Still, he felt a fatherly need to protect her.

Her skin was pale, a common trait for a redhead. And the sun had brought out her freckles that danced lightly on her cheeks. She was a beautiful young woman. He realized that she wasn't that much younger than him. He acknowledged to himself that if it were a different time, he'd be attracted to her.

She glanced over at him and caught him staring again. He made a face and mouthed, "I'm sorry," then dropped his eyes to his plate. He took another bite and glanced back at her. She was listening to Joey talk but caught his eye and offered a faint smile.

There was no way he was going to let Joey harm her. No. Fucking. Way.

Bob strained to hear their conversation but could only grab bits and pieces. He thought he heard Joey say, "a couple more days." Jessica didn't say much, but it was easier to understand her when she did because she was facing more in his direction. He did pick up, "I wonder where he is." Then, Joey said something, but he couldn't tell what. He did hear her response. "The sooner the better. You need to convince him he's wrong about you."

They finished their beers and rose to return to their cabin. Jessica stopped at Bob's table.

"Hi. You're new. I'm Jessica and this," she motioned for Joey to come back and introduce himself, "is Joey."

"I'm Bob."

The name sparked a reaction from both. Could this be Mason's partner? Bob picked up two distinctively different yet subtle reactions.

Joey tensed. Jessica looked relieved.

"Are you Mason's friend?" she asked.

"Guilty as charged," he answered. "Have you seen him?"

"Not since lunch. He's probably off exploring," she said. "Do you live in Bangkok, too?"

"Nope. Tampa."

At the mention of Tampa, Joey's stomach knotted. He remembered that Amanda was from Tampa and her father was the one who hired Mason.

"So how do you know Mason?" Jessica asked.

"My company hired him to do some work for us. He and I clicked."

"He should be back soon," Jessica said. "If you see him, tell him we're looking for him."

"Sure," Bob said.

Jessica and Joey returned to their cabin. Joey had a new worry. Mason must have told Bob everything he knew. Why else would he have come all the way to Malaysia and show up now?

Mason was not around for dinner. That troubled Jess. The only thing that made sense was that he'd changed his mind and headed to the mainland.

"He's probably just out somewhere," Joey told her. "Let's just hang close. I really want to talk with him."

They stayed at the table for the rest of the evening. Bob sat nearby. Joey knew that Mason wouldn't be returning but played his role. He asked other guests if they had seen him. None had since lunchtime.

At about ten o'clock, Umar told everyone in the restaurant that he was getting ready to turn off the power for the night. The guests all rose and headed back to the bungalows.

It wasn't a night for making love, though Jess did snuggle up to Joey. She eventually fell asleep. But not Joey. He always had a plan and now he knew that he needed a new one.

He loved this girl and he had no reason to doubt her loyalty to him.

He was sure that she would see the danger in his waiting to be charged with murder. Innocent people are executed in America all the time. She would realize, he knew, that Malaysian justice is far swifter. Charged, tried and executed in months, not years. He was confident he could convince her to run away with him.

He also knew that she had money. Wallace had left her an insurance benefit, at least. They likely could live off her money for the rest of their lives, if she were willing. And, of course, if they could get at it.

Depending on how much the homicide detective in Penang knew, though, simply getting rid of Mason might not have been enough. The detective knew her name or he wouldn't have been able to track her credit cards. They needed to move swiftly to get to her money.

A new plan started to form in his mind. They should give the appearance of waiting for Mason another day. Every day that they stuck around after he went missing would make them less obviously connected to his disappearance. But then they had to bolt.

Joey was convinced that they needed to head back to the mainland to focus on two things. First, put some distance between them and Perhentian Kecil. But just as importantly, Joey felt, was to move Jess' money into accounts with a new identity. God how he wished he could turn to Big Willie. But that was off the board.

Then the next best thing became obvious to him. Big Willie's Singapore family was probably even better at these kinds of financial issues. And they already knew who he was.

When he and Jess got to the mainland, they'd need to head south. Mason was a private detective with no legal authority. Their passports – her real one and his fake one – would not be flagged entering Singapore.

They'd go there and meet with the Chirathivats. Joey thought again about how much money Jess might have. Again, he told himself that it was likely to be a million dollars. That would be enough, he was sure, to interest the Chirathivats.

They'd take a healthy cut, but it would be worth it. They could put

298

him and Jess in a safe house, create new identities for them and create a scheme for moving and hiding her money.

With new identities, they could relocate almost anywhere. The more he thought about it, the more he liked it. He just had to convince Jess. He was sure he could do it. In fact, he was sure she already was with him. He didn't doubt that she loved him even if she hadn't actually said it.

He decided that first thing in the morning, he'd convince her that they needed to leave before Mason returned with the police. In reality, he just wanted to put distance between them and Bob and head to Singapore.

Day 24

J oey kissed Jessica awake. When she opened her eyes, he was there smiling down at her.

"Good morning," he said. "I have an idea that I want to talk with you about."

She sat up and he told her he thought they should leave on the first ferry back. They'd be in Kuala Besut by mid-afternoon. Then he told her why.

"Listen, I think you were probably right," he said. "I bet Mason went to the mainland to call the cop in Penang. They could be here by the afternoon. They'll arrest me, Jess. I'm being framed. I just know it. You do to. I know you do."

"Running only makes you look guilty," she answered.

"This isn't America. I could be convicted and hung before we know it."

Jessica was not all in, though. The doubt was written all over her face. Joey pressed on.

Bob, he told her, would probably wait for Mason, but they shouldn't tell him – or anyone, for that matter – that they were leaving. They should just abandon their stuff in the bungalow and leave.

"Seriously? I don't know, Joey. You know how that makes us look?"

"Well, let's not say anything for now. Let's go eat breakfast. Who knows, maybe Mason is back. After breakfast, I'll run to the jetty and get our ferry tickets. We can decide after I get back if we want to say anything."

One cabin over, Bob was awake and worried. It was highly unlikely that Mason had gone to the mainland. And he certainly hadn't been out last night chasing a skirt. No, Mason would stay close to Joey. Bob was sure of that. It only left one real option. Joey had done something to Mason. He was most likely dead. It was a cold, sobering thought.

Bob headed to the restaurant to find Umar. None of the other guests seemed to be up yet.

"Good morning, Mr. Bob," Umar said cheerfully. "What you want for breakfast?"

"Just coffee for now, Umar. Listen, Mason's still not back. You said you saw him head up the beach yesterday afternoon. What's up there?"

"D'Lagoon. People go there to snorkel. Snorkeling very good."

"Did Mason look like he was going to snorkel?"

"No. He just walking. Maybe he take trail to other side of the island."

"There's a trail up there?"

"Yes. About fifteen-minute walk to trail. Trail go back into jungle, then becomes two trails." He made a V with his fingers.

"The trail forks?"

"Yes. Right trail goes to D'Lagoon. Left trail crosses island. Trail not used, though. Much better trail there." Umar pointed to where Bob had seen Joey approach from the day before.

Bob had a sick feeling. He was all but certain now Joey had found a way to lure Mason to the trail and kill him. He was unsure what to do. That's when he saw Joey and Jessica walking toward the restaurant for breakfast.

"Hi Bob. Any sign of Mason?" Joey said, much more chipper than yesterday.

"No. Still not here. What do you make of it?"

"Beats me. Maybe he met someone."

Bob gave no reaction.

"I'm sure he'll come rolling in sometime today," Joey added.

He and Jessica sat in their usual seats and told Umar what they wanted. Bob decided he should eat something, so he ordered a couple scrambled eggs, toast and a plate of fruit. Umar refilled his coffee.

THE NEXT BEST THING

Jessica was silent. In fact, she didn't utter a word the entire time they were eating. Joey made comments from time to time, but even he stopped. Finally, Joey stood and Bob heard him tell her, "Listen, I'm going to go do that thing we discussed." He turned and walked to the beach. He flagged a young man in a boat and headed south toward the jetty.

As soon as Joey was on the boat, Bob moved to Jessica's table.

"We have to talk," he said. "Did Mason tell you why he was here?"

"Yes."

"How much did he tell you?"

"All of it, I think."

"And…"

"Joey says it's not true."

"Wait, you told Joey? Did Mason tell you to do that?"

"Mason said not to, but I've gotten to know Joey and I don't see how he could possibly be the right guy. Then he and I talked about it yesterday and I know what probably happened."

She told him the story about the tailor and Joey being framed.

"It all makes sense," she said.

"No, it doesn't. Joey is lying to you. He's never even been to America."

"Yes, he has. He spent most of his childhood there. That stuff about living at a church school in Melaka is crap."

"Jessica, let's go look in Mason's cabin. I'm sure he has a photo with him of Joey at the school when he was sixteen."

She stared at him a moment, then said. "Okay."

They got up and walked to Mason's bungalow. Inside it only took Bob a moment to find Mason's file. Stuck in the file was a blow-up photo of Joey, one of the Pastor and his wife, and a class photo. It was clearly taken in Malaysia. There were about a dozen kids in the picture, all but Joey looking 100 percent Malaysian. It was taken outside, and she could see a Malaysian sign in the background.

She sat on Mason's bed, staring at the picture. It was true. Joey was raised in Malaysia. Tears welled up in her eyes. Suddenly, she doubted

302

everything he had told her. No, she was beyond just doubting him. In that moment, she realized Joey had killed those girls, had taken Bob's daughter's life.

She looked up at him. Tears streaming down her face.

"Where is Joey going?" Bob asked her.

"To the jetty to get ferry tickets for the first ferry. He wants us to sneak away later this morning."

"Go put on some walking shoes and meet me back here. Quickly."

She left and Bob glanced around Mason's cabin. He knew Mason would have a weapon somewhere and that he probably didn't have time to grab it when he followed Joey up the beach. Bob was certain now that Joey had killed Mason. He had to find Mason's gun before Joey got back.

He looked first in Mason's backpack, but nothing was there. He next checked the tiny bathroom. Not there either. There was a small closet area that Mason had hung a couple shirts and a pair of pants. Nothing. He was getting frustrated.

Think, Bob told himself. Mason would want the gun where he could grab it quickly if he needed it. Near the bed, in all likelihood. He checked the mattress and discovered a Glock 17 with a magazine in it and a second mag lying next to the weapon lodged between the mattress and the wall. He took the Glock and the extra mag. He pulled a big shirt from Mason's closet and put it on. It hung baggily and covered his pockets. No one would be able to tell he was armed.

He heard Jessica come back up the steps and joined her.

"We've got to get moving. Umar saw Mason head up the beach a few minutes after Joey yesterday. The only thing up there is a trail that either goes to a place called D'Lagoon or across the island. Umar said no one uses that trail. Then, right after I got here, I saw Joey come from the other trail across the island just below the Turtle. We got to go find Mason before Joey gets back."

Bob and Jessica headed up the beach, just as Joey, then Mason had the day before.

"Do you know where this trail is?" he asked as they neared the point.

"I think so. We're almost there. Joey and I went snorkeling up here yesterday with Mason. I remember seeing it."

A minute later, the trail entered the jungle to their left. Bob couldn't tell where it went once into the jungle. The trail seemed to head toward a hill that rose at least one hundred feet from where they stood. They headed into the jungle.

There was an eeriness about the jungle. It took Bob back to the war. There were all those sounds that Bob figured to be monkeys, birds, bats, millions of insects and even frogs. It can be disconcerting to go from the sound of the gentle surf to the symphony of the jungle in a mere hundred feet or so. But that's how overwhelmingly dense jungle can be.

Bob and Jessica headed up the trail. Walking the path required looking down because of a thick undergrowth of roots. But looking down was also where they might see hints that Mason had come this way. You couldn't focus just on the ground in front of you, though. This was the jungle and you didn't want to stumble on to something that might hurt you.

Most animals are not aggressive unless provoked. Bob remembered from his Vietnam days that he didn't want to spook a giant monitor lizard. They were docile – until they weren't. If they sink those razor-sharp teeth into you, you're going to end up in bad shape. Same with monkeys. Who knew what other creatures might be nearby? He could certainly hear scurrying just out of sight. Probably the monitor lizards, he told himself.

They were about ten minutes up the trail, just passed the fork and near what appeared to be the top of the hill. They crested it and Bob stopped. He saw signs of blood on the trail. He squatted and looked closely. He brushed aside leaves and saw the ground stained dark in about a three-foot circle. He knew from his days in Vietnam that it was blood – a lot of blood.

"This isn't good," Bob said to Jessica. She knelt and as a surgical nurse immediately knew Bob was right.

"Oh God. Where is he?" she said, standing to look around.

"Mason!" Bob called out, but they both knew Mason wouldn't be answering. Bob surveyed the jungle around them. He saw the flora squished and torn in a narrow path moving away from the trail. They peered into the jungle but didn't see anything.

"Wait here," Bob said. "I'm going to see where this leads."

"I'm a nurse, Bob. There's a chance he's still alive. I need to be there."

They worked their way through the jungle vegetation about fifty feet off the trail and found Mason. His throat had been slashed just like the girls. The eyes in his lifeless body stared up at them.

"Oh fuck," Bob mumbled. "Fuck. Fuck. Fuck."

Jessica started to sob, the enormity of everything crushing in on her.

"Nothing we can do," Bob said, answering her unasked question. "There are no police on this island. I say we get out of here and back to the mainland as soon as we can. We'll call Bo – he's the detective in Penang Mason was working with. He'll take care of it."

At that moment, Joey seized Jessica from behind. His powerful left hand held his knife to her throat.

"I'm sorry about this Jess," Joey whispered into her ear. When I said I loved you, I meant it. I really did. But now you know the truth. I wanted to spend the rest of my life with you, Jess, but it's not going to happen now, is it?"

Bob couldn't believe he didn't hear or sense Joey sneaking up on them. He must have been returning from the jetty and saw them heading up the beach. He probably had the boat drop him at the D'Lagoon. They had been so focused on Mason and the jungle was, well, loud. They just tuned everything else out. He looked over at Joey holding Jessica. They were just four feet from him.

She squirmed and he held the knife tighter against her throat. A small amount of blood started dripping down her shirt. She wasn't crying. Her eyes were wide open and what he saw in them was anger more than fear.

"You can't do this, Joey," Bob said, holding his hand up, palms facing toward Joey, before lowering them. "Put down the knife so we can talk."

Joey looked at Bob.

"Come on, Joey. Let's talk this out."

"I have nothing to say to you. Here's what's going to happen. I'm going to do Jess. When I do, you'll lunge at me. But I'm a lot younger and stronger than you. I'll sink my knife into you. I'll pull it out and do it over and over again. You'll both die right here."

The look on Jessica's face changed. The reality of the predicament she was in wiped away the anger so that only fear remained.

"You don't have to do this, Joey," Bob said. As he spoke, he nonchalantly slid his right hand into his pants pocket and felt the cold metal of the Glock. "What do we both want? You want to get away somewhere where you won't be found. I just want Jessica safe."

His hand encircled the pistol's grip. His finger went into place. The Glock has no safety. If it is ready to fire, it would fire once he pulled the trigger. Bob had chambered a round and cocked it back in Mason's cabin. Doing that had made him nervous, but he had figured it was worth the risk. It was a good call. The gun was ready, if he were.

"Let's call a truce, Joey," Bob said as he stared not into Joey's eyes, but Jessica's. "If you agree to let her go, we can let you leave the island and find a good place to hide. Hell, I'll even give you money. I'm a rich guy, you know. How about a million bucks? We can all just walk away."

Joey seemed to give it some thought. It didn't take long, though, to realize that Bob would probably spend another million tracking him down.

"That's not going to happen, and you know it," Joey said. Bob, who had not taken his eyes from Jessica's, gave his head a sharp downward shake and yelled "now!" She got the message. Jessica violently twisted back and away from Joey. Bob pulled the Glock from his pocket and rapidly fired a round. It struck Joey in the upper shoulder and he went down in pain and disbelief. Bob stepped on his left forearm while pointing the Glock at Joey's head.

"Take the knife," he said to Jessica. She bent to remove it from his fingers. Joey gripped it tighter, so Bob applied more pressure through his shoe to Joey's arm. Joey cried out and released the knife. Once Jessica held it, Bob removed his foot from Joey's arm.

"You're bleeding, I think you might be bleeding enough to bleed out. What do you think, Jessica? You're the nurse."

"I think if he doesn't get help, he'll die," she said, a coldness in her voice that Joey had not heard before.

"So, Joey, you're the piece of shit who killed my daughter."

"Fuck you," Joey uncharacteristically said in a hiss. The pastor and Mrs. Helen would have sent him to bed without dinner for language far less foul.

Joey pulled himself into more of a sitting position. It freed him to move his left hand up to press against the gunshot wound in his right shoulder. He thought the pressure might stem the bleeding.

"I'm sure you remember Amanda Anderson. Sweet girl. She was the light of my life, you piece of shit. She was all I had left in the world. What was she to you?"

Joey said nothing.

"You don't know? You fucking don't know? Here's how it went down, Joey. You screwed my little girl, then you slit her throat just like you were about to slit Jessica's. You watched without feeling a goddamn thing as the life left her body. Why would you do that?"

Joey shook his head, but not with remorse.

"Sure you do, you motherfucker. You cleared a couple thousand dollars through that fat Thai back in Penang. You killed my little girl for two grand."

He turned to Jessica. "He's pretty strong. I don't think this gunshot wound is going to do the job."

She just shook her head.

"Hmmm," he said, bending over and pulling Joey's hand from the wound so he could inspect it. "This hole is too clean."

At that moment, Joey lunged for the gun, summoning all his strength. The unexpected move threw Bob off balance. He tumbled to his butt, dropping the gun. Joey stood up and shakily staggered toward the Glock. At that moment, Jessica picked up a stone and swung it at Joey's head, connecting with his right temple. Joey went down in a heap.

Jessica stood over him, crying softly. Bob picked up the pistol. They stood there solemnly for a moment.

"I have to finish this," Bob softly said to Jessica. "You should start heading back down the trail."

She looked at Bob through tearful eyes and gave a small nod. She turned and made her way back to the trail, then down the hill toward the beach. She steeled herself to hear a gunshot at any moment.

Bob saw Joey's pearl-handled knife on the ground. He was sure that it was the knife that Joey had used on Amanda, all the other young girls and most certainly Mason the day before. He picked it up and felt the weight of it in his hand. He knelt over him as the younger man started to regain his consciousness.

"Oh good. I wouldn't want you to miss this," Bob said. He held the younger man's gaze, showing him the blade. Terror seeped into Joey's mind.

"Is this the knife you used to kill my little girl?" Joey gave a small nod. "I thought so. Rot in hell," he said as he pulled the blade across Joey's throat. He leaned into it to make sure that the cut was deep. Joey's eyes widened and Bob realized that Amanda had probably made the same face at Joey. Then his eyes rolled back in his head and he was gone.

Bob wiped the knife on Joey's shirt, then closed it and put it in his pocket. He also pocketed Mason's Glock. He wasn't sure what he would do with either, but that decision would be for another time.

He moved swiftly back to the main trail, then jogged down it to the beach. Jessica was there, ankle deep in the surf.

"Is it over?" she asked him. He nodded that it was. Bob rinsed his hands in the surf to remove the blood, He pulled the gun from his pocket, leaned back and tossed it as far as he could out into the South

China Sea. He then did the same with the extra mag. Finally, he took the knife from his other pocket. He cocked his arm to throw it, as well, then stopped. He slipped it back into his pocket.

In a strange yet powerful way, the knife was his last physical connection to Amanda. He just couldn't throw it into the sea.

Jessica told him that he couldn't wear the bloody tee-shirt back to the Turtle. He took it off and rinsed it in the surf, as best he could. The blood was fresh, so a lot of it came out. Not enough, though. He'd carry it back then burn it later that evening.

"You ready?" Bob asked Jessica.

She nodded yes. Fifteen minutes later they were back at the Majestic Turtle. The walk was long enough for Jessica's tears to stop flowing.

"We need to decide what we do next," Bob said outside her bungalow. "But I need a few minutes."

"Me too," she answered softly.

They agreed to meet in the dining area in thirty minutes and each went to their huts.

Bob used the hose to take a cold shower in the tiny bathroom. He was having a hard time figuring out just how to feel. He had killed before when he was a soldier, but even then, he had done nothing so cold-blooded.

Yet, he had no second thoughts, felt absolutely no remorse. His mind flashed back to the day that Fitz, standing in his office, told him that Amanda had been murdered. He had promised her that day that he'd get the person who did it. And he had.

It didn't bring her back, but in that moment, Bob remembered what Mason had said when they met at the hotel in Bangkok. Mason had called taking revenge the next best thing. At that moment, Bob felt it was just that. He wasn't happy, but he did feel closure.

Then he thought about Mason, the man who led him to Joey, without whom Joey would have escaped to kill again. Mason deserved better than to die at Joey's blade. He would forever be in Mason's debt.

As he thought about the ex-CIA officer, it dawned on him that there were likely things in Mason's cabin that would tie him to Bob. That could be a problem. Jessica, too, probably. He decided that he would sneak back into Mason's hut and remove anything that might connect them.

He put on clean clothes and walked to the Majestic Turtle's restaurant. Jessica was there. She, too, had changed clothes. It was lunchtime.

"Will Joey be joining you?" Umar asked when he approached the table.

"Not today," Bob said. "He went out looking for Mason."

They gave their lunch choices to Umar and asked that he bring them two cold Tiger beers.

"He can't do that," Jessica told him. "It's a Muslim thing. We brought the beers. Umar is letting us keep them in the refrigerator. If we want one, though, we have to get it ourselves."

Bob got up, followed Umar into the kitchen area, saw the refrigerator and took out two ice cold cans 'of beers. He returned to the table where Jessica was sitting.

"What's next for you?" he asked.

"I want to get as far away from here as I can," she said. "When I left Seattle, I thought that I might volunteer as a nurse some place that really needs it. There's an awful famine in the Sudan and Ethiopia. I think I'll go there and be a nurse again."

Bob said he thought that was a great idea. He said focusing on doing something good would help put all the ugliness of Joey behind her.

"I hope that's so," she said. "But right now, I just feel numb. I've been such a fool."

"Cut yourself a break, Jessica. You were taken in by a master. Truly. And you got to him, too. Just in the end, you know, he was always going to look out for himself."

Jessica stared out toward the sea. She was taking a mental inventory of her life. She knew she was smart but couldn't help but wonder how she had made two such awful choices in men.

Joey, a psychopath, made Wallace's dallying seem tame. My God, she thought again, she had been sleeping with a serial killer. How does that happen? At least Wallace never killed anyone. She considered her late husband in a new light. He was a good-hearted man. He just couldn't keep his manhood in the pants. Maybe she could learn to forgive him.

Jessica told herself that she had to learn from this god-awful experience. But learn what? To be careful? That wasn't who she wanted to be. She wasn't going to live her life fearing what might happen. She had no answers. At least, not today.

They sat quietly for a bit, taking small swigs on their beers. Eventually, Jessica broke the silence. She picked up where they had left off.

"What about you? What do you do next?"

"I got to wrap all this stuff up as best I can." He looked at her. "Should be me, not you. In fact, I think you should get out of the country before I do anything."

She wasn't about to argue that point. "Can't happen quickly enough," she said.

"I'll call Mason's detective friend, Bo, when I get back to the mainland. I'll tell him everything and where to find Mason and Joey's remains. I'll ask that he keep you and me out of it, as best he can. I think he will. I'll also call the guy at the State Department who's been helping. He needs to know that it's over. I'll tell him everything. He and Mason were old friends. They were in Laos together in the Seventies."

Bob told Jessica that he had another piece of business to take care of for Mason. Mason had asked him to consider helping the young man, Haziq, who provided the big break in the case. He explained that Haziq was trying to save four-thousand dollars to buy the restaurant he manages.

"That's a lot of money to these people," he said. "Mason said his time is running out. I'm going to give him ten thousand. I would have given Mason more than that in a bonus. He was an incredible detective."

"Mason would like that," she said.

Bob said the hardest thing he needed to do was go to Bangkok and meet with Mason's assistant, Boonsri. She had worked for Mason for years.

"She was dedicated to Mason," he said. "She going to be devastated. I'll do whatever she needs. I'll even sponsor her coming to the States if she wants."

Day 25

J essica left for the mainland after breakfast. It was eerie for Bob being there with little to do, knowing that Mason's and Joey's bodies were less than a mile away in the jungle.

After seeing her off, he entered Mason's bungalow and began a close inspection of what was there. There wasn't much, but there was Mason's journal and the manila folder with his case notes.

Mason sat on the bed and read through the journal. He had kept track of all his expenses, as he said he would, but he had also used the pages to record his thoughts. The first few days, the personal entries were short. The first entry was on his flight from Bangkok to Penang when he wrote about his meeting the night before with Bob:

Met the new client last night. Seems like a solid guy. I could feel his agony. It reminded me of when I lost Sylvie.

Once the nightmares started, the entries became longer and more agonizing. Bob didn't even know that Mason was having these flashbacks in his dreams. By the end, Mason was clearly in deep pain emotionally.

Tonight's dream showed me more people I killed with that goddamn bomb. There was a man, probably in his thirties. He was dressed well. I suspect he had a professional job. Maybe an accountant or a banker. He was sitting at a small table on the far side of the restaurant with a young girl, maybe a teenager. She was clearly his daughter. I couldn't tell, of course, what they were talking about, but they were having a wonderful time. Lots of laughing. Then there was a flash and I saw their mangled bodies lying about five feet apart. They were obviously dead, but the little girl's eyes bore into me. That's when I woke up. Goddamn it! I've cried more from these flashbacks in the past week than I've cried, well, ever.

As I learn more about Joey, I wonder if his crimes were any worse than mine? I mean, really. He was orphaned as a young boy, then taken in by a loving couple, but they abandoned him and left him to live on the street. No skills. No real way to earn a living. No wonder he started stealing. I don't know why he stopped snatching purses and started killing young girls. Maybe it was just the money. The way he made a living. I don't know. It's easy to judge him because he killed those girls.

But what about me? I'm not just a killer. I'm a mass murderer. I took out more innocent people in one day than any IRA terrorist has done. Joey couldn't hold a candle to me. Why has this not bothered me till now? It's been fourteen fucking years! I killed all those people. I only wanted to kill one guy and I just didn't care about all the others. What's wrong with me? We think Joey is a sicko, but maybe I'm the goddamn psychopath.

Will I even be able to kill Joey? I don't know. Taking out bad guys has never been a problem before. Maybe I should insist that Bob do it. I doubt I'd be having these nightmares if I had just focused my revenge on the general. An eye for an eye. Bob has killed in combat before. He can do it and probably should. Then again, I'll do it if I have to. Joey deserves to die. What about me?

Bob took the journal. There was no reason to share Mason's inner turmoil and certainly no reason to drag Bob deeper into the case. That would be unavoidable if the authorities were to find the little notebook.

Later in the day, Bob walked to the island's one and only dive shack. He signed on for a snorkeling trip that afternoon. He was here. He might as well take advantage of it. Besides, it might get his mind off everything else.

The snorkeling was spectacular. Wherever the boat dropped him and the three strangers in his group, he could see rich and plentiful coral for hundreds of feet around. And my God! The tropical fish, big and tiny, were so abundant and colorful. It was awe-inspiring.

Off one isolated, white sand beach, he swam upon a half dozen giant sea turtles lumbering along about six feet beneath the surface. A magnificent sight. He even glimpsed the famed blacktip sharks hanging out near the bottom. There were three and they weren't the least bit interested in him.

The next morning, one day after Jessica left, he was on the first ferry back to Kuala Besut.

Epilogue

Amal – would he ever be just my gym buddy again? – sat silently across from me, sipping his tea while slowly shaking his head back and forth. I had held the story in a secret place for most of my adult life. I'm not sure why I never told anyone. Perhaps it was that I had no one I cared about enough to tell. That didn't explain spilling it all to Amal.

Perhaps I feared that if I told one person the story would soon spread and define me. I didn't want that. I certainly didn't want to discuss it with friends and associates. Hell, I never even told a shrink! I was quite sure that telling the story would imprison me.

So why did I confide it to Amal? Good question. I think it was as simple as the time was right. I'm an old man. I have no family left and few real friends. I don't care what people might say or think about me. Those days are behind me.

When I started telling Amal, the story just flowed from me. In a strange way, it felt good to confide it. That Amal was only a casual friend might have made it easier.

People thought it was the loss of Amanda that changed me. That certainly was a big part of it. I'll never get over losing her. After she was taken, all that mattered to me was getting my revenge.

Revenge can be cleansing, but taking it exacts a toll on your soul. It was years before I could daydream about Amanda without reliving Joey's final moments. The blood squirting up and soaking my shirt as I watched him die.

I don't regret what I did to Joey. Not at all. I'm glad I did it. Who

EPILOGUE

knows how many other families he would have ruined? No regrets. I did the world a favor.

— — — — — —

"Did you ever hear from Jessica," Amal asked.

"No. Never did," I said. "But I did search for her online a few years ago. It's amazing what you can find now. I knew her entire name, where she was from, her age and that she was a nurse. It wasn't hard. Took maybe five minutes before I was looking at a photo of a much older Jessica. She's still striking. It brought a smile to my face. There was a lot about her online. She has lived a truly meaningful life."

Bob told Amal that Jessica stayed in famine-stricken Africa for more than ten years. She eventually ran a camp for a quarter-million refugees. That led to her testifying at the UN. When her mom got sick, Jessica returned to Seattle. While she nursed her mom, she wrote a book and advocated for a quicker and greater famine relief. About ten years ago, she met Bill Gates at a conference in New York where they were both speakers. He was so impressed, he hired her on the spot.

Amal asked if he kept Mason's journal.

"Maybe I should have," Bob said, "but it just didn't feel right. I built a small fire on the beach the night Jessica left. One by one, I ripped the pages and fed them to the flame. The case files from Mason's cabin, too."

And why this day to finally share the story, Amal asked?

Yesterday, Bob told Amal, was the anniversary of the day it all ended.

"I mark the day every year. I pour myself a glass of Jack Daniels –Mason's drink – and think back to that month. I recall how it started with excitement because I thought that maybe the State Department was coming to offer me an ambassadorship. It was possible. I had given the Reagan campaigns a lot of money. And then the horror when I suddenly realized why Fitz was there."

He said he recalls the first meeting with Mason in the hotel bar at the Bangkok airport and the awful next day in Kuala Lumpur. "Morgues are cold, terrible places," he told Amar. "I pulled the sheet back and

317

saw my sweet girl. It's an image I can't forget. Nobody should have to do that."

"I can't even begin to imagine," Amal said.

Bob again praised Mason and how the ex-CIA officer had quickly tracked Joey down.

"And I remember every single thing about that last day we were all together on Kecil. I can smell it, Amal. The fragrance of the jungle. And hear it. The constant rhythm of the surf, the cacophony of the jungle itself. Have you ever been in a jungle?" Amal shook his head no. "It's the original surround sound.

"When I think of my life, Amal, taking revenge on Joey was the most remarkable thing I've ever done. Remarkable might not be the right word. I don't mean remarkable in the usual sense. I mean it's the first thing that pops into my mind when I think back on my life. I guess most people would think that sad. But I don't feel that way. When he took my girl's life, he punctured my soul. It left me empty.

"No, killing Joey didn't bring Amanda back. But Mason was right. Revenge was the next best thing. At least it was for me."

The two men sat in silence for a bit. Finally, Amal broke it.

"What happened to the knife?"

Bob reached into his right pants pocket. When he withdrew his hand, it held the five-inch, pearl-handled switchblade.

"Never without it."

Acknowledgments

Special thanks to **Patricia Graffy**, the first person to read my book nonstop cover-to-cover. Pat is my cousin. She gave me awesome feedback that helped me refine the early versions of the story. She also was always there with heartfelt support and was quick to respond whenever I needed to bounce something off her.

Thank you as well for my great team of beta readers. In addition to Pat, the beta readers were **Pete Pepinsky**, **Arlene Carter** and **Ken Dishman**. Each brought unique skills and perspectives that made the story better and the mistakes fewer.

Another set of thanks to a retired CIA officer who served in Southeast Asia at about the same time as my fictional Mason Ray would have. I'm honoring my pledge to keep him anonymous, but he knows these thanks are for him. You were gracious with your time and helped me better understand the CIA and how it operated at the time.

Finally, thank you to the people of Malaysia. They were friendly and accommodating to me on my first visit in 1987. When I returned in March and April 2019, virtually everyone I met went out of their way to help me. I was especially taken by the hospitality afforded me by **Baharom**. He was at ABC when I stayed there in 1987 and is still there today. Older and wiser now, of course, but still has that wonderful smile. He spoke freely about the times in my story. It provided an added level of detail that I found helpful. It was great to reconnect with him after all these years, and to meet his son, **Thakif**.

Please Write a Review

If you liked this book - or even if you didn't - please take a moment to revisit Amazon and write a review.

Until I became a self-published author, I didn't know how vital reviews are to writers. I've written lots of reviews myself. I thought I was simply sharing my take on the book with others thinking about buying it.

In fact, the number and timeliness of reviews is far more vital to a writer's success. It is one of the ways Amazon decides if a potential reader will even see a book when searching for their next read. Of course, they also give weight to the score the reviewer gives. If you are torn between four stars and five, be generous and round up!

If you want to go above and beyond, please give me a social media boost. Post that you just finished a great book by a new author. A link to the Amazon listing would be awesome.

About the Author

Wiley Brooks started his career as a journalist working for daily newspapers. By age 30, he had become an award-winning executive editor of a morning paper in central Pennsylvania. He later became a sought-after crisis communications expert for companies both large and small. Since 2003, Wiley has presented workshops to business and government groups on how to write more clearly and concisely. *The Next Best Thing* is his first novel.

In 1987, Wiley took a four-month sabbatical to backpack around Southeast Asia. It was on that trip that he first got the idea for *The Next Best Thing*. He didn't get serious about writing it, though, until 2018. He has returned to Southeast Asia several times over the years, most recently spending part of March and April 2019, revisiting the locales in the book.

Wiley was born in Tampa, FL, but has been living in Seattle since 1983. He is happily married to Marianne Bichsel. They have three adult children and two grandchildren. His first grandchild, a beautiful, sweet young girl named Amelia, died unexpectedly of a rare and aggressive form of leukemia. She was just twenty months old at the time. When he wrote of the pain of losing a child in the Prologue, he was thinking of Amelia.

Made in the USA
Middletown, DE
03 August 2019